CHRISTINA DODD IS

"MY GO-TO AUTHOR."
—Jayne Ann Krentz

"A MASTER ROMANTIC STORYTELLER."
—Kristin Hannah

**"SEXY AND WITTY, DARING
AND DELIGHTFUL."**
—Teresa Medeiros

"MY GO-TO AUTHOR." —Jayne Ann Krentz

PRAISE FOR CHRISTINA DODD'S NOVELS

Chains of Fire

"The urgency of the plot ratchets up the emotional drama, giving the story an exhilarating edge." —*Romantic Times*

Chains of Ice

"High-stakes action and high-adrenaline adventure provide the literary fuel for the latest addictive addition to Dodd's scorchingly sensual the Chosen Ones series."
—*Chicago Tribune*

In Bed with the Duke

"In Dodd's triumphant return to historical romance, she offers all of the elements her fans crave: deliciously clever writing, sexy romance, and a swashbuckling plot."
—*Booklist*

Storm of Shadows

"A riveting new series...the action and romance are hot!" —The Romance Readers Connection

"Fabulous urban romantic fantasy...a stupendous thriller."
—*Midwest Book Review*

Storm of Visions

"The taut, suspenseful plot, intriguing characters, and a smooth, natural style show that Dodd has earned her place on the bestseller list." —*Publishers Weekly*

"Ms. Dodd plunges readers into a fast-paced tale with intriguing paranormal elements, and treats them to a deliciously steamy romance that's sure to grab the reader's attention...suspenseful, packed with danger-filled action, and never slows as the story unfolds." —Darque Reviews

"*Storm of Visions* definitely hooked me...quirky, unusual, fun, tense, surprising, sexy, and wild!"
—Errant Dreams Reviews

continued ...

CHRISTINA DODD

Taken by the Prince

A SIGNET SELECT BOOK

SIGNET SELECT
Published by New American Library, a division of
Penguin Group (USA) Inc., 375 Hudson Street,
New York, New York 10014, USA
Penguin Group (Canada), 90 Eglinton Avenue East, Suite 700, Toronto,
Ontario M4P 2Y3, Canada (a division of Pearson Penguin Canada Inc.)
Penguin Books Ltd., 80 Strand, London WC2R 0RL, England
Penguin Ireland, 25 St. Stephen's Green, Dublin 2,
Ireland (a division of Penguin Books Ltd.)
Penguin Group (Australia), 250 Camberwell Road, Camberwell, Victoria 3124,
Australia (a division of Pearson Australia Group Pty. Ltd.)
Penguin Books India Pvt. Ltd., 11 Community Centre, Panchsheel Park,
New Delhi - 110 017, India
Penguin Group (NZ), 67 Apollo Drive, Rosedale, North Shore 0632,
New Zealand (a division of Pearson New Zealand Ltd.)
Penguin Books (South Africa) (Pty.) Ltd., 24 Sturdee Avenue,
Rosebank, Johannesburg 2196, South Africa

Penguin Books Ltd., Registered Offices:
80 Strand, London WC2R 0RL, England

First published by Signet Select, an imprint of New American Library,
a division of Penguin Group (USA) Inc.

First Printing, April 2011
10 9 8 7 6 5 4 3 2 1

Copyright © Christina Dodd, 2011
All rights reserved

SIGNET SELECT and logo are trademarks of Penguin Group (USA) Inc.

Printed in the United States of America

For my dear friend Emily March.

We've laughed, we've consoled, we've partied, we've supported each other through thick and thin, we've hung out in culverts, we've plotted evilly and well.

May Eternity Springs flow forever.

ACKNOWLEDGMENTS

Leslie Gelbman, Kara Welsh, and Kerry Donovan, my appreciation for your constant support. More appreciation to NAL's art department, led by Anthony Ramondo. To Rick Pascocello, head of marketing, and the publicity department with my special people Craig Burke and Jodi Rosoff, thank you. My thanks to Frank Walgren and the production department and, of course, a special thank-you to the spectacular Penguin sales department: Norman Lidofsky, Don Redpath, Sharon Gamboa, Don Rieck, and Trish Weyenberg. You are the best!

Thank you to Roger Bell, retired Air Force pilot, for his help with ballistics, and to Joyce Bell for critiquing in all conditions and in all places, and always knowing how to conjugate lie and lay. I truly appreciate it.

Chapter One

England, 1837

"So, Grimsborough, this is your little bastard."

Eleven-year-old Saber stood on the thick rug in the middle of the big English room in the big English manor. He stared narrowly at the tall, elegant older woman with the sneering mouth and the pale yellow hair, the one who dared insult him. In his native tongue, he said, "In Moricadia, I kill people who call me names."

"What?" the woman asked. "Grimsborough, what did he say?"

The shadowy figure behind the wide, polished wood desk did not look up from his writing.

Five finely dressed girls, ages five to twelve, stood lined up by the fireplace, and one of them, the skinny one in the middle, said in awestruck tones, "He's so dirty."

"And thin," said another.

Saber shifted his attention to them. *Soft, silly English girls.*

They stared at him as if he were a trained dancing bear, and when he glared, the littlest's brown eyes filled with tears. She popped her thumb into her mouth and slid behind her sisters' skirts.

"Look, he's tired." The eldest spoke with authority. "He's swaying on his feet."

Then in unison, the four eldest girls smiled at him. Kindly, sweetly, as if nothing ugly or brutal ever touched their lives.

Saber hated them. He hated the lady, hated the uniformed servants standing at attention, hated every single one. Most of all, he hated the evil man in charge, the man behind the desk, the one he knew had to be the viscount . . . and his father. Again in his native tongue, Saber spit, "Stupid English wenches."

"What did he say?" The sneering English lady looked between Saber and the viscount. "What did he mean?"

For the first time, the man spoke. "Bring him to me."

Two of the man's absurdly dressed servants grabbed Saber's arms and propelled him around the desk to face the man.

Grimsborough gestured for the candelabra to be brought closer, and when the light struck his face, Saber thought he looked like the older woman. Not in his features, which were sharp and strong, but in the aristocratic lift of his chin and contemptuous curve of his mouth.

The English lady drew in a sharp breath. Because,

although Saber didn't realize it, he and Grimsborough looked alike, also.

Grimsborough examined the skinny, filthy, tired child as if he were a bug squashed beneath his shoe. Then he reached out a pale, long-fingered hand and slapped Saber across the face with his open palm.

The sound of flesh against flesh echoed like a gunshot. Saber fell sideways.

One of the girls gasped. Another one whimpered.

The woman smiled in satisfaction.

And Saber lunged for Grimsborough, fists swinging.

The servants caught him, dragged him backward.

The contemptuous man waved for him to come forward again.

The servants didn't let go of him this time.

Grimsborough put his narrow, patrician nose so close it almost touched Saber's, and his soft, deep, menacing tone raised prickles of fear along Saber's spine. "Listen to me, lad. You are nothing. Nothing. My bastard by a foreigner, and if I had had another son, your filthy feet would never sully the floors of my home. But God in His infinite wisdom has blessed me with nothing from this marriage but *daughters*." He glanced at the girls, so colorfully clothed, so sweet in their innocence, and he despised them. "Five *daughters*. So you will live here until you're fit to be sent to school. And never again will you speak of your betters in that insolent manner."

Saber shook his head, shrugged, and gestured helplessly.

"Don't pretend with me, lad. Your mother spoke English. Every servant who works in your country speaks English. So do you."

Saber didn't quite have the guts to swear at Grimsborough, but he spoke Moricadian when he said, "English is for the ignorant."

Saber never even saw the blow coming, but it snapped his head sideways and his ear rang.

"Never let me hear you speak that barbaric tongue again." Grimsborough's voice never rose.

Saber lifted his chin. "I hate you," he said in clear, plain English.

"I hate you, *sir*," Grimsborough said with chilling precision.

Saber's gaze was full of loathing.

"Say it." Grimsborough's frigid green eyes held nothing: no spark, no interest . . . no heart.

Saber glanced toward the elegant, sneering woman. She stood terrified, looking at her husband the way a mouse looks at a snake.

Saber glanced at the girls. Four of them stood with their heads down. One, the middle girl, stood with her hands clasped at her skinny chest, staring at him, and when their eyes met, her lips moved in appeal: *Please.*

He looked back at Grimsborough. This man who was his father scared him—and he wasn't afraid of anything. But he couldn't give in. Not quite. Straightening his shoulders, he said, "I hate you, *sir*, but my grandfather told me I had to come to this damp, cold island and go to your savage schools and learn everything I could about mathematics and languages and statesmanship so I could go back to Moricadia and free my people from cruel oppression."

The eldest girl stepped forward as if he interested her. "If you want to free your people, shouldn't you learn how to fight?"

He swung a contemptuous glare on her. "I already know how to fight."

"You'll need an army. Do you know how to lead an army?" She looked him right in the eyes, not at all impressed with his bravado.

"I know how to lead," he retorted; then grudgingly he added, "But I will have to learn military tactics."

"Then we are in accord in one thing—you will cease to be an ignorant savage and become a civilized gentleman." Grimsborough gestured to the servants. "Take him away. Clean him. Give him over to the tutors and tell them to use any means necessary to teach him what he needs to know. I will see him here in six months. Please note, I expect an immense improvement, or I will be unhappy."

Saber felt the little shiver that raced through the room at the idea of anyone incurring Grimsborough's wrath.

Picking up his quill, Grimsborough turned back to his desk and ignored the servants, his wife, his daughters, and Saber.

"We will begin with a bath," Lady Grimsborough said decisively.

At the mere idea of this woman seeing his naked body, Saber struggled, lunging against the grips of the servants.

The second-to-the-eldest girl, a pale, soft, silly thing dressed in pink and ruffles, begged, "Mama, he's so skinny. Please, can we feed him first?"

"Do you not have a nose? Can you not smell him?" Lady Grimsborough waved her scented lace handkerchief before her face.

Saber had learned to fight in a hard school, and he

swung on one servant's arm, knocked the feet out from beneath the other, broke free, and raced toward the door.

The head servant, the one who was dressed in black and wore white gloves and a face with no expression, tackled him around the knees. The two footmen leaped on top of his back, crushing him into the flowered carpet.

His father's unemotional voice intoned, "A few good canings are in order. Thompson, I trust you'll handle the matter."

The man in black and white helped haul Saber to his feet, then dusted off his white gloves. "Yes, my lord. Immediately, my lord."

"Clearly the little bastard will survive without a meal for a few more hours." Lady Grimsborough eyed Saber as if he were a plucked chicken ready for the pot.

In a cold, clear voice Grimsborough said, "As of now, his name is Raul. Raul Lawrence."

Clearly dismayed, Lady Grimsborough asked, "Lawrence? Surely you don't intend to—"

"Adopt him? Indeed I do. He is Raul Lawrence, son of the Viscount Grimsborough, and he is to become an English gentleman. Wife, please ensure that everyone in the household realizes how quickly he or she will incite my displeasure should the boy be given the wrong name or title."

Once again that shiver rattled the room.

Saber had left a country where he roamed free, and landed in hell.

And his father was the prince of darkness himself.

Chapter Two

Three months later

For the first time ever, Thompson, the butler, stepped into the drawing room during Saber's dancing lesson. In that sonorous tone that so annoyed Saber, he announced, "Mr. Lawrence, your father wishes to speak to you."

Saber stopped waltzing so abruptly that his middle sister—he knew her name now; she was Belle—squeaked and stepped all over his feet. "Why?" he asked.

"We do not question Lord Grimsborough's wishes. We simply do as we are told as quickly as possible."

Saber cast him a look of alarm.

Thompson had a hard hand with a cane and demanded total obedience when teaching etiquette, but this time, as Saber passed him on the way to Grimsborough's office, he placed a comforting hand on Saber's shoulder.

So whatever it was, it was bad.

Saber searched his mind, trying to remember what he'd done that warranted a visit to his father. Since his arrival, he'd seen Grimsborough only from afar, and that was enough for him. He'd learned his father terrified everyone in the house: his wife of fifteen years, his daughters, his estate manager, his servants from Thompson on down to the lowliest scullery maid. Grimsborough wasn't an unusually cruel master; nor was he a lecher or a pervert. He seemed uninterested in anything but his own enthusiasms—collecting books, observing theatrical melodramas, and horse racing. Yet he carried with him a darkness. Wherever he walked, the sunshine seemed to dim, the air to cool. When he turned his attention to an unfortunate culprit, that person, noble or common, shrank away, trying to avoid the touch of his shadow.

Saber wasn't afraid of him, or so he told himself. And in a way, it was true. He was far too busy to be afraid of his father: He had discovered that he really was the ignorant savage Grimsborough had called him. He spoke Moricadian, English, Spanish, and French, but he was illiterate in every language. He knew how to barter, how to do figures in his head, but not how to read the numbers. He knew how to tell a story that had his sisters hanging on his every word, but not how to write it down. He could sense north and south, east and west, but didn't know how to read a map.

He knew how to ride. . . . Ah, now, *that* he did better than anyone, and he quickly discovered his father's Thoroughbred horses carried the wind under their hooves.

So for three months he had absorbed, gulped, feasted on learning, driven by the belief that the sooner he knew how to be the military leader who would destroy the evil leaders of Moricadia and allow him to take over the throne, the sooner he could go home.

He'd also been driven by simple competiveness— even his youngest sister knew more about history, art, literature than he did.

He couldn't bear that.

He had also been taught the social arts: bowing, dancing, mincing, this fork, that spoon, flowers, smiles, the Correct Phrase for Every Occasion spoken in the Correct Tone.

He despised every bit of it.

But Ella, his eldest sister, had pointed out that a prince needed to know diplomacy, that after the battle was won, he would have to bow, dance, mince, eat, and flatter.

He hated that she was right.

The girls made his life bearable. That was all. Bearable.

For every night, his heart ached for his homeland, for the wild Pyrenees mountains. He dreamed of his grandfather's stern face as he enjoined him to run away to England and live another day. He remembered his mother's comforting scent as she held him one last time before putting him on the horse and waving good-bye.

Every moment he was not busy, he longed for his house in the woods, decrepit and tumbledown, for the spicy smell of pines, for the wild winter storms and the grand summer days, for the vistas that stretched across mountains and glaciers.

No one ever knew, but at night, he cried. He, Saber of the royal and honored House of de Barbari Jinete.

And now he was walking to see the man who had created all this hell—his father.

Thompson rapped on the tall, dark door of the study, then opened it and stepped back to allow Saber to precede him.

Saber stepped into the room. The door closed behind him.

He was alone with his father.

As before, Grimsborough sat behind the desk, writing on some papers spread before him, but today the curtains were open and the watery English sunlight was shining from over his left shoulder, leaving him in silhouette. He looked up and motioned for Saber to come and stand facing him, the wide expanse of the desk between them. "I got a letter today." He lifted the smudged, torn paper off the pile of other smudged, torn papers, and read, "'My lord, if you would find it in your heart to convey this news to my beloved son, Saber.'" He looked up, his green eyes cold. "She doesn't realize your name is now Raul Lawrence."

Anxiety coiled in Saber's belly, and he didn't protest this insistence on his English name. All he cared about now was the contents of that letter. "Please, my lord. What does she say?"

"'His grandfather was killed by the de Guignards while out foraging in the woods.'"

A fist squeezed tight around Saber's heart.

"'Tell him the dirty thieves used him like prey, chasing him down, stabbing him with spears—'"

Saber couldn't breathe, couldn't think. He saw red. He felt faint.

"'—then hung him from a tree and cut out his entrails. I waited until it was dark and cut him down.'"

A shriek built in Saber's brain. Didn't she know how dangerous that was?

Of course she did. She knew what the de Guignards would do to her if they caught her.

"'I buried him in the graveyard next to the castle where the last true king rests—'"

The shriek built and built, and at last burst forth. Saber sank to his knees, screaming out his rage at the murdering de Guignards, his grief at his grandfather's death, the terrible images in his brain. He tore his hair; he ripped his clothes; he beat on his chest: He did what was proper in Moricadia for the death of the beloved leader of his renegade family.

Vaguely he heard the door fling open. Thompson's voice, urgent and concerned.

An answer from his father.

Then ... the kick to his ribs caught him by surprise. Pain exploded across his chest. He flopped like a rag doll over on his side, robbed of his breath and aware of only one thing—the agony of broken bones.

Another kick followed to his rump, dangerously close to his balls.

Instinctively, he rolled, protecting his equipment with his hands.

Another kick to his thigh.

He scrambled away.

Another to his ribs. Another. He felt hard shoe leather and heard a hateful voice saying, "Never. Never. An Englishman never—"

Through the roaring in his head, Saber couldn't comprehend the words.

Another kick, to his shoulder this time, then Thompson speaking, begging—

Abruptly, Grimsborough grabbed Saber by his torn shirt, half lifted him off the floor, and stared into his eyes. In his usual cool, precise, crisp tone, just as if he hadn't almost killed his son, he said, "Do not ever let me hear such a sound out of you again. Englishmen do not wail like heathens. They do not cry like women. They show no emotion. They feel no emotion." He shook him. "Do you understand?"

Saber stared, mouth open, trying to get air, trying to comprehend the kind of beast who held him, who bred him, who counted it a crime to mourn a beloved grandfather.

"Do you understand?" Grimsborough repeated.

Saber knew he should defy him, should stand up for his right to grieve. But he coughed and tasted blood. Each breath was an agony. He was barely conscious, and all he could see were those compelling eyes, so like his, yet like a viper's, cold and soulless.

He nodded.

Grimsborough dropped him.

Pain streaked along his nerves, but he remembered. He made no sound.

"Get him out of here," Grimsborough said, then turned his back and walked away.

Murmuring encouragement, Thompson slipped an arm under Saber's shoulders, helped him get to his feet and out of the room.

In the corridor, Saber collapsed in shock and agony.

He learned a lesson that day, a hard, brutal, painful lesson. A lesson ingrained for life.

Conceal your feelings. Never give in to emotion.

For Grimsborough wanted a son only if that son was like ... him.

So when, five months later, Grimsborough called him in and read him another smudged letter, Saber didn't make a sound.

What was the point? He had lost the most important thing in his life.

His mother was dead.

Chapter Three

Ten years later

At the top of the hill, twenty-one-year-old Raul Lawrence sat straight in the saddle and with a slight smile observed the charming scene.

Young women from Belle's boarding school floated like colorful dandelion puffs across his father's lawn at Grimsborough Abbey, twirling their parasols of pale pink, yellow, and blue. He recognized Belle from afar; she led the largest group on a tour of the gardens, pointing out the climbing roses, the paved paths, the tree swing he'd built for his sisters not long after he'd arrived from Moricadia.

That had been ten years ago, and every moment he was absent from his home was a heartache to be borne stoically, alone and in silence.

Yet although he never imagined it possible, there were things about England he loved. His sisters, his friends, his horses, Thompson, even his stepmother ... poor woman. They had made his exile bearable, and he was heartily glad for each and every one.

As he watched, a young lady strolled arm in arm with Belle, gazing bemusedly at her friend.

Raul understood that. Belle, with her soft, dimpled smile, her kind heart, and her unexpectedly clever mind had a tendency to bemuse them all.

He had been spotted, for one of the servants hurried up the hill toward him.

Raul dismounted. He pulled his present for Belle out of the saddlebags, handed over the reins, and started down toward the gardens.

As he got closer, the young lady with Belle glanced up toward him.

He stopped in his tracks.

She was the most beautiful woman Raul had ever seen. Above medium height, with a generous bosom and tiny waist. Golden skin that glowed beneath a wide-brimmed hat. Cornflower blue eyes surrounded by dark lashes. Thick, blond hair, the color of ripe wheat, coiled in a bun at the base of her neck. Lips meant for kissing, for lascivious action, and a dark beauty mark set close to the left corner of her mouth.

She was perfection.

Then he noticed the flared nostrils, the narrowed eyes, the pursed lips as she surveyed him. ...

He knew what that meant. She didn't approve of him, of his parentage, of his reputation.

Whoever she was, she was a prig.

Belle followed her friend's gaze and squealed, "Raul!"

Opening her arms, she rushed toward him, embraced him, laughed and cried at the same time. "I have missed you."

"And I you, my dear girl." He hugged her hard, cherishing her for the moments they had left. "While I was up at Oxford, I searched for exactly the right gift for your eighteenth birthday, and I found it . . . here." He presented her with the flat silk sack.

She pulled the strings apart and removed the Kashmiri shawl, its colors softly glowing in harmony, brilliance, depth. "Oh . . . Raul," she whispered, smoothing her hand across the material. "This is beautiful. So special to me." She looked up at him, her eyes brimming with tears. "Thank you."

She knew. Somehow, she knew.

But Belle was always the sister who could read his heart.

Taking it from her, he shook it out and wrapped it around her shoulders, then offered her his arm. "Shall we greet your guests?"

She put her hand on his, and as they turned, her face lit up. "Victoria, this is my brother, Raul Lawrence."

Victoria blinked as if startled. "Your brother?" She flashed him a look from the top of his top hat to the gleam of his shining boots. And she dropped into a curtsy. "Mr. Lawrence, an honor."

So. She had disapproved of him even before she knew his true identity.

Ah, a challenge.

He enjoyed a challenge.

"Raul, this is my dearest friend forever, Victoria Cardiff."

"Miss Cardiff." He bowed, his lips unsmiling. Yet his

eyes were amused, and that, he was pleased to note, quite annoyed young Victoria.

"Victoria and I met at school and she is an absolute dear of a soul," Belle told him.

"You do me too much honor, Belle"—Victoria lowered her gaze—"for you are so sweet it's easy to be kind."

"She is, indeed." He heard a shriek from across the garden, looked up, and saw Arianna and Lucy bearing down on him at a run, while Madeline and Ella followed at a more sedate rate. "Excuse me, ladies." He strode toward his two youngest sisters, grinning broadly.

Arianna was now sixteen, with her mother's blond hair and blue eyes. She looked like an angel.

Raul knew she was not.

Lucy was fifteen, the tallest of the sisters, with her father's dark hair and eyes, a girl who covered her tension with a hard-earned air of serenity.

After a round of kisses and hugs, he greeted the two eldest girls.

Now Belle joined them, and all his sisters stood together, looking at him, laughing with the pleasure of having him home.

Always he was aware, in the midst of the bacchanal of joy, of Victoria, watching gravely, observing as if he and the girls were exotic birds and she a scholarly eyewitness.

Gathering his sisters close, he herded them toward Belle's dearest friend forever.

She was not dressed as well as the other girls at the party. Her gown had been turned and remade, with dark marks at the seams. The style was from five years ago, and her bonnet was . . . well, the brim shaded her fair complexion, but the straw drooped as if it were weary.

They surrounded her, laughing, drawing her into the center of the family. They liked her, it was easy to see, and that was interesting, for he had great respect for his sisters and their judgment. They had, after all, grown up in his father's household, where acute observation of temperament meant the difference between receiving Grimsborough's attention and being neglected.

Neglect was much preferred.

Yet Victoria treated his sisters with reserve, as if she didn't dare trust their friendship, as if all her life, she had stood by herself, on the outside looking in.

Bleakly amused at his insight—or was he simply assuming she was the same as him?—he flashed Victoria a sharp predator's grin.

Deliberately, she took a step back.

The two of them spoke quite well without words. And no one else realized they were communicating at all.

"It's time for us to dress for the ball tonight." Belle grabbed Victoria's arm. "Come on, Victoria, it'll be fun!"

For the first time, Raul saw Victoria waver uncertainly. She seemed not to agree, and yet a wistful longing settled on her features.

The other girls surrounded her, called a farewell-until-later to Raul, and carried her away.

All except Ella, who stepped to his side and placed her hand on his arm.

He put his hand over Ella's and they strolled after the hurrying, chattering girls.

For him, Belle and his other sisters had been the cushion that had softened the shocks of his existence, and in turn he had done what he could to cushion them.

He was the son, and the focus of Grimsborough's attention, but with a father like theirs, the girls had been ignored, insulted, exposed to cruelties. Grimsborough's careless contempt for his daughters, based on nothing more than their gender, had left its marks.

Their mother had done what she could, but during Raul's sojourn in England, she'd suffered at least two miscarriages as well as a stillborn birth, all boys. The strong, handsome, scornful aristocrat he had first met had faded into a thin, sad woman beset with grief for her lost sons.

So as the eldest, Ella had taken responsibility for protecting her younger sisters and, when she could, Raul. She mothered and worried about and tutored her younger siblings. He respected her goodness even while he wondered how she could stand sacrificing so much of her youth for her family.

Now Ella said, "Belle convinced Miss Cardiff to allow the girls to dress her in one of Lucy's as-yet-unseen gowns. They are the same height, and with a few adjustments for Miss Cardiff's figure and greater maturity, she will be charming tonight, don't you agree?"

"Indeed, she will." He would readily admit that. "But does she have no gowns of her own?"

"She does, and they're all in the same pitiful condition as the dress she's wearing. Her stepfather has had his own children with her mother and begrudges every dime spent on her."

Ah. That explained the practiced reserve.

Ella continued. "When it came to a choice between clothes and school, she took school. She is to go to the Distinguished Academy of Governesses and learn to earn her living. She has a true talent for languages, a strong will, a good sensibility, and I believe will have a successful life in service."

He nodded. He'd heard of the Distinguished Academy of Governesses, owned by Adorna, Lady Bucknell. "A bastion of female career guidance and education."

"Indeed. Her mother, who is, I think, a poor creature quite cowed by the stepfather, took a stand and insisted Miss Cardiff be allowed to go, rather than stay home and tend to her siblings."

So he'd been right about Victoria. She was used to being on the outside looking in. "No wonder Miss Cardiff has that excessively upright backbone."

"I think it more likely she's the type who responds to a challenge by growing a shell."

"And pincers? Like a crab?" Suspicion struck him. "Why, my dear Ella, are you telling me this?"

"I wanted you to know she has nothing to look forward to, and you could perhaps cease your peacock posturing."

He turned to her with a laugh. "Is that what I've been doing?"

Ella did not laugh back. "Miss Cardiff is very beautiful, yet she has a reputation that must remain polished beyond dispute."

He understood her warning. He didn't like it, but he understood it. "Of course. I wouldn't dream of besmirching her with my inglorious addresses."

"Inglorious, are you? I hardly think that. Nor do you." As always, Ella saw him and his character far too clearly. "Modesty ill befits you, King Saber."

"You mock me with the title, but it is sweet to hear my true name again."

Her already serious face grew somber, and she tugged

him to a halt. "Belle says you'll be leaving us soon to return to Moricadia."

He touched Ella's cheek with his forefinger. "Belle is very perceptive."

Ella took a difficult breath. "So you are going to claim your throne."

"It's not as easy as that. I know from the newspaper reports that the de Guignards are still firmly in charge, but I don't know what is left of the resistance. And my family? I've heard no word from anyone since the letter announcing my mother's death. But that's not to say Grimsborough hasn't kept the letters from me."

At the mention of her father's name, even Ella's mouth twisted in dislike. "I would almost say it was a certainty. His determination to sever any ties between you and Moricadia is remarkable only in its steadfast cruelty."

"There is nothing remarkable about Grimsborough's cruelty. It's the one trait we can all depend on."

"I don't wish to pain you, but in Moricadia . . . could it be there is no resistance left? That your family is scattered?" Her wide eyes were anxious.

"That is what I fear." And he did. All the long years in England, he had worried, hoped, tried to think of a way to investigate the families in Moricadia without attracting the attention of the de Guignards, the usurpers of his throne. Yet their police tortured and murdered any native Moricadians they suspected of insurgence, and he always knew that when he returned home, he had to appear innocuous. So he confined his investigations to questioning visitors who returned from Moricadia, and that had yielded him no information at all.

"What can one man do against these beasts who hold

all the power?" She squeezed his arm. "I confess, I fear for you."

"Don't fear. I'll find my family. If necessary, I'll re-unite them, but my family is remarkably resilient. They know the hidden places of the mountains and forests." Remembering his childhood in those places, he smiled. "I must believe that somewhere, they're still alive."

"You have said that for two hundred years, since the de Guignards murdered King Reynaldo, they've tried to claim that this time they exterminated the remnants of his line, and every year your family fruitlessly fights to recover the throne. Why should your return change that?" In her own way, Ella was aggressive, determined that he realize the challenges ahead.

"With no money and no backing, there was never a chance for my family, but when I return, all that will have changed." He grinned at her. "Have I not succeeded in using the education Father chose for me in all the best ways possible?"

"You've made your fortune?"

"Horses have been good for me. I know them, I know which ones will win, and with my winnings, I know how to buy and breed. Yes, I've made my fortune."

"I'm glad. I only wish . . . Oh, well." She shrugged. "No matter. So you plan to return and win your throne or be killed?"

"There's always a chance I'll be killed, but there's a legend among the Moricadians that when the ghost of Reynaldo rides, it foretells the return of the one true king."

"Is the ghost of Reynaldo riding?"

"No, but I haven't returned yet."

She smiled and hugged his arm. "I wish you wouldn't

go, but I know you'll never be whole until you are in your home country."

"What about you, dear sister? What is your fate?" For she was far too solemn for him to feel easy.

"I'll marry. I'll have children. I'll be widowed young and live out my life in peace."

His niggling disquiet grew. "You're not even married and you're hoping to be widowed?"

She tugged his watch out of its pocket. "Aren't you supposed to be meeting with Father?"

"You're changing the subject."

"You'd better hurry. He doesn't like to be kept waiting."

"Definitely changing the subject."

"There'll be time later to talk." Ella pushed him. "Go on. I have to go get dressed myself." She walked away, then turned back to him. "Promise me one thing."

"Anything."

"Promise me that no matter how dreadful your interview with Father, you'll stay for Belle's party."

He hesitated. Ella only suspected the interview would be dreadful. Raul knew very well that when his father heard the news Raul intended to give him, he would be in a cold rage.

"Your departure would ruin this party for her, and she's had little enough joy in her life," Ella insisted.

"Yes. I know. Very well. I will stay."

"And say farewell to us before you leave forever."

"That I would not fail to do."

Ella walked back to him, reached up, and smoothed the midnight dark hair off his forehead. "I don't care what the gossips say about you. You're a good man, and wherever you go, remember—we girls love you dearly."

He took her hand and lightly kissed her fingertips. "If I am a good man, the credit goes to you and my sisters."

"I think not. The goodness is at the bedrock of your being, built there by your character."

God, he hoped that was the truth.

But as he stepped into his father's study and looked at Grimsborough's dark visage, so like his own, he didn't believe it for a minute.

Chapter Four

As always, Grimsborough sat at his desk, writing on some papers that held his complete attention.

Raul knew his father wasn't putting on airs with his imperious ways. Grimsborough simply saw no reason to politely acknowledge a visitor before he had reached a stopping point. In his own opinion, and in the opinion of his wiser servants, no one on earth was as important a personage as the Viscount Grimsborough. Yet Raul had reached the glorious moment where what and who his father was meant nothing to him.

So he seated himself in the chair before Grimsborough's desk and waited without apparent interest for his father to finish whatever occupied him.

When his father put down his pen, a portentous silence followed.

Raul glanced up.

"So!" Grimsborough sounded irritated. Because Raul was studying the shine on his boots? Or because the figures on his sheet of paper didn't add up to his satisfaction? "You say you're done with school."

"I *am* done with school. I have learned everything I need to know there."

"I suppose you think you should go on the Grand Tour."

"Not at all." Grimsborough still made the mistake of assuming that Raul was like other young English gentlemen: vapid, self-absorbed, convinced that the world revolved around them. While in fact Raul knew very well that if he wished the world to revolve around him, he would have to work to create that world.

"Good." Grimsborough *was* one of those English gentlemen: no longer young, but still self-absorbed. "Because it's come to my attention that you've shown a talent with horses."

"All Moricadians are good with horses. It's a talent bred into me by my ancestors."

As Raul knew it would, his claim on Moricadia goaded Grimsborough into snapping, "Nonsense. You're only half Moricadian, and your bent comes from being around superior English horses."

"As you say." With studied indifference, Raul straightened the crease of his trousers.

Satisfied he had quelled Raul's brief rebellion, Grimsborough went right to the point. "My wishes are that you should take over the direction of my racing stables."

"Those are your wishes?" Raul hated that his father could aggravate him with such ease and without even realizing he had done it. Raul should be bigger than this . . . but this was his father, the man who had ordered him beaten, forced civilization on him, and almost killed him, and all because of a careless union with Raul's mother. Careless on Grimsborough's part only; Raul knew his mother had loved the man who had so betrayed her. For that, he almost pitied her, and yet . . . he missed her still. He would go for months without remembering. Then he would dream about her, and the grief would catch him by the throat.

He hadn't been there to hold her hand while she died, to whisper of a son's love—and that had been his fault. It was all his fault.

"I'd pay you a commission, of course, based on the amount of your winnings." Grimsborough clearly believed he was making a concession.

Raul almost smiled. Almost. "Is this a test, sir, to check my worthiness?"

"What do you mean?" Grimsborough seemed truly puzzled, as he undoubtedly was.

"Your minions have drilled into me the wonder of your generosity in allowing me to join, despite my bastard birth, the ranks of English gentlemen."

Grimsborough nodded pontifically.

"I've learned that a gentleman spits on the idea of earning lucre through any kind of honest labor." Raul had watched noblemen, old and young, lose their homes, wreck their families, flee to the continent, or go to debtors' prison rather than earn a living. He scorned them— but Grimsborough didn't know that.

For the first time in his life, Raul saw Grimsborough warily pick his words. "Of course, while it's true that most English gentlemen carefully eschew the appear-

ance of work, there are men who do work because circumstances demand they do so."

"But not the son of the Viscount Grimsborough.
Indeed, I know that as your bastard, I should be even
more careful than men who were legitimately born to
the ranks. So I'm afraid I must refuse your generous offer." Raul scrutinized his father, not seeing the cracks
in Grimsborough's composure, but knowing they were
there.

Irritation at having his wishes balked sent a whipcord
of color into Grimsborough's sculpted cheeks. "Then I
shall have to cut off your allowance."

"As you wish." Raul stood, satisfied with every aspect
of the interview.

"What do you think you're going to do without your
allowance? You have no money of your own." With deliberate malice, Grimsborough added, "Your mother's
family clearly hasn't contributed to your support. In
fact—your mother's family hasn't written in years."

Remembering his conversation with Ella, Raul asked,
"How many years, sir?"

"What?"

"When you told me of my grandfather's death, and
again of my mother's death, a pile of letters sat at your
elbow. So someone did write." Resentment put a bite
into Raul's voice. "For how long, sir, was my family
ignored?"

"I judged it better to cleanly sever your ties with
Moricadia." Not an answer, but it told Raul so much.

"A clean amputation, you might say."

"Exactly." Grimsborough seemed to believe Raul
approved.

"Where are the letters now?"

"I gave them to Thompson to burn. Why?"

"I'm returning to Moricadia, sailing on tomorrow evening's tide, and I would like to know the situation I face." Raul twirled his watch fob. "But perhaps not knowing is better."

"Mori . . . Moricadia?" In the first spontaneous movement Raul had ever seen from him, Grimsborough came to his feet. "What do you intend to do in Moricadia? There's nothing there!"

"You are very wrong. Moricadia is famous for its gambling houses, its spas, its pleasure seekers—and its racetracks. I have purchased a castle with extensive stables. My hostler, my handler, my horses have preceded me. I shall make a fine living among the *bon ton.*"

Grimsborough strode around the desk and came to a halt in front of Raul, his nostrils flared, his green eyes lit with cold fury. "Where did you get this money for horses? For travel? For a castle? Have you been stealing from me?"

Raul held his temper as he held his horses, with a steady hand and a fine eye for the winning move. "How would that be possible, sir? You've gambled away most of your fine fortune, and word is out on London streets—loan no more to the Viscount Grimsborough, for that way lies penury."

Grimsborough flung his head back in shock. Lifted his hand to slap his son.

Raul looked into his eyes, his own gaze icy with warning. "I would not do that if I were you."

The silence that followed was long, fraught with shifting power.

Grimsborough's hand dropped.

He was, possibly for the first time in his life, afraid of another person.

"Very wise," Raul said.

Raul's taunt infuriated his father, and, putting his face close to Raul's, Grimsborough said, "You owe me for your education! Your clothes! Your life! I demand that you give up this ridiculous scheme to return to—" He caught his breath, his eyes becoming a pale green as an old memory returned to him. "Wait! You still think you're some kind of Moricadian royalty, don't you? Well, let me tell you, my lad, when I seduced her, your mother was nothing but a serving maid in my hotel. When I left her, I told her to send word if she was with child and the child was a son. I heard nothing until you arrived on my doorstep. God knows what happened after I left her. She no doubt prostituted herself."

Raul swallowed the bile in his throat. "My grandfather wouldn't have allowed such a thing."

Grimsborough drew himself up to his full height—only to discover he no longer overtopped Raul. Wild with rancor, he said, "Ha! Your grandfather was nothing but an old peasant with aspirations. I don't even know if you're mine."

A scurrilous insult, and one both men knew to be false.

They stared at each other from identically colored eyes, two men who shared nothing but blood and bone—and an abiding hatred for the other.

"All the better reason for me to leave England. Farewell, Father. I hope that our paths never cross again." Raul strode toward the door. Turning, he faced his father again. "By the way, you might want to find yourself a new butler. Thompson is going with me to Moricadia."

"You worthless bastard." Grimsborough's words slashed at Raul.

Raul paused. Took a grip on his suddenly precarious temper. "A bastard, certainly. The bastard son of the biggest wastrel in all England. I wonder, Father, what you will do next."

Grimsborough hissed like a dying snake.

With a bow, Raul walked out, wanting desperately to leave this house forever, but bound by his promise to one sister and his affection for the others.

Bound, when he would rather be free.

Chapter Five

Smiling, nodding, Victoria made her way through the ballroom, then up the stairs, never slowing to speak to the other revelers until she could step outside the open door onto the long balcony that rimmed the upper story.

The night was warm, clear, and moonless. The fresh air had enticed the small groups who stood in the light of the open windows and gazed out over the midnight gardens.

Composure determinedly intact, Victoria turned to the right, got to the corner of the stately home, then turned right again toward the darkest corner, where the sound of the music and conversation faded. There she walked more slowly, taking care not to stumble over chairs artfully placed in conversational poses, toward the stone railing, and stared blindly into the moonless night. She listened oh so carefully, and when she had heard no voices, no footsteps, no sound, she took a breath to ease the constriction of her chest. Then, with careful deliberation, she broke, one by one, the ivory stays of her white lace fan. Staring at it as if it were the focus of her ire, she said, "You . . . insufferable . . . ass." Her voice was quiet, intense . . . shaking. She took another breath. "How dare you . . . ? As if I want *you* . . . You're rich and you're ugly and you're old and you're fickle and—" Another long breath. "Fifty years old. Fifty! And I'm barely eighteen. Puny, bony, gray complexioned, and married. Disgusting! Have you never heard there's no fool like an old fool? Do you imagine I'm here looking for a patron?" She put her fingers to her face and realized angry tears wet the fingers of her borrowed white gloves. Tears of anger. Tears of humiliation.

The first time Lord Meredith rubbed his elbow against her breast, she had thought it was an error.

The second time, she flushed, excused herself, and moved away.

This was her fault. All her fault. She should never have allowed Belle and her sisters to dress her up like a fancy doll. The gown was the height of fashion: a glowing azure silk, cut with a wide skirt that gathered at her tiny waist, puff sleeves that bared her shoulders and back. She should have realized that some vile man would interpret it as an invitation.

But she was always careful. Always. A girl in her position couldn't afford scandal. Foolishly, she had thought herself safe here, in her friend's noble home. She had imagined that men who would take advantage of a woman left virtually alone in the world would respect the reputable circumstances if not the impoverished female.

Her mother would be pleased to know this lesson of propriety had been thoroughly learned, and with no damage to Victoria's good character.

She took another long breath as she tried to ease the constriction of the corset that pinched her waist so harshly. Then, as she remembered Lord Meredith's touch, she shuddered and her skin crawled. "I wouldn't have a man like you. . . ." Lord Meredith wasn't here to listen, but she berated him anyway. "I wouldn't have any man. . . . Cretin! Inbred buffoon!"

Yes. She had to take every care, for if she failed to safeguard her reputation, no one would hire her as a governess and she would suffer only two choices—living forever in her stepfather's home on his grudging charity, or taking a man like Lord Meredith as her protector.

Both options were unacceptable.

She stared at the broken, shredded fan, then threw it as hard as she could.

The lace caught the breeze, flapped here and there like a wounded bat, and landed in the bushes far below.

"Unspeakable!" she said.

A man's voice spoke from behind her. "An illuminating display, Miss Cardiff."

She whirled to face the witness so well concealed by the darkest shadows at the edge of the house.

She couldn't see him, but she knew who he was. She would recognize that voice, the way he spoke her name, anywhere. "Mr. Lawrence. I didn't realize you were there." If she had, she would have walked to a place where she could enjoy her rage in private.

"That had occurred to me." His voice sounded vilely

amused. "Miss Cardiff, if you're going to be a governess, you're going to have to learn to control that temper."

How did he know she intended to be a governess?

Someone had been talking about her.

Or he'd asked.

Either way, she was annoyed. "I assure you, Mr. Lawrence, I keep my temper under very firm control." *Usually. When I know I'm being observed.*

"Really?" His steps were silent, but his voice was closer. "I would have sworn I just observed a violent flare-up."

He was a swine. But what did she expect? She knew what he was. The bastard son of the Viscount Grimsborough, shoved down society's throat: a horseman, a gambler, a philanderer from whom no woman was safe. "What are you doing out here?" Did he have a woman with him in the shadows? Was he seducing someone and she interrupted?

"What was I doing out here?" His voice grew hard, moody. "Much the same as you, Miss Cardiff, much the same as you."

He was out here to cool his temper? What would make him angry? When she'd met him that afternoon, he'd been irritatingly entertained by her and by his sisters.

"Your display made me long for a fan to break," he said. "That looked satisfying."

He was right. It was satisfying, although now she was sorry she'd destroyed the pretty, frivolous thing that had cost her so much of her meager allowance, the one piece of her costume that was truly hers.

He moved to stand beside her at the rail, and she could see him now, a dark shadow clad in black with a touch of white at his cravat, a face barely visible in the darkness, and eyes that observed her with nerve-racking intent.

She was tall.

He was taller.

She took a deep breath.

He smelled good, clean, like cut grass and fresh air.

Out here, alone, in the dark, he behaved like a gentleman.

But would a gentleman make her bunch her fists in the silk of her skirt, aware of the rasp of thin, cool thread against the delicate skin of her fingers? Would a gentleman make the sounds of music and conversation fade from her consciousness? Would a gentleman make the memory of Lord Meredith diminish to insignificance?

She thought not. "I should go back in."

"To be further accosted by some doddering old fool?"

So much for her hope that he hadn't heard her tirade. Gathering her skirts, she said, "I shall take care to avoid doddering old fools."

"And run away now to avoid me."

"Don't flatter yourself," she snapped. *Hm.* Perhaps her control was not so firm as she had hoped. "I am not avoiding you, sir; I'm doing what any young lady would do when surprised by a gentleman in a lonely place. I am retreating to protect myself from gossip." Then, trying to inject some humor into the simmering atmosphere, she said, "I suppose I should be grateful that a prince has found me tonight, but unfortunately, I've never believed in fairy tales." She started to walk away.

His hand unerringly caught her wrist and yanked her to a stop. "To what are you referring?"

She blinked in surprise and . . . *Oh, dear* . . . Had she

spoken hastily and in malice? "I'm referring to the stories you told your sisters about being an exiled prince." Stories that had caused her a great deal of private amusement. "Now, if you'll excuse me—"

"Belle told you I was a prince?" He did *not* sound equally amused, and he didn't let her go.

Belatedly, Victoria realized he might not relish his sister's gossiping about him. "She said a king, but I thought since I was referencing a fairy tale—" She was babbling, she realized, because he held her wrist.

"How many other giggling schoolgirls did she tell?" For the first time since he'd joined her, she heard the crack of rage in his voice.

His grip on her wrist remained the same: loose, but inexorable. She felt a chill slide up her spine. "No one. I assure you, sir, she meant no harm."

"And how many did *you* tell?"

Now her rage crackled. "No one! Why would I?" She wrenched herself out of his grasp. "I don't find you interesting, and I assure you, I didn't take her story seriously."

He stepped in front of her, stopped her when she would have stormed off. "You have a waspish tongue and not a lot of good sense."

Beatings from her stepfather and her harried mother's advice had taught her to tame that waspish tongue.

She'd had no choice.

Yet here she was, thoroughly angry, defiant in the face of Mr. Lawrence's aggression. Why this bastard Grimsborough son made her rage, she didn't know. Perhaps she cast him in the role of villain, putting him in the place of Lord Meredith. Which was foolish beyond belief, yet despite her attempts to stop them, words bubbled up in her and she flung the truth in young Lawrence's face. "I don't understand you. You're the illegitimate son of the Viscount Grimsborough, raised in his household, given the kinds of opportunities most of us would kill for."

"And a father most men would kill to avoid."

Victoria knew what he said was true. In the depths of night, she and Belle had shared stories of the fathers who had ruled their lives, who dismissed them as unimportant, who sought to crush them with indifference. And Belle had told Victoria that Grimsborough had been one hundred times worse to his son because Raul *was* his son. But right now, Victoria wasn't in the mood to be fair. "Are you *never* satisfied with your lot? To be better educated, better fed, better clad than your fellow Englishmen, yet still you expect worship for imaginary royal blood coursing through your veins."

"A waspish tongue," he repeated, "and not a lot of good sense."

Outraged, she said, "I am one of the most sensible women I know!"

"You're a fool of unimagined proportions."

He pushed her toward the rail, lifted her off her feet.

With a shock, she realized he was right. She was a fool.

It was fifteen feet to the terrace and the marble floor below. If he let go—

Chapter Six

As Victoria teetered on the rail, she flung one arm around Raul's neck. She wrapped her fist in his cravat, crushing the starched knot. Opening her mouth, she prepared to scream.

And he kissed her. Not the first gentle, pleasant kiss of her girlish dreams, but a hot, angry, openmouthed kiss that swallowed her shout and shocked her senses.

He wanted to murder her. She could taste it in his rage.

And she could taste something else.

Passion.

Not like the slimy Lord Meredith, but a searing heat, burning away all the extraneous emotions, catapulting her into sensuality, setting her innocence ablaze.

She scrabbled for balance. For freedom. Started to bite his marauding tongue.

But before she could, he jerked his head up, muttered, "Bite me and I'll throw you over the edge."

He sounded so furious, so menacing.

Then, belying his threat, he swung her around, put her feet on the floor. With his arms around her, he pushed her back, and when he had her trapped between his body and the wall of Grimsborough Abbey, he kissed her again.

Each kiss was brief, bitter, sharp, volatile, like gunpowder set alight, as if Raul and Victoria were two elements that together resulted in explosion after explosion. Each kiss tasted of restlessness, of frustration, of a longing to fly free.

His? Hers? She didn't know. She knew only that each time he lifted his head, thought returned to her mind, she suffered the burn of shame, and she tried to speak, to shove him aside.

Then he kissed her again, and another detonation set her on fire.

At last he stopped, and in the darkness, she could hear him panting.

She was panting, too, torn apart by a need she had never imagined.

The granite was cool and rough against her exposed shoulder blades.

He held her tightly, too tightly.

She should scream, cry, struggle. . . .

But she liked this.

Why? What perverted part of her liked feeling his chest heaving against hers? How could she experience the warm sense of safety in the arms of a man who had threatened to toss her off a balcony? What madness made her experience an affinity to a bastard driven by some unexplained rage to lust?

It was as if she understood him. As if she, Victoria Cardiff, sensible and prosaic, had found the one mate who would allow her to be the woman she truly was. . . .

Then he sighed. Relaxed. His grip around her waist loosened, became a warm cradle of comfort. He leaned into her again, but this time he cupped her throat in his hand, nudged her chin up with his thumb, found her mouth with his, and kissed her . . . differently. His fury had evaporated, become something *more*. His fingers stroked the hollow behind her ear, caressed the sensitive, satin skin of her jaw.

His lips pressed against hers, no longer rudely invasive, but coaxing her in gentle strokes, reminding her how he had looked when she first saw him: too handsome, with sunshine gleaming on his dark hair, turning his tanned skin golden, making his green eyes glow with sinful promise. For the first time, their passion no longer felt dangerous, no longer seemed as if it would blow them apart with its violence, and with the transformation, the tight anger that held her in its grip eased.

Distantly, she heard the music of the party, knew that somewhere people were talking, laughing, eating, drinking, behaving as civilized human beings should. As Victoria herself always did.

But out here . . . the warm air was redolent with the rich scent of night-blooming nicotiana, the darkness enclosed them seductively, and the slow heat of Raul Lawrence made her blossom, made her reach for him with her body, with her heart. She eased herself against him, tilted her face to better fit their mouths together, and answered him with the touch of her tongue to his lower lip.

"Witch," he whispered against her mouth. "I knew . . . when I saw you today . . . you would enchant me."

His kiss this time was deep, intimate, seeking something. Seeking *everything*.

And she gave it to him, allowing him the freedom to discover the way her breath quivered in her lungs, her startled reaction to his tenderness, the drift of desire that rose with every brush of his tongue against hers.

Her previous tension had slid away. Now it returned, no longer incensed, outraged, but more of a striving toward some unseen goal. She didn't exactly know where they were going, only that she wanted to get there soon . . . and with him.

It seemed to her that this man was *like* her: wounded, yet fighting, seeking comfort and giving strength, and for the briefest moment she wondered how it was possible, when they had so little in common, that their souls combined with such sweet heat.

After many long moments, he once again lifted his head. His fingers caressed her throat, then fell away.

He put distance between them. Not a lot. But enough to allow the chill of reality to touch her.

What was she doing?

She still held his cravat in her fist. Her arm was still wrapped around his neck. Her lips stung and her skin felt hot, swollen, as if this new thing he had set alight had burned her from the inside out.

And suddenly, she saw herself as others would see her—an opportunist, using her friendship with Belle to advance herself into the position of mistress to a wealthy man. In other words, she was behaving exactly as Lord Meredith had believed she would.

With a whimper of horror, she loosened her grip on Raul.

He stepped back. "Miss Cardiff." His voice was concerned. *Concerned*, as if he feared she would demand something from him: jewels, a home fit for an opera singer. "Miss Cardiff, I must beg your pardon for my inopportune act."

He was *apologizing. Apologizing* for the things they had done together.

Brittle anger galloped over the top of the horror. "You! You!"

He waited, but when she said no more—how could she? She was incoherent with shame—he continued. "I had no right to mock you and your temper when mine is so uncontrolled. I freely admit my fault."

He was not only apologizing, but he had been the one to call a halt to this impetuous display of . . . of . . . insanity.

For that, she wanted to slap him.

Instead impulsive words burst from her, too loud, too harsh, cruel and unjust. And she knew it. But she didn't care. She knew only that she wanted to hurt him as he had hurt her. "You, Mr. Lawrence! Do you imagine you are somehow better than Lord Meredith? Forcing a kiss on me, threatening me with death, making me respond when you know I have no experience, possibly ruining me for any decent employment? And why?"

"Again, I express my regrets." His voice was not quite as conciliatory now. "My father made me angry."

"Your *father*, your real *father*, made you angry? Isn't that too bad?" She took a breath, knowing she would regret her temper. She always did. But right now she had a choice: Say the wrong thing, or cry. And she would not cry, not in front of Mr. Lawrence. "I know men like you."

"Do you?"

No. Not like him, really. Like her stepfather, who

would gladly have kept her at home for the rest of her life to care for her stepsiblings, until she was bitter and old and all the bright, shining promise of the world had passed her by. But she couldn't be fair now. Not to Mr. Lawrence, who had *apologized* for what had felt to her like the meeting of two souls.

She was the world's biggest fool. "Men like you," she said, "are bullies who use their power to enforce their will, who can't control their anger, who make excuses for their brutality." She braced herself, waiting for him to slap her as she so richly deserved. Waiting for him to prove he was as ruthless as she claimed.

Instead, he said, "How you must hate knowing a false prince, a brute, and a bully made you respond to his kisses." His drawl mocked her, drove the righteous fury from her lungs.

Because it was true. She had responded. Exalted. Explored.

And she was ashamed. Ashamed of her passion, and ashamed of the hot words that had betrayed so much of herself and lashed so brutally at a man who had done nothing so dreadful except to give her pleasure. To give her a taste of what she could never have.

Gathering her borrowed silk skirt in her hand, she whirled and stalked toward the ballroom.

Chapter Seven

On the road in Moricadia
Three years later

One of Victoria's two charges sidled up to her and tugged at her arm. "Miss Cardiff, the forest has eyes."

"What, dear?" Victoria pressed a cool, wet rag to Mrs. Johnson's bruised arm.

"This forest has eyes," said Effie urgently.

Victoria glanced up.

The trees hovered hard against the edges of the road to the Moricadian capital, and beyond those edges, little sunshine pierced the dense canopy of green. Victoria could see why the fanciful sixteen-year-old might think so. "It certainly looks that way, doesn't it?" Victoria asked.

Shivering, the girl huddled close to her mother. "I saw them. Eyes watching me."

"No, dear." Her mother smoothed Effie's blond hair back from her thin face. "It's just your imagination."

"They hate us," Effie said.

"Oh, Effie. Don't be ridiculous." Maude, who was seventeen and imagined herself the height of sophistication, sat in the carriage, her dignity, her clothes, and her imagination intact. "The trees are not alive. Are they, Miss Cardiff?"

Victoria looked around.

The road to Tonagra, Moricadia's capital city, was well tended, but steep and winding, with unexpected drop-offs and narrow places that had made Victoria hold her breath. An unexpected falling log had rammed the lead traveling coach, tearing one wheel off its axis, making the coach careen off the road and almost over a precipice, bruising Mrs. Johnson and making Mr. Johnson bluster in his anxiety about his wife.

Victoria and the Johnson daughters had been in the second coach and had barely stopped in time. The third coach—the baggage coach—and the three maids who attended the Johnson women had arrived late to the scene. All the Moricadian men had leaped out and gone to work to right and repair the coach. The native driver insisted the accident was just that, a random occurrence.

But Victoria looked now at the log.

It had been freshly sawed and dropped. To disrupt their passage? But why? And the forerunners were muttering among themselves. They were all strong men, tall, thin, with smooth, dark-tanned complexions, black hair, and dark eyes.

They reminded her of . . . of Raul Lawrence. Stupid to be thinking of him, but this was, after all, where he had removed himself and his horses. This was the country where he had claimed to be a king.

The letters she'd received from dear Belle had confessed their father was furious with his ungrateful son, that all ties had been cut, that the girls had been forbidden to communicate with him, but word from English people doing the Grand Tour was that Raul supported himself in a splendid manner.

Victoria was *so* glad for him.

She took a calming breath, erased the sarcasm, and tried again.

She was glad for him. Calmly, coolly glad for him. Truly, she was.

The kiss—or rather, those kisses—had happened a long time ago; three years, to be exact. But for months after, she had spent the nights awake, thinking what she should have said, what she should have done, how hard she should have slapped him, the way she should have shamed him with her quiet reproachfulness, thinking up any scenario except the one where they kissed passionately and then flung bitter words at each other like two spoiled, emotional children.

If occasionally, very occasionally, she had even recalled the forbidden thrill, the sweeping passion, the dangerous edge of his ardor . . . well, she was over that now. She hadn't thought of Raul Lawrence for a year, or at least not for many months, and when Mr. Johnson had announced he had been hired by a gentleman in Moricadia who wished to have his financial advice, Victoria's gasp had not been an indicator of dismay on her part.

Although right now—once more, she looked at the fallen log—perhaps her trepidation had been for good reason.

"Miss Cardiff, if you would." Mr. Johnson gestured her to him.

Rising, she walked to his side.

Mr. Johnson was a big, barrel-chested man with a florid face and a loud voice, common to the depths of his bones. He was also so shrewd about finance that his knowledge bordered on genius, and while their two-year journey through Europe had ostensibly been to see to his daughters' education and polish, he'd used the time to consult with men of wealth and property about how to increase and preserve their wealth and property. His work had proved an education for Victoria, for once he discovered her mathematical skills he used her as an accountant, and while he did, he explained the complexities of the European economy.

For a young woman who had been raised in hopeless servitude, his instruction provided the first glimmer of light in the long blight of her life. She knew she could never work as Mr. Johnson did; she knew she was *not* a financial genius, and in any case, women were not encouraged in such intellectual pursuits. Yet Victoria absorbed his every word, asked questions, and ultimately learned how to invest her salary. If all went well, her savings meant that someday she could function as an autonomous woman, travel for her own pleasure, perhaps buy a small home of her own in the English countryside. . . .

Okay, that was rather depressing—to realize that by the time she achieved such an independence, her likely companion would be a cat. She liked cats, but to dwindle into old age alone . . .

She shook herself.

Better that than to be like her mother, a slave to the man she called her husband.

Mr. Johnson flung himself into speech as he flung himself into everything: bluntly and without introduction. "I see, Miss Cardiff, you already comprehend my problem."

She inclined her head, not comprehending at all but knowing full well that Mr. Johnson would enlighten her.

"The accident was no accident, but sabotage, the work of desperate men who wish to topple Moricadia's government."

Appalled, she asked, "But why?"

"Because of some mumbo jumbo about a true king coming to free the people from their onerous overlords."

Raul! Victoria's jaw sagged. The blood drained from her face. *Raul Lawrence!*

"Yes." Mr. Johnson took her shock to be a civilized person's amazement at such superstition. "Not that the people here aren't exploited. I did my research before agreeing to this job, and the people are indeed oppressed. But ignorant, too. Rumors claim the ghost of the last true king has been seen riding the roads, taking his revenge on the ruling tyrants. They say it's a sign that the new true king is ready to depose the de Guignards."

"The de Guignards," she echoed faintly.

How was it possible that she had come to Moricadia to hear . . . this? This tale that sounded so much like Mr. Lawrence's own conceit?

It wasn't possible, of course. Mr. Lawrence couldn't be a deposed *king*. Perhaps he was a liar, although he hadn't seemed the type to . . .

Well. One minor kiss, or even a dozen rather intense kisses, didn't mean that she *knew* the man. She most certainly did not. He might well be a liar.

"The de Guignards are truly dreadful rapscallions, keeping the Moricadians in poverty in both the countryside and in tenements in the lower parts of the cities. So I suppose it's not surprising the rebels have stirred up the people." Mr. Johnson stroked his mustache.

But a more likely scenario was that Mr. Lawrence must have heard this myth when he was a boy and took it too much to heart, for according to the tales Belle had told, Mr. Lawrence had claimed he was the true ruler of Moricadia, and when he returned, he would take his country back from the usurpers.

"Stirred them up so they're attacking visitors to their country?" she asked. "You told us this country thrives on the money they make off their visitors."

"Yes, in the gambling houses. The mineral hot springs. The racetracks. If the rebels drive off their tourists—well, I've taught you what happens then."

"Yes. If they drive off the tourists, the government will be deprived of their income, and they will fall." She glanced at the Johnson family. Victoria had grown fond of them. "Do you fear violence?"

His shrewd, heavy face settled into worry lines. "Perhaps. Prince Sandre was the victim of a humiliating joke. His cousin Jean-Pierre has taken control of the government, brought in mercenaries. His master of the dungeon is known for his inventiveness. Yet it is Jean-Pierre who is *feared*, and for good reason. The man is cruel clear to the bone. As soon as the men clear the lead coach off the road, I want you to take Mrs. Johnson and the girls to the Hôtel de Tonagra. Check them in, get them settled, and I'll follow when the coach has been repaired."

"Of course."

"Here." He offered her a pistol. "It's loaded. There's one shot. If you must use it, make it count."

She stared at the gray metal barrel, the polished wood

butt. Before they left England, Mr. Johnson had insisted she learn to shoot. He said he needed someone of good sense who could handle firearms. Obviously, that did not include his wife and daughters. Maude was vain and selfish. Effie was young and silly. And Mrs. Johnson was a peahen who babbled so constantly Victoria didn't know how Mr. Johnson bore it. Yet he adored her, adored his children, and he would do anything to protect them from the dangers of the world.

Living with the Johnsons had been a revelation for Victoria. No matter their faults, no matter their annoyances, no matter their fights—and there were many—they were a family, united against the world and led by a loving father.

It was good to know men like him existed.

It was difficult not to be jealous.

But these two years had been a time of deepening maturity for her. Traveling through Europe, educating and polishing the Johnson children, becoming fluent in languages, and discovering a way to support herself when inevitably she grew old: Those events had changed her life. She was not the same girl she had been, given to occasional storms of anger and frustration. She was not helpless anymore. She controlled her own destiny, and now Mr. Johnson trusted her with his family's lives.

Taking the pistol, she hid it in her skirts. Nodded to him. "I'll manage with one shot."

"Good girl. Once we get to the city, we'll be safe." He patted her on the top of the head, his attention already back on the horses and men dragging the coach out of the way. "Keep your guard up. Around this place, the trees have eyes."

Chapter Eight

The hotel lobby was warm, lofty, elegant, decorated with potted plants and vases with flowers, and with red carpet rolled from the door across the long marble floor to the elaborate polished wood desk. There, two men dressed in the height of fashion stood behind a leather book placed on a stand. They frowned, disapproving of this young, single woman who dared to breach their respectable establishment, but Victoria took no heed of their censure; in her two years spent traveling through Europe with the Johnsons, she had been forced to deal with a great many surly foreigners. As she walked between the two rows of pale pink marble columns, she glanced about her, examining the lush artwork, the stylish dining room through the broad arched doorway, the man standing on the bottom step of the curved stairs. . . .

It was him. Raul Lawrence.

Her gait slowed.

Bad luck. The worst. Impossibly bad. The first person of quality whom she viewed here could not be the one man she wished never to see again.

She glanced once more.

She was mistaken. That wasn't Mr. Lawrence. The resemblance was striking, but . . . no. He did not look the same.

Good clothes: black trousers and black coat, carefully fitted, shining black boots, a formfitting white shirt. But his body: leaner through the hips, bulkier at the shoulders, in some indefinable way tougher . . . Long, dark hair pulled back in a severe style that bared his face. Skin molded closely to the broad forehead, high cheekbones, firm chin.

It couldn't be him. Mr. Lawrence had been a youth, angry and wild. This was a man, focused, intent.

Another glance, one that lingered this time.

But his lips . . . Ah, it must be Mr. Lawrence, for she remembered those lips only too well; they were as full and velvety-looking as before. And the way he watched her: head tilted down like a bull about to charge, his green eyes veiled, smoldering . . . and still promising sin.

She jerked her gaze away from his, faced forward, kept walking steadily toward the desk.

She should greet him. After all, it had been three years since their encounter, and he was her best friend's brother.

But he had *stared* at her in a manner that bespoke a heated remembrance of those moments on the balcony, of the angry words they had exchanged.

She stopped at the desk.

The clerks looked down their noses at her. "Welcome to the Hôtel de Tonagra, Miss . . . ?"

She said crisply, "My employer, Mr. Johnson, sent his family ahead with me to check in."

The noses became level. One man turned to pull a sheaf of paper from the shelves behind him. "Mr. Johnson and his family are here? Now?"

"Mrs. Johnson and the children are here. Mr. Johnson's traveling coach was hit by a falling tree. You may wish to send help." She viewed the two men coldly. "I am Miss Cardiff, their governess. The ladies are waiting at the door in the second coach. You may also wish to send assistance to them. They are badly shaken by the accident that so threatened their father."

She wasn't surprised to see the men jump into action. She knew how to use her voice to force obedience out of hotel clerks across the continent. "The luggage coach is following close behind," she added.

One man picked up a whistle and blew it twice.

Servants rushed from doors and cubbies toward the entrance and the waiting coach.

There. Victoria had completed her mission for Mr. Johnson.

Now to deal with Mr. Lawrence and his reaction to her—and her reaction to him.

She hoped Mr. Lawrence didn't carry a grudge. Yes, that evening three years ago, she had been sharp-tongued in a manner that embarrassed her now. She had let her temper get the best of her in a way she had never done since. She had said things that, in the lonely, dark hours of the night, she had regretted.

But he had done things, too. Said things. Rude things. Unforgivable things. Surely he remembered that—

although in her experience, men were not fair in their recollections or their opinions.

Still, as she had walked into the Hôtel de Tonagra, she had effectively given him the cut direct. She hadn't meant to. She had been so shaken by his unexpected appearance that the good manners she impressed on the Johnson girls had left her, and she . . . Well, she was rude. Unacceptably rude.

She had herself under control now. She would nod to him as soon she turned, and smile politely. She would beg pardon, give the excuse that she was so shaken by the incident on the road and so involved in doing her duty, she had failed to note him.

He would pretend to believe her.

The incident would be over.

But when she turned toward the stairway, a man and a woman stood there, he in a green plaid suit, she in a rose satin gown, observing the bustle of the Johnsons' arrival.

Victoria looked around the lobby, seeking that lone, dark-clad figure.

Raul Lawrence was nowhere in sight.

"Did you see that gentleman?" she asked the desk clerk. "The one who stood on the stairway when I walked in? He was tall, clad in black. He had long, dark hair and green eyes."

The desk clerk scrutinized her as if she had spouted two heads. "Miss Cardiff, I have been observing the lobby all day, and have seen no one who fits that description."

"No one?" She leveled her gaze at him. "Surely gentlemen in black suits are not so rare."

"Here in Moricadia, our guests take the waters,

party, gamble. They relax, and they dress accordingly."
He glanced significantly at the colorful couple who had
taken Mr. Lawrence's place.

"Yes, but . . ." Other guests wandered in from the dining room, confirming his statement. Everyone, young
and old, babbled cheerfully in different languages, wore
bright, fashionable garb, and observed the Johnsons' arrival with avid interest.

Mrs. Johnson appeared at the entrance and waved
her handkerchief at Victoria. "Miss Cardiff! Miss Cardiff! Come at once. We need you to direct the servants."

As Victoria hurried toward the family, she continued
to look around.

But she could see no sign of Raul Lawrence.

Had she so thoroughly offended him?

Or had she imagined him after all?

Chapter Nine

Maude rushed into the suite Victoria shared with her charges, her cheeks bright with excitement. "Father wishes you would come to help him."

"Does he?" Victoria smiled at the pretty, plump girl with the carefully coiffed brown hair and the sparkling blue eyes. "Is he recovered from the accident?"

"You know Father. He's fuming, but he's healthy as a horse. He says he needs help with his figures." Maude twirled the curl that rested on her shoulder. "You'll put him into a good mood, won't you?"

"I can't promise that. But I will certainly assist him with his accounting." Victoria nodded to the three maids who had unpacked under her direction. "Take our traveling clothes and have them cleaned and pressed, and have them returned by tomorrow morning." She'd learned to be firm with the foreign chambermaids, give them time limits, or they took advantage of the foolish English tourists.

These girls curtsied and nodded, and the spokeswoman said, "Yes, Miss Cardiff. It will be as you say." Then, turning to the others, she translated . . . something. Victoria hoped it was her message, but despite her gift with languages, she hadn't been able to comprehend the Moricadian speech. She had thought it would be similar to Spanish or French, but instead it seemed distinct, not derived from Latin at all, but from some far older tongue, a language created when the world was young and all of mankind was primitive and savage.

Victoria stood, straightened her collar and cuffs, and prepared to attend Mr. Johnson. When she turned back to Maude, the girl was holding her needlework frame, ready to go. "You want to listen while your father and I do a stranger's accounting?" Victoria asked. "When instead you could take your maid and explore this glorious hotel?"

"I like to spend time with my parents," Maude said quickly.

Victoria sat back down. "All right, what's going on?"

"Why would anything be going on?" Maude did innocence badly, and when Victoria continued to interrogate her with her gaze, Maude collapsed on the sofa. "Oh, all right! There's a ball."

"When?"

"Tonight!"

"Where?"

"Here at the hotel. They have one here every Thursday night for their guests. Everyone comes and dances until the wee hours of the morning." Victoria shook her head, but before she could speak, Maude rushed on. "Oh, Miss Cardiff, this is our last stop. Next, we're returning to England, and when that happens, I shall have to be that most boring of creatures, a debutante. I can't have fun. I can't dance with too much pleasure. I can't talk knowledgably about my travels or drink wine or kiss a prince in the darkness. Because my father is an accountant, and for me to marry well, I must be exemplary. You know it's true, Miss Cardiff. You know how dreadful it will be. I'm beautiful and I know it, and I will make a good match, I promise, but let me have one evening of champagne and laughter and dance. Just one, and I swear I'll be good for the rest of my life."

It was as if Maude spoke directly to Victoria's heart. A mere three years ago, Victoria had felt exactly this same way before a ball. She had given in to temptation, enjoyed a few hours of youthful joy, then . . . Ah, but there was no reason to think Maude's desires would turn out to have the same consequences as her own. Except . . . this country might soon suffer a revolution.

But Mr. Johnson said they were safe in the city, and he believed it. If he didn't, they wouldn't be here.

The question was—did Victoria agree with him? She had seen Raul Lawrence today; she knew she had. If he was in the heart of the city, if he was the center of the revolution, then they were in danger.

But he'd been here three years. What had he been doing in that time? Had he discovered that being mythical royalty was more difficult than he imagined? That leading a bunch of uneducated natives to overthrow their cruel overlords involved more than he planned? Or had he discovered the good life—he certainly had been dressed well—and given up on his dream?

Seeing Victoria's hesitation, Maude produced her ultimate argument. "I just want to dance with young, handsome men who are interested in me not because of my father's money, but because I'm pretty! Is that such a crime?"

Victoria smiled. Trust Maude to make Victoria pointedly aware of the difference between them: Victoria had wanted freedom; Maude wanted to be admired because she was pretty. Still, who was Victoria to judge Maude to be more foolish?

"You may ask your father if he will consent to the ball." Victoria rose again.

"And you'll back me?" Maude jumped to her feet.

"The answer will be in the capable, loving hands of your parents," Victoria said firmly.

"But you know you have influence on Father."

Yes, the influence of a sensible woman on a man surrounded by flighty females. "Come. You know your father does not endure waiting well."

Maude huffed in impatience, but she gathered up her needlework again and followed Victoria to Mr. Johnson's suite. Victoria knocked.

Maude pushed the door open and barged right in.

The oppressively luxurious room included a large sitting room with a desk, a fireplace, and a comfortable grouping of chairs upholstered in embroidered black velvet. Beyond, the bedroom contained a velvet-curtained bed on a tall dais, a Persian rug, dark wood floors, and wallpaper so busy it made Victoria's head swim.

Mr. Johnson observed her and grinned. "And they say I'm vulgar."

"This is an interesting place," Victoria said with careful neutrality.

"Bah. It's decadent. I wouldn't have brought the family if I'd realized." He glared through lowered brows at Maude. "What do you want?"

"Nothing, Father, but to spend some time with you." With a curtsy, she took a chair next to her mother and pulled the needle out of her crewel, then took a stitch.

"What's this about?" Mr. Johnson asked Victoria.

Book in hand, Effie poked her head out of the window seat. "She wants to go to the ball tonight."

"What?" Mr. Johnson roared.

"Thank you very much, Effie tattletale." Maude glared at her sister.

Effie made a moue of satisfaction and ducked her head back into the window seat.

"You are not going to go to some ball in some debauched foreign country where who knows what kind of reprobate will try to dance with you," Mr. Johnson yelled.

"Don't shout, dear," Mrs. Johnson said placidly.

"I am not shouting!"

Victoria moved to the doorway of the bedroom, where the three maids clutched Mrs. Johnson's gowns and cowered. "You might wish to hurry and put those clothes away so you can be gone."

One maid, the one who spoke English, Victoria assumed, translated into rapid Moricadian, and the three started moving furiously to finish their task.

Victoria nodded in satisfaction, then returned to sit at the desk, where Mr. Johnson's account books were open and waiting.

"We're working-class people, but you have a chance to marry well, maybe even a title—if you have a sterling reputation." Mr. Johnson was still roaring.

Maude, who was more like her father than she realized, stomped her foot. "Papa, I want to have fun *now*!"

Mr. Johnson's color turned from ruddy to purple. "Fun! That's not what I want for my daughters!"

"There's going to be music and dancing. And at midnight, a great buffet of fantastical food! And handsome men from all over the world!" Maude tossed her needlework aside. "Everyone's going. I want to go, too!"

Mrs. Johnson continued to sew.

Victoria leafed through the pages, trying to understand why Mr. Johnson had been summoned to handle these accounts, whatever they were. It looked as if someone with a lot of wealth intended to transfer it all out of the country.

She looked back at the title page, trying to find the owner, but only a stylized sketch of a boar graced the page.

"Maude, why can't you be more like Effie?" Mr. Johnson gestured toward the window seat. "She doesn't want to gallivant with strange men all night long!"

Mr. Johnson's blatant and unflattering comparison brought Victoria around in her chair.

Maude's face flushed an unattractive red and her resemblance to her father became marked.

Luckily, Effie slid out of the window seat and said, "I'd like to go to the ball, too."

Maude turned on her sister. "You can't go. You're only sixteen. And a tattletale!"

Mrs. Johnson placed her hand on Maude's arm. "Quiet, dear. Your father is thinking."

He wasn't thinking. He was floundering at this unexpected development. "You're too young. It's out of the question."

"I'm too young in England, but I'm not too young here." Effie so seldom asked for anything, she had the advantage here. "Please, Papa, I have that new gown you bought me in Venice, and if I don't wear it soon, it will be out of fashion."

"Horrors," he muttered. His color had begun to subside.

The crisis was over for the day.

"Miss Cardiff," he said, "you're the only woman who has any sense in this room. What do you think? Should I allow the children to go to a ball in a strange country with a bunch of disreputable strangers?"

Victoria looked beyond Mr. Johnson to see Mrs. Johnson concentrating on the needlework, and took her cue from Mrs. Johnson's slow nodding of her head. "It's not as if your daughters will be unchaperoned. I'll be there caring for them every moment, and you and your lovely wife will also, I know, keep a watchful eye out. Although perhaps you'll have time for a turn around the room yourselves?"

He stared at her forbiddingly, then swung around to Mrs. Johnson. "I know what you're doing. You women think you can handle me."

"I don't know what you mean, dear." Mrs. Johnson sounded as absentminded as usual.

"All right, then, damn it. We'll go."

The girls jumped up and down and clapped their hands.

He turned on them and pointed a beefy finger. "But if I see you step one toe out of line—"

Maude stopped her celebration at once. "No, Father, we'll be absolutely perfect!"

He continued. "If Miss Cardiff has one complaint—"

"She won't, I promise." Effie was still hopping on one foot.

He charged on. "We'll come back to the rooms at once!"

"We know, Papa." Maude grabbed Effie's hand. "Let's go tell the maids to iron our dresses."

The girls started backing toward the door.

"You go ahead and work, Papa," Effie said. "Miss Cardiff will help you."

Right before they disappeared into the corridor, Maude said, "Who knows, Papa? Maybe we'll find our prince at the ball."

Mr. Johnson stood shaking his head and staring at the empty doorway. "What a couple of ninnyhammers I've raised."

"That's a natural dream for a young lady," Mrs. Johnson said.

"And it's not impossible," Victoria said. "Today in the lobby, I saw Raul Lawrence, the son of the Viscount Grimsborough, and when he was in England, he claimed to be the true ruler of Moricadia."

From the bedroom, they heard a crash.

Victoria came to her feet at the sound.

Mr. and Mrs. Johnson swiveled to face the door.

The maid stood there, the one who spoke English, a silver tray in hand, broken glassware and plates at her feet. She stared at Victoria in horror, then said, "Pardon. I'm so stupid." Dropping to her knees, she scooped up the broken pieces with her bare hands, cutting herself in her haste.

Victoria hurried to her. Kneeling beside the maid, she caught hold of the woman's wrists. "Please. It's not such a terrible accident. Don't distress yourself so much."

The maid, who was surely no more than twenty, seemed to take no comfort from that, but grew even more round eyed and upset.

"What's your name?" Victoria asked.

"Amya," the girl said.

"It was a silly mishap," Victoria said, "and of no consequence."

The other maids hurried over, clucking with distress as they cleaned up the mess.

Victoria wrapped her handkerchief around the girl's bleeding fingers. "I swear, this is no reason to be unhappy. Mr. Johnson will pay the expenses." Victoria glanced at Mr. Johnson.

He nodded his agreement.

"If there're any repercussions, please, we'll help you."

Amya nodded repeatedly.

But she trembled under Victoria's grip, and Victoria worried what the hotel would do that the girl was so frightened. "Amya, you mustn't worry so much. Mr. Johnson will protect you."

"I am not worried for myself, Miss Cardiff, but for you." Amya's concerned eyes filled with tears.

"For me?" Victoria was puzzled. "But why?"

"You know . . . so much. I wonder—how soon can you leave Moricadia?"

Chapter Ten

Among the tumult and dust of the horse race, Raul Lawrence stood absolutely still, watching, waiting for Halcón Guerra to make his move. The colt was in his prime, a beast of unimaginable speed. The Welsh jockey knew his animal, rode him with an artistry that took every scornful European jockey by surprise.

And the horse would lose, because Raul decreed it so.

It wasn't yet time to win.

Almost. But not quite.

Raul could see Dafydd holding Halcón Guerra back, handling him with a delicate care that sympathized and promised at the same time. The jockey kept the colt in check until the last second, then allowed him to leap ahead to finish second.

"Ahh." In the box beside Raul, Baron Halse Huber

grunted with pleasure. "My horse beat yours once again. Perhaps you'll see your way to selling the colt to me . . . for two thousand guineas."

Raul smiled and bowed to the portly German. "My price is seven thousand guineas."

Baron Huber snorted. "I say. Are you insane? That price for a Thoroughbred that has never fulfilled his potential?"

"He will, and then the price won't be so low."

The baron brayed with laughter. "Would you care to bet on that?"

Raul covered his face with his hand; then, when he knew he had control of his expression, he pushed his hair out of his eyes. "As you wish, Baron, but do not say I didn't warn you." He gestured the man who recorded the wagers over, and took on not only the baron, but every other monied fool who believed he knew his way around the racetrack.

Raul *had* warned them all that Halcón Guerra would win, more than once.

They all laughed.

So when the time came, they would get what they deserved. Perhaps next time, they would recognize the better gambler—but probably not. Fools who bet against a professional gambler were, after all, where Raul made the bulk of his fortune.

Raul caught sight of his majordomo as Thompson stepped into the stands, and he tensed.

What was Thompson doing here? Grimsborough's former butler had made the transition to being Raul's right-hand man, organizing his home, his accounts, his servants, and the very, very constant task of maintaining security. For in this country ostensibly ruled by Prince

Sandre, the dreaded secret police pried and prodded into every attic, every bedroom, every lovers' tryst, and Raul guarded too many secrets to ever rest easy.

"Baron, gentlemen, if you'll excuse me? It appears the message from my mistress has arrived." Raul smiled and bowed, and moved to meet Thompson. Clapping his hand to the man's shoulder, he walked with him toward the stables, and when they were out of the crowds, he asked, "What has happened?"

The last three years had been good for Thompson. He had discovered an affinity for intrigue and a love for the mountains and forests of Raul's homeland. He still dressed like the stiffest of butlers, but it was now a disguise. In the high mountain air where intrigue ruled their lives, he had blossomed from a mere servant into one of Raul's most important weapons in the upcoming fight. He spied, he rode, he schemed. He had grown strong and tough. He was the man to whom the people came with information, and now, in a low voice, he said, "One of the maids from the Hôtel de Tonagra walked all the way to the castle."

The journey was eight miles, not a far distance, but the road was rough and the climb steep. For that reason, Raul had chosen it for his home base—it was close to the capital city that he needed to conquer, yet when he chose, they could make the way very, very difficult for a force to move on them.

But Thompson's tone made it clear the maid had made the trip for a reason, and so he asked, "Why?"

"She said an English lady, very beautiful, had seen you and claimed that you were purported to be the true king of Moricadia."

Raul didn't stumble, didn't show any exterior sign of

stress. But he knew the truth. Victoria Cardiff, foe, friend of his sister, and one hell of a kisser, had seen him, recognized him.

And he had recognized her.

He shouldn't have. Victoria Cardiff had not been on his mind the last three years. He'd been busy: returning to Moricadia, locating his family, establishing his credentials with the de Guignards, finding the castle he would use as his home base, becoming the gambler to beat in the casinos. Women had not been a concern; he had used them as covers for his activities and to maintain his image. He had no time for serious romance; he had a duty to his heritage, to his dead grandfather and his dead mother, and to the country. He took those duties seriously.

Then . . . there she was, Miss Victoria Cardiff, walking into the hotel. He had never in his wildest imaginings thought to see her there. How was it even possible? When he left England, she had been going to attend the Distinguished Academy of Governesses so she could teach children or some such ghastly duty. Probably catch the eye of some young banker and decide marriage was less onerous than work, marry the banker, have his children . . . Of course, the husband would be boring, a bad lover, an indifferent conversationalist, the kind of man who was shocked by his wife's hidden passions, and, being Victoria, she would put poison in his tea.

If he had thought about Victoria Cardiff at all, and he hadn't, that would have been the fate he imagined for her.

Instead, he strode through the lobby of the best hotel in Tonagra and saw her, and like it or not, he remembered the way she looked, the way she moved, the way she kissed. . . .

In an instant, his focus shifted from conquering Moricadia . . . to conquering Victoria. He became a predator, all instinct and dominance, hunting the woman who had escaped him once.

She would not escape him again. Because she had come into his territory.

She was his.

Chapter Eleven

But Raul had goals—to bring down the de Guignards, free his people, and establish his family in their rightful place as the rulers of Moricadia. It was too dangerous for him to claim Victoria, for if he did . . . she would distract him.

He knew that. He hated that. It was why, after seeing her at the Hôtel de Tonagra, he had disappeared behind one of the hotel's massive flower arrangements . . . and watched her.

She had not so much lost her youthful dewiness as subdued it with a severe hairstyle, a painfully plain gown, a mousy hat, and an expression meant to frighten the unwary. And the way she spoke to the desk clerks, like a barrage of bullets ripping holes in their composures. She was in training to become a severe old woman in wire-rimmed glasses, with a tight line for a mouth.

But beneath her traveling cape, he caught glimpses of her figure—the lush breasts contained by some torturous device, the tiny waist he remembered spanning in his hands. He supposed he'd touched many women who were equally repressed and equally well-endowed, yet none whom he cared to save from a spinster's fate.

Victoria Cardiff had been a beautiful challenge before, one the youthful Raul knew he could easily vanquish.

Today, only a seasoned man could see beyond the masks she wore and tear them aside.

Only Raul could find the heart of this woman.

In a low tone, Thompson asked, "Sir? About the maid?"

Raul focused on Thompson, and with equal care to any who might be listening, he said, "Is she one of ours?"

"Never before, but she knew the truth about you. She knew where to come to deliver the message." Thompson looked grim.

"Word is getting around. My return has become more than a rumor. We knew it would." In two months, as the leaves turned to gold, they would make their move. Raul would take back his country. Inevitably, as the army gathered, more and more people learned their intentions, and the chances of the de Guignards' discovering the truth were growing greater and greater. The longer they could put that off, the better. But . . .

"The maid's report—it might be a trap," Thompson said.

"No, no trap. The truth. Victoria knows Belle. She knows me. She's heard my story."

Thompson had known nothing about Miss Cardiff—no one knew—and he'd never seen a woman truly concern Raul one way or another, and he stood still in astonishment. He then hurried to catch up. "You remember her? From your sister's party?"

"As do you, apparently."

"I remember every person who attended any function in your father's house. It was my job, sir, as it is my job now to watch your back." *Ah*. No matter how informal Raul's household was when compared to Grimsborough's, Thompson would never lose his starch.

"I thank you for that."

Always, Thompson focused on the issue at hand. "Do you believe Miss Cardiff's comment was malicious?"

"Not at all. In my father's house, she took care to assure me she dismissed my claims to royal blood."

"Good heavens," Thompson said blankly. "I had no idea any woman was ever rude to you."

"Yes, well, Miss Cardiff was the first. And the last." At the memory, a small smile played around Raul's mouth.

"What do you want me to do about her?" Thompson asked.

"First, transport the maid back to the hotel."

"To watch and listen."

"Exactly."

They entered the cool, dim stables. The familiar smells of leather, of straw, of warm horseflesh and horse manure filled Raul's head. Wherever they were, the stables were his home. "How long will Miss Cardiff be in the city?"

"A week, maybe more. Her employer is acting for one of our nobles, transferring cash out of the country."

"Who?" Raul paused, well back from the stall where Dafydd groomed Halcón Guerra.

"I don't think even her employer knows for whom he's working."

"So. Whoever it is, is keeping it a secret." Raul doffed his hat and ran the rim through his fingers. "Have we perhaps begun to frighten the wealthy leeches of Moricadia more than the de Guignards themselves have frightened them?"

"We have, indeed. But this woman could ruin everything."

Raul stood, thinking, struggling against his baser instincts.

Thompson did not help. "I think we should take her, hold her until we've finished our business." The business of revolution, he meant.

But Raul needed to *concentrate*, and Victoria Cardiff's living in his home would not expedite sensible thought. "I won't proceed unless it becomes absolutely necessary."

"Why not? At such a delicate juncture—"

Raul gestured sharply, and although he didn't realize it, for a moment he looked so much like his autocratic father that Thompson winced. "No. I've burned my fingers on that dish before. I won't do it again." He proceeded toward the stall.

In a low, urgent voice, Thompson asked, "Do you wish to know if she repeats her tale?"

"Yes, because then I'll have to do . . . something." Raul hung his hat on the peg on the wall.

Dafydd had removed the colt's saddle and was grooming him, crooning a love song to his mount.

Raul took the brush out of the jockey's hand, took over the brushing and the singing. Halcón Guerra stood still, trembling from the strain of the race, and Raul stroked his neck, his haunches, humming wordlessly, reassuringly.

Dafydd struck a hostile pose. "He wants to win."

"He will," Raul said.

"If he doesn't win soon, he's going to lose heart."

"I understand." No one appreciated the colt the way Raul did; they had everything in common. Raul had been in Moricadia for three years, making the kind of fortune that would support an army, digging deep into the de Guignard secrets, learning the back roads, organizing his people. Every moment had been filled with background work, and now—he wanted to win. *They* wanted to win. Soon . . .

From the door of the stall, one man's hateful voice spoke. "Look at that. Raul Lawrence, son of the Viscount Grimsborough, grooming a horse."

Raul didn't pause, didn't flinch, didn't in any way show the depth of his repulsion. "Bastard son of the Viscount Grimsborough, Jean-Pierre, *bastard* son. I worked in my father's stables whenever he wasn't looking. How do you think I developed my own stables?"

"I've wondered exactly that." Jean-Pierre de Guignard stepped into the stall, his riding whip over his shoulder. "You're an enigma, Raul Lawrence, and I don't like enigmas. Not in my country."

"Your country?" Raul lifted a polite eyebrow. "Does Prince Sandre know you've claimed it?"

The left corner of Jean-Pierre's mouth twitched down. "Prince Sandre is glad to share with his family members, especially with the man who enforces his laws."

"Prince Sandre is well, then?" Raul asked politely.

"Very well. Why should you doubt it?"

"He hasn't been seen in public recently. There are rumors. . . ."

"Unfounded," Jean-Pierre said.

What Jean-Pierre didn't say was that Prince Sandre's recent humiliation had left him a recluse, afraid to go out, for inevitably laughter followed him. Quiet laughter, usually, suppressed titters or meaningful coughs, but during his last public appearance, the crowd of Moricadians had burst into jeers and shouts of, "Pig! Roasted pig!" and "Candlestick!" Jean-Pierre had sent the mounted royal guard through the crowd, but they had scattered like leaves before the wind, and Prince Sandre had slinked back into his palace to brood.

That vacuum left Jean-Pierre as the power in the kingdom. Jean-Pierre, with his dark hair, handsome face, muscular build—and eyes so light as to be almost white. In Moricadia, people said his eyes were that color because of his mother and the sexual activity for which she was most famous . . . and with so many men. Prince Sandre had been heard to claim Jean-Pierre was like a dog on the verge of rabies, and Sandre bragged about holding the chain.

Raul believed Jean-Pierre had broken free. No chain bound him, and everywhere he went, he inflicted pain and madness. Every day another Moricadian father was thrown into prison for poaching; another mother was accused of stealing to feed her starving children, and brutally and publicly beaten. The intent was not only to quash the recent upturn in crime, but to force the Moricadian rebels to show their hand before they were ready.

That was not going to happen.

But just as Jean-Pierre intended, the rebels suffered for every injustice.

Saber suffered.

There was no justice in Moricadia as long as Jean-Pierre remained in charge.

Now here he was. What had drawn Jean-Pierre's attention to Raul? Had he already heard about Victoria Cardiff's assertion?

"I recently—today, in fact—took a ride out to your castle," Jean-Pierre said.

"Did you? But surely you knew I would be *here* today!" At the track, where Raul was every race day.

"Yes. But I was curious why I—or indeed anyone—had never been invited to a party or a tea."

"You say you went out there. Do you understand why I'm not throwing parties to show off my home?"

"Yes. The castle is quite, shall we say, atmospheric. In a Gothic way. A rickety drawbridge. Black dungeons. Cobwebs hanging from the chandeliers . . ." Jean-Pierre strolled forward to pet Halcón Guerra.

The colt shied and retreated.

Raul calmed the colt, and assured Jean-Pierre, "You should have seen it when I moved in. It's much improved."

Jean-Pierre chuckled. "That's good, because my next curiosity was to wonder on what you spent your money."

"On what do most men spend their money?"

"You don't support a mistress."

"Instead I help a great many good"—Raul paused significantly—"friends."

"Yes. Women always speak well of you." A fact that did not seem to please Jean-Pierre. "Still, my visit never gave me an answer to my main question. Why would an

Englishman move to a country such as ours, settle down, and buy a tumbledown former royal palace?"

It was time to stop answering his questions, time to draw a line in the sand. "I did that three years ago."

"I have just recently become the man who enforces the de Guignard rule."

"True. You got the job only a few months ago, isn't that correct? When your predecessor was found hanging from a tree."

Dafydd edged out of the stable.

Thompson picked up a leather bridle and hung it on a nail.

They underestimated Jean-Pierre's control. Jean-Pierre stood there, slapping his boot with his riding whip and smiling. "Yes. That was a fortunate turn of events for me."

Plain speaking indeed, since the man he replaced was his cousin.

"If my predecessor did not wonder about a man such as you," Jean-Pierre said, "then he was a fool who deserved to be hanged."

"Hanged by the Reaper, a wraithlike figure who has galloped along the midnight roads, fulfilling the age-old prophecy that when the ghost of the old king rode, the return of the new king would soon follow."

"A man in a costume, nothing more!" Jean-Pierre snapped.

"Yes, of course. You don't think I'm dullard enough to believe in ghosts or prophecies, do you? I'm an Englishman, and above all the superstitious nonsense." Which, since Raul had helped facilitate the Reaper's rides, was truer than even Jean-Pierre realized. "I'm also a horse breeder." He gestured at Halcón Guerra. "I gamble. I occasionally seduce a wealthy woman. I chose to live here, in Moricadia, because I can indulge in those activities to great profit."

"You are exactly the kind of man Moricadian casinos need to thrive," Jean-Pierre said.

"Yes. So why the curiosity?" Raul had to know. "Why now?"

Jean-Pierre's eyes narrowed on Raul's face. "You remind me of someone . . . someone I have met before."

Chapter Twelve

Raul's mind raced. No rumors of his Moricadian descent had accompanied him here; Grimsborough had bidden his household to keep Raul's background secret—he didn't want anyone to know the shame of his son's foreign blood.

Of course, he was implicitly obeyed.

It was true Raul carried the look of the last Moricadian king, but he downplayed his features with a dark fall of hair that swept his shoulders, and so far, no person had made the connection between him and the royal family. He was determined that Jean-Pierre would not be the first. Looking right into Jean-Pierre's gaze, Raul used his green eyes as a distraction. "Have you visited England? Perhaps we met there."

"I've never visited England, so no. No, you remind

me of someone I met long ago. . . ." Jean-Pierre stared back at Raul, examining him with all the weight of his curiosity.

Raul lifted his hands, then let them fall. "I am puzzled as to when."

"It niggles at me, like a sore tooth. I'll remember soon enough. Until then, I look forward to my next visit to your home."

"Next time, I'll send an invitation."

"That's not necessary. I find it's so much more fun to simply . . . drop by." Jean-Pierre tipped his hat, turned on his heel, and strode from the stables, his boots making a hard tapping on the wooden floor.

Thompson stepped out of the stall and watched him leave.

Raul reflected on that sound. "We didn't hear him coming, did we?"

"No, sir, we didn't," Thompson said. "He must have been walking very lightly."

"He's good at tiptoeing around. Did he overhear anything he should not?"

"I reflected on that, and no, he did not." Thompson continued to look out the door, and lowered his voice. "But I wonder—*does* he remember you?"

Raul grinned, then chuckled, then leaned against the wall and laughed and nodded.

Thompson was patently unamused. "May one ask from where, sir?"

"I believe he might have been at the event that got me exiled from Moricadia." Raul sobered at that memory, but the grin never quite left his lips.

"What event is that?" Thompson's precise diction grew even more crisp.

"In those days, I ran a bit wild."

"I remember, sir."

"No, you don't understand. As a boy, I was a hellion. Then my actions forced me to come to England. It was a hard lesson I learned, that what I did had consequences. That and the homesickness kept me subdued." Raul was now quite sober. "But before . . ." Raul shook his head at the remembrance. "The de Guignard family was famous for their autumn picnic. They climbed into gaily decorated wagons—decorated by their loyal, loving subjects—and rode to a clearing in the forest where a beautiful white tent was pitched—again by their loyal, loving subjects—where they feasted on wild boar—"

"Killed by their loyal, loving subjects?" Thompson suggested.

Raul inclined his head, and returned to grooming Halcón Guerra, taking comfort in the colt's warmth and appreciation. "If their loyal, loving subjects didn't play the part, there was hell to pay. All through our long history, my family have been warriors, so we handled the boar hunt. We had our horses, but they were precious to us, and we didn't risk them in pursuit of a gift for the cursed de Guignards. We had a few firearms, but they were contraband, and the de Guignards were watching, so we didn't risk being caught with them."

"Your family hunted wild boar on foot?" Thompson was clearly appalled. "With spears? My God, that's medieval!"

"You're in a primitive country, Thompson." From Thompson's expression, it was obvious he knew that all too well. "We were a large family, and all of us, boys and girls, learned very early to be tough. Food was scarce, the winters were hard, the de Guignards oppressive. Yet for all that, my grandfather and my uncles wouldn't let us boys hunt with them. The boars were too dangerous. So the men installed us in trees and told us to stay put, and they put the bay hounds after the boar."

"Are boars really as vicious as one hears?"

"When a boar is cornered, it comes out fighting. It's low to the ground, it's fast, it's heavy, and if it gets past the spears, it will gut a man."

"I say!" Thompson's expletive was the disbelief of a civilized Englishman.

"When I was seven, I saw the boar charge my grandfather and rip his leg to shreds with its tusks. For the rest of his life, he limped. The son of kings, hurt in the service of the children of French usurpers." Even all these years later, Raul's gut burned at the memory. "They didn't care. Their loyal, loving subjects roasted the boar, brought the produce from their gardens and fields, and fed their oppressors."

"I'm surprised the de Guignards didn't suffer a poisoning."

"They used Moricadian children as tasters."

"You?"

"No. I was the kingly heir, and deemed too precious to risk. As you can imagine, *that* irked me, as did my cousins' taunts." Remembering an important point, Raul added, "Their loyal, loving subjects dug and built the latrines, too, so the de Guignards could deposit their royal shit."

In a voice heavy with suspicion, Thompson asked, "What did you *do*, sir?"

"I was ten, it was Prince Sandre's first year as ruler, and I wanted revenge for my grandfather—so I hatched a plot." Even now, even knowing the disaster that followed, Raul smiled. "Do you remember what I looked like when I arrived in England? Short, skinny?"

"Starving," Thompson said.

"That, too. The night before the famed de Guignard picnic, I climbed a tree, got onto the roof of the tent, and cut a slit in the silk big enough to push through a cow's bladder filled with de Guignard excrement gathered from the latrines—"

"Oh! Sir! No!" Thompson rubbed his forehead.

"I was ten. At the time, it seemed like a good idea." Any further explanation was fruitless.

Either Thompson remembered being ten, or he didn't.

"My plan worked like a charm. The de Guignards sat down to eat; I got on the tent, slipped the bladder through the hole." The memory was so good, even now Raul was in ecstasy. "It hit actually *on* the boar and exploded, blowing shit over everybody, especially Prince Sandre, who, I swear, had his mouth hanging open when it landed."

Thompson gave a quickly muffled bark of laughter.

"It was perfect . . . except that I had no experience with material, with silk, and I didn't realize that when I leaned against the slash I had made, it would rip and I'd go through it like a hot knife through butter."

Thompson's expression looked exactly the way Raul remembered Prince Sandre's—as if he had a mouthful of excrement.

"Yes. The silk split wide; I went down and landed flat on my back, on the table, on the boar, looking up at a bunch of furious, shit-covered de Guignards. They grabbed at me. I rolled in the pig grease and slipped out of their hands. I ran up and down the table, trying to make a leap for the entrance."

"How did you escape?"

"My grandfather was a shrewd old bird. He suspected I was up to something, and he tormented my cousins until one of them confessed. So while I was leaping, my relatives collapsed the tent. I got out of there, and before winter set in, my mother and grandfather sent me to England for safety." Old, familiar guilt squeezed at Raul's heart. "They found and killed my grandfather. Then my mother died."

"Not your fault, sir."

"Maybe so. Maybe not. The de Guignards didn't need an excuse to hang an old man, and perhaps my mother did not die of grief and hunger. But I know what I owe to my family and this country." Raul would pay his debt or die. And he had no intention of dying.

"Was Jean-Pierre de Guignard at the banquet?"

Raul reflected, trying to bring the memory into focus. "He would have been my age, down at the end of the table, but . . . yes. Very possibly."

"So he *does* remember you." Thompson's voice was heavy with foreboding.

"I don't much look like the little savage I was then."

"No . . . but you still look like yourself."

"There's nothing I can do about that, Thompson."

The two men gazed at each other until Dafydd slid back into the stall and noisily cleared his throat. In his distinctive Welsh accent, he said, "Look, sir, Mr. Lawrence. I'm just a jockey. I don't know anything about politics, but guys like me know about men like that who just left. He's the kind of guy who likes a little guy like me, because he can rip my leg off and chew on it like a drumstick."

Raul didn't insult Dafydd's intelligence by disagreeing.

"I'm clearing out," Dafydd said. "Now."

Raul made up his mind. "Stay for the next race?"

"For what purpose?" Dafydd asked suspiciously.

"To take him to the finish line first." Raul stroked Halcón Guerra's neck.

"Do you think you should?" Thompson asked.

"Dafydd is Halcón Guerra's jockey. Halcón Guerra won't work for anyone else like he does for him." Raul nodded at Dafydd. "We'll need the cash soon, and there's no use waiting any longer. There'll be the purse, which will be hefty, plus I'll sell the colt for eight thousand guineas before the day is over. For right now, it's a good sum, guaranteed money in hand."

"I don't know, sir." Dafydd stroked his thigh as if Jean-Pierre already had set his teeth in the muscle. "I want out of this heathen place."

"I'll give you ten percent of the purse," Raul said.

In Dafydd's mind, that settled the matter. "Done."

Raul clapped him on the back, then moved with Thompson out of the stall. He collected his hat and the two men moved toward the door.

"What should we do about the woman?" Thompson asked softly. "About Miss Cardiff?"

They stepped outside.

Raul tilted his face toward the sun, let the light bathe him, warm him. "We do have to do something about her, don't we?"

"With Jean-Pierre sniffing around you, I would say it is imperative to somehow quiet her."

"Yes." For the first time, Raul allowed the floodgates of his memory to open wide, and all the soft sensations of holding Victoria seized him: her surprised lips opening beneath his, the soft weight of her breasts against his chest, the scents of lavender and vanilla in her hair. The remembrance spun him into a whirlpool of desire, and swiftly, before Thompson could see his face, he donned his hat and started walking back toward the stands. "I'll take care of Miss Cardiff. In fact, in pursuit of that goal . . . I believe it's time to disrupt the prince's ball."

"Is it really, sir?" Thompson's voice rose with his eagerness as the long-anticipated plan was announced. "I'll let the men know. This will make them *very* happy."

"Go, then, and tell them." As he watched Thompson walk with speed and determination toward the road, Raul's own excitement rose.

For so long, he had remained a master chess player, moving himself and others into position, keeping himself guarded in word and deed. Everything he did and said was aimed at one goal—to take back his country from the tyrants. He had created incidents aimed at undermining the de Guignards' control, at shaking their iron-fisted grip on the vast flow of money that flooded the country's gambling houses and spas. But those moments, while exhilarating, had been brief and heady.

Now, tonight, he was starting the first careful steps toward revolution—and at the same time—his heart pounded, his mouth dried—he had no choice.

Tonight, he would take Victoria.

Chapter Thirteen

Victoria's first indication that something was very wrong occurred when she returned to her room after bringing Maude and Effie to their mother to have their ball gowns inspected. Mrs. Johnson had approved, Mr. Johnson had scowled and tugged at his cravat, and Victoria had left the family with Mrs. Johnson's maid, who would make the finishing touches to the girls' costumes.

Now Victoria entered the suite she shared with the girls, went to the dressing table, and lifted the small, white lace cap that awaited her there.

The cap was an important part of her costume. The dark blue silk was a gift from the Johnsons, a beautiful material, but modestly cut, and the white collar and cuffs were stiff with starch. But, although at the age of twenty-one she was firmly on the shelf, she was still pretty, so she wore the lace cap as a badge so every gentleman would know she was not an available female, but a chaperone. She didn't sigh about that; it was the way things were.

But as she stood in front of the mirror, she heard movement in the closet, and turned in time to see a maid walk out with an armful of gowns. "What are you doing?" Victoria asked sharply.

The maid jumped guiltily. "I'm taking the gowns to be ironed."

Victoria recognized her. She was Amya, the one who spoke English, the one who had dropped the tray earlier today. "They *are* ironed."

"No, Miss Cardiff, the girl who was supposed to do it is lazy. She did a bad job. I will do them myself. You'll be more satisfied."

Victoria had examined the gowns when they came back, and while the work wasn't the best she'd ever seen, it was by no means the worst, either.

"We are training," Amya added, as if that explained everything.

Victoria surrendered. "All right. But please be careful. Some of the girls' gowns are quite expensive."

"Yes, miss, I am the best." Amya edged toward the door, opened it, then fled into the corridor without shutting it behind her.

Victoria stared after her. Something niggled at her, something odd.... Each and every gown the maid had held was made of dark cloth—brown, black, a second dark blue. Going to the closet, she checked the hooks.

Her suspicions were right. The maid had taken only *Victoria's* gowns to be ironed. Had she stolen them?

But why steal the cheapest, the plainest of gowns? It didn't make sense.

She stepped out the door to follow the maid.

At the same time, Maude stepped out of her parents' suite, bright-eyed and impatient. "Here she is, Mother. Now let's go!"

The mystery, if there was one, would have to wait.

Maude and Effie hurried over to the place on the side-lines where Victoria had seated herself in the midst of the rest of the chaperones.

"Can you believe it? The prince won't make an ap-pearance tonight." Maude petulantly wadded handfuls of her rose velvet in her fists.

Victoria set aside her needlework. "Don't wrinkle your skirt, dear."

Maude opened her fists and smoothed them along the luxurious material. "According to the girls to whom I spoke, he hasn't been seen at a ball for most of the summer, ever since some humiliating incident visited on him by ghastly rebels. Can you imagine ruffians doing something mean to a noble prince?"

"I heard some people say he's not actually a prince, but from a family of usurpers." Effie, ever more thought-ful than her sister, looked troubled.

"That's stupid. He's single. They should leave him alone so he'll come to the ball." Maude's color was high with indignation.

"Girls," Victoria interceded gently. "There are an abundance of gentlemen here, some quite handsome, and no doubt some quite—"

"Wealthy!" Maude said.

"I was going to say, some quite good dancers, I'm

sure. Rather than worry about Prince Sandre, I suggest you bend your mind to having a pleasant time. This is our last stop before returning to England, and the rules for young ladies will be much stricter there. Especially for you, Effie, since you are not old enough to make your debut."

"Quite right, Miss Cardiff." Effie whirled, her satin gown appropriately modest for a girl her age, yet handsomely done by Italian artists and seamstresses. "Maude can mope if she likes. I want to dance tonight."

"I want to dance, too!" Maude said.

"Please remember, when you are asked, to bring the gentleman to meet your parents or, if they are otherwise occupied, to meet me. We will maintain some semblance of propriety here." Victoria cast a cold eye over the assemblage.

"Miss Cardiff, Father is right." Maude shook her head in a spooky imitation of Mr. Johnson.

"About what?"

"He says for such a beautiful woman, you're an incredible stick-in-the-mud."

"He hired me for the latter quality," Victoria said dryly, and didn't allow herself to feel hurt.

Was that why Mr. Lawrence had fled rather than speak to her today? Because she had incorporated the starchy qualities of a strict governess and chaperone?

But it was silly to think that. He simply hadn't remembered her. For all that it hurt to realize those kisses that had been a seminal moment in her life meant nothing to him, had been an incident among dozens like it . . . Well, it was undoubtedly the truth, and any other explanation was pure vanity.

And Victoria Cardiff did not indulge in vanity.

Not that any of it mattered. She glanced toward the crowded dance floor. He was here. Mr. Lawrence, whirling madly to the strains of the waltz, a beautiful lady in his arms. She was bedazzled, if her expression was anything to go by, and rightly so—when Raul Lawrence tossed back his fall of dark hair, he looked like one of the poets in the best romantic tradition.

Victoria adjusted her cap, picked up her needlework again.

She hoped he made no move on Maude and Effie. Then she would have to step in. And she smiled, enjoying the thought a little too much.

The hotel ballroom shone with polished woods, gilded frames, crimson velvet curtains, and gold-fringed tie-backs.

It was, to Victoria's eyes, vulgar and overdone. But she'd learned Europeans were different, more flamboyant and aggressive, with naked, undraped statues and immodest fashions. She hoped this place was simply the pinnacle of indelicacy, and not a country where all who visited were tainted by scandal. That would be a very difficult thing to explain to any proper English suitors for Maude's or Effie's hands.

Yet the more she watched the assembly, the more she wondered. Gentlemen twice outnumbered the ladies, and while some women seemed perfectly respectable, others were less so, laughing too loud, drinking too much. Victoria even saw the occasional skirt lifted to show a silk-clad ankle. The doors opened onto the darkened terrace, and as Victoria watched, she saw more than one couple slip out, laughing. Even the chaperones gossiped among themselves rather than watching their charges, a gross negligence of duty.

Victoria put her needlework aside. She wished now that she hadn't urged Mr. Johnson to allow the girls to have a bit of innocent fun before they returned home. She feared any fun they had would not be so innocent after all.

If she hadn't been watching so closely, she wouldn't have noticed the masked, dark-clad men slipping into the crowd from the open doors. At first she thought they must be servants preparing some kind of play to entertain the guests. But they moved aggressively, pushing the gentlemen aside, smiling cockily at the women.

Nerves prickling, Victoria slowly came to her feet.

More men came in, right through the doors where, when she entered the ballroom, she had seen guards standing at attention. At the time she had thought it inappropriate to put them where they could be so clearly seen wearing pistols and clutching swords. Now she wondered where they had gone.

The dark-clad men started moving counterclockwise around the ballroom, pushing the guests to do the same. They were like spoons stirring the soup, creating eddies of people who stumbled and grumbled, then gradually grew worried.

Victoria started to go to find her charges. Then, with a thought to safety, she backtracked, got the needle out of her embroidery, and moved purposefully toward the dance floor.

But she was cut off. It was almost as if the men deliberately targeted her, catching her up, widening their circle, pushing her back toward the walls.

Something crashed—one of the servants had dropped a silver tray full of glasses.

The music screeched to a stop.

The smell of spirits and slowly burgeoning panic filled the air.

Victoria caught a glimpse of Maude, still unaware and smiling. Of Effie, looking frightened and fleeing toward her parents. Of Mr. Johnson, holding Mrs. Johnson in one arm, extending a hand to Effie, looking around for Maude . . .

But not for Victoria. His focus was narrow and always on his family.

As it should be.

She stumbled.

One of the masked men caught her, steadied her, then twirled her into another's arms. And another.

Their grips were impersonal, but they moved her inexorably toward an open door that led into the depths of the hotel.

She didn't know what was there; she knew only she didn't want to go. But the mass of people moved her in that direction. Another man grabbed her.

And she stabbed his hand with her needle.

He yelped satisfyingly, jerked his hand away, and not so satisfyingly took her needle with it. Then, with real intent, he shoved her through the door and into a darkened corridor.

A faint breeze ruffled her hair, and she smelled fresh air.

The man loomed menacingly between her and the ballroom.

In the ballroom, a woman screamed.

Picking up her skirts, Victoria ran.

Chapter Fourteen

If Victoria could get outside before that man caught up with her, she could circle around through the gardens and into the ballroom, and make sure Maude found her parents. The girl was barely a young woman. God knew what these men would do with her. . . .

Victoria ignored the fear hammering inside her, for if they caught her . . . what would they do with *her*?

But she should not to be so selfish, so involved in her own safety. Maude and Effie needed her.

Gasping, she reached a large, dimly lit room. She glanced around.

The kitchen. Why had she been herded toward the sinisterly empty kitchen?

And where were the cooks, the scullery maids? Where were the servants?

A quick glance back into the corridor showed nothing, but the darkness would cloak any pursuit. Seeing the open door, she sprinted out into a small, walled garden. The scents of rosemary, of lavender, of thyme and basil and sage rose from the ground.

The cook's herbs grew here.

The gate stood open, and Victoria hurried toward it, then paused to listen. Faintly, in the distance, she heard men's shouts and women's screams. But here . . . she heard nothing. Nothing behind her, nothing on the other side of the wall. Cautiously she stepped out.

She stood on a wide dirt path lined with tumbledown shacks. After the extravagance of the rest of the hotel, the sight of them provided Victoria with a shock. Whatever the hotel stored here, they did not value.

A quarter mile of path ended with a tall building, a farm building of some kind. She picked her way toward it, still straining to hear a sound, any sound.

The eerie quiet lifted the hair on the back of her neck.

Or was it the sense of being watched by unseen eyes that frightened her?

She reached the wooden wall, put her hand against it, and walked until she reached another door. Cautiously she pushed against it.

It opened silently.

She peered inside.

A lantern hung on a hook against the far wall. Dimly, she could see horses in their stalls, hear the soft whoosh of their breathing. The stable. She'd found the stable. No one was in sight. No one made a sound. But again, where were the servants? A stable boy should be guarding the horses. . . .

Warily, she stepped inside. "Is anyone here?" she called softly.

The horses pricked up their ears, turned to look at her, but no one answered. Probably the boy had heard the commotion and run out to see what it was all about.

She let out her breath on a soundless sigh.

She was safe.

Except . . . she had a duty to go back.

But she wouldn't go unarmed. There were weapons here.

Her gaze roamed the walls where the tack and the tools hung.

An ax.

Too heavy.

A pitchfork.

Too long and unwieldy.

An iron hook, small enough for her to hide in her skirts, heavy enough to fend off an attacker.

Perfect.

She tiptoed toward her weapon. Lifted her hand to take it off the wall.

Strong fingers grasped her wrist, and a man's voice said, "No, I'm afraid that's not going to do at all."

She looked up—into a black mask with dark, gleaming eyes.

She opened her mouth to scream.

A cloth descended over her head, muffling the sound. She was lifted, carried, thrown like a sack of potatoes over the back of a tall, broad horse.

Her captor mounted, put his hand firmly on her back.

And they rode into the night.

The sack over Victoria's head was thin; she could

breathe, could feel the cool air as soon as they left the
stables. It covered her to her knees, and when she tried
to rip her way out, she found it was strong enough to
obstruct her movements. The horse was high, with a
smooth gait that ate up the ground. They rode through
the forest; she could smell pine needles and loam.

But what good did it do her to know that? All she
knew of this country was the hotel, and that was in
chaos. This man who had her . . . She swallowed in fear.
Absurd though it seemed, this man who had her had
deliberately set a trap for her. He had wanted her cut
from the pack so he could take her . . . wherever . . . and
do . . . what? Rape? Murder? Torture? Why? What did
she have that any man would want?

She tried to hold herself up, away from the horse,
tried to ease the pressure as the blood pooled in her
head.

The horse's gait slowed to a walk.

The man, whoever he was, picked her up by her waist
and sat her upright before him. Their speed increased
once more.

Her head swam as her equilibrium righted itself.
"What do you want?" she asked.

The sound of her voice was muffled, she knew, but
she also knew he heard her.

He didn't answer.

She hadn't even screamed. *Damn* her English reserve. She had looked into that masked face, she had
fought him, but she hadn't shrieked loudly enough to
get anyone's attention. Not that there had been anyone
to hear, but still, she swore if she lived through this, she
would take every opportunity to scream her head off.

She could scream right now. She could feel hysteria bubbling up in her throat.

But what good would it do? The horse was climbing; she could feel the way he strained, the way the rider adjusted and guided. The air was cooler, the wind in the trees singing in muted melancholy, but she heard not a single human voice.

They had traveled into the wilderness, away from the city.

Her back hurt. Her skirts flapped. She was blind. She was frightened. As if sensing her discomfort, her abductor supported her back, but she didn't allow herself to relax.

She was an Englishwoman. Englishwomen did not cooperate with their kidnappers.

It seemed like forever, but she thought it another half hour before she heard a man's voice hail them.

He was speaking Moricadian.

For the first time, she remembered that her kidnapper had spoken to her in English.

Was he an Englishman?

No. No Englishman would behave so shamefully. No Englishman, except for . . .

But no, that was unlikely in the extreme.

The horse's hooves struck on stone, the sound echoing upward.

More voices, men and women, all speaking Moricadian. Light showing through the cloth.

Victoria's heartbeat picked up speed.

The horse slowed. The rider dismounted and pulled her off and into his arms in one easy movement. He walked, still holding her, inside a building, through a large room filled with voices, laughter, and the scent of food. He climbed stairs, leaving the voices behind, into alternating patches of dark and light. He turned sideways as if passing through a door. Light leaked through the cloth. A woman spoke, saying something that elicited his grunt of approval.

Finally, *finally*, he put Victoria on her feet and stepped away.

In a flurry, she ripped the bag off her head.

She was in a bedchamber, shabby and worn. Flames burned in the fireplace. There was a wooden chair. A short sofa. A water pitcher and basin. Food and wine on a tray resting on a small table.

She whirled toward the heavy wooden door. Saw it shut. Heard the click. As she flung herself at it, the key turned in the lock. She was locked in. Alone. Angry, scared, bewildered.

And more afraid when she saw, laid out on the bed, her dresses. . . .

She had been kidnapped.

Chapter Fifteen

The click of the latch brought Victoria out of a deep sleep into the bright Moricadian morning—and the sight of Raul Lawrence as he stepped through the door of her prison.

She sat straight up on the short sofa, blinking, staring. "You!"

"Very eloquent, Miss Cardiff." He bowed and shut the door behind him.

Outrage bubbled in her veins. "I admit that for the slightest moment, I did suspect you, but I thought no Englishman could be so despicable as to kidnap a woman."

"You're wrong on two counts."

"Two?" Her mind must still be fuzzy, for she hadn't a clue what he meant.

"Englishmen are as despicable as any other man, especially when confronted with a prize as beautiful and valuable as you." He strolled forward, untying his cravat as he went. "And I am no Englishman."

That brought her to her feet.

But the sofa was short and she'd been scrunched up on it for hours, ever since she'd realized there was no way out of this room—looking out the window at the star-speckled sky had proved this castle sat on a crag and the room was at the top of the castle—and it was useless to pound on the door and shout. Now she hobbled a few steps, trying to straighten up.

Of course, the contemptible man laughed. "You could have slept on the bed."

"Certainly not! And what do you mean, you're no Englishman?" Until she was fully awake, she refused to broach the "beautiful and valuable prize" comment.

"I'm Moricadian. I'm a Moricadian prince. As you so foolishly proclaimed in your employer's hotel room, I'm the heir to the Moricadian throne."

She might be fuzzy with sleep, but she wasn't stupid. "You know I said that?" She made the next leap of logic. "You kidnapped me because I said you were a *prince*?"

"Yes."

"That's why the girl dropped the dishes?" Victoria had discovered that indignation enabled her to stand up very straight.

"Yes."

"And took my clothes?" Including her undergarments, which she'd discovered neatly stacked in a drawer.

He tossed the cravat on the floor. "I thought you'd want all that feminine stuff."

"You arranged this because you think someone cares

if you go around claiming you're the heir to the Moricadian throne?"

He moved so quickly she didn't have time to avoid him. Grasping her arms, he loomed over her. "I have done everything in my power to hide the truth from the tyrants who would torture me, kill me, and drag my mutilated body through the streets of Tonagra behind my own horses—and I have been successful. I don't intend to ruin my chances to rescue my people from oppression because the one Englishwoman who can spoil my plans doesn't know how to keep her mouth shut."

Incredulous, she stared at him.

His face was stern, his green eyes glowed, and the way he held her reminded her of those moments on Grimsborough's balcony when she thought he was going to toss her over the edge.

Who was this man? She barely knew him—but right now, she knew he frightened her.

But in her time, other, more worthy men had frightened her.

She knew what to do.

Lifting her chin, she said steadily, "The authorities are going to suspect you of fomenting the trouble last night."

"That's where you're wrong." He relaxed, but he didn't let her go. "I was at the party. Didn't you see me? I was dancing with the newest Belgian heiress when the trouble started. I was pushed outside and fled, as did so many other men and women. After two hours of stumbling about in the dark, I returned to the ballroom and offered my assistance in catching the rebels. I was quickly corrected—they were not rebels, but merely foreign youths playing a rude joke. I helped by questioning servants and jumping at every loud sound. Then I excused myself, told Jean-Pierre de Guignard that I intended to spend the week hunting, smiled feebly, and rode home."

"But . . . that's not all the truth!"

"Yet no one looks more innocent and cowardly than I."

He had thought of everything. Everything! The man was clever as well as dangerous, and she would do well to remember that. "What do you mean, calling me a beautiful and valuable prize?" Of all the stupid questions, why had that popped out of her mouth?

She thought she heard his teeth grind. "You're beautiful. That you know."

"I'm passable," she corrected, "and I've reached the age of being a spinster."

He snorted. "You've reached the age where you're no longer a twit. You're a woman, and a damned fine-looking one. A man, if he were so inclined, could take you to the Mediterranean pirates and sell you for a tidy sum. I suppose you're still a virgin?"

Her face flamed. "Mr. . . . . Lawrence!"

"So you are. Yes, a tidy sum. Or I could keep you here as my plaything, tame you myself."

"I am not a wildcat!" The place where he held her, his hands to her arms, grew hot, as if his touch were causing friction.

"How would you know? You just admitted you're a virgin."

"I most certainly did not!"

"So you're not a virgin?" He grinned as he watched her struggle with the answer.

Finally she settled on, "Whether I am or not is not your business."

"My dear Miss Cardiff, I would like to make it my business." His smile faded. "But the fact is, I don't have time for you right now. I'm planning a revolution."

"So take me back to Tonagra."

"And what would you do, Miss Cardiff? Go straight to the police? Do you know what they'd do to you? They'd question you."

"About you? I wouldn't tell them anything."

He laughed harshly.

"I wouldn't," she insisted. "I swear, and my word is my bond, because, unlike you, Mr. Lawrence, I am proud of my English background."

"Your word is worth nothing." Before she could speak, he shook her slightly. "Not because you're a liar, but because the de Guignards would take you into the royal palace, drag you down to the deepest dungeon, interrogate you, torture you, rape you, extract every bit of information you ever knew or surmised about me, my background, my location, my fortune, my compatriots . . . and when you were begging for death, they would kill you."

Chapter Sixteen

Victoria stared at Raul in shock.

She had thought he was the only barbarian in this civilized country, yet his words held the ring of conviction.

"No one would ever find your body." Grimly he watched her, judging the impact of his words. "This is not a game to be lightly played. Money and power are at stake, and the de Guignards will do anything to keep both." He removed his hands from her arms. "So you are staying here."

"Here."

"With me."

"This is *your* room." Last night, when she had been stuck here alone, before the fire had burned down, she had inventoried the room. In addition to the bed (big and old with a new, overstuffed feather mattress), the regrettably short sofa, the food and wine—which she had left untouched for fear of drugs or poison (she was sorry, because now she was thirsty and starving)—the bedside table, and the wooden chair, there was a privy room furnished with modern porcelain fixtures and a large closet full of a man's clothes. Further examination of those clothes proved they were made by London's most exclusive tailor. Moreover, the chest of drawers in the closet contained men's cravats, collars, and cuffs.

He was apparently pretty good at interrogation himself, for he followed her thoughts with little perplexity. "Were you embarrassed when you handled my undergarments?"

"No, I certainly was not." It was true. By the time she found them, dawn was breaking and she was numb to shame. But she added loftily, "I was searching for a weapon. I only wish I'd found one."

"I can show you how to make a weapon out of a dozen things in this room."

Was he jesting? He didn't appear to be. She cast her gaze around. The chamber was furnished in quite an ordinary manner. What could she use for a weapon? "Last night I looked out the window"—to see if she could climb out—"and discovered this is a castle, is it not?"

"It is indeed, one of my family's castles." He strolled to the window and fondly gazed out into the distance. "It's in deplorable shape, but ideal for our campaign, full of secret passages, nooks, and crannies where we can hide firearms and ammunition, dungeons hidden beneath false floors."

She didn't care about the revolution. "A castle has many bedrooms. I'll move elsewhere to sleep."

"Allowing you to do such a thing would be stupid on my part." Turning back, he stripped off his collar and cuffs and flung them on top of his cravat. "I intend that you shall be occupied and watched during the day, and locked in with me at night."

"I can't stay here with you. My reputation is at stake!"

"You can trust me. I promise not to tell." He softly flicked her cheek with his finger. "After all, I have proved to be trustworthy. No one knows about the kisses we shared so long ago."

She did not want to talk about those kisses. "I swear I won't try to escape."

His face grew stony. "You're an Englishwoman, Miss Cardiff. You believe a vow to a heathen like me means nothing—"

"That's not true!"

"—and that your duty as an Englishwoman is to make your escape."

That *was* true. But she knew how long the ride had been to arrive to his castle, and she'd gazed out at the dense, impenetrable gloom of the forest. It was true she would escape if the opportunity presented itself, but ... how would she find her way back to Tonagra? If she got lost, would she ever be found? And what kind of predators—animal and human—existed out there in the wild?

Perhaps she could bribe one of his servants. . . . "How long do you intend to incarcerate me so immorally?"

"You're rather jumping the gun, aren't you? We haven't done anything immoral yet."

"Nor will we, sir! Now I demand to know—"

"You'll stay until I have control of the country."

"How long will that be?"

"No more than two years." He took one look at her and burst into laughter. "If you could see your expression!"

In her most forbidding teacher's voice, she said, "Yes. I'm sure it's sidesplitting. Now—could I have a more precise timetable?"

"Two months. Certainly before the first snow flies."

"Two months!" She stared at him, appalled. "Are you mad?"

"Your error of judgment left me no choice."

"No choice?" She paced across the room to confront him. "You sound like a child. Of course you have a choice. Send me back to the Johnsons. We'll leave for England at once and I'll never darken your door again!"

"The Johnsons are gone," he said.

Her agitation fled. The blood drained from her face. Her hands fell limply at her sides.

They had abandoned her.

"Perhaps you should sit down." With his hand cupping her elbow, he led her to the chair and eased her into it.

"Of course they're gone. How could I not realize that? That demonstration of yours at the ball—Mr. Johnson would never risk the lives of his family for any reason. Certainly not for their governess." She understood. She truly did.

"It's not such a great loss, then, if they have so little sense of responsibility or affection."

"I'm not a gambler. I have money saved, but not enough. Not yet. I need a job." She spoke through lips that felt numb. "What will I do in a strange country with no references and no ability to comprehend the language?" Stupid concerns, she supposed, for the moment, while she was trapped in a castle with a rebel. But when this was over and she was free—what would she do? How would she return to England? How would she explain her disappearance to any prospective employer?

Raul poured from the pitcher and handed her the goblet. "Drink."

She took a sip and recoiled. "This is wine!"

"And good for shock." He watched her a little too acutely, as if he could see her pain.

She required a lot of herself, not the least of which was that no one ever see the emotions that roiled beneath her surface. Early in life, she had comprehended that feelings left her vulnerable; pretended indifference gave her protection from hurt, and she took care to present a serene facade.

Now the same man who three years ago had blasted his way through her well-practiced indifference held her in his power, and she couldn't bear to have him see her pain that the people with whom she had lived and traveled had left her behind without a backward glance.

She took another sip of wine, then put down the goblet. "Thank you. I'm better. I'm hungry and thirsty. That explains my former light-headedness."

"I'm sure you're right."

She intended to tax him about the cynical edge to his tone, but he yanked the tail of his shirt out of his trousers and pulled it over his head.

The sight of his bare skin scandalized Victoria to the point she couldn't take her gaze from it. The sturdy structure of his shoulders served as the bracing over the muscled breastbone and ribs. The narrowness of his belly and waist confirmed her earlier observation of him—he had taken an already athletic frame and refined it further, until he was nothing but solid strength on a manly form. And he had hair. Not a lot, but a dusting of dark hair formed a narrow "T" across his chest and down to his waistline. If only ... if only she were not so acutely aware of that manliness, and that form.

He himself seemed totally unaware of her fascinated gaze, as he dropped his shirt on top of his other laundry.

She should have scolded him for his immodesty, pointed out that this was exactly the reason she needed her own bedchamber. "Who's going to pick all this up?"

"Pick what up?"

"Your cravat. Your collar and cuffs." She pointed. "Your shirt!"

For the first time in the conversation, he looked confused. "The person who always picks it up?"

A satisfying flush of irritation brought her to her feet. "Men like you always leave someone else to clean up the mess."

"First, Miss Cardiff, I beg that you not liken me to other men you've met during your brief and lackluster existence. I may drop my clothes on the floor, but when it comes to *messes* ... I clean up my own." With that speed of movement that had caught her by surprise before, he wrapped his arm around her waist and pulled her close, proving he was not unaware of his actions or their effect on her.

He had been baiting a trap.

"What do you think you're doing?" She was afraid she knew.

"Offering you a job."

"A job?" *A job?*

"You said you needed one."

"Yes, but—"

"Everyone in my castle works."

"I don't want to be in your castle, and I certainly don't intend to work for you."

"It's not for me. It's for the cause. *Everyone* in this castle works for the cause. It's necessary. I've made a lot of money through the years, but I'm financing a revolution. I can't feed idlers."

"Put me on the post coach and I'll be out of the country and off your hands."

"This is an easy job, one I think you'd find pleasurable." He grinned again, that swashbuckling slash of a pirate's grin. "I'm offering you the job of my mistress."

Chapter Seventeen

Victoria slammed her forehead into Raul's face. She felt his lip crack with the impact.

He yelped and leaped backward.

She felt an unholy and never-before-experienced satisfaction of knowing she had hurt another human being. "You're right. There are weapons here I hadn't previously recognized."

"Damn it, that hurt," he said in a calm tone. Then, "Yes, with the proper incentive, your best weapon is yourself."

She felt a swell of pride—and she hated that. Hated to think that his praise meant anything to her. Hated it even more that he thought so little of her that he offered her a job as his mistress and believed she would accept it. "Do you not remember what drove me out onto the balcony during Belle's debut ball?"

"Lord Meredith was window-shopping in your store."

Victoria had spent three years becoming a gracefully aging, impressively composed spinster. And one quarter of an hour with Raul Lawrence whisked all of her polish away as if it had never been. She had been shocked, angry, embarrassed, aroused, and violent, and his turn of phrase—"window-shopping in your store"—made her gaze roam the room seeking another weapon.

That tall iron candleholder. If she removed the candle and used it, pointed end out, like a battering ram, she could pierce Raul's chest and crush him against the wall.

The image somewhat settled her ire, and she asked, "What makes you think I would yield to you and not to Lord Meredith?"

He laughed, then winced and dabbed his lip again.

She was not amused. "You're young and handsome, yes—"

"You've noticed!"

"—but Lord Meredith had money and wasn't likely to be killed by his own foolish ambitions."

Raul's smile disappeared. "I said before you have a waspish tongue and not a lot of good sense."

The phrase set off her alarms. She had heard it before. He reached for her.

She refused to yield an inch. In a warning tone, she said, "Your lip is already bleeding."

"You can kiss it better." Slowly he slid his arms around her.

"Or I can make you afraid to go to sleep."

He paused. He scowled. "Have you thought that chal-

lenging a man who holds you in his power is a logically
unsound concept?"

"Yes. I know." Although she hadn't done so foolish
a thing since her stepfather had slapped her mother
for not training Victoria in proper respect. But something about Raul—the way he treated her like an intelligent person—made her bold. If she had assessed
Raul Lawrence incorrectly ... Well, the gilded rope
ties that held back the bed curtains would make a
good garrote.

Raul loosened his grip.

She stepped away.

"By the way," he said, "Lord Meredith's conceit hurt
him badly. Late that night, on his way to bed, he was
waylaid by someone who forcibly took exception to his
behavior to you."

"You? I mean ... you were that someone?"

"Why so incredulous?" Raul dabbed at his lip again.
"He was bleeding more than a little when I left him."

"You hit him?"

"He insulted you, a guest in my father's house."

In the world of men as she knew them, that made
more sense. Raul wasn't defending her honor, but his
father's. "You a minute ago insulted me in exactly the
same way, when you asked me to be your mistress!"

"You encouraged me."

She drew herself up to her greatest height. "I did no
such thing."

"You *did*. You're alive, you're intelligent, you're well-
spoken, you're spirited."

"I'm *alive*?" A half laugh escaped her. "You have low
standards indeed, sir."

"Actually, I have very high standards." He stroked

his chin and studied her. "Something about you sets you apart."

"Because I'm the only woman ever to tell you no?"

"There is that."

She would have called him conceited, but how could it be conceit when it was true that he attracted women without even trying? For no reasons other than a striking physique, a superficial attractiveness ... and because when he looked at a woman, she knew she had his whole attention. And he would willingly use that attention to bring her an excitement she would treasure the rest of her lonely, barren life.

Oh, no. Victoria could not think that. If she did, she'd forget what she knew of honor and propriety and take his job offer. "My beauty, no doubt, also draws you," she mocked.

"I know a lot of beautiful women. You are the one I want to bed. But if you're sure you won't be my mistress—"

"Absolutely not!"

"—we'll have to find another job for you."

She was *not* disappointed that he gave up so easily. "Nor am I picking up your soiled laundry."

"No, I think probably Thompson does that. Also, I have a cook." He disappeared into the closet and called, "Perhaps you could act as his scullery maid."

"No." She crossed her arms over her chest.

"I have a housekeeper." He came out minus his boots and socks. "Perhaps you could act as the under-housekeeper."

He was leading up to something, she could tell. "You have a job in mind?"

He snapped his fingers in fake wonder. "I have an idea!"

"I'll wager you do."

"You're a governess of two young ladies of less-than-noble origins. It's well-known that on your journey through Europe, you polished those girls and their parents to such a shine they'll be accepted, if not welcome, in English society."

"*I* am well-known? I doubt that. To whom have you been speaking?"

"Gossip travels faster than any traveling coach."

"But not about the governess."

"When the governess is pretty, most certainly there is gossip."

"Hm." She didn't know whether to believe him or not. Then a dreadful thought struck her. "Do *you* have a child who needs tutoring in etiquette?"

"No. No wife, no mistress—obviously—and no children, legitimate or otherwise. My own circumstances taught me to be careful to not produce a child on the wrong side of the blanket."

She was very pleased to hear that, although why she cared, she could not tell. "Then who . . . ?"

"I have relatives."

"Relatives," she repeated.

"Most of the people living in my castle are relatives. Cousins, mostly, and second cousins, and cousins once removed. And others. It's a far-flung family with noble roots and ignoble manners." He sat across from her, rested his elbows on his knees, and leaned toward her, as earnest and charming as any gentleman trying to persuade a lady to accept his plans.

Unfortunately, he was wearing only his trousers, which distracted her and detracted from the "gentleman" aspect.

He continued. "There are rumors that my family are descendants of Attila the Hun, who ravaged France and spread his seed far and wide. They say one of his unwilling women stole Attila's scimitar and, pursued by his wrath, fled to the Pyrenees, to the site of modern Moricadia. There she gave birth to her son in the forest. The soil absorbed her sweat and her blood, and only the wild beasts heard his first cries. She raised the boy to be a warrior, and when Saber was fifteen, he forced the mountain tribes to join him and unite to form his kingdom. Saber took the green-eyed dragon as his emblem and used the sword to impose his rule."

"Saber," she repeated.

"His name." Raul tapped his bare chest. "My name."

"Where's the scimitar?"

"No one knows."

"You don't look like I would imagine a descendant of Attila the Hun to look." Although Raul *did* look like a warrior. She could imagine him riding a horse, controlling the beast with his thighs. He would swing a scimitar, his hair whipping in the wind. All would fear him . . . and love him.

"It's been seventy generations since that first baby was born. I don't have the look of a cruel Asian conqueror, but my mother said that *her* mother said I was born with Attila's hair." He took a handful of ends and showed her. "Black, straight, plentiful."

"Beautiful hair," she said.

As if he were taunting her—he wasn't, was he?—he lifted his arms and ran his fingers along his scalp, pushing his hair away from his face.

She did not long to touch it. Or him. "How did your family lose control of the country?"

"More than two hundred years ago, my ancestor, King Reynaldo, welcomed an upstart French count and his men into the palace in Tonagra. They were treated as honored guests, they feasted, they drank, and when Reynaldo and his guards slept, the de Guignards slaughtered the guards." Raul's green eyes grew cold and bleak. "They threw Reynaldo into his own dungeon and secured the country."

She knew she would be happier if she remained ignorant, yet still she asked, "What happened to King Reynaldo?"

"They hanged him, then beheaded him. As a lesson to any of his family who might imagine that they could somehow recover the country, they put his head on display on a spike in Tonagra."

She shivered and rubbed her arms.

Raul nodded. "Yes. The de Guignards are and always have been stained with cruelty and dishonor. The French king granted them the country as a principality—it wasn't his to give, but he didn't let that stop him—to be theirs and to pass down to their heirs as long as they retained control."

"If they lose control?"

"Then the French take the country as their own. But the de Guignards would never willingly let that happen. No, they cleverly proclaimed the natural warm and cold springs to be therapeutic and constructed spas to attract the wealthy to the country. Realizing they had not yet tapped into all the riches that could be theirs, they built gaming halls, casinos, hotels. The money flows in; they put it in their coffers. . . ." He gestured widely. "It stays there. The Moricadian people are starving, ready to revolt, and if they do, it will be a bloodbath. The de

Guignards might die, but too many Moricadians will die with them. My family is ready to fight for them, and we will win the day."

"Then you'll be king."

"It's what I have trained for, sacrificed for, planned for, my whole life."

Seeing Raul like this—his face strong, his gaze direct—she believed him.

"When I'm king, I'll keep my kin close, and to say the least, they haven't had the advantage of a proper English education. In fact, most of them are no more learned or mannered than the Moricadians we hope to help. So to have a proper court, I need a governess for them."

"I see. Perhaps we can come to terms. My salary was forty-eight pounds a year. You believe I'll be here two months—shall we say four pounds a month and two pounds for every week over two months?"

"Four pounds a month? That's blasted expensive." He had the gall to look indignant.

She began to enjoy herself. "You get what you pay for. Although I admit, I did help Mr. Johnson with his accounting work."

"Did you?" Raul had been giving her the Moricadian history, persuading her, coaxing her to do his bidding. Suddenly, his charm changed to something quietly, deadly serious. "Whom did he come to Moricadia to work for?"

"I don't know."

"You don't know, or you won't tell me?"

She didn't like the tone of the question, didn't like realizing Raul had masks he could don and discard at will. "Why do you care?"

"Because information is power. Whoever it was is moving his fortune out of the country."

How did Raul know so much? He really was a man to be treated with care, for if he wore a mask . . . how did she know which was the true Raul Lawrence? "I saw the books, but there was no name."

Raul searched her face as if he could somehow pry the information from her. His fist clenched on his knee. "All right. Your employer left the country before he finished the job. Until whoever it was finds another consultant, the money will remain here. For that, let us be grateful." His fist loosened. The easy charm returned to his face, his bearing. "Now—will you take on the task of civilizing my relatives?"

Why not? The Johnsons had left her. She had to work. "For four pounds a month? Yes."

"Done." He offered his hand.

She took it, surprised—and suspicious—at his easy capitulation about her salary. "Half in advance," she added.

"As you wish." But he distracted her by trapping her hand in both of his and holding it while he looked in her eyes.

His fingers were calloused and warm, and he used his thumb to caress her palm.

The pleasure of that small gesture made her gasp and yank her hand away. "I told you I would not be your mistress."

"I know." Long and lean and contented, he stretched back in his chair. "You rejected my offer of that particular job, and I'm glad of that."

She had the feeling he'd somehow manipulated her into the exact position he desired.

His face settled into the expression of a pasha contemplating his new concubine. "If you had consented, I'd be . . . fulfilled. And that would be good, but to be a mistress is, in essence, a salaried position. I never thought you'd take the offer. You have too much pride to give yourself for money."

"I have other ways of earning a living," she told him impatiently.

"I know that." He stood. "So now, when you come to me, I'll know you're there because you're irresistibly tempted."

"I have never been irresistibly tempted in my life." Yet at his challenge, a kind of fear rose in her. Because she'd kissed him once and been swept away, and that, perhaps, left her vulnerable. She was like the person who had suffered pneumonia and was now so weak that she contracted every disease. . . . No, that wasn't quite right. Because she didn't fear her weakness with other men.

The disease to which she was susceptible was called Raul Lawrence.

"You've never been irresistibly tempted because I've never tried to seduce you."

"I thought we agreed that wasn't going to happen."

"No. You refused to be my mistress. But we will be together, in all the ways that count." He put his hands to the waist of his trousers.

"Your confidence is misplaced, sir!" She watched as he loosened the buttons. "I am not the kind of woman who . . . not the kind of— What are you *doing*?"

"I was up all night dancing, fomenting, kidnapping, riding back and forth, and playing the fool." He dropped his trousers and stepped out, leaving him clad only in a white linen undergarment that covered the essentials and no more. "I'm going to bed. Want to join me?"

She turned her back to him . . . but not before she got a good look at his thighs.

"So what did you think of your forbidden view of me?" He was laughing at her; she could tell.

In her most crushing tone, she said, "In my opinion, you're excessively muscled for a gentleman."

"Proof positive I am no gentleman."

She heard rustling, realized he could be sneaking up on her, turned quickly, and got a flash of bare buttocks as he climbed into bed. She covered her eyes with her hands. "What am I supposed to do while you sleep off your bacchanals?"

"You could join me in bed."

With her hands firmly over her eyes, she said, "I believe we already covered that ground, and the answer is no."

"Then . . . Thompson, who is a quite excellent English butler and my right-hand man, is waiting outside the door to conduct you on a tour of the castle."

Slowly, she lowered her hands.

Raul reclined on the pillows, hands clasped behind his head, the covers over his belly, his chest broad and bare. He looked young, handsome, insouciant.

"Thompson has been standing outside the door waiting for me?"

"Yes. Why?" Raul's eyes grew wide, as if he were innocent—which he was not.

Thompson had been waiting for her? Raul had known she wouldn't take his offer? This whole discourse had all been nothing but a play that mocked her, her morals, and her beliefs? He had been stripping to *seduce* her? "You're a swine." She stormed to the door, yanked it open, and turned back. "I hope I don't disturb your slumber as I arrange my bedchamber to my own satisfaction."

Chapter Eighteen

"**I**'m bored." Prince Sandre de Guignard pulled a
card from his hand and put it on the discard pile.

*Bored? Of course you're bored. We're from the most
powerful family in Moricadia. We are the two most
powerful of the de Guignards. And we're holed up in
your suite in the private quarters of the palace, playing
cards.*

But Jean-Pierre didn't say that. Instead he suggested,
"We could attend one of the balls at the Hôtel de
Tonagra. You always enjoyed those before."

But Prince Sandre snapped, "Before what? Before
I was disgraced and humiliated in front of the entire
country? The entire world? And that was your fault,
Jean-Pierre; don't think I don't remember that."

Jean-Pierre played a card. "Yes, Your Highness, and I appreciate your kindness in allowing me to retain my position as your most humble servant."

"Sometimes, Jean-Pierre, I don't think you're humble at all." But Prince Sandre, dark haired, blue eyed, trim, and athletic, didn't really believe it.

For Prince Sandre had lifted Jean-Pierre from his position as the son of the de Guignards' biggest slut to being in charge of security and quashing the rumors of revolution. It was true, Jean-Pierre had been spectacularly unsuccessful in keeping Prince Sandre safe, but by the time Prince Sandre had recovered from the "incident," enough people had been tortured and hanged to satisfy Sandre's desire for vengeance.

Or had they?

Sandre's behavior puzzled Jean-Pierre.

He had thought Sandre would come back from the incident in a white-hot fury. He had expected to be dragged to the dungeons and, at best, left to rot. At worst, he thought Sandre would rip out his intestines for a rats' feast.

Instead, Prince Sandre had continued to be a pitiable figure, cowering in his rooms studying his books, unwilling to go out in public for fear he would be mocked, occasionally traveling in a secret coach to the spas, there to sit in an icy spring while complaining in a voice two octaves too high.

So Jean-Pierre ran the country as it was meant to be run—with the clear intention of crushing the rebellion right out of the Moricadian peasants. For rumors were rife among them that the true king was coming to free them from de Guignard oppression, and Jean-Pierre intended to kill those rumors, and the people who spread them.

But in his spare time, he was reduced to babysitting his princely cousin, a man who now wallowed in cowardice. He told Prince Sandre, "We have a prisoner in the dungeon. I was going to hang him in the morning in the public square in lower Tonagra. Would you like to hang him now instead?"

"I won't go out in public!" Sandre sounded like a petulant child.

"It's night. If you wear a cloak and a broad-brimmed hat, no one would recognize you." Indeed, it had been long enough since Sandre had been out in public that he could disappear completely and no one would know. . . .

Jean-Pierre's thought surprised him. Shocked him. He lived to serve Prince Sandre.

Yet . . . what did Sandre expect? It was Sandre himself who had turned Jean-Pierre into this monster who killed and tortured, whose mere appearance caused men to cower and women and children to flee. Sandre had taught Jean-Pierre ruthlessness. If Prince Sandre were as smart as Jean-Pierre had always believed, he would have known the results of that training could be deadly . . . to him.

Jean-Pierre considered his prince.

For the moment, he looked like the old Sandre, anticipation and cruelty sparkling in his blue eyes. "Yes. Yes! How delightful! A nighttime hanging. I'm sure the fellow is fearing the morning. Let's in all charity erase his fear."

Jean-Pierre tossed the cards—a winning hand—rose, went to the door, and summoned the nearest of the palace guards.

The man moved briskly, but nothing could hide the terror in his eyes.

"What's your name?" Jean-Pierre asked.

"Your honor, I'm Salazar."

"That's right. You're new." Recruited after Jean-Pierre had had to kill one of the other guards for trying to stab him. "I have your wife in the dungeon, don't I?"

"Yes, your honor."

"Well, good news. While you're down there, you can visit her. But first, tell Bittor to bring Aguirre up. We're hanging him tonight."

Salazar stared and swallowed. "Bittor . . . I'm to speak to Bittor?"

Bittor was the leader of the royal guard, more monster than Moricadian, thin as a whippet, with long white teeth and dark, soulless eyes. He frightened his fellow guardsmen, and with good reason.

Rumors abounded that he liked to torture women in imaginative ways.

They were all true. Jean-Pierre had witnessed his brutality. "Bittor is in charge of the dungeons, and of you. Don't worry; he won't hurt you. Not until I tell him to." Jean-Pierre smiled as Salazar turned and almost ran away.

Then he sobered. He'd lost too many of his hand-picked men. Some he'd had to kill for stealing or suspected treachery. Some had disappeared, he supposed into the rebel forces. That was why he'd recently taken to keeping the guards' families in the dungeon. And yes, that kept them under control, but it also made cowards of them all.

He'd been forced to hire mercenaries: a hulking Prussian with white blond hair and his troop of a thousand handpicked killers. They were Jean-Pierre's army, and they kept the palace and the country secure.

He sighed. Keeping the Moricadians subdued was a heavy burden . . . and one he carried alone.

He looked again at Prince Sandre. And if he was carrying the burden alone, why did he need his cousin?

Jean-Pierre and Prince Sandre rode into lower Tonagra like a chill wind, bringing fear like a gift. The guard rousted the peasants out of their homes, assembled the shivering crowd around the gibbet, and dragged the screaming, begging prisoner up the stairs. They put the noose around his neck, dropped the trapdoor from under his feet.

The hanged man jerked his feet and clawed at the noose . . . but only briefly.

Prince Sandre gestured at the gibbet. "Look. He's already dead. What is wrong with the people in this country? Have they no spirit? Have they no pride? Why don't they fight? They used to fight."

"They're starving and hopeless," Jean-Pierre said.

Prince Sandre turned toward Jean-Pierre, and for a moment the gleam in his eyes was as virulent as Jean-Pierre remembered. "So?"

"You asked a question. I answered it. It wasn't a critique. It's a fact." Another fact—that cruel gleam in Sandre's eyes no longer frightened Jean-Pierre.

Nothing frightened Jean-Pierre anymore.

He started toward the horses.

"It's boring. I'm bored." Prince Sandre trailed behind him like a whiny child. "I almost wish the Reaper would return."

"He's gone," Jean-Pierre snapped. "And I would think after what happened to you, you'd be glad of that."

"What about our family? Where are they, I say? A year ago, we would have had a dozen de Guignards to cheer every punishment. Now there's only you and me."

"They've fled the country." Jean-Pierre bared his teeth. "They're afraid."

"I know." Prince Sandre sounded grieved, and sighed. "I suppose I could go back and work on my accounts."

Jean-Pierre mounted his horse, looked down at the prince. "Don't you have a bookkeeper for that?"

"Yes, of course!" Prince Sandre swung into the saddle and busied himself adjusting the reins. "But this concerns the wealth of the whole country. No one can be trusted with all the money from the casinos and the spas. No one."

"I suppose not. But such a sedentary occupation on such a promising night seems a waste."

"We could go back to the palace and play cards," Prince Sandre suggested.

Jean-Pierre couldn't bear it. *He couldn't bear it.*

Where had the charming master of cruelty he once served gone? Not long ago, Prince Sandre had not been satisfied to end the night unless he had danced, drunk, debauched a virgin, and tortured a prisoner. Now he liked to sit alone in a room and stain his fingers with ink, or to play cards in an endless ritual that involved complaints of boredom if he always won and petty tantrums if he did not.

Jean-Pierre felt the bubble of madness rising in him, tearing at him, trying to get out. He didn't dare kill his prince; that would be the end of whatever honor he held dear. So *something* had to be done.

Inspiration struck. "Shall we go see what Bittor is doing?"

"Does he have someone down in the dungeon?" Sandre asked.

Jean-Pierre waved a hand at the hanged man. "His wife."

"Does she have valuable information?"

"Probably not, but what does that matter? Bittor can make her confess to anything."

"Let's do that. I'm in the mood to get my hands dirty." Prince Sandre spurred his horse up to the road toward the palace.

Jean-Pierre followed, his grin flashing—it was good to see Prince Sandre up to his old tricks.

At the sight, the Moricadians recoiled in fear.

Chapter Nineteen

Raul heard voices. *Victoria's. Thompson's.*

A thump. A curse in Moricadian.

Prospero.

Another thump.

Another curse, more vicious this time, and Thompson's reproving tone.

Then tapping, a constant, annoying tapping.

Without opening his eyes, Raul judged that he had been asleep two or three hours, that Victoria was doing something meant to torment him, and that he didn't care. Whatever it was, it could wait. He needed another three hours' sleep, and nothing less than the start of the revolution would interrupt him.

Then he slid back into his dreams.

When he woke again, the room was so quiet his first

thought was that Victoria had escaped. Then he opened his eyes, and knew she had not.

Because she had made changes throughout the room. She had taken a long iron pole—it had a spike on one end, so it was a lance of some kind—and hung it over the window by iron hooks driven into the mortar. On it she had placed a moth-eaten blanket, pulled to one side and secured with another hook and a rope....

Curtains. Curtains hung over the window. Why, he didn't know. This castle sat atop a rocky crag in the middle of the forest, and this room sat in the top tower of the castle. They were up so high not even the eagles could gaze in to watch her undress, yet nevertheless . . .

And on the floor. From somewhere she'd unearthed a carpet woven, by the looks of it, in medieval Spain.

Actually, except for the worn edges and faded colors, it didn't look bad.

Where had she found it? In the attic? In the dungeons? Could no one control her wanderings?

Silly question.

He sat up—and grinned.

Never mind the curtains. Never mind the carpet. There it was, the cause of the thumping . . . the short sofa had been replaced by a sofa long enough for Victoria to comfortably stretch out and sleep. It was both a statement to the residents of the castle and a challenge to him.

He was up for the challenge—noticeably and inconveniently up, considering Victoria was nowhere in sight, and also unwilling.

But soon she would be willing, and then . . .

Tossing back the covers, he dressed and went in search of his guest. Went *hunting* his guest.

Hanging over the rail on the landing over the great hall, he scanned the downturned faces. Thompson sat at one of the long side tables, his accounting spread out before him.

Hada, his housekeeper, inspected the spoons, slapping the ones not clean enough to meet her approval to the side, and occasionally speaking sharply to the three girls who swept and dusted and cleaned the glass chimneys on the lamps.

At this time of day, the population of the castle was slight, yet nowhere among his dark-haired kin and help was that one golden head.

Damn the woman. Where was she?

He strode down the stairs, irritated and, more than that, worried. He would not be a fool about Victoria; she was too intelligent for a woman, and he didn't underestimate her ability to slip away or, more likely, charm her way out of the castle. And then . . . there was peril in that forest unlike any she could imagine.

Thompson rose to greet him. "Sir, I apologize for the earlier disturbance, but—"

"I know exactly whom to blame. Where is Miss Cardiff?"

"She's in the kitchen with the children."

Raul stared at him, narrow eyed. "With the children," he repeated.

"The children are teaching her Moricadian, and she's teaching them English . . . among other languages."

"I see." Raul's irritation rose. "And are we trusting the children to guard Miss Cardiff?"

"She has access to only two exits, one into the great hall"—Thompson indicated the stairway that led down to the kitchen—"and one that leads into the courtyard, where the men are practicing their bowmanship. I felt as if both of those circumstances would deter Miss Cardiff from escape." His cool tone never changed, but Raul didn't make the mistake of thinking he was pleased.

"You're right. I apologize." Raul realized he had been indeed foolish; Thompson was the antithesis of irresponsible, and it was he who had first suggested Victoria should be acquired for the purpose of curbing her tongue.

"Of course, sir." Thompson was not so easily appeased.

"Amya's with her, too." Hada had made no bones about eavesdropping on the conversation. "Not that Miss Cardiff is too fond of Amya right now."

"Amya?" Raul thought. "The maid from the hotel? The one who reported Miss Cardiff's faux pas?"

"That's the one. She's not good for much except being a lady's maid, so I put her to work for Miss Cardiff. But apparently Miss Cardiff is carrying a grudge." Hada scowled at a spoon and slapped it on the table with the others. "When she saw her, she was not happy."

Raul lifted his brows in surprise. "Miss Cardiff was rude?"

"Damn, no. She was so polite, she almost gave Amya frostbite." Hada chuckled. "Scared the poor timid scrap of a thing to death."

Raul grinned. "Yes, I can see her doing that."

A young, fragile-looking woman, Hada walked with a limp so extreme Raul had had a special shoe built to give height to her left side. But for all her apparent frailty, she ruled the household and all the women who worked in it. As her husband said, *Hada has a fearsome way with words.*

Prospero was right, and no one challenged Hada with impunity.

"The men are out in the field?" Raul asked.

Hada snorted. "At last. After sleeping like babies and snoring like great, fat bears."

Raul grinned at her. "Celebrated when they returned, did they?"

"Yes, my liege. For hours." Hada looked weary. "You'd think they'd brought the House of de Guignard down, rather than prodding it with a sharp stick."

"It's a start." Raul proceeded down the stairs to the kitchen, where the newly installed iron stove glowed red, the cook swore at his two minions, and Victoria Cardiff sat at the end of the long servants' table, Amya standing at her right shoulder, a dozen children at her feet.

Raul paused in the shadows, observing Victoria hungrily.

She wore a different dress, brown wool, clean and ironed. She wore her hair in a chignon at the back of her head; it was damp, and the blond tints were subdued, the color of old gold coins.

Sometime while he slept, she had bathed and changed, and a smile tugged at his mouth. She must have felt abhorrently grubby, else she would not have consented to use his warm water and his soap. How she must have hated settling into his house in such a way!

And how he wished he had been there to lift the bucket of warm water and sluice it over her breasts, her belly, her thighs.

Soon, tonight, he would start the slow process of seduction, knowing that when he did, she would have no chance. For in her kisses, he had tasted a hidden, heady passion . . . for him.

Now she pointed at the steer carcass rotating before the fire and said, "Beef."

"Beef," the children repeated; then they shouted, "*Govadine!*"

"*Govadine*," Victoria repeated. Pointing at the pans hanging on copper hooks from the ceiling, she said, "Pans."

"Pans," they said, then, "*Scovrada*."

"*Scovrada*," she repeated. Looking around, she saw the cook glaring evilly at the children, and said, "The witch who cooked Hansel and Gretel."

The children looked bewildered.

"Miss Cardiff, if you do not mind?" Amya said.

"Yes, Amya, if you would please translate my little joke."

Hada was right. Victoria's coolness made Amya shiver.

But the maid turned to the children and spoke quickly, translating "Hansel and Gretel" into the Moricadian version of the folktale.

The children caught on quickly, laughing uproariously while Cook scowled.

Raul stepped into the light. "Pray to God, Miss Cardiff, he doesn't quit. Good cooks are difficult to recruit when I offer so little in the way of fame or fortune or exquisite settings, and you don't want to be subjected to the meals my people would produce."

At the sound of his voice, the children came to their feet and pelted toward him, all grubby hands and grinning faces. He picked up two of the littlest, twin three-year-olds who let him hold them for as long as it took them to realize their mother stood on the stairway. Then they struggled to get down and run to her. The other kids, two four-year-olds, two five-year-olds, four six-year-olds, one seven-year-old, and two eight-year-olds, hung on his legs and his hands, grinning up at him.

Amya curtsied, her brown eyes round with awe.

Victoria stood, taking particular care to straighten her skirt and ignore him with all her might.

Irritation gave an edge to his voice. "I suggested you teach my adult relatives manners, not teach the children English."

"I'm afraid you're mistaken, Mr. Lawrence. They are teaching me Moricadian. And they are very good teachers indeed." The tone of her voice made them wriggle with delight, and she deliberately offered her hands to the children.

Two of the littlest girls willingly joined her. Victoria's gesture was natural, friendly, yet as she walked past him, he knew she was using the children to put a distance between her and him.

"Previously, I hadn't been able to understand a word, but I had been trying to relate it to one of the romance languages—French or Spanish. It actually reminds me more of German or Russian." She chatted to keep him at a distance, too, using the same cool tone she'd used on Amya.

Did she really believe that was going to work on him?

"They say it's the language of Attila." He stayed close on her heels, taking care not to trip on the other children who clustered around him.

"The language of Attila, seventy generations later," she said.

"Yes." He could almost see her mind arranging the words she'd learned into some kind of order, utilizing her linguistic skills to comprehend the world into which she'd been so abruptly thrust.

He had told her he admired her intelligence; he did, but more, at the sight of her surrounded by children, he felt the tight pinch of possessiveness.

Jealous of a dozen children ... for with them, she showed pleasure unguarded by the wariness with which she viewed him.

Before she left the kitchen, she stopped by the cook. "Thank you for your forbearance. I have greatly enjoyed watching you work, and look forward to tasting your creations."

He turned his back.

But as she climbed the stairs, Raul noted Cook turned to watch, and Raul scowled at him. He didn't like the man's interest, or the knowledge that men, all men, so blatantly responded to her beauty.

In the great hall, the pace had picked up. Hada directed the maids as they set the tables in preparation for dinner. Thompson had gathered up his accounts and stood in the foyer, speaking to the footmen about requiring the returning soldiers to properly scrape their boots.

Victoria made her way to an open window, picked up one of the moth-eaten tapestries that had previously hung on the wall in the upstairs gallery, and seated herself. Looking like a proper English young lady, she began to mend it.

He wanted to grin at the sight of his chosen woman acting like the chatelaine of his castle; he was not so foolish.

Still in that maddeningly cool tone, she said, "I am in

your home. I have no method of escape even if I knew the way."

He stood over her. The scent of lavender mingled with her own scent, lingering like an enticement in the air. "So?"

"So stop stalking me."

Chapter Twenty

"I simply came to inquire after your well-being." Raul seated himself beside her.

Victoria shot him a rightfully scornful glance.

For although he knew better than to admit it, he *was* stalking her, watching her as the royal cat observed an unwary mouse that had by mistake wandered into its kingdom. It was a game he was playing, and he should have been ashamed ... but he was not.

"Have you explored your accommodations? Made the changes you require?"

"I made some changes," she acknowledged. "There are more I intend to make."

"Of course. I want you to feel at home here."

"Ha." She created a starburst that both patched the

base material and made the patch look like part of the original design.

"What a world of mockery you put into that one little syllable." Her long, slender fingers moved with deliberation and dexterity as she exhibited her skill and distracted him from her true passions.

What she had been before when in England—so young, so pretty, so proud—was nothing to the dimensions he could see in her now. She'd put her years to good use, exploring countries, learning languages and accounting, sharpening her skill at managing her employers and her students.

Yet she didn't try to manage him. Oh, they played a game of manners and incivility, but those were merely words, for it seemed as if the two of them saw each other stripped of any charade. To pretend any different would have been an insult.

"Did Thompson perform proper introductions?" he asked.

She selected a new color of thread from her kit. "He did." A pause. "You have a great many relatives."

"When the men come in, you'll have many more to meet." He had no doubt she would handle the courtesies with aplomb.

"You come from a prolific family."

"It is a matter of fact that while the de Guignards believe they've wiped us from the face of the earth, we continue to grow. You see, in old Moricadia, when a woman was widowed or a man lost his livelihood through calamity, they became part of the king's family."

She glanced up sharply. "And by extension the king's responsibility."

"Precisely. And because over the years the de Guignards have so blithely and indiscriminately butchered and maimed the men of this country—"

She finished his sentence. "You're related to everyone."

He inclined his head. "It gives me a very large and talented pool from which to pull my commanders, my sergeants, and my soldiers."

"I can see that it would." She observed as more and more men and women poured in from their day of training in the forest. "That's a great deal of responsibility for you." Lifting her hand, she said, "I know—such a large family makes the task of recruiting and training your army easier."

"Exactly." He gestured Prospero over. "Prospero is not of my blood, but he is a fierce warrior, one of my top commanders, and worthy of honor."

Prospero swaggered over to them ... but then, Prospero swaggered everywhere. He was squat and broad shouldered, with legs bent as if he'd grown up with a horse between his knees. His face was round, and flat; his nose looked as if someone had smashed it with a frying pan; and a gold tooth winked in his mouth when he sneered. He wore a wide-brimmed hat tilted rakishly to the side, but he didn't remove it when he placed his fist over his heart and bowed to Raul. "Saber, my prince."

"Prospero, this is Miss Victoria Cardiff, the young lady you, um, met last night." Raul scrutinized her as she absorbed the fact that this was one of the masked men at the ball.

"The one with the needle." Prospero rubbed the back of his hand and glared.

"I didn't realize that was you." She smiled tightly into

Prospero's face. "But then—if I had it to do over, when you grabbed me I would stab you again."

"I thought you were that kind," Prospero said.

"What kind is that, Mr. Prospero?" She injected a chill into her voice.

"Stubborn and saucy. Why else would Saber have wanted you?"

Raul appreciated the fact that looks could *not* kill, for if they could, he would right now be a shriveled corpse.

With great precision, Victoria said, "Mr. Lawrence *tells* me he brought me here to keep me from making trouble for him with the de Guignards. And I *told* him, and I tell you now, if you could convince him to get me out of the country, I promise never to return; nor will I remember one moment of my stay here."

"Convince him?" Prospero gave a sharp bark of laughter. "Not likely."

"It would be so much easier if no one had to watch me," she said.

"Yes." Clearly, Prospero considered her a liability. "But I take my orders from Saber."

Raul observed the exchange without a hint of anxiety. "You see, Miss Cardiff, my people obey only me."

How irritating to find he had set her up to discover one man's undying loyalty, and how even more irritating to suspect the attitude was prevalent among all his subjects. "They obey you because they fear you!"

"No, lady, I don't fear him." Like Hada, Prospero didn't hesitate to interrupt. "He's my commander. My king. He's going to free me, my wife, and my children from the de Guignards. For that, I owe him all my loyalty, and if necessary, I will pay with my life."

"Admirable," she said sourly. She had imagined she

could bribe one of Raul's servants to help her escape. But how could she fight that kind of fervor?

A man of about thirty years joined them, and his resemblance to Raul was marked in the shape of his face and the color of his hair. Only his eyes were different, large, golden brown, and warm. He greeted Raul in the same manner, with his fist over his heart and a bow, but he also bowed to Victoria, and smiled. "Welcome, Miss Cardiff. I hope you'll enjoy your stay with us."

Raul introduced him. "Miss Cardiff, this is Zakerie, one of my blood kin. The men are going to give me a report on the day's progress. Perhaps you'd like to join the women in the great hall proper?"

"If it makes no difference to you—and I don't know why it would; I know little of warfare and have no one to tell if I did—I'll stay here as long as I have the light."

"As you wish." Raul didn't look at all surprised.

And that surprised *her*. He was very much the imperious commander. Would he not assume that a woman shouldn't be exposed to the activities of war?

Then they started speaking . . . in Moricadian.

Oh. Mr. Lawrence thought he was so clever.

But she was even more clever.

Once more she picked up the tapestry.

Chapter Twenty-one

When the men were finished, Prospero flashed Victoria a grin that ridiculed her ignorance of their language, bowed, and walked to the sideboard. He bumped Hada out of the way and helped himself to a piece of bread.

She scolded, but poured him a goblet.

Zakerie also bowed to Victoria, but without the mocking grin, and went to greet the steady stream of soldiers entering the great hall.

Raul waited until they were out of earshot to ask, "How much did you understand of our conversation?"

She slanted him an artful glance. "What makes you think I understood anything?"

"I heard you with the children, and I know that one

of the reasons the Johnsons hired you was for your language skills."

She paused, her needle in suspension. "And how do you know that?"

"I told you." He leaned back in his chair, stretched out his legs, and enjoyed matching wits with the one woman he knew to be his intellectual equal. "Gossip about the pretty new governess in town."

"I don't like being gossiped about." She used the needle to stab the tapestry.

"Few of us do, but if you're aware, you can bend the gossip to your own liking. It's a skill I developed in England, and I've made much use of it here, misdirecting the de Guignards' suspicions."

"I see." As her hair dried, a strand slid free and hung by her cheek, its natural wave a charming hint of enticement. In an unconscious sign of anxiety, she took it in her fingers and twisted it. "What else did this gossip tell you?"

"That for two long years, as you've traveled through Europe, men of all sorts—handsome men, wealthy men, noble men—have tried to entice you with jewels, with property, even with wedding rings, and you would have nothing of them."

"I assure you, the accounts are vastly exaggerated."

"I think they are not."

"The few who did pay me attention were not welcome." Her generous mouth became a thin, strained, straight line. "I didn't want them."

"Do you want to know what I think?"

"No." She clipped off the word.

"That you were waiting for me."

"Think differently, sir." Her eyes flashed blue fire,

and she tucked the poor stretched and tortured strand of hair into her chignon with a briskness meant to erase all sign of softness from her persona. "I have no wish to ever again be under the thumb of a man as his unpaid servant and dogsbody. I am independent. I intend to stay that way."

He could not doubt her vehemence. "You hate being here."

"You have a conceit if you think I welcome this time, trapped here with you."

"I *do* have a conceit. Because whether or not you like it, you catch fire in my arms."

They were both nettled, snapping at each other until he wanted to catch her up and make her cease talking and start . . . burning.

"It has been a very long time since I *caught fire* in your arms." She belittled their kisses with a withering scorn.

But he wouldn't allow that. "A very long time." He leaned toward her, put his hands on the arms of her chair, trapping her there. "Yet all the long nights since, I've been haunted by the memory of your essence, begging for me to release it."

She didn't look away from him. *Couldn't* look away from him. "My *essence*, as you call it, does not willy-nilly call forth across time and miles to any man."

"Only to me." He leaned closer, inhaled deeply.

She smelled like lavender and defiance and long, slow nights of heated desire.

"Yes," he said. "It calls forth only to me."

Her hands rose, ready to box his ears.

He gazed at her in warning.

Their eyes locked.

The two of them froze.

Memories and desire rose between them, palpable as heat and smoke rising from a fire.

He wanted her. He wanted to grab her, take her away from here, away from the great hall, away from his people, his war, his world. He wanted to entrap her in a place where only the two of them existed. He would feast on her. He would make her realize what lust was, what life could be when the two of them tasted each other, loved each other. . . .

Her arms relaxed. Her hands fluttered and settled in her lap. And she said, "I didn't understand much."

"What?" What was she talking about?

"When you were speaking to Zakerie and Prospero. I didn't understand much of your language." She spoke quickly, leaned back hard in the chair, her color high. "'Men'—I understood that. I think I caught a few names. And you kept saying one thing—it sounded like the Bulgarian word for 'knife.' I thought perhaps you were actually talking about knives."

"Very good." He wasn't complimenting her about her translations. He was admiring her quick change of subject, of atmosphere, her skillful diversion of his attention from *her* and what would happen when she yielded to him.

She knew what he meant, but stubbornly didn't acknowledge it. "So *noz* means 'knife'? I translated correctly?"

"That's right." Again he leaned back, releasing her from the prison of his body.

There was, after all, time for that later.

He continued. "Prospero, Zakerie, and I were discussing our defense class. The de Guignards have hired skilled mercenaries equipped with swords. Of course, most Moricadian men don't know how to use swords."

"Because they've never handled them?"

"That's right. The de Guignards don't even like to allow their subjects to own knives. But what can they do about that? Since time immemorial, men and women have carried their own short, sharp blades for use with each meal. So to counter the mercenaries and their swords, Prospero is working with the men, teaching them to smash through any attack and get in close, and then ... well ... Moricadians know how to use knives." Raul looked as satisfied as a cat that'd been into the cream.

"What about firearms?"

"Firearms are expensive. I've invested in rifles, but we have enough to arm only a third of our troops. So Zakerie is training the women in their use." His gaze sought and found his cousin in the open space of the now-bustling great room, and observed him thoughtfully. "He's very good, and the women show remarkable marksmanship."

"The women? Really? How progressive of you." Victoria didn't know what she thought of the idea of women in battle, or of seeing them dressed in men's clothing.

"In my family and my country, women are fierce defenders of their homes and themselves." Raul's lip curled in disdain for the de Guignards. "So many have lost their husbands and brothers and fathers that they've had to be."

That, Victoria understood, and admired. Women always did what was required. "So the women shoot as well as the men?"

"Don't be ridiculous." He smiled, inviting her to join

him. "They shoot better. I can't begin to tell you how much the men resent those occasional shooting matches where they discover their wives and daughters, their aunts and nieces, can hit the target at three hundred yards."

"That is very impressive." She did smile, imagining a group of Moricadian men sulking as the women made them look like fools. "I can shoot a pistol." She didn't know why she offered the information. Probably it was foolish to warn him. But he so admired these women and by extension must think Englishwomen were silly puffballs.

She didn't want him to think that about her.

"Can you? Can you shoot with any accuracy?"

"Mr. Johnson, who taught me, told me to make every shot count, but he also explained I had to be close enough to aim. He said pistols are notoriously inaccurate and if the distance was farther than thirty feet, I might as well throw the weapon."

"Then Mr. Johnson was a good teacher."

"Yes. I'm good for a distance of forty feet." She warmed when he laughed, then asked, "Do Moricadian women handle swords and knives, too?"

"Not in this battle, they will not. Women are naturally not as strong as the men. In hand-to-hand fighting, facing the mercenaries and their swords, we'd lose them. We'd lose them all. So our strategy is to allow the women to hide in the trees or behind rocks, for them to use the natural cover of the land, and from cover, to pick off the soldiers the de Guignards send after us."

She understood and appreciated his tactics. "You're imitating the kind of fighting the English colonists did in America."

"Exactly." His eyes admired her in the most flattering manner. "We hope to enjoy the same success as the American Revolutionists."

A chime sounded.

Rising, he offered her his hand. "I'd be honored to be your dining partner."

There was little she wanted less. To be the cynosure of all eyes—she, who had been the governess, who had practiced the fine art of pinning on a spinster's cap and disappearing while in plain sight!

But she had no choice. She had to eat, and Raul would insist, and better to face his people behind a facade of composure than to have anyone, most especially Raul, realize her fears.

So, rising, she took his arm and walked with him toward the tables.

Chapter Twenty-two

The great hall had filled with men and women in rough clothing. The men stood in clumps, drinking ale and wine, laughing, comparing old scars and new wounds. The women, even the ones who had come in from training, helped set the table and pour the drinks.

"You're nervous," Raul said.

Victoria had been so proud of her calm demeanor, but he must have felt the slight tremble in her fingers. She was used to having men ignore her, and now this man—handsome, accomplished, and by all accounts royal—paid attention to her. *Close* attention.

She hated that. Hated that he knew her so well. Irritation made her snap, "What did you expect? I don't know this place. I don't know the language. I don't know these people."

"They're good people."

"That makes it worse." She looked down at the polished wood planks beneath her feet. "I'm foreign, and an object of curiosity. But more than that, among good people, your sleeping arrangements are guaranteed to cause gossip and laughter . . . at my expense." Bitterly, she said, "This kind of scandal is always at the expense of the lady."

"That is an unfortunate truth. Nevertheless, I'm keeping you in my room." He halted at the ornate, high-backed chair at the center of the head table.

"I never doubted your heartlessness." She stopped beside him.

"If you believed I was truly heartless, would you not be a fool to confront me?" His deep voice was musical with amusement.

"I am a fool." For more reasons than he could imagine.

The people turned, saluted Raul with their goblets, and cheered and laughed. "*Drachon!*" they called. "*Drachon!*"

Victoria's gaze fell on the embroidered cushion that decorated the back of his chair. "Dragon," she translated.

"My family's heraldic seal, and the symbol of Moricadia."

Victoria gazed at the mythic creature that flew on broad and mighty wings, breathed fire from its nostrils . . . and stared at her from glittering green eyes. Yes, the dragon did remind her of Raul. Perhaps, if she had known of this creature, she might have been more cautious, and the kidnapping might never have taken place.

But she knew that was foolish, for she didn't believe in dragons.

Of course, until yesterday, she hadn't believed that Raul was a prince, either.

Raul lifted the pewter goblet Hada handed him and returned the salute to his people.

More cheers.

"Does your appearance always create such a sensation?"

"Last night's incident at the ball signals the beginning of the revolution. The de Guignards simply don't realize it yet." He offered the goblet. "Drink."

She took a sip.

It was wine—warm, red, and hearty.

She handed the goblet back, only to see him turn it and, smiling at her over the rim, sip from exactly the same spot she had.

Her breath caught.

The great hall quieted. Then a buzz started, and Victoria recognized the various notes: excitement, dismay, fascination.

"I promise you," he said, "there'll be no comments about our sleeping arrangements."

It was at times like these when she saw the king and artful diplomat he would become.

Raul held up his hand.

Again the hall quieted.

"This is my guest, Miss Victoria Cardiff from England." He waited while the men bowed, the women curtsied. "She is not yet fluent in our language, and I would take it as a favor to me if you would speak to her in English." He turned to Victoria and in a bitter voice he said, "Everyone in Moricadia understands a little English, French, and Spanish, and almost all of them speak a little, also. Language is necessary for a Moricadian to have a chance to work at one of the hotels—and that is the only way to make enough money to live without starving."

"I find that, for those in service, a grasp of languages is an unassailable advantage." Her answer included more than a little snap to it.

How *dared* he insinuate she had never known need or desperation? She, who had suffered under her step-father's hostile domination for every moment of her youth?

Then she realized how closely he watched her, how well he read her anger and her anguish, and smoothly withdrew her emotions from sight.

She was, after all, Miss Victoria Cardiff, not some sensitive female who demanded attention and nurturing.

What Raul thought, she did not know, because he turned again to speak to his people. "Miss Cardiff is a governess, and she has agreed to teach us etiquette."

Prospero lowered his goblet. "Etiquette?"

"Etiquette," Raul repeated.

"Have you lost your mind, my king?" Prospero's tone was deferential. The words were not. "What in the hell do we need etiquette for?"

The men muttered in agreement.

The women were silent, watching, indecisive.

Raul spoke to the women. "When the day arrives that we move into the royal palace in Tonagra, we must become not warriors, but courtiers accomplished in the business of diplomacy."

Prospero shook his head. "I respectfully suggest we cross that bridge when we come to it. For now, every moment should be spent in training to fight."

"My wish is that you attend the classes and treat Miss Cardiff with all honor."

Fists clenched, Prospero glared at Victoria.

She wanted to point out that teaching etiquette wasn't her idea, that she didn't care if Raul's court was the laughingstock of Europe. But she recognized Prospero's challenge, and looked steadily back at him, refusing to lower her eyes, to back down from his hostility. In a slow, metered tone she said, "It would reflect well on Mr. Lawrence if, when he is ruler, his family eats with silverware and refrains from issuing sounds from their bodily orifices."

"I *speak* out of a bodily orifice," Prospero retorted.

"Exactly," she said.

Everyone laughed.

Everyone except Prospero, who turned ruddy with rage.

When Raul stopped chuckling and caught his breath, he said, "Ah, Prospero, I've discovered myself it's not wise to match wits with Miss Cardiff. She makes one feel like an unarmed man."

Prospero was trapped, angry and foolish and unable to take it out on Victoria. So he pointed his stubby finger at Hada. "Woman! Pay attention. I need more ale."

Hada tossed a glance at Victoria that promised retribution, then carried the pitcher over and filled up his goblet.

"She's not his servant," Victoria said to Raul.

"Worse. She's his wife." Raul touched her lightly on the arm. "Don't worry. Ultimately, she holds the reins."

Raul pulled out the chair next to his.

Victoria seated herself.

He seated himself.

The arrangement was medieval—the head table across the head of the hall, two long tables down the sides, spoons at each place, and knives, long, curved, and wickedly sharp, provided by the diners themselves. Zakerie and Prospero sat at the head table at Raul's right hand. Hada and Thompson had seats at Victoria's left—not that either of them sat for more than a minute at a time. The fighting men sat on long benches. Thompson and Hada directed the women who served the meal: huge platters of skewered sausages, peppers and onions, the spitted beef, mountains of roasted potatoes, round, flat loaves of bread, and golden mashed carrots with herbs.

The conversation, the laughter, the savory smells slowly relaxed Victoria. The moment with Prospero had been tense, and he made it clear she would pay for her cheek, but she had no doubt she could deal with him.

After all, she understood and taught children.

Thompson carried the platters to the head table.

Raul served her, explaining that the sausage was spicy, the bread was dark and wheaty, the carrots were one of cook's specialties. But he refused to allow her to drink from her own goblet, insisting that she share his, and every time she sipped, she was aware of his satisfied gaze on her.

The man had a way of putting his stamp on that which he coveted.

As a proud, independent woman, she shouldn't like being a "that"... but as a woman who had never been able to depend on anyone except herself, his assumption of responsibility for his entire family—and the way he included her in that family—reluctantly warmed her.

And why was she listening to his voice and smiling? Why was she trying to learn his language to please him?

Because she hadn't slept well the night before.

Because the food and wine were stealing her common sense.

Because obviously she was exhausted.

Tomorrow she swore she would be back to normal. Tomorrow she would defy Raul again.

As the meal wound down, she leaned back and surveyed the great hall. It was full to the rafters, yet by her calculations, there were no more than one hundred and fifty men and a third fewer women, and that seemed inadequate for the plans Raul had made. When he turned to her and inquired after her comfort, she asked, "Is this your whole army?"

"We also have soldiers out on patrol, spies in the city, men and women in place in the hotels and in the royal palace," Raul told her.

"While I don't pretend to understand war or battles, it seems that as a revolutionary force, it's alarmingly small."

"Think of the Spanish Armada, crushed by Queen Elizabeth's tiny fleet." Raul's voice rumbled, low and comforting.

"How many mercenaries are you facing?" she asked.

"A thousand men."

"And the de Guignards themselves? Are they fighters?"

"Every rat, when cornered, will come out fighting."

"Then you're outnumbered five to one."

"Four to one," he said.

Prospero must have trained his hearing, for he leaned across Zakerie. "The woman is right. We need more men to win this battle. My king, we *could* have more fighting men."

"No, we couldn't," Zakerie snapped at Prospero.

Victoria looked among the three men, at Prospero's frustration, Zakerie's bulldog determination, Raul's still expression, trying to comprehend what they would not say. "What do you mean?"

"Prospero believes we could join forces with my cousin Danel," Raul said.

His calm forbearance served only to build Victoria's frustration. "If it's possible, why would you not?"

"Danel is challenging my right to be king," Raul told her.

Prospero sat forward again. "I know Danel. He's a proud man, but if you would simply go and talk to him—"

Zakerie interrupted, "I know Danel, too. He's my cousin, too, my blood kin."

Prospero drew back as if he were a cur who had been reprimanded. Raul might mean it when he said Prospero was part of his family, but for Zakerie, clearly blood was thicker than water.

"I grew up with Danel. I was his second in command, and when he heard that Saber had returned, he called him a usurper and swore to kill him the same way the de Guignards killed Reynaldo." A lock of Zakerie's dark hair fell over his forehead, and his amber eyes were earnest.

"Why would he do that?" Victoria was trying to discern not so much who was right and who was wrong, but why they disagreed on such a basic issue.

"Danel is older than me, and legitimate, with no foreign blood in him. Some believe age brings wisdom; ergo Danel is wiser than me. Some believe it's important that your parents be married at your birth." Raul gave a world-weary shrug. "But that which sways most of those who will not support me is my English blood. I'm not full Moricadian. So while I was abroad, it was assumed he would lead the revolution and be crowned king in my place."

Now she understood Danel's claim, if not the dissension among Raul's commanders. "I see. So this divides your family."

"It does." Raul looked stern and distant, as if everywhere he turned, he ran into this insurmountable wall.

She wanted to talk more, to listen to the voices, to analyze the situation in depth—but a yawn caught her by surprise.

Raul chuckled softly. "You need your sleep."

She had, incredibly, forgotten what she faced at bedtime—a night in Raul's room. With Raul. She straightened. "No! That is . . ."

Rising, he put his hand under her arm and lifted her to her feet. "Come, my dear. It's time to beard the big, bad wolf in his very own den."

Chapter Twenty-three

"**G**ood night." Raul lifted his hand in farewell to the room. "Miss Cardiff and I are going someplace private, where she will tutor me in etiquette."

Victoria flushed, glowered, and looked less panicked and more imperious—she would have been glad if she had realized it.

Laughter followed as he escorted her out of the great hall. He knew his people were watching, speculating, judging.

Some of them would say that since he was going to be king he could take whatever woman he wished.

Some would say he should cleave to his own kind, take a Moricadian woman as mistress and, eventually, as wife.

Some would wonder what he intended with this

woman who was so unlike any woman they had ever seen.

For Victoria was different from any he had ever taken to his bed. Victoria learned languages at an amazing rate, spoke her mind, analyzed his battle plans, observed the dynamics of his family . . . and was beautiful, graceful, and intelligent beyond her years.

But what no one knew except him . . . and her . . . was that he had never touched Miss Victoria Cardiff except in the most innocent of ways.

Not that his intentions had been innocent. But she had been. He'd been the first man to taste her. He'd been the only man to realize that beneath that cool facade, she was a woman of passion, a woman who disciplined herself, hid the truth about herself. He'd been the man who wanted her so much he risked dishonor to have her.

If he were a good man, he wouldn't be delighted to now be taking her to his bedchamber to seduce her.

But he wasn't a good man. More to the point, he didn't think he would succeed. Not tonight, anyway.

He opened his bedroom door for her.

Tired, yet defiant still, she lifted her chin at him.

He ushered her inside, and shut the door behind them.

She turned on him.

He braced himself for her attack.

Instead she asked, "How well do you trust your cousin Zakerie?"

Astonishing how she managed to distract him *and* cut right to the heart of his disquiet.

"You think I should talk to my cousin Danel." He held out his hand, indicating she should precede him.

"Am I so obvious?" With every assumption of ease, she seated herself on the chair by the fire.

A good tactical move. Amya had made up the sofa as a bed for Victoria. She had laid out Victoria's night-gown. If Victoria had sat there, it would look as if she were extending him an invitation—and he would have taken it.

Instead, he pulled up the footstool and seated him-self at her feet. "As Zakerie said, he was Danel's second in command, and when I came back to Moricadia and Danel refused to support me, Zakerie abandoned him because he believes I am the one who should be king."

She chewed her lip. "He believes it? Or he says he believes it?"

Raul took a long breath. "Yes, I, too, had doubts about his loyalty. I've wondered if he was true to Danel. I've wondered if he's selling me to the de Guignards. But I've twice set a scenario wherein he could betray me, and for a profit, and he steadfastly remains loyal."

"I see why you trust him. I fear it indicates cynicism in my personality, but ... when a man turns his back on profit, it probably indicates he *is* loyal."

"That's not cynicism. That's a shrewd reading of the human character."

She stifled a yawn. "Pardon me. I *am* interested in our discussion."

"I fear a short night, a long day, and the wine have contributed to your weariness." He indicated the sofa. "Perhaps you'd like to ..."

"No." She blinked and straightened. "How dangerous is Danel to your cause?"

"In England, I studied classical warfare. I know the strategies; I know how Alexander the Great beat the

Persians at the Battle of the Granicus." He was discussing warfare with the woman he wanted to seduce.
Madness.

Yet he was interested in her opinions, valued her clear
vision. So he continued. "Classical warfare doesn't win
the day in Moricadia. Danel knows the people, knows
the terrain, knows how the de Guignards think. He's a
natural tactician; no one could lead the battle for freedom as well as he. But if all goes his way, he could be
king. Why would he give that up to support me?"

"I wonder why these two men you trust so much disagree so heartily about Danel. I ask myself—if you join
forces with him, what would each man have to gain?
What would each man have to lose?"

"An astute observation. Have *you* studied diplomacy?"

"All women study diplomacy. It's how we survive."
She smiled at him, then caught herself, hastily sobered,
and looked down at her clasped hands. Gathering her
thoughts, she returned her attention to his face, but
without the smile. "If a meeting could be arranged without either Zakerie's or Prospero's knowledge, and in a
neutral setting—then you *must* meet with Danel. You
need him, and the only way to know whether he truly
wishes to supplant you is to see for yourself."

To talk to Victoria was like talking to a friend with no
stake in the game and his best interests at heart. "Thank
you." He placed his fist over his heart in the gesture of
honor she must now comprehend. "I value you."

The always composed Victoria jumped to her feet.

Her alarm brought him to his feet, also. Was his respect really so frightening?

Wide-eyed, she wavered for a moment, rushed over

and grabbed her nightgown, and clutched it to her chest. Turning to face him, she said, "I'm glad I could help." Rushing into the closet, she shoved the door closed.

He heard the slap of something against the door, probably some great weight she'd placed in there earlier to protect herself against such a moment, and him—as if anything could keep him out if he wanted in. He wasn't proud of himself, but the idea of holding Victoria Cardiff in his power made him want to laugh.

Walking to the fireplace, he used the implements to rake up the coals, then placed seasoned branches and, when the fire began to consume them, larger pieces of wood on the flames.

He heard her come out, but took care not to turn until he knew she was under the covers on the sofa. He faced her then, seeing the golden flames shimmer across her tightly braided hair and dance in her wide, tired blue eyes.

If he were any kind of gentleman, he would leave her alone tonight.

Such restraint was beyond his control.

Going to the sofa, he knelt beside her.

She had pulled the covers up to her chin and clutched them tightly. She viewed him as if he were a mountain goblin. Not a flattering image, but one that amused him even while he struggled against the demon inside—the one that demanded he lift the covers and help himself to the woman fate had so neatly handed him.

Although some would say—*Victoria* could say—that fate did not kidnap her, transport her to the castle, or lock her in his bedroom.

And if he settled into complacency, if he assumed

that as king he had privileges above all other men—who was he then?

Prince Sandre? Or worse—Grimsborough?

No, he wouldn't take Victoria.

She would give herself to him. Every night, she would release a little bit more of herself until she was his, completely and without reservation.

He had studied her; he knew how to seduce this woman.

He brushed his knuckles up her cheek, tucked her hair behind her ear, then feathered his fingertips down her jaw until they reached her chin. He outlined her lips, watching as she first tried to turn her head away, then grew still, hypnotized by pleasure.

Her lids drooped. Her mouth opened slightly. Her breathing grew deep and slow.

He circled her lips again and again, rousing the nerves so close beneath the plush, rosy flesh. Moving without urgency, he leaned down and brushed his lips across her eyelids, shutting them completely. He kissed her cheek, then gradually replaced his fingers with his mouth on hers.

Her eyelids fluttered. Her breathing deepened.

"Shh," he whispered . . . and he kissed her.

For the first time in three years, he felt her breath, tasted her essence. For the first time ever, she responded to his tenderness.

Exactly as he had planned.

With unhurried precision, he explored the contours of her lips with his, increased the pressure of the kiss, slipped his tongue into her mouth and sighed with a very temporary contentment. She tasted pure, fresh, clever, like past excitement and new passion.

She tasted as if she were *his*.

Again he stroked her cheek, taking pleasure in the velvet of her skin, and tangled his fingers in the rebellious strands of silky blond hair.

And she responded, her hand rising to grasp his wrist as if she needed him to stabilize her in a universe spinning out of control.

Her gesture broke his carefully nursed self-discipline.

He paused, his lips barely above hers.

Didn't she know better than to trust him?

Apparently not, for she closed the space between them, kissed him the way he had kissed her, with sweet warmth and tentative restraint.

And in response, passion rose in him, clawed at him, surprised him in its violence.

He closed his eyes, fighting for control as she supped on his mouth, tasted him as he had tasted her, kissed him inexpertly . . . kissed him until he was insane with need.

Who was Victoria that she could destroy his conceited intentions so easily? What about this female wrapped in white cotton that buttoned all the way to her chin made him *want* so much his world turned red with heat and desire?

She ended the kiss.

Too soon.

Her hand fell away. She leaned back against the pillow, sighed with contentment.

He waited for her to say something. To do something. To explain her actions, to demand he explain his.

Nothing.

He opened his eyes. And stared.

Her fingers rested against her forehead. Her eyes were closed. Her face, her body were relaxed.

She was asleep.

Chapter Twenty-four

Terrified instinct brought Victoria to consciousness with a start.

Someone loomed over her. Someone angry.

She opened her eyes, sat up in a flurry.

"Sorry." Raul stood next to the sofa by her head, fully dressed, adjusting his cravat, tall, dark, and obviously not sorry at all.

She glanced around. Morning sun was slipping through the window, the birds were twittering in the trees outside, he'd tossed clothes all over the floor.... His day looked perfect. What was he mad about?

"I'm going into Tonagra to complete the sale of a colt," he said, "but before I leave, I wanted to warn you—I haven't discussed the matter of Danel and my doubts about my current strategy with anyone but you. I pray that you keep these matters to yourself."

"Wha . . ." She blinked at him, not completely awake, not completely over her fright. . . .

Then she remembered—their private time in the room, the way they'd discussed his strategy, his family, his misgivings. He'd confided in her, and now he was accusing her of possibly gossiping about it.

Rage wiped the cobwebs from her mind. "If I know something is a secret, I don't tell it. Why would you think . . . ?" Then she realized. "You think that because in Tonagra I mentioned you were a prince, I am a scandalmonger? I assure you, sir, had I realized you were truly of royal blood, destined to reclaim your throne"—she still couldn't quite comprehend it—"I would have never said a word. Ever!"

His white smile flashed in his olive skin. "I do trust in your ability to keep a secret. It was my mistake not to speak to you when I saw you in the lobby and warn you to remain quiet. I apologize for that."

She nodded grudgingly.

"So it makes sense that I would warn you now, does it not?" He pushed a diamond pin into the folds of his cravat and secured it.

"Whatever we say in this room will remain private between us; I swear it."

He searched her face as if looking for something, and nodded. "I swear, also." Walking to the door, he opened it, hesitated, then turned back to her. "Is it so hard to believe I'm a king?"

"Yes. You seem very normal to me."

He laughed. "You're good for me." Stepping out, he shut the door behind him.

She stared after him, trying to comprehend what that had been about. Not the words—she understood those. But his early hostility—what did he have to feel hostile about? He wasn't forced to remain here against his will. And last night had been almost civil between them, with talk and . . .

Her eyes narrowed.

And what? Although she'd been sleepy, she remembered the discussion about Danel perfectly well. She remembered him putting his fist over his heart, remembered her panic, remembered changing in a flurry into her nightgown, going to the sofa, lying down, Raul coming over, kneeling beside her, and caressing her face. . . .

His touch had been like nothing she'd ever experienced—indeed, like nothing she'd ever imagined. He hadn't been hurried or rough. He'd been slow, careful, treating her as if she were delicate, like a glass ornament, like something dear to him.

Sliding back onto the pillow, she remembered. . . .

She'd relaxed under his touch, blossomed like a flower in the sun.

He'd stroked her lips—she stroked them now—and that had felt less relaxing, more sensuous. She'd almost wanted to suck at his fingers.

She hadn't. At least, she didn't think she had. Because after he'd closed her eyes, she had drifted, awash on a sea of sensation. He had kissed her; she was sure of that. And . . . and she'd kissed him, too. She'd held his wrist; she could remember the strength of his bones, the texture of his skin, the feel of his muscles as they shifted in her grip.

But beyond that . . .

Had she gone to sleep? That seemed impossible. How could she go to sleep? She didn't trust any man, much less Raul Lawrence, who three years ago had so violently kissed her, and who only two nights ago had kidnapped her.

Her blood curdled when she imagined what he had done to her while she slept!

Then her indignation died.

She knew very well he had done nothing. He wasn't the kind of man to take advantage of a sleeping woman.

In fact, he wasn't the kind of man who ever *had* to take advantage of a sleeping woman. It was more likely some more experienced woman than Victoria had taken advantage of him.

The difference was, he would like it.

Yes, he was a vile man, but he was too handsome for his own good, and also—she sighed and admitted the truth—he was an honorable man.

One always knew where one stood with Raul Lawrence.

A knock sounded on the door. Amya stuck her head in. "Miss Cardiff? Our king believes you are ready to rise, and sent me up to assist you." The girl's voice trembled as she spoke, and she looked as if she expected Victoria to throw a shoe at her.

Victoria sighed. She was going to have to forgive the girl for betraying her to Raul. After all, it wasn't Amya's fault that with his looks, his body, and his royal blood, he commanded loyalty from every young woman who drew breath.

"I've brought fresh water in which for you to wash," Amya said.

"Come in." Victoria rose. "Although I don't truly know how to utilize you. You realize I usually dress myself."

"Yes, miss, but I'm here so you don't have to." Amya took the water into the privy room, then came back and curtsied. "Which gown would you care to wear today?"

"The black, please."

She went in the closet and came back with both the black and the brown Victoria had worn the day before. "I'll clean and press the brown as soon as I'm done here," she said.

"Thank you." Victoria went in and washed, and returned to discover the sofa returned to normal, the blankets folded and put away, flowers in a vase, and fresh undergarments as well as the black gown laid across the bed. Victoria would be well cared for during her sojourn in Mr. Lawrence's castle.

As Amya helped her don her clothing, she said a little less timidly, "I can dress your hair." She eyed Victoria's simple braid with an assessing eye.

"I wear it simply. I like it that way." There was no use in becoming accustomed to luxury.

"Yes, but I can fix it so each strand gleams with gold."

By that Victoria could assume Amya missed her work at the hotel—and it was Victoria's fault she was no longer there. "I'd like that," she said.

"My king asked that you teach your first etiquette class today directly after the noon meal." Amya led Victoria to a stool and went to work on her hair. "He says it will allow everyone to enjoy a relaxing time during the heat of the day."

Everyone except me.

As Victoria went through the morning, dragging another small chest out of a storage room, showing the children how to repair the tapestry, teaching them a hundred English words while learning two dozen words in Moricadian, she kept her doubts to herself.

But when she stood at the head of the great hall and faced two hundred hostile pairs of eyes, she knew she was right.

She would not enjoy a relaxing time teaching this class.

In fact, if the way Prospero was looking at her meant anything, she'd be lucky to come through unbloodied and unbowed.

Chapter Twenty-five

"Miss Cardiff?"

At the sound of Thompson's voice, Victoria looked up from the letter she was writing. "Yes?"

"Mr. Lawrence sends word he won't be back in time for the evening meal. In fact, he'll be very late." Thompson glanced at the great hall, now rapidly filling with warriors weary from the day's training. "Will you take a tray in your room?"

She considered the options. She could take the tray, run away, hide behind closed doors while Prospero and his miserable friends exulted in their rout of her.

The idea ground at the edges of her pride.

Or she could sit at the head table next to Raul's empty chair, knowing she was the cynosure of all eyes, while they ignored her, while they made rude comments about her, and she would be unable to choke down a bite.

That scenario reminded her far too much of her days in her stepfather's house. "What would you suggest, Thompson?"

"It's no trouble to send Amya up with a tray." Thompson's eyes gleamed with pity and comprehension. "And I believe Mr. Lawrence will be back tomorrow for sure."

She nodded. "Thank you. In that case, I would appreciate it." She corked the ink with a steady hand, gathered up the sheets of paper covered in her small, neat handwriting.

"May I post your letter for you, Miss Cardiff?" Thompson asked.

"Oh, Thompson." She laughed openly at him. "You are ever Mr. Lawrence's faithful servant. Do you really think I trust you to post it?"

"I would post it." Then he conceded, "After the revolution."

"Yes, so I assumed. I can do it then." She looked at the sheets. "In fact, then I can probably give it to my mother myself."

"Will she worry when she doesn't hear from you?"

"No, she's never traveled. She has no idea how long it takes for letters to make their way across the English Channel."

"Very good. I would hate to think an action of mine contributed to a mother's distress."

"Be at ease, Thompson." Victoria turned toward the stairway, then back to him. "And, Thompson?"

"Yes, miss?"

"I would appreciate it if you didn't inform Mr. Lawrence of the debacle today. I'll make his people respect me or I won't, but I'll handle this on my own."

He hesitated, clearly uncomfortable with her request. But she observed him steadily, not giving an inch, and finally he inclined his head. "As you wish. I'll send Amya up with your tray."

She nodded and climbed the stairs, went into Raul's bedchamber, and shut the door behind her. Going to the sofa, she stretched out and wearily rubbed the stiff muscles of her neck.

As she suspected, the etiquette lesson had been an unmitigated disaster. Raul's people resented her, resented the notion that they could be improved, and Prospero had made it clear that he wouldn't take instruction from a foreigner.

She covered her eyes with her hand, trying to block the memories.

Raul would be pleased to know this room was now her sanctuary.

The click of the lock woke Victoria from her unplanned slumber.

Candlestick in hand, Raul stumbled in. He looked young, handsome, happy, rakish, with his jacket off, his white shirt unbuttoned, his collar and cravat flapping. When he saw her eyes were open, he put his finger to his lips in a shushing motion. With elaborate care, he shut the door behind him.

She lifted herself on one elbow. "Where have you been?"

"What a wifely question. If you're going to ask wifely questions, you have to perform wifely duties." He leered at her. "Want to?"

Her eyes narrowed on his flushed face. "You've been drinking."

"Is it obvious?" He cupped his hand in front of his mouth and blew, then pretended to wither from the smell.

She stifled her amusement.

He waggled his finger at her. "Be careful, Miss Cardiff; you almost smiled."

"You're amusing." When Amya had come in with the dinner tray, she had gently woken Victoria, pulled the pins from her hair, helped her into her nightgown, coaxed her to eat a few bites of bread and butter, then pulled the blankets over her and covered the dinner tray with a clean white napkin. While Victoria sought escape in sleep, Amya built up the fire, then quietly shut the door behind her when she left—and Victoria had heard the key turn in the door.

Even Amya locked her in.

But now the fire had burned down to a pile of glowing embers, and no light slid through the window. Victoria squinted through the shadows toward the clock on the mantel. "It's late."

"Very late." He smiled blissfully. "I was at the casino."

"What were you doing there?"

He put the candlestick down on the bedside table, then came to loom over her in that exasperating, irritating way he had. "I was gambling." So suddenly she blinked in astonishment, he plopped himself down on the carpet and grinned into her face. "And I was *stealing*."

All trace of her sleepiness vanished. "Stealing what?"

"Everything!" He gestured widely, wafting the smell of whiskey toward her. "Every last bit of wealth the

Tonagra gambling hall has won for the last month." He grinned triumphantly.

"*You* did this?"

"No. My people did it." He pouted like a little boy who'd been cut out of the game, then brightened. "But I *planned* the whole thing."

Grasping the blanket to her chest, she sat all the way up. "You really stole their entire take for the month?"

"Every last gold franc and lire and pound. Every banknote. Every voucher. The de Guignards were going to transfer the hoard to their accounts tomorrow, but now all they're doing is running around looking foolish and trying to convince the frightened tourists that they're safe and should remain in the country." Happiness spilled from him in wild exuberance.

"What were *you* doing while your people were pulling off this theft?"

"I was *gambling*. And *winning*. At the tables. In *plain sight*, and without a care in the world. And after my people were done and the money was secure, I found out"—he grinned—"that I couldn't collect my winnings, so I threw the *biggest* tantrum you've ever seen." He wore his hair tied back in a black ribbon; now he pushed his fingers through the strands and tore the bow from its moorings, then winced in pain. But that didn't stop him. He waggled his finger at her. "Jean-Pierre de Guignard doesn't like me. *He's* the one who got me drunk."

"Why?" she asked in alarm.

"He was trying to appease me, he said, assure me I could collect my winnings as soon as they discovered the *lousy rotten* thieves. I asked how long that would take. He assured me it would be soon. I said soon wasn't soon enough." Raul frowned as if he couldn't quite make sense of his own sentence.

"Was he possibly suspicious of you?" Did this man know no fear?

"He's suspicious of everyone. If he'd *really* suspected I was behind the theft, I'd already be missing my teeth and my eyes, and all my fingers would be shattered and my balls would be ripped off and I'd be screaming in agony and—"

"Please!" She held up a hand. "No more."

"Sorry." Catching her hand, he kissed her knuckles. "Sorry. You're so easy to talk to, I forget you're a lady."

She sighed at his less-than-flattering explanation. "Yes, I see how you would."

"Here's the thing. Here's my *strategy*. I know there's one thing authorities never expect, and that's that the thief will call attention to himself, so I just kept complaining. Loudly. Over and over. You should have heard me! To shut me up, Jean-Pierre finally put me in his own carriage and sent me home." Raul flopped flat on his back on the floor and laughed uncontrollably.

She leaned over the edge of the sofa and laughed with him. She didn't know why. In the normal run of things, she didn't approve of theft.

But he was so pleased with himself, so unguarded. He was almost innocent in his pleasure, and something about his spirit called to her.

When he finished laughing, he looked up at her. "Do you know what I'm going to do with that money?"

"Fund the revolution? Buy more firearms?"

"*No*. No, no, no. This money is for *after* the revolution. This money will fund the government, feed the people, get us through the first winter until we can reassure the tourists that they'll be safe here. When they're back, we'll use them to become a rich country. To be secure from the large countries that would absorb us and use our income for their people rather than ours." He laughed again. "The theft—it went better than I could ever have imagined, and Jean-Pierre will be busy for the next fortnight trying to track me down."

"He won't be successful, will he?"

"The money's gone, out of the country, and Jean-Pierre believes I'm just a wild, worthless gambler and horse breeder who is thinking of emigrating to the Caribbean, where I'll be safe from the rebels who are chasing away the travelers I make my living from fleecing...." Raul looked up at her, boyishly charming and oh, so smug.

Then, as his gaze searched her face, his smile faded. He caught a loose strand of her hair in his grip, held it as if it were made of gold.

Suddenly, the midnight silence pressed in around them. Suddenly, she remembered that they were alone, that she was his captive, that he had pressed kisses on her unwilling mouth, had vowed to seduce her into his bed....

He remembered, too.

Passion flared in the depths of his eyes. All trace of the boy disappeared, and wildness took possession of him.

Danger. The warning reverberated along her nerves.

Slowly, he sat up, never releasing her from his gaze.

He became once more a man, a victor ... in need of his woman.

Slowly, she retreated, heart racing, hypnotized by his intensity.

He followed, stalking her. Heat rolled off him in waves.

Her back struck the back of the sofa. She clenched the blanket in her fist, holding it before her like a shield.

He gathered her head into his hands, slid his fingers into her hair.

The rasp of his skin against her scalp felt possessive.

He kissed her. *Kissed* her as he hadn't last night, forcefully, thoroughly, opening her mouth with his lips.

The first thrust of his tongue startled her. The second warmed her. With the third, blood pulsed furiously in her veins, taking the desire he fed her and spreading it through her body. She caught her breath, too surprised to do anything . . . and unwillingly aroused.

Like a warrior with a conquered woman in his bed, he possessed her with his mouth. He ran his hand down the contours of her body, acquainting himself with her as if he had every right to take her as a prize of victory.

Of course, he did not. She knew that. She knew she should be outraged to be reduced to nothing more than a trophy, but he was so intent on *her*. He wanted *her*. When she felt him clench his fist against her hip, holding the material of her nightgown as if he feared to lose her, she found her own exultation rising to meet his.

His revolution hadn't even started, yet already he had won every skirmish. The enemy feared him, and didn't even know who he was.

He was, already, a victor.

But he had not won the victory over her, and when his hand cupped her breast, when his thumb circled her nipple, shock rolled through her.

She boxed his ears, swift and hard. "Sir, you go too far!"

"Damn it!" The single candle barely lit the taut hollows of his face, the grim lines of fury as he struggled to contain his anger ... and his lust.

But when he felt her backing away, he lost the battle. Reaching for her, he snagged her wrists, pushed her back down on the sofa.

She struggled, wanting nothing so much as to slap him again.

Probably that wasn't smart. Probably such an action would only goad him to further ferocity. But he wasn't the only one whose temper was roused....

No, not her temper. What was roused was ... something else. Something foreign to the proper Englishwoman and governess Miss Cardiff.

As he thrust her arms above her head, leaned into her, she fought because it felt too good, too right. Because his touch transformed her into a different person: earthy, lusty, a woman who heard the call of his body to hers and responded.

Again he kissed her, thrusting his tongue in and out, in and out, until he had imprinted himself on her, until she was weak with need, until the gown she wore was a feeble barrier, too thin to keep them apart.

When she moaned against his mouth, he said, "Yes." He pulled his cravat from around his neck.

And she was so foolish she didn't realize what he was doing—until he tied her wrists together.

"No!" She fought him anew.

He held her with one hand now, and used his other hand to roam her body, exploring where he would: her breasts, her belly. He even pressed the cleft between her thighs, molding the cotton material to her until it grew damp from her arousal. Then her face grew hot with mortification and she lunged at him, throwing him off balance.

He hit the floor flat on his back, dragging his cravat—and her—with him.

They sprawled together, limbs tangled, and before she could catch her breath, he rolled on top of her. "You never learn," he snarled, and, keeping her hands above her head, he put his mouth to her throat.

He didn't retaliate for her attack; she had thought he would. Instead he used his mouth like a sexual weapon, savoring the place where her vein beat against her skin, nipping at her earlobe, sliding his tongue in a slow loop around the shell of her ear.

He was heavily muscled, weighing her down. The tufts of the rug easily penetrated her thin nightgown to rasp against her back, her buttocks, her thighs. He smelled of whiskey, of saddle and horse, and of Raul. . . . *Why* did she already know his scent? She didn't want to, but somehow she knew she could find him anywhere: in the dark, in a crowd, across a continent. . . .

His wicked, knowing mouth roamed farther, down to her breast, where he tasted her through the material, drawing her nipple into his mouth and sucking hard, then, when she was whimpering, letting it go and blowing on the wet cotton.

Now her struggles were not against him, but against herself. Because she wanted to wrap her legs around his body, take him inside, and learn how to move with him, mate with him.

He suckled at her other breast, creating a madness that battered at her resistance, at her pride.

How could she fight him when he enlisted her own body against her? He performed every depraved act, invading her privacy, showing her facets of herself she was better off not knowing. All these years traveling in Europe, she had imagined herself to be the embodiment of true spinsterhood, impervious to temptation. Now Raul stripped away her innocence, destroyed the lies she had told herself. She hated him for that . . . and wanted him regardless.

His knee worked its way between her legs, compressing the nerves and making her tighten her thighs around him.

"Burn for me," he said, and pushed against her again, and again.

She moved with him, panting with explosive need. "Please." She didn't know what she was asking for; she knew only that when she said that, he lifted his head from her throat.

His eyes flared; his teeth clenched. He braced himself and watched as yearning and passion carried her past wisdom. He let her use his body to seek pleasure, showed her in tiny increments of knowledge how to inch closer and closer to orgasm. Pressing his hand between her legs, he gently squeezed.

Flames engulfed her, and she did burn for him.

Chapter Twenty-six

In Victoria's opinion, Raul knew more about torture than any de Guignard. Every night for six nights, he returned from his work with his troops. At dinner, he fed her from his own hand, insisted she drink from his cup; then, when the evening meal was over, he led her to his room . . . and seduced her.

He never removed her clothes, or his. Instead he proved, over and over, that he could drive her mad with need.

She resisted. Of course she resisted.

He became very good at the use of a cravat to control her, and in a way, she didn't mind that. At least when he tied her, she knew she was behaving in a manner befitting a civilized woman. When he tied her, she was fighting him.

It was the times when he no longer needed the cravat that shamed her. It was when he drove her to the cliff edge of passion and then pushed her off. Night after night, he showed her that she could fly ... and when she came back to earth, the ties were gone, her wrists were free, and he was observing her. He never said a word, but they both knew the truth—he could far too easily destroy her resistance. She didn't have to like him; he made her want him.

She'd cried last night, begged him to take her.

But no, that wasn't what he wanted. He would not take her.

He wanted her to give herself.

She hadn't yet sunk that far.

The only thing that helped her survive the night torture was that he was suffering, too. Maybe he was suffering more. She didn't know. She hoped so, because while every night she came again and again ... he got no satisfaction at all.

She hadn't seen his easy smile in days.

She was glad.

If only she didn't have to teach that horrible class today. She could only imagine how pleased Prospero would be to see her swollen eyes and hear her scratchy voice. She considered hiding in her room, letting Prospero crow in triumph.

But she always spent the morning with the children. They eased her wounded spirit, made her remember that she was not one man's plaything or another's object of scorn, but a governess, beloved among those who mattered most—the children.

These children were loved, but they'd been raised in adversarial circumstances. Every day they knew the de

Guignards could brutally take their parents from them. Their education had been neglected as the adults concentrated on the necessary tasks at hand, first staying alive, and then winning the revolution. So they basked in Victoria's attention, and more than that, they loved teaching her Moricadian.

Every day she learned more words and more phrases, and every day she comprehended a little better. They, of course, learned English so quickly that she'd sought out the dilapidated schoolroom, cleaned it up, and started teaching them to read and write.

Most of them absorbed everything eagerly.

But not Prospero's son. At first, Victoria thought he had been listening to his parents and was being deliberately stupid. Then she saw his expression when his four-year-old sister recited the words Victoria put on the slate.

He truly couldn't comprehend.

She thought it might be his eyesight, but when she questioned him, she discovered he was the best shot of any young hunter.

So, remembering the teachings of the Distinguished Academy of Governesses, she quizzed him about his numbers.

The boy was a mathematical genius. When she recited long columns of numbers, he told her the answer almost before she finished—and he was always right. She taught him multiplication in one sitting, division in another. More important, he understood the concepts at work, his brain leaping from one conclusion to another—and everything she taught him, he kept in his head.

He couldn't write, but what did that matter? When she remembered Mr. Johnson and the work she'd done for him, she knew Prospero's boy could hire someone to put down the numbers. All he had to do was figure them out in his head.

She ate her noon meal with the children, and found great comfort in the fact that she never had to say a word about their manners. All she did was eat slowly, neatly, pass the dishes, carry on a polite conversation, and the children imitated her.

That was a victory in which she could exult, and she was glad.

She'd enjoyed no such victory with their parents.

Every day was another withering defeat at their hands.

And after that, every day she spent the late afternoon at the writing desk in the corner of the great hall, helping Thompson with the household accounts—she had, after all, learned a lot from Mr. Johnson, and she was glad to put it to use.

"Victoria." Raul's warm, deep voice startled Victoria.

She dropped her pen. Ink splattered across the paper. She caught up the blotter, and with a steady hand, she dabbed up the excess, trying to save the words she'd so carefully written. When she was satisfied, she turned to face him.

He looked thinner than he had, and grimmer, his face gaunt, and she realized the warmth in his voice was a chimera, for his eyes were ice-cold. He smelled fresh, as if he'd bathed in a mountain lake, and perhaps he had, for his shoulder-length hair hung in damp strands, and the rough clothing he wore to work with his troops was wet across his shoulders, at his waist, and where the hem of his trousers tucked into his boots.

"What are you doing?" He didn't wait for her response, but reached for her letter.

She moved it smoothly out of his way. "I'm writing my mother, giving a truthful report of the events here in Moricadia."

"All of them?" He lifted an eyebrow.

"My mother feared I would come to a bad end, so I've refrained from telling her I sleep in your bedroom." With her direct gaze, Victoria challenged him. "Even knowing I sleep on the couch would not comfort her."

If Raul experienced guilt for making her conceal the truth from her mother, Victoria saw no evidence of it. "Would you like Thompson to post your letter?" he asked.

She laughed briefly, bitterly, folded the pages, and put them in the reticule that hung at her waist. "Thompson and I have had that discussion. I'll take care of this."

"As you wish," he said indifferently. "Hada is serving the evening meal. Will you join us?"

She wanted to say no, that she would take a tray in her room, that she couldn't stand to look forward into that room of sneering faces, then turn and see his un-smiling expression.

But he presented his hand to her, and as she stared at the upturned palm, she realized his invitation wasn't truly an invitation; she had no option. She would take her place at his side.

She gave him her hand, and the shock of her bare skin against his stopped her breath.

She wished she wore gloves. A barrier would make his touch less onerous . . . but then, the clothes between them at night hadn't protected her from experiencing passion in his arms. Perhaps the only thing that could protect her from him was distance. If she could hold out for another week . . . and then another . . .

No. She needed a different goal.

If she could hold out for just tonight . . . that would be victory.

With a desperate assumption of ease, she walked at his side to the head table. She nodded to Prospero—at night, they pretended to be on speaking terms. She murmured a greeting to Zakerie—she was glad to see him, for his easygoing manner put her at ease.

Raul held her chair.

She sat and braced herself for another evening spent pretending to eat while wishing she were elsewhere.

He seated himself.

The chairs next to her were empty as Thompson coordinated Hada and the women as they placed food on the table, poured ale and wine, and made sure their men were comfortable.

Victoria didn't know what made her speak. It was probably no more than the determination to carry on a normal conversation. Or maybe she was tired of trying to be invisible. "Raul?"

"Yes?" He offered her his wine goblet.

She took it, cradled it in her hands. "You said the women shoot better than the men?"

"Yes."

"Are any of them in charge of . . . anything?"

He viewed her as if she were speaking a foreign language.

"The women go out all day, practicing to fight in the revolution like men. At night, they come in tired and dirty. But they don't get to eat and drink and relax like the men. They have to fetch and carry and perform traditional women's tasks." Around them, the conversation slowly withered and died. "So I was wondering—in the

field, are any of them in charge? Are any of them commanders, or are they subordinate to Zakerie and all the
other men?"

Raul stared at her as if she'd grown horns.

Zakerie had his fingers pressed to his forehead.

Prospero glared, his eyes as dark and shiny as obsid-
ian.

Thompson stood off to the side, watching.

Victoria looked toward Hada, who stood unmov-
ing, expressionless, a pitcher of ale balanced against her
waist, a platter of meat in one hand.

Raul leaned back in his chair and laughed, a single
note, harsh and derisive. "No, none of the women are
commanders. They haven't had the training needed."

Of all the things Victoria abhorred, it was bias and
injustice, and this was prejudice at its most odious. And
really, what could these men do to her if she spoke frankly?
Imprison her? "You said so many have lost their husbands and fathers to the de Guignards that they have
had to protect their homes and their families in any way
they can. You insinuated that you admired the women
who were willing to fight. And you said they were being
trained to shoot. Can they not be trained to command?"

The women who stood while the men sat looked at
one another as if seeking support.

"Are the men not also so trained before becoming
sergeants and such?" Victoria insisted.

"She's right," Zakerie said. "The men *are* trained, and
I've got two women whom I leave in charge when I have
duties elsewhere. They do everything I would do, and
better."

Prospero slammed his goblet on the table. "A man's
nature makes him more able to lead!"

"It seems that a man's nature makes him more able to throw a tantrum," Victoria said coolly. "Is that a leadership quality to be admired?"

Thompson stepped to the table. "Mr. Lawrence, if Hada took over the entire household in the position of butler—and she is admirably capable of handling all situations and crises—I would be available to work in the field more often." His voice was eager. "I do enjoy going into the woods and coordinating the operations there."

Babble broke out and swiftly rose to a roar as everyone offered their opinions.

Raul relaxed back into his chair and asked indolently, "What have you done?"

"All I did was ask a question."

"A question that needed to be asked, obviously." Picking up her hand, he kissed her fingers.

Almost at once, the furor faded and Victoria once more found herself the center of curious eyes.

"I'll take the opinions everyone has expressed this evening under advisement, and tomorrow make a decision about which of the women to put in command." Raul nodded to Hada, and then to Prospero. "But for now, Thompson is right, and I'm sorry I was obtuse. Hada, if it pleases you, you may take over the running of the entire household."

With typical reticence, she nodded and set to work at once directing the women in the dinner service.

Prospero leaned forward and spoke to Victoria. "Hada loves to be outdoors."

Victoria shifted her startled gaze to Hada. She was frail, short, and thin, and her limp was fearsome.

"Do you know why she works indoors rather than training the women in shooting?" he asked.

"No, we've never really spoken about our lives." Because Victoria took care not to share memories or ambitions with the people she met in Moricadia.

It seemed Prospero wasn't as oblivious as she'd imagined, for he said, "Because you don't want to make friends here."

"No. I don't want friends here." She refused to pretend otherwise, and met his gaze head-on.

He nodded knowingly. "When I met Hada, she was twelve years old. She was whole and beautiful, she ran wild, and she was the best shot in the country."

Victoria drew back. She already knew she didn't care to hear, because so clearly Prospero was determined to tell her.

But he leaned closer. "When she was fifteen, she was out hunting, looking for something to feed her family. Now, you need to know—no Moricadian is allowed to take meat from anywhere in the country. The de Guignards say it belongs to them. Prince Sandre and his men caught her shooting a rabbit, a little rabbit"—with his hands, he showed her the size—"for even the rabbits are half-starved in this country. So the prince declared a hunt, and he and his men chased her through the woods. They were on horseback. She was on foot. They toyed with her until she was exhausted, until she couldn't run anymore, until she fell. Then they galloped over the top of her. One of the hooves crushed her hip, another her leg. They left her for dead and rode off, satisfied they had done justice."

Horrified, Victoria stared at him, then at Hada.

Hada saw her reaction and started toward the head table, her gait lopsided and painful.

"She didn't die, but she'll never again be able to run,

to shoot, to be the woman she should have been." Prospero's eyes shone with hate. "She bore me two children, but she can't have more. With our last child, she almost died."

Painful tears pressed at the back of Victoria's eyes.

"Prospero. Enough." Raul made a slashing sign across his throat.

Prospero paid no heed, but continued to speak to Victoria. "You come here and you want to change everything. When you've suffered the way we've all suffered, when you see your mother starve and your friends die, then you'll understand why we are as we are. Then we'll listen to you!"

Hada reached the table, leaned across, looked into her husband's eyes. "Prospero. I will not allow you to make me an object of pity. Never for any reason. So hold your tongue."

"Woman!" He stood and stared down at her. "You don't tell me what to do."

She looked back. "Someone has to."

And he backed down. "I've got to go on patrol." Taking his goblet, he stomped toward the door.

Victoria stood. "I'm going to bed."

Chapter Twenty-seven

Victoria didn't care what people thought. She just wanted to be alone.

Of course, that wasn't possible.

Raul caught up with her before she left the great hall. As they climbed the stairs, he placed his hand in the small of her back to steady her, and he entered the bedroom on her heels. He shut the door behind them and turned the key in the lock.

As she had done every night, Amya had prepared the room. She'd placed bed linens on the sofa, laid out Victoria's nightgown, lit the fire. But every night, she added something to the ambience—a vase of flowers, rose petals floating in the basin of warm water. Tonight Amya had lit candles throughout the room, creating a warm glow that made even her tormentor look . . . compassionate.

She couldn't stand that. Snatching up her nightgown and a blanket, she fled into the closet. She changed in the dark, wrapped herself in the blanket, and returned to the bedroom.

He was still there, standing in the same spot, waiting. Waiting . . .

She faced him, upset and angry, wanting him to go away, ready to fight him if necessary.

But the ruthless swine surprised her. "I'm sorry about the letter to your mother." He offered her his hand. "When the revolution is over, you can post it."

Oh, no. He wasn't going to coax her out of her distress. And she was not about to touch him. "When your revolution is over, I'll go and see her."

"Yes, of course you will." He dropped his hand. He strolled to the window, braced his arm against the wall, and looked out. "You and your mother are close?"

"Not at all." She didn't know why she confessed such a shameful thing—maybe because that first night he had confided in her—but she added, "I don't think she ever worries about me, but still, because she's my mother . . . I write."

"You travel the world and your mother doesn't worry about you?" He turned back with a frown.

She scrambled onto the sofa, although not because she thought he intended to seduce her. Not right now. Right now, he was getting close without coming near. "I'm her eldest, the only child of my father. After his death, she struggled to make a living, but we almost ended up in the poorhouse."

"That would have been a death sentence to you both."

"Exactly. So she married my stepfather." She sank

down onto the pillow, pulled the covers up to her chin, huddled there, and wished she'd never started this conversation . . . and wished she could stop right now. Oh, Raul's younger sister Belle had made some guesses, probably pretty good ones, but Victoria had never told anyone the truth about her and her mother. Now she couldn't seem to stop. "My stepfather married her to have a wife to tend his house and take care of his children by his first wife. They've since had children together. I have eight step- and half siblings."

"So your mother had to divide her attention between a lot of you." Raul came and sat on the floor beside the sofa. "Still, she's your mother."

She turned her head and looked at him.

His green eyes gleamed with something that looked like affection. His hair fell like black silk onto his shoulders. He was so handsome he made her heart ache. "You were fond of your mother?" she asked.

"She loved me," he said simply.

"Oh, my mother loves me. I didn't mean to insinuate she didn't." Maybe her heart ached for more reasons than she could imagine. "But I was a difficult child, ungrateful for my stepfather's charity and wanting more than was my right, and she was caught between him and me."

"You've had to be too strong."

"Only as strong as I've needed to be," Victoria corrected.

Finally, he made his move, the move she'd been expecting all evening, the move she had braced herself to reject. Slowly, he eased himself onto the sofa with her, trapping her between the back and his body. She stiffened, but he did nothing except pull her into his arms

and hold her . . . hold her until his warmth penetrated
the chill that held her in its grasp. Hold her until she
relaxed against him, put her head against his chest, and
listened to his heartbeat. Hold her until the world vanished and only the two of them remained.

It was afternoon when Raul returned to the castle. He
tossed his cravat and cravat pin on the table in the entrance hall.

Thompson hurried to his side, took Raul's collar and
cuffs, and asked, "Tired, sir?"

"A long day." Raul rubbed his neck. "But profitable
in many ways, and successful in so many others."

"Viento won his race?"

Raul nodded his satisfaction. "With two horses in two
weeks in the winner's circle, the eyes of the breeding
world are turning to Moricadia. And with two sales to-
taling over sixteen thousand English pounds, I have attracted Jean-Pierre's concerted attention."

"Is that really a good thing, sir?" Thompson had
grown more anxious in the last weeks.

They all had. Witness the scene last night at dinner
between Victoria and Prospero, with Prospero snapping
at Victoria, Victoria's flight from the table, and then her
unhappy confession of estrangement from her mother.
A week ago, she would have never told him so much
about her personal life, and to him, it was a sign that, despite her unwilling presence here, they had grown close.

He frowned.

When had that happened?

He had intended a seduction, not a romance. Not
love . . . He had a revolution to win. He didn't have time
for love.

"Sir?" Raul's long hesitation made Thompson even more anxious.

"As long as I continue to appear at the gambling halls and the spas, it is good to keep Jean-Pierre's attention." Raul put a steadying hand on Thompson's shoulder. "Then he doesn't notice the spies I've set in place in the hotels and in the palace, or hear the gunshots echoing in the most remote parts of the forest."

"I hope you're right, sir."

"Not too much longer, Thompson. We're almost ready." He started up the stairs to the great hall.

"Sir!"

Thompson's urgency stopped Raul in his tracks.

"Miss Cardiff asked that I not tell you about the class you have her teaching, but you're here, and it's been a week, and nothing has improved."

"She's having trouble teaching them? *Victoria Cardiff* is having trouble teaching a class?" Raul could scarcely believe that.

"If I may, I'll keep my promise and not tell you. . . . I'll show you." Thompson gestured Raul to follow him.

They walked toward the entrance to the great hall and stood behind the wall. Raul could hear voices— many voices speaking Moricadian, then Victoria saying, "I can't yet comprehend so much of your language—but I suspect you know that."

Prospero's voice answered her. "You should learn faster, teacher. We all know English. We've had to learn it to serve the tourists who come and think *we* are ignorant."

Victoria answered steadily, "It is a very great shame that English tourists consider you ignorant; that's foolish on their part. But that doesn't mitigate the need to learn manners that will please all nationalities."

Prospero laughed rudely. "We have our manners. They're good enough for us. They're good enough for everyone."

Raul peeked around the corner at the great hall.

The way his people sat, stood, talked, laughed—they were like wolves closing in for the kill, and Victoria was that kill.

She knew it, too, but stood straight and tall at the front of the room, not retreating, not surrendering, but persisting in the task he had assigned her.

Raul turned to Thompson. "She hasn't been able to teach them at all?"

"Nothing."

"Why not?"

"From the first, it's been a mob on the attack."

"Because she was rude to Prospero?"

"No one likes change, and change is coming. It's easy to blame Miss Cardiff."

"But what about the women? Why don't they support her? Why doesn't Hada support her?"

Thompson looked uncomfortable. "Because she has no authority here. In fact . . . I believe the problem originates with the women."

"The women?" *The women?* "Why wouldn't the women like Victoria? Especially after last night, when she spoke up for their cause?"

"They despise her. Despise her because they say—sir, forgive me; I am repeating what I overheard—she's a failure as a woman."

Raul felt as if he'd wandered into a strange forest filled with twisted branches and dark hollows. "Why is she a failure as a woman?"

Thompson squirmed in discomfort, like a schoolboy

who'd been caned. "She sleeps in your room, but you don't want her."

"What?"

"They know you're not having sexual congress."

Raul would have laughed at Thompson's formal terminology. But he wasn't amused. "How do they know that?"

"There's been discussion among the people living in your household about your foul mood."

"My foul mood," Raul repeated.

"They know . . . That is, they believe that if Miss Cardiff were making you . . . happy, you would be . . . more pleasant."

"For the love of God, what a bunch of gossips!" Raul knew his people watched him, and certainly his nightly confinement with a beautiful, passionate woman *was* disturbing his sleep and making him wonder if she could outlast him in this contest of wills. But to have them take it out on Victoria . . . He had never imagined such a consequence would fall upon her head. "Miss Cardiff asked that you not tell me about the problems she's having?"

"That's right. She said she would make them respect her, or not. I believe her pride won't let you interfere."

Raul pushed his hand through his hair and thought hard. "Then for the moment, I won't. Frankly, Thompson, I would back Miss Cardiff in any fight." He walked toward the back stairway. At the door, he turned. "At least, in any fight where I am not her opponent."

Chapter Twenty-eight

Today would be different.

Today, as Victoria stood before Raul's people, she resolved to find the right words to make them realize the importance of her mission. For today she had been in Raul's dilapidated castle for ten days, and as she watched the warriors, male and female, eat their lunch, and burp and scratch, she more and more realized how desperately they needed her help.

More important, she wanted to be able to face Raul in the light of day and tell him she had successfully begun the task he had assigned her. She couldn't stand the idea of failure. Not when Raul had turned her world upside down and made her so uncertain of herself.

Uncertain because, when he shut the bedroom door at night, she never knew which man she would face.

Would he be the darkly seductive lover, insistent on her surrender? Or the gentleman who coaxed a wretched confession out of her, then held her in his arms and made everything better?

She had to know she could teach these people, or who was she? Not Victoria Cardiff, controlled and expert governess, but a woman tempted by the night and a man until she craved him without ceasing . . .

No, today would be different. She would accept no other solution.

She faced Prospero—for if she won him, she won all—and said, "Today we learn to how to greet one another, and to eat with forks."

Prospero lolled in his chair, goblet of ale in hand, and loudly asked, "Why should we learn these things you value so much? They're worthless, and we have a revolution to win!"

Victoria waited until the approving tumult had died down. "Because, Prospero, once your revolution starts, it will be won or lost in the matter of a few days, a week at most. Then the king will be in his palace, you will be his courtiers, and the eyes of the world will be on you. Right now—this is all the time you have to learn the bare basics of courtesy."

"We're courteous," he said belligerently.

She almost laughed at the irony of Prospero saying that to her. But she understood him, and his pride. "You have a rough courtesy, yes." She raised her voice, making sure it projected to the far corners of the great hall. "But the reason you're willing to die for this revolution and this king is because you know you're living in circumstances so cruel and backward you and your children have no choice but to stay here."

Hada stood against the far wall, watching and listening.

Victoria continued. "If you went out to Italy or France or Denmark, you would be like a peasant from a thousand years ago who had suddenly been brought forward and deposited in the modern world. England, Spain, Prussia—they have newspapers. They have railroads. Would you know how to behave on a train? You have no idea. Learn what I can teach you, if not for yourself, then for the sake of your children and your king."

She must have struck a chord, because Hada limped forward, her gait a bitter reminder of the de Guignards and all the cruelty of which they were capable.

Prospero watched his wife, breathing hard, almost trembling with suppressed emotion. Turning back to Victoria, he said, "It's you that's the problem. You're so proud of your travels and your sophistication—but do you know the trouble with you?"

"No. Tell me." As if she could stop him.

His voice rose as he, too, projected into the depths of the great hall. "You don't have a stake in the revolution. When you can, you're going to leave. Before the battle starts, Saber plans to get you out of here, and you're going to flee without a backward glance. We'll be here, fighting and dying, and you won't care. You sleep with our king in his room every night, but you don't care that he's determined to lead the charges, that he insists on traveling beneath his family's banner, that the de Guignards will aim for him first, that he could be shot and killed, or worse—captured, dragged into their infernal dungeon, and tortured."

Victoria suddenly found it hard to breathe.

"Do you know what the de Guignards do to people? Have you ever seen a man who's been stretched on the rack until all his joints are torn apart? Do you know what happens when they put two knots in a rope and pull it around a man's face until his eyes pop out?"

Victoria couldn't speak. Faintly, she shook her head and tried not to imagine Raul . . . like that.

"I have. Everyone here has seen torture."

Raul's people were turning their heads away, looking toward the entrance, squirming in their seats as if wanting to get away. From Prospero's recitation. From the pain and the memories.

Hada stopped behind her husband, put her hands on his shoulders, and observed Victoria with dark, expressionless eyes.

"From the day we were born, we were dragged into Tonagra to see the prisoners before the de Guignards hanged them. I saw my own father . . ." Prospero stopped projecting his voice. He bent his head, closed his eyes, reached up, and gripped Hada's hands.

For the first time, Victoria saw him not as an obnoxious nuisance, but as a man racked with recollections too agonizing to bear. "I am sorry, Prospero."

His eyes sprang open. He glowered, rejecting her sympathy. His voice rose again. "You natter on about manners while we're facing death. So no, I don't want to join your modern world. Not until I've finished the job I have to do here first."

Hada lifted her hand off his shoulder. She slapped him on the back of the head. Once. Hard. "Shut up."

He turned on her. "What did you do that for?"

"She's right," Hada said. "You know she's right."

"You think this woman is right?" He rubbed his head and grudgingly admitted, "Maybe she is. But I don't want to learn from a snooty—"

Hada boxed his ears. "She might be snooty, but she's teaching your son his numbers." She turned to face the other women. "I know there are many things about Miss Cardiff that make us doubt her usefulness to us and to our king. But she's teaching our children—all our children—to read. We didn't ask her. She hasn't asked for praise or for money, just took on the task, and you all know the children love her."

One by one, the women started nodding.

Victoria stood quietly, recognizing this breakthrough for what it was—a change in policy led by the mothers of the children she tutored.

Of course. Who else but the mothers would give a good education the value it deserved?

Hada turned back to Prospero. "*You* might not want to join the modern world, but this is what I've been fighting for—a chance for our babes to learn. So you respect Miss Cardiff and be trained in what she can teach us."

"Stupid idea to learn manners," Prospero muttered.

Hada pressed her fingers into his shoulders until he turned to face her. "Maybe so, but the king has decreed it, and, Prospero—he has seen the childish way you've been acting."

Prospero stared at his wife in shock.

"He sees more than you think." She turned to face Victoria. "Go ahead. We'll listen. We'll learn. Teach us to eat with forks."

Chapter Twenty-nine

Amya finished pinning Victoria's hair up, then accepted the last bucket of warm water from the scullery maid and poured it into the tub. "Is the water temperature comfortable, Miss Cardiff?"

"It's good, thank you, Amya." Victoria relaxed against the tall back of the round wooden tub and let the heat work its way into her bones.

Eyes closed, she listened as Amya made the sofa into a bed and laid out her nightgown, stoked the fire, and set the screen.

Victoria was weary. Tired of fighting the adults in her etiquette class. Tired of lying awake at night, struggling against the clawing need Raul created in her. And now . . . wishing she could ignore those fatal words Prospero had thrown at her, and what they ultimately meant.

You have no stake in our struggle. We all could die. Our king could die.

She hadn't thought . . . Yes, she had known Raul would go off and fight. But he was so alive, so vital, she had assumed he would win, be triumphant, lead the victory parade, be crowned king, and when all that had happened . . . she would be free. It had been her goal—to stand strong against his seduction for another day, another week, another month, and then she would be free, body untouched, heart intact.

Please, God, heart intact.

"I'll return with your rinse water," Amya said softly, and left, shutting the door quietly behind her.

"Thank you," Victoria said to the empty room.

Prospero had cruelly torn the veil from her eyes.

Yes, victory was possible. She even believed Raul's plan would succeed—*should* succeed—but Raul could be hurt. Tortured. Killed.

Success or failure, life or death, when the revolution was over, she would be free. Body intact. Heart intact. To grow old by herself . . .

Today Raul had once again gone into the city to pester the de Guignards, so she had spent the whole afternoon with Raul's people, teaching them how to greet dignitaries and noblemen, to muffle their bodily functions, and yes, to use their forks. Once they set their minds to learning, they seemed determined to make up for lost time.

So, thanks to Hada, Victoria would succeed in her goal. She had started Raul's people on their road to respectability . . . while her own respectability clung precariously to life.

For so many nights, she had had to fight both Raul's

seduction and her own weakness. She fought because Miss Victoria Cardiff always knew the right thing to do, and preserving her virginity until marriage was the right thing to do—and since Victoria Cardiff had no desire to wed, the maintenance of her purity had previously been automatic, like brushing her hair a hundred strokes each night.

It spoke volumes for her current conundrum when she considered she hadn't performed that nightly ritual since she'd arrived at Raul's castle.

The latch on the door clicked.

She thought it was Amya.

Then . . . then when no one spoke, she *knew*.

Goose bumps rose on her skin. Slowly she turned her head toward the entrance.

Her instinct had not steered her wrong.

Raul stood there, steaming bucket of water in hand. He looked as if he'd been to the opera, wearing black and white in a suit cut to display his body like a frame. He should have appeared as if he were the epitome of civilization; instead, his eyes glowed dark green and primitive, like the tangled forest outside their window . . . or like a dragon's on the prowl.

He shut the door behind him and leaned against it.

Reaching behind him, he turned the key.

"No," she said.

"I'll listen when you say yes." He stalked toward her, one slow step at a time, and her world trembled as if thunder shook the ground.

She couldn't tear her gaze from his, couldn't look away from the fall of black hair that framed his face, the way the flames bathed his features with rosy light and dark shadow.

She pulled the small square of wash linen over her chest—it was barely the size of a handkerchief, and almost useless. She sank deeper into the water.

He put the bucket down. Knelt by the fire and stoked it higher.

She realized she'd been holding her breath and inhaled, tried to be Victoria Cardiff and not a creature who thought of nothing but passion, longed for nothing but passion. But when he turned back to her, prudence fled, leaving only fear and . . . *passion.*

He stripped off his cravat, his collar, his cuffs. He pulled off his shirt and his undershirt. He was graceful, his muscles sharply defined. He teased her with the sight of his bare chest and broad, bare shoulders, and she waited for him to remove his trousers.

But disappointment seared her, for he acted as if the thought had never crossed his mind, as if he didn't know that like a withered old maid, she wanted to see him, his body—and the source of his drive to possess her.

Yet the way he watched her made her feel anything but withered, and when he picked up the bar of lavender soap Amya had placed beside the tub, Victoria caught her breath.

She knew what he intended now, and every respectable impulse in her rose in protest . . . and faded as anticipation took command.

He plunged his hands into the water, worked up a rich lather, then paced around her, his gaze fixed on her body half-revealed in the shimmering water. Finally he stood behind her; she waited, not knowing what to expect . . . until he placed his soapy fingers on her neck and moved them in slow, firm circles.

The silence in the room was thick, rich, warm with

promise. Each breath she took heated her from the inside out.

He moved around to the front, kneeling before her as if in worship of her beauty.

And the way he leaned forward, looked deep into her eyes . . . he did make her feel beautiful.

Not that he wasn't interested in her naked body beneath the lapping water. But he was making it clear, very clear, that it was *she*, Victoria, who held him enraptured.

His soapy hands slid down her arms. His fingers entwined with hers; he pushed his calloused palm to hers, a firm pressure that felt somehow incendiary, as if he were rubbing her intimately.

He dipped their joined hands into the water, released her, again reached for the soap and lathered his hands. Again he moved behind her. With his arms under her arms, he lifted her out of the water and pulled her against him.

Never had she known the shock of bare skin against bare skin.

Water and bubbles sluiced down her body as he rubbed her, first on her chest, then her belly, then her breasts. . . . *Oh, God.* Her breasts, her nipples, every sensitive inch of skin . . . She trembled, caught between the heat of him against her back and the pleasure of his hands on her body—the unique sensations he created made her jittery, jumpy, torn between the need to run from this cataclysmic event . . . and the need to embrace it. Embrace him.

His hands rubbed her belly again, her thighs, between them. . . .

She couldn't explain why she allowed this. Perhaps it was the nights of silent seduction. Perhaps it was the perfume of the pine-scented smoke that gave a tang to the air and clouded her vision. Perhaps it was too many years of loneliness . . . but she wasn't so much lonely as alone. In truth, she had always liked being alone, being the only person responsible for herself.

With Raul, it wasn't necessary.

With Raul, she could relax the stiff spine that had carried her through years of living with her stepfather, years of school, years of supporting herself, making sure everyone knew she was proper, so proper.

With Raul, she knew he would climb the castle tower to have her. If only that weren't true, she would have the strength to hold him off.

But with Raul, she felt like a fairy princess and an earth goddess, all at the same time.

No one knew what was happening in this room. No one knew she wanted Raul: wanted to lie in his bed with him, taste him, let him taste her, let him teach her the meaning of pleasure.

As his hands slid between her legs and opened her to temptation, she moaned, a long, slow, languid sound, as if together they were making music.

The sound gave him pause, made him lean his face into her hair, inhale as if she were an intoxicating perfume. His lips grazed her cheek, and the knowledge of his longing washed over her.

She turned her head, caught his mouth with hers, then kissed him as his hands moved on her, touching places no man had ever touched, setting off thrills. . . .

She could kiss him forever. He kissed like a man who needed kissing. He kissed, and in his kiss she tasted long years of facing a world that cared not at all about his loneliness. His kiss was like hers, a mere half kiss until the two of them were together. Then they were whole. They were one.

When he released her, her knees gave way and she slid back into the tub.

He picked up the bucket of warm water and poured it over her, rinsing the soap away.

She could scarcely breathe for the desire that sped like a drug through her veins. When he picked up the towel and offered his hand, anticipation made her bite her lip.

She should be afraid that tonight was the night his control would shatter.

No, that wasn't true.

She should be afraid that tonight was the night her own control would shatter. For his sinful lips silently promised bliss; his green eyes burned with experience and knowledge; his broad hands had already proved their mastery of her body.

She placed her palm in his.

He pulled her from the tub and dried her: her shoulders, her breasts, her back. . . . The long, slow strokes of the rough linen set her nerves on edge, and when he knelt before her to dry her thighs, her calves, her feet, she blushed. Or maybe the heat she experienced was lust, for to see this powerful man on his knees before her naked body was an aphrodisiac so strong she extended trembling fingers to stroke the beautiful shining black of his hair.

He looked up then, his expression wild and fierce. He flung the towel away. Moving quickly, he wrapped one arm around her thighs. Pulled her close, while his other hand urged her to part her legs, then slid into the blond hair over her slit.

She closed her eyes, ready for his touch.

But no—not his touch, his breath.

Horror made her gasp and try to spring back.

His arm was an iron bar holding her in place, holding her upright. His dark head leaned into her, a contrast to her pale skin. His tongue licked at her, explored her, *tasted* her with every evidence of enjoyment.

He was a god. He was Poseidon; pleasure broke over her like a wave, drowning her in passion. He drove her from peak to peak, taking her higher and higher. She writhed, trying to fight the relentless rhythm.

But he knew exactly what he was doing.

Her eyes were wide, her senses filled with the sight of the leaping flames, the scent of the lavender soap, the sound of her own desperate panting, the slick, warm feel of his tongue that thrust and thrust, outside, inside. . . .

Climax seized her, swirled her in ever-decreasing circles until she was dizzy and blind with rapture.

When she came back to the room, she realized her fingers clutched the silky strands of his hair. His cheek rested against her belly; his eyes were closed; a half smile lifted his lips.

He looked like a satisfied man.

He was not, of course, except . . . every day took him closer to his goal of seduction.

He was, in the end, a hunter who had spotted his mate, tracked her, trapped her, and knew that soon she would consent to be his in every way. Because she couldn't resist this. Resist him.

Her fingers fell away.

He lifted his head, saw the satiation, the wonder, the amazement. Still in silence, he stood, took her hand, and walked her to the sofa. Lifting the nightgown, he put it over her head, helped her slide her trembling arms into the sleeves, buttoned her up to the base of her throat. Lifting the covers, he watched as she sank down. He tucked her in, moved beside her, put his head onto her pillow. With memories and blankets between them, he looked into her eyes and whispered the first words he had spoken tonight: "Imagine how good you'll feel when I'm deep inside you."

Chapter Thirty

Raul rose from beside the sofa. Walking to the tub, he removed his boots and stripped off his trousers.

Taking a black tie off his end table, he lifted his arms and bound his hair at the base of his neck—and at the sight of his silhouette against the fire, Victoria forgot how to breathe, how to move, forgot she should shut her eyes in virginal embarrassment.

He was glorious, a man at the peak of his health and strength, and even if she hadn't known he was of royal blood, she would have recognized him by the power he exuded. His rugged face looked as if it had been sculpted of stone. His taut chest and belly were lightly dusted with dark hair and rippled with muscle. His bottom was high and tight, and his powerful legs could control a horse with ease. She saw the whole man—but she focused on the single element that could make them one.

His erection jutted up, strong and glorious, declaring all too clearly his desire for her.

Stepping into her bath, he sank into the water, and only then did she remember to shut her eyes. She listened to the splashing as he used her lavender-scented water. She tried to mock the thought of Raul, so brawny and masculine, smelling like swaths of purple fields in Provence.

But nothing could erase the vision of Raul's silhouette burned into her brain, or ease his words from her mind. . . . *Imagine how good you'll feel when I'm deep inside you.*

Now she lay beneath the Raul-scented blankets, smelling the essence of him where his head had rested on her pillow, feeling the memory of him against her lips, tasting him in her mouth, longing for him in the moist recesses of her body. . . . Everything sexual in her ached, swollen with need, damp and willing, and only a small piece of her mind argued against surrender.

Because it would be surrender. She knew that. He intended to imprint himself on her, possess and keep her as long as it pleased him, and when she gave in . . . no, if she gave in, she would be his plaything, his mistress, with no rights and no future.

The splashing stopped. She listened to the whisper of the towel as he dried himself. Listened as he strolled barefoot across the room. Listened to the rustle of the feathers in the mattress when he climbed into bed.

She wanted to open her eyes, to go to him, because . . . *Oh, God.* When he kissed her, she could think of nothing but the pleasure he could give her. *Would* give her. He walked like a man who knew women in every intimate way. He smiled like a man who loved to seek out a woman's secrets. When he gazed at her, those green eyes smoldered with promise, and her dream of a small house in the country where she could live alone and unencumbered by relationships faded to nothingness. . . .

If only she could escape him.

But she was stuck here, spending every day in his castle working for his cause, every night in his bedroom trapped in a bubble of heated sensuality.

He was right.

She was going to give in. Why not here? Why not now? Because now . . . might be the only time they had.

Today Prospero had made her look at the truth she so desperately did not want to see.

Raul was leading a rebellion.

Even if the rebellion succeeded, he could be killed. If the rebellion failed, he *would* be killed, and in the horrible method befitting a heinous criminal.

At the thought, her eyes opened, and she stared into a darkness lit by fire and the single small flame of the night candle.

What would she do if Raul was killed? Mourn every day of her life for what she had not dared to take?

Yes. That was exactly what she would do. Because she was every kind of a fool.

But she was his fool.

Throwing the covers aside, she stood.

She knew he was awake. She could feel him watching her as she put one foot in front of the other through the faint moonlight, across the threadbare carpet to the bed. Yet he didn't say a word, didn't encourage or reject her.

He simply waited—and it occurred to her he was very good at waiting. He had been waiting for his throne his whole life. He had been waiting for her to come to this decision since the moment he'd seen her at the hotel. Maybe before ... Maybe he had been waiting for her since the kisses on Grimsborough's balcony.

Maybe this was inevitable.

Three pillows propped him up. His hands were clasped behind his head. His powerful arms, trained to swing a sword, bulged with muscle. His chest was bare, the covers resting on his waist.

She put one knee on the feather mattress, then the other. She knelt beside him.

His patience was frightening—and at an end.

"Take down your nightgown." His low voice was rough, abrasive with demand. "I want to feel your nipples against me when you kiss me."

She froze.

Yes. She had been right. He was insisting on a full surrender. She would give everything, and never would she be able to claim she had not known what she was doing.

He'd left the very top buttons of her nightgown undone. Now, hesitantly, she opened the buttons over her breasts and down to her belly. With excruciating care, she slipped first one shoulder, then the other out of the gown.

She shouldn't have cared what he viewed. After all, less than an hour ago, he had seen her, touched her, washed her, all of her. But this was her showing herself to him, voluntarily, and that took so much more confidence. Confidence in the way she looked, but more than that, confidence in what she was doing.

If only he would help her ...

She clutched the light cotton tightly over her chest, waiting breathlessly, but he said nothing. Did nothing. Except for the glint of his eyes, she might not have known he was alive.

But he was alive, radiating heat, need, seduction. With every breath, she took him into herself, making him a part of her. If she wanted him truly inside her, she would have to take him.

Hesitantly, she slid her arms out of the sleeves and lowered the nightgown to her waist.

He reached for her, grasped her shoulders, and pulled her across him.

Victoria had never imagined that she would melt from heat and desire. Her hands rested against his shoulders; that felt like opportunity. She stroked him curiously, amazed at the strength inherent in his muscles and bones. His arms were steel and velvet, and beneath her his chest rose and fell, pausing between as if each breath were agony.

His mouth was so close. She had only to stretch a little and she could taste him once more. And tasting him was like savoring the finest wine: heady, intoxicating, the prelude to other pleasures. So she stretched until their lips were close, so close, and she thought, *When I do this, there's no turning back.*

So she kissed him.

Chapter Thirty-one

Kissing Raul was like kissing a dragon, the warm brush of flame in Victoria's mouth, in her veins, in her womb.

The nightgown clung to the swell of her hips, and he rested his hands under the cloth. His fingers gripped her as if he needed her close, and she wished he would caress her.

But he didn't move, wouldn't move unless she asked.

Reluctantly, she drew her lips away from his. Rising onto her knees, she pushed the nightgown completely off and onto the floor.

In the rosy light of the fire and the candle, his eyes smoldered as he gazed at her nude body. She sank back on her heels, and his gaze followed her with mouthwatering intensity. He reached above him toward the shelf on the headboard, and as he did, his arms, chest, and belly tensed.

She stared, so fixated by the play of muscles beneath the skin she didn't notice what he fetched until the renewed scent of lavender captured her attention.

He held a small bottle in one hand and poured golden liquid into his cupped palm. "Lavender oil," he said. "Lavender is said to be relaxing."

She laughed, a little hysterical at the idea that she could relax here, now, poised on the brink of passion.

He smiled back at her, reading her mind as he was wont to do. He nudged the bottle into her fingers, and when they had closed around it, he rose on one elbow and brought his hand over her thighs. Turning his fist, he dribbled the oil onto her legs, then flattened his hand on her belly and smoothed his palm across her skin. Swiftly, he caught trickles of oil before they slid off her thighs onto the sheet, and using both his hands, he massaged her thighs with a deepening pressure that oddly made her relax and tense at the same time.

So, while he kneaded her legs and hips and belly, she pressed her knees together, trying foolishly to safeguard her most private and feminine of places.

Yes, he had already touched her there, kissed her there, but to open herself freely, to know he could look on her, caress her . . .

But she *wanted* him to touch her.

That was the conundrum.

She wanted his hands on her, his fingers in her, his mouth on her. From all the nights she had been in his castle, he had trained her in pleasure. Now she sought it like an addict.

He could have easily used his strength to separate

her legs, but he didn't. Wouldn't. Instead, with his gaze on her face, he rubbed her, waiting, still waiting for her to regain the courage that had brought her to his bed.

In the end, it wasn't courage that made her open her knees, but the desire he so easily commanded.

She eased her legs apart, a slow yielding, and as she did, his calloused palms, slick with oil, found their way to her inner thighs and slid up and down, so sensitive to her responses that every time he touched her, she wanted more. He was a magical creature, so similar to the dragon that symbolized his royal blood. He knew her and what she craved before she knew it herself, and he created a simmering frustration that made her clutch the smooth sides of the glass bottle in utter frustration.

At last she whispered, "Please."

He lifted his eyebrows inquiringly, as if he didn't know *exactly* what she wanted.

"Please," she whispered again. "Touch me . . . there."

"Where?"

"There. Down there. Please . . ."

"Show me."

She didn't want to. He should know where. He *did* know where. But his insistence was part and parcel of his determination that she submit.

She pointed her finger down to show him. "There."

His hands skated up her legs.

For one ecstatic moment she believed he was going to vanquish frustration.

But his hands came to rest at the tops of her thighs. His thumbs slid up and down along the crease where her thighs met her body. "Here?"

"No. I mean, yes." Her legs flexed as chills ran up her spine. "But closer to the middle . . . and in front."

"Show me," he said again.

She bit her lip, then lightly touched herself.

"There?"

"Yes." She trembled, waiting.

"What do you want me to do?"

"If you could just . . . stroke me?"

"Like this?" His thumbs moved in tiny circles, closer and closer, until they met and gently lifted the sensitive bit of flesh. They slipped up and down, up and down.

She forgot to be shy. "Yes."

"You like this?" He used more pressure, more speed.

"Yes. Please. Raul. You make me . . . want to . . ." Unbidden, a moan broke from her. She undulated her hips, using every womanly instinct to offer him an invitation.

He didn't take that summons. Instead he used his skillful hands to smooth oil everywhere, in each secret place front and back. At last he swirled his finger around the entrance to her body. Swirled, and waited, and swirled, building heat and need with each circle.

"Please," she said again.

"You know the rules."

He would not enter her. Not without an invitation.

She panted, trembled, knew what she had to do. Grasping his hand, she pressed it against herself.

That was all he needed. His finger slipped inside, easing his way with oil and a man's sure knowledge of her body. As a second finger joined the first, he used more care, opening her tight passage and gently bullying his way through her discomfort. As he did his knuckles brushed her already sensitive clit.

Sobbing with need, she climaxed hard, so hard he wrapped his free arm around her back to hold her in place, and all the while, he used his fingers to enter her, over and over. And when the climax began to ease, he put his mouth to her breast.

Dragon fire licked through her and started the whole process again.

At last, she was too exhausted to come anymore. Or perhaps he simply allowed her to rest, knowing what the future held.

He eased her onto her back and reclined beside her.

Her heartbeat slowed. Her breathing calmed.

He had, once again, brought her to glory.

But she wasn't yet his. He had so much control—too much control—and he managed to keep to his plan to make her give herself to him.

She sat straight up.

Or . . . he didn't really want her and this was all a cruel hoax.

A quick glance at the covers over him reassured her. He did want her. She simply had to discover the means to make their union possible. She crossed her arms over her chest, knowing she looked pouty and not caring a bit. "I don't know what to do next."

Her snappishness didn't seem to affect him at all. His answer was smooth and deliberate. "Whatever . . . you . . . want." Using his foot, he eased the covers off his bare body. "Use your imagination."

She turned her head to look, looked again.

The vista made time slow.

He shouldn't have seemed threatening, not stretched out on his back, but he was tall and broad, big and bold, a man so virile the memories of other men, civilized men in suits and gloves, men she had admired . . . vanished from her mind. Raul was *here*. He was *now*. He was *naked*. And yes, he all too obviously wanted her.

She looked down at her hand. Somehow, through all that had happened, she still retained the bottle of oil clasped so tightly in her palm her fingers ached from the pressure.

Inspiration struck.

Uncorking the bottle, she dribbled a light stream of oil from his breastbone to his lower belly.

But she didn't know how to handle what she'd started. With the cork in one hand and the bottle in the other, she didn't have a hand free. Should she cork the bottle? Then do what with it? And while she fretted, the oil was gliding in tiny streams down his sides toward the sheet and the mattress.

Propelled by an absolute unwillingness to let Amya see the proof of their decadence, Victoria's brain sputtered up a single idea. Spreading her arms, she leaned down and slid her body along Raul's, south to north, smearing them both with oil.

"Damn it!" He caught her shoulders and held her still. "Where did you learn that?"

Appalled by her own depravity and pleased at his response, she said, "You said I should use my imagination."

"Someday I'll be grateful for that imagination. Right now, you've pushed me to the edge." He plucked the bottle and cork out of her hands, put them together, and tossed the bottle on the floor.

Dismay made her protest, "You'll break it!"

"If I don't break it pretty soon, the anticipation is going to kill me. And no, I'm not talking about the blasted bottle." His voice scraped along her sensitive nerves like a rasp in the hands of a master.

She wasn't the only one suffering. Thank God. She

wanted this to be just as difficult for him as it was for her. More difficult. She wanted him to *suffer*.

Lifting her arms, she took the pins out of her hair, dropping them one by one off the edge of the bed. She heard a ping; one of them must have hit the glass bottle. When the last pin was out, her hair fell around her shoulders. She shook it out; some of the strands fell in front, most of them fell behind, and one of them found its way into his hand, where he buffed it like a miser polished a piece of gold.

This time when she rubbed herself on him, she moved like a snake, back and forth, up and down, unhurriedly spreading oil over his skin while learning how he felt beneath her, and completely, totally aware of the hard thrust of his male member against her belly and chest.

It was the most purely sensuous experience of her life.

When he groaned in tortured agony, she at last smiled. Sitting up, breasts proudly thrust forward, she put her hands on him. She let her fingertips ride up and down the ripple of his ribs. She found his male nipples and circled them, rubbing them until they hardened.

When he tried to reach for her, she batted his hands away. "No. You said it was up to me. So . . . let me do it." Completely brave now, she straddled his thighs and used the palms of her hands to stroke oil down the sides of his belly.

He writhed as if in agony.

"Does it hurt?" she asked.

"No." He shook his head emphatically.

"I didn't think so." For his behavior reminded her of her own only a few minutes ago—he *wanted* her to touch him. To touch him where he was most sensitive, to stroke his male member with her hands and in her body until he climaxed with all the violence that he had visited on her.

Before she was finished with him, she would use every lesson he'd taught her to frustrate him . . . and satisfy him.

She stroked his thighs, opened them, and stroked again, slid her hands up to cup the base of his male member and discovered his balls. The way they moved in her hands, the way Raul strained beneath her, everything about his anatomy fascinated her. She had never imagined that making love could create such sweet madness in him . . . and in her. For even as she explored him, her own passions rose, trying to break free.

Tonight she had left the governess Victoria Cardiff far behind.

Lubricating her hands in the oil on his belly, she stroked them along his member and marveled at the silky texture of his skin, the swollen rivers of his veins, the ridged cap, and the single, pale drop of fluid that seeped from the hole at the end. He was too big, the concept of this inside her was overwhelming, and yet she had the oddest sensation that right now, she was in control.

"Do you know what to do with that?" He sounded both strained and amused.

Still stroking him—her fascination with the texture and the strength that flowed through his manhood did not cease—she said, "Of course. I'm a virgin, but not unworldly."

He laughed. "You're one of the most unworldly women I've ever met."

"I am not!" She couldn't believe he could insult her so thoroughly. "In the last three years, I've visited eleven countries!"

"And never been tempted. Not even once?" He used his forefinger to lift her chin.

She jerked her head back. "There's more to civilization than the relations between a man and a woman."

"No. In the end, what happens between a man and a woman is all that matters." He looked as if he believed it, this man who fought to regain his realm, who sought to deal with presidents and parliaments, with dictators and kings.

He spoke, he believed, and something inside her changed, never to be the same. She was more valuable. More vital. An essential part of the unbroken chain of life and love that stretched back into the mists of time and forward into the unseen future.

She took deep breaths, trying to apply intelligence and logic to this feeling, to subdue her sense of triumph.

But intelligence and logic apparently didn't work when she was naked.

She didn't understand it, but all she wanted was to make him happy. "Have I not proved how tempted I am with you?" Putting her face down, she rubbed her cheek against the head of his organ.

He flinched. His hands rose as if he wanted to grab her and take her. In a voice strained with need, he said, "It's time."

It wasn't a command or a suggestion, merely a fact.

It *was* time.

He reached up to the top of the headboard again and brought something down, something that looked small and crinkly and like skin.

"What's that?" she asked.

"I'll wear it and you won't get with child."

"Oh." She watched as he smoothed it over his up-standing body part. "Is it comfortable?"

"Whatever I do with you is wonderful," he said fervently; then with his hands on her hips, he helped her move up into position.

It seemed so awkward: hovering over the top of him, trying to make their bodies match up. They were both covered with oil and damp with desire, and if she'd thought about it, she would have said this would be easy. But although she was half-mad with confidence and beyond thought with tenderness and craving, the act of impaling herself caused a stab of pain that caught her unawares.

He was ready for her instinctive retreat. He caught her when she tried to move off, held her in place.

The pain eased, and she remembered—"I knew this would happen. You're too big."

He understood how to distract her with his voice and his touch. He respected the late hour, speaking quietly. "No. Trust me. This will work." His fingers smoothed the hollow of her throat, a touch so light it brought every nerve to life. "Slowly. Slowly. We have all the time in the world."

She hadn't thought that when he was inside her, it would be so alien, so intimate in a way she had never imagined. She put her hands against his chest to brace herself, but his skin was slick with oil . . . and that was a remembrance of pleasure. She caressed him as she had before, and all the while he rocked against her, pushing more and more deeply.

He had a care for her virginity, moving his hips away,

then up, in a gradual motion that soothed and reminded her of the passion he had the power to incite.

She moaned softly as pain and pleasure mingled, until her body molded around his and they became one.

When she rested on him and he was all the way inside, touching the deepest part of her, he released his hold on her hips and commanded, "Ride."

Chapter Thirty-two

Victoria woke when something depressed the mattress beside her. Her eyes fluttered open to see Raul, knee on the bed, leaning over her, smiling like a lover. With his fingertips, he pushed the hair out of her face. "How are you?"

She blinked at him, at the sunshine streaming through the high, narrow window, and the events of the night came back in a rush. She plastered the covers to her chest and sat up on a horror-struck inhale.

"How are you?" he asked again. "Are you sore? Would you like me to call Amya to bring another bath?"

Victoria glanced at the tub, still filled with cold water, sitting before the ashes of the fire, and realized that last night, no one had been allowed through the door to empty it and take it away. "Oh, no. *No*. Everyone in the castle is gossiping about what we did last night." She was blushing. All over. She was pretty sure her toenails were blushing. The things they had done last night. The things *she* had done last night! She had ridden him until the two of them were gasping and straining, and finally she had collapsed on top of him, exhausted by the physical effort, the emotional tumult, and the pleasure. Such a surfeit of pleasure.

Raul had held her, embraced her, cradled her until she slept.

Then sometime in the predawn hours, she had woken to his gentle seduction, one so thorough and so exhaustive she had died and been reborn.

That must be why she felt as if today she were a different woman: tender, shy, uncertain, easily given to tears and laughter, open to feelings that had never before touched her.

His voice was prosaic, and he didn't seem shy—she couldn't imagine such a thing—but he kept touching her as if he couldn't believe she was so close and so *his*. "Everyone gossips all the time. They have no idea what really happened in here." Her wide-eyed dismay must have impressed him, because he added, "No one knows what we did, Victoria, and unless you tell them, they never will."

She let out her breath. "That's true. I am no more ruined than I was before last night—which is to say, completely ruined."

"No one in England knows where you are, and I promise my family won't tell where you slept."

She didn't have his faith in people; in her opinion, no one in the world could refrain from good gossip. But she could hope that she wasn't important enough to have gossip trek so far as England. Although Raul had certainly heard enough gossip from her travels with the Johnsons. . . .

"Today I'm going into Tonagra to finalize the sale of Viento, and I need to spend time gambling, dancing, and gossiping, like the worthless rake that I am." He used the backs of his fingers to gently rub her cheek. "I have to keep making appearances or Jean-Pierre de Guignard will get suspicious."

"Is he particularly suspicious of you?"

"He's particularly suspicious of everyone, especially after the incidents those nasty rebels have caused." Amusement put a crease in his cheek. "Tourists are leaving, and worse, word is getting out that there's trouble in Moricadia, and they're canceling their travels here altogether. We are the royal family, the de Barbari Jinete, and we have successfully created chaos for the de Guignards, sending them on the chase in a dozen different directions, after real problems and imaginary, distracting them from the real threat right under their noses." Raul's smile grew broad and warm. "I had no idea this would be so much fun."

Disquiet constricted her throat.

He was trying to get himself killed.

Not that he was doing anything different than he had been doing, but the shift that had occurred yesterday seemed to actively involve her in his fate and the fate of his crusade.

What was she doing here?

"I won't be back until late," he said. "I didn't want you to worry."

"I won't," she mumbled.

"You do know how to crush a man's fragile ego."

"I wasn't trying to—"

"I know. That's the worst part." Catching the back of her neck, he pulled her close and kissed her.

She resisted. For a moment. Then, as she had last night, as she had every night, she yielded. More than yielded. She gave everything in her . . . to him.

And why? Why was she giving herself to him with her whole heart? Why did she care if he got killed?

When they pulled apart, he was breathing hard and color rode high on his cheekbones. "You make me forget sanity."

"I wasn't trying to do that, either."

"Yet you're a natural." He touched her cheek again, then walked toward the door. "You had a long night. Go back to sleep."

"Raul?"

"Yes?"

"Why did you tell me where you were going?"

He spoke as if the answer were patently obvious. "Because now it's your right to know." He shut the door behind him.

She stared at it, confused and perturbed. Her right? What did he mean, her right? She didn't have any rights when it came to him and his whereabouts and what he was doing. She didn't *want* any rights. She didn't know if she really liked what had happened between them last night. The whole thing had been hot and sweaty, and she was still oily, and despite what she'd said to Raul, she ached between her legs because she had . . . she had ridden him.

All right. "Liked" was too mild a word for what she felt about last night. Some of it had been painful and some of it had been embarrassing and far too intimate and required emotions she had avoided most assiduously. She had been alive as she had never been before, closer than she'd ever been to another human being, wild and reckless, and right now she could be with child—except he had taken care of that problem.

Her fists clenched.

If she didn't get out of bed right now and act as if nothing had changed between them, everyone in the castle would know what had happened. And the consequences, Victoria well knew, would be insupportable.

She glanced at the clock ticking on the mantel and gave a gasp of dismay. It was past nine. The children would be wondering where she was.

Hurriedly she rose, grabbed her nightgown off the floor and flung it on the sofa, picked up the bottle of oil and placed it on the headboard. She performed a hasty wash using the water in the pitcher, dressed, and painfully labored to comb the tangles from her hair. Pinning the strands atop her head, she peered into the small mirror on the chest of drawers—and grimaced.

She didn't look like herself. She was too rosy, too glowing. She looked thrilled and surprised and terrified. But on one thing she could depend—no one in the great hall ever paid her any heed. They never did.

But children weren't like the adults. They noticed things.

She had to act normal, as if between yesterday and today, nothing had changed—when in fact the world had tilted sideways.

As quietly as possible, she opened the door. She peered down the corridor and, when she saw it was clear, she slipped out of the bedroom and hurried toward the classroom. To her surprise, the children were there, working together in small groups, teaching one another their letters and numbers. She stepped in, and they came to their feet and jabbered excitedly, pleased to have her with them, determined to tell her what they'd been doing.

Victoria laughed and relaxed.

She knew what to do with the children, how to behave . . . who she was.

She praised them for their self-discipline and reestablished their schedule. She made sure she took the time to allow them to instruct her in Moricadian, for not only did she learn the language—she could now comprehend a lot of conversation—but in their eagerness to teach her, they learned English more quickly. When it was time for the noon meal, they all traipsed down to the great hall together, two of the youngest holding her hands.

The children went down the stairs to eat in the kitchen.

She saw some sideways glances as she settled in her seat, but surely that had more to do with the upcoming class than with any speculation about her rosy glow. Raul had promised no one would know what they'd done last night; she had to believe he was right.

Lunch was the usual—hearty food and a lot of loud talk about battles, fighting, knives, and rifles. That left Victoria alone to think about . . . *things*. Which wasn't so good, since the *things* that came to mind involved the slow rotation of Raul's calloused palms around her nipples, the way he'd looked when he climaxed, like a man who had scaled the highest mountain peak, what he was doing right now, and whether he would live through the day.

He would live through the day.

She knew he would.

And at the same time, she suffered from a fear that sliced through her peace and kept her restless and on edge.

When she heard the scraping of benches across the floor, the meal was over and everyone moved into place for her class in etiquette.

As she stood before them, she was glad to face them in the role she understood so well: that of being a teacher. "Today we'll learn how to address a duke, an earl, a baron, and a man rich but not titled, and, of course, royalty, for in Mr. Lawrence's court"—she corrected herself—"in King Saber's court, you will have many visiting kings, queens, and princes."

"Not for a while." Prospero scratched his cheek, then hastily lowered his hand. "They'll want him able to prove himself as ruler first."

"You're probably right." She nodded. "But from what I've seen of your king and the loyalty you hold for him, as well as what I've heard of his plans for after the revolution, I think after the first winter, he'll be well established, and then they'll come for the spas and the entertainment."

"That'll give us time to polish our manners, too." Prospero sagely nodded back.

"Having an English gentlewoman in the court will help prove we're civilized enough," Amya said.

Victoria started in surprise.

Amya timidly asked, "Won't it?"

"While I appreciate your confidence in my influence, I believe yesterday Prospero"—Victoria indicated him with a wave of her hand—"said the current plan is for me to leave before the start of the revolution."

Prospero looked at her as if she'd taken leave of her senses. "But that was yesterday."

"Today is different," Hada said.

Alarm skittered up Victoria's spine. "Why is it different?"

Hada said, "Because last night, you and our king were mated."

Chapter Thirty-three

Victoria staggered back.

Raul had betrayed her.

He had bragged about her capitulation. About the things they'd done in private. After promising no one would know.

"Mr. Lawrence told you we had ..." She swallowed. She couldn't say it. "Your king *told* you—"

"No!" Hada hastened to assure her. "He didn't tell us. He's not that kind of blackguard. But he didn't have to say anything. He was smiling and cheerful. He was whistling when he left. So we knew...."

Prospero suggestively thumped his fists together and grinned.

Victoria looked around the room.

Everyone grinned.

They weren't being disrespectful. Several of them inclined their heads to her. A few put their hands over their hearts. They were glad she had made Raul happy. They didn't seem to understand that to be a man's mistress was a disgrace. She was grateful for that, but what she and Raul had done was so private, so profound, so ... decadent. He had assured her no one would know what had passed between them, but these people comprehended, if not the details, then certainly the basics.

Victoria always maintained a wall between herself and the rest of the world, and in this matter especially, she wanted privacy.

Too late.

If only Raul could have not been so obviously happy!

Knowing that they knew, she could scarcely bear to stand here and look them in the eyes.

But she couldn't run away, either. That would be undignified and ... and how would she ever face them again? No, she had to stay here and do her job.

And she did, ordering them to their feet to bow and curtsy and greet. She finished the class, holding dignity before her like a mask and all the while suffering an agony of mortification.

After an hour, she dismissed them—more than that she couldn't bear. As they departed, rambunctious as always and obviously without a clue she was distressed, Hada asked if Victoria wished to consult with the cook about dinner.

Victoria stared at her wildly. "Why would I want to do that? No!" She held up her hand in the signal to stop. "I don't want to know." Because the mistress of the house approved the menu for dinner, and she did not wish to be cast in that role. "What I want is to go for a walk outside."

"You're upset, because I think you realize now your life is no longer your own." Hada spoke convincingly, like someone explaining the facts of life to a child.

"Yes, it is!"

Hada laid a soothing hand on Victoria's arm. "Listen to me. We Moricadians are Saber's people, his orchestra, his to command. We play our parts, and we make music so sweet it brings tears to your eyes. But we wait and we watch for the principal singers to take their place on center stage. It is the voices of the hero and the heroine that capture the attention of the world. And that's as it should be. That's the way we want to see the opera. We want to hear our music, we want to know we helped bring the show to the stage, but we want to hear the voices sing the aria while we sit, dumbstruck with awe."

Victoria worked through her distress, trying to comprehend. "Are you saying I'm one of the principals?"

"It matters not what I say and what I don't. You are what you were born to be."

"No." Victoria didn't want to hear what Hada was telling her. She didn't want to be center stage. And anyway, when had Hada turned into a wise woman? Just because she'd been almost killed when she was a young woman, just because she'd recovered to find her whole world broken and rearranged, didn't mean she could go around offering sage advice and thinking Victoria would be comforted. Victoria liked her life as it was. Yes, she was on her own, but no one ever disappointed her—and she never disappointed anyone.

No one ever told her she didn't have the voice to sing.

Desperate to be alone, she insisted, "I would really like to go for a walk outside."

Hada seemed to understand, but still she hesitated for a long moment. Then she stepped aside. "Please be careful. There are more dangers in the woods than you can imagine."

Victoria didn't wait for Hada to change her mind. Picking up her skirt, she donned her straw bonnet and hurried toward the door. One of the footmen sprang forward to open it for her. She strode into the courtyard. Then, as if she expected no objections, she walked over the drawbridge and out the gate.

No one hollered at her to stop. No one paid her any heed. Overnight, she had become someone they trusted.

She had become one of *them*.

And she needed out. She needed fresh air, solitude, a chance to ease the panic that drove her.

She hadn't been beyond the gate since the day she'd arrived, and that night she'd been nothing but a package swaddled in cloth and thrown over a horse. Since then, all she'd seen of the world outside the castle she'd gained by looking out the windows. Nearby, she heard grunts and thumps as the men practiced hand-to-hand combat. Farther away, she heard the thunk of arrows as they hit a target, accompanied by manly shouts of encouragement and, beyond that, the occasional gunshot. So she walked away and into the forest, and drew her first long breath of freedom.

The woods were dense and green, an untouched alpine Eden. The pines reached their needled arms toward the skies, the sunshine filtered through in bursts of gold, and the silence enveloped her like an embrace.

She left the castle far behind, following a path many

feet had worn into the ground, through the brush and toward a knoll growing like a stony knee from the forest floor. She could see the sun shining brightly above, and, drawn by the heat and the light, she climbed the steep, rugged path. Her governess clothes withstood the snags from branches and outcrops, and her sensible boots helped her make the ascent without slipping. When she reached the top, she was panting and triumphant.

Then she looked at the view, and her breath caught.

Untouched forest and mountains undulated toward the vivid blue horizon, majestic and blissfully quiet. In the distance, a hawk floated on the same breeze that ruffled her hair and breathed peace into her face.

She found a boulder, a peach-colored slab of chunky granite, and perched herself in the sun-warmed center. Slowly her panic dissipated.

She put her hand on her chest. Her heart stopped racing and returned to its steady, pragmatic pace. She felt . . . almost normal, as if the weight of too many expectations had been lifted from her.

Since her father had died on that horrible day lost in the mists of her memory, she had been alone, without true connections or responsibility. Not that she didn't care about her mother and her siblings; she did, and they cared about her, but in a haphazard way that always left her an outsider. She hated her stepfather. At school, she made good friends. But at no point had she been the center of anyone's life, and she told herself that was fine with her.

Suddenly, she found herself important. The *center*.

What had Hada called her? One of the principal singers. The heroine.

No. *No.* Victoria had made the decision to join Raul in his bed because . . . Well, just because. But that decision did not include her becoming some sort of guide—or, heaven forbid, the inspiration—for Raul's people in the next few weeks. Never had the thought crossed her mind that she would stay through the revolution and beyond. These simple Moricadians were making too much of the night between her and Raul—which they wouldn't be doing if he hadn't been happy!

She didn't know the solution. Raul's people were so involved in the pursuit of their goal that they were giving everything to their victory. They trained all the time. They spied, they masqueraded, they schemed. Although for the most part they thought it was silly, they learned etiquette. Most of all, they knew they could die, they knew their families were in danger, but they believed the world they would create would be better than the world of poverty and fear they currently inhabited.

So what could she do? Whine that she didn't want the responsibility they thrust on her? Ask that they go back to being rude so she didn't grow affectionate toward people who insisted on putting themselves in the line of fire? Tell Raul he needed to stay safe because . . .

Because why?

It didn't matter. She couldn't tell Raul anything. He wouldn't listen.

Her concerns for herself were piddling compared to his for his people.

She didn't want to be the heroine. She most certainly didn't deserve to be the heroine.

But for the moment she had no choice. She would return to the castle and play the part.

And when the revolution started, she would leave Moricadia, and she promised herself she would never look back.

On that decree, she started her descent.

After all, she didn't want to be gone too long. Hada would worry about her.

She found the descent tougher than the ascent. The gravel on the steep path gave way under her feet, and she almost fell half a dozen times, catching herself on branches and rocks. The last ten feet dropped off precipitously. She was hot and tired, and she gazed at the slope and wondered at the desperation that had driven her to climb so high. On an indrawn breath, she started down, moving fast, using her hands to steady herself. She was almost on level ground, only five feet left to go, when she slipped, slid the rest of the way, and landed hard, her hindquarters in the grass.

Dirt cascaded down around her, and she sat there, feeling foolish, dusting herself off, paying no attention to her surroundings . . . when two massive black leather boots stomped into view and halted at the edge of her vision.

Startled, she looked up.

A man stood over her. Short, powerful body. Greasy dark hair braided on either side of his broad, flat face. Blackened teeth and wide, red lips. Pistols across his chest, a sword and two daggers at his belt. Fists on his hips, he grinned with such malice, she braced herself to run. "Look at what we have here," the pirate said. "Cousin Saber's sweet-mouthed little mistress come to pay us a visit."

Chapter Thirty-four

When Raul spoke of his cousin Danel as a natural tactician and a possibility to be king of Moricadia, Victoria had never imagined this flea-bitten, smelly, round, and squat fellow. He was loud and disgusting. His contingent of men was loud and disgusting. All of these traits became apparent as Danel lifted Victoria face-down onto his horse, mashing her bonnet. He took his place behind her, and galloped toward his camp.

Worse, as they rode into his camp and circled the perimeter, Danel smacked Victoria's bottom and shouted, "I've captured the queen! I've captured the queen!"

Victoria was *really* tired of being flung around like a sack of grain and carried away against her will, and if she lived through this, she was going to somehow make Danel sorry he was born.

It was suppertime and the full deputation of his people was there, about seventy men and women watching, laughing, and cheering as he stopped the horse and
shoved her off.

She landed on her feet and staggered backward, re-
gained her balance, and jumped away from the prancing
hooves. She would have said Danel was trying to kill her,
but he handled the beast with such skill she knew she
was never in any danger.

The camp was built in a small clearing in the forest, and
consisted of two dozen tents surrounding a large central
fire pit where a pot full of some questionable stew bubbled. A variety of tree stumps served as tables and chairs,
and the tallest stump on the far end was dressed up with
a rug and some cushions. One sizable tent of different
colors of grimy velvet and a few gilded tassels stood
nestled under the trees. This didn't look like a respected
group of rebels; this looked like an impoverished Gypsy
encampment. Danel didn't look like a candidate for the
throne; he looked like a man who drank too much, ate
too much, lived hard, and never cleaned his teeth. And
he had hit her as if she were a strumpet off the streets.

Shaking out her skirts, she stalked away toward the
cooking pot and the woman stirring it with a long spoon.
She pointed to herself. "Victoria."

The woman, tall and thin with a black braid that fell
to her waist, pointed to herself. "Celesta."

Picking up a metal bowl, Victoria held it out. "Please,"
she said in Moricadian.

Celesta looked startled, glanced at Danel, and when
Victoria said, "Please," again, she filled the bowl, tore off
a piece of bread and placed it on top, and handed her a
spoon.

Victoria glanced around.

Like some petty sheik of the desert, Danel had seated himself on the rug on the stump. He grinned at her—grinning evilly seemed to be his stock-in-trade—and indicated the cushion that rested at his feet.

Fine. They needed to talk.

She walked over and seated herself.

At once, Celesta came over with two horns of some thick, brown, foaming brew.

Victoria thanked her, then took a cautious sniff. The ale—she assumed it was ale—smelled like roots and barley, and when she tasted it, it was strong enough to make her worry it would melt her teeth.

Maybe that was what had happened to Danel's. . . .

Danel drank his to the bottom of the horn. Wiping his hand across his mouth, he cleaned off his mustache; only the two long ends still hung heavy with mustard-yellow foam. "Drink up!" he told her. "It will cure you of worms and whatever else ails you."

"That is certainly a worthy objective." With every appearance of ease, she took a drink, then a bite of stew—venison, she thought, and some vegetables she didn't recognize—and a bite of the flat, gritty bread. Looking him right in the eyes, she said in English, "Thank you for inviting me to your camp."

She knew he understood her when he roared with laughter. "No wonder Saber adores you . . . That upstart rampallian."

"He doesn't adore me, and yes, he is a rampallian." Whatever that meant. It sounded bad. Still staring Danel in the eyes, she added, "Being a rampallian runs in his family."

Danel grinned again. "Do you seek to insult me?"

"I seek to discover why you haven't joined with Saber to end the de Guignards' reign of terror."

Instantly, Danel's mood changed from geniality to rage. The little tyrant leaped to his feet and strode across the camp, kicking at roots and rocks, shouting in Moricadian and waving his arms in wild gestures.

Victoria watched him, and she watched the reaction from his people, too.

No one cowered. They stepped out of his way.

Celesta continued to stir the pot.

They weren't afraid of him and his temper.

By the time he stomped his way back to Victoria, she was eating her stew. "I didn't understand you," she said. "Pardon me, but my Moricadian is not yet good enough."

He glowered at her. "*The children* haven't taught you enough?"

"They're doing their best." So he had a spy, perhaps more than one, at the castle. She repeated her question. "Now, why haven't you joined Saber in defeating the de Guignards?"

"*He* should join *me*." Danel pointed his thumb at his chest. "I'm older. I'm legitimate. I'm Moricadian. All the time Saber was hiding his yellow-striped toady ass in England, I fought the revolution. *My* people, *my* family fought the revolution. I know how to fight. I know how to win." He spun in a circle. "But did my family celebrate me for my struggles? For my victories? Some of them did." He held out his arms to embrace the camp. "The loyal members of my family are with me still. But when that reeking pustule of a cousin returned from England, some of my family, deluded with the belief that that half-breed was the true king, abandoned me to serve him."

Victoria ate and watched, enjoying the drama and

the fireworks like an onlooker at a play. When Danel stopped and glared at her, she put down her spoon and clapped. "That was magnificent!"

He radiated indignation. "Woman! My wrath is not a jest to amuse a simpleminded female!"

"I think you're more than just angry. I think you're hurt." She watched the play of emotions across his face: rage, anguish, embarrassment ... and again rage.

This time, Celesta shook her head. His people stepped back.

And Victoria knew that by accusing him of sentimental emotions, she had overstepped her bounds.

She put down the bowl.

He kicked it aside, sending it and chunks of food flying. He kicked the spoon. It clinked when it smacked a rock. He kicked the mug, splashing beer from her hem to her nostrils. Reaching down, he grabbed her by the arms and hauled her to her feet. His brown eyes glowed yellow with temper; he shook her and he shouted into her face, "You are going to get me what I want! You are the bait that will bring Saber to me. He will fight for you—and he will die!"

She flinched from the bad breath and the spittle-driven malice.

Perhaps she had read Danel wrong. Perhaps he was truly as evil as she had feared.

He shoved her toward the large velvet tent. "By the time Saber gets here, I'll have tupped you in every way possible, and he can die knowing you carry my babe in your belly!"

She shoved back, fighting Danel, kicking and shoving, shrieking and struggling, and all the while he held her against his fat belly and laughed.

He pushed her inside the tent.

She ran to the far corner, bent, and then straightened.

He stalked in, unbuckling his sword belt as he came. His pants dropped to his fat, hairy knees.

She lifted the pistol in one hand and pulled back the hammer with the other.

At the click, he froze in place, his aghast expression a comedy that did not amuse her in the least.

"Get out." She steadied the heavy piece with both hands.

"Where did you get that?" He looked down at the holsters that crisscrossed his chest, his horror escalating as he realized—"You stole my pistol!" He groped himself. "You stole both my pistols!"

"Yes, I did, while you were pushing me around. Did you think I would allow you to rape me with impunity?" She was as furious as he had been earlier.

"You would have liked it! All my women like it!" He honestly seemed insulted.

"Get out," she said again.

"Don't be foolish, woman. You don't know how to use that!" He believed it.

His mistake. She lifted the pistol and aimed.

A split second before she shot, he slammed himself full-length onto the floor.

She pulled the trigger.

The pistol discharged with a roar.

The velvet behind where he had stood wavered, blasted by the bullet.

He sat up and stared at the smoking rupture. Incredulously, he said, "You could have killed me!"

"I will kill you"—she picked the second pistol off the floor—"if you don't get out of here and leave me alone."

He stood up, pulled up his pants. "This is your last chance!"

She aimed.

He ran out, tearing through the flap like a ferret through a rotting log.

She heard the babble of voices as his people dashed to his side. She stood, waiting to see if they were going to rush the tent.

Nothing happened.

The din died down.

Finally, after she had waited in the dim, smelly, grubby tent for more than an hour, someone lifted the side of the velvet and shoved a fresh bowl of stew and a spoon through. A horn of the bitter ale followed. The hand—it was female—waved at her, then disappeared.

Victoria smiled wearily.

She recognized that hand and the gesture. That was Celesta.

The food was safe, untainted.

Victoria sat. She pulled the bowl toward her and ate and drank. She looked at the bed, calculated how long it had been since the furs and blankets had been cleaned, shuddered, and leaned against the brace on the wall. And she waited for Saber to come and rescue her.

She had no doubt that he would.

He was, after all, Moricadia's true king, and a dragon of unimaginable power.

Chapter Thirty-five

In the morning, Victoria came out of Danel's tent, feeling grubby and tired from sleeping upright with a pistol in her lap.

The sun was peeking over the trees and into the glade. The air was still and clean, with the faint scent of wood smoke to give it spice. Danel's people sat in front of their tents or drank from tin mugs and horns, and looked at her with interest and without hostility.

Danel stood in front of the central fire, scratched his fat belly, and grinned with disgusting cheer. "Ah! The queen arises. All hail the queen!"

She relaxed. She had guessed right. He wasn't the type of man who could hang on to his ire, and this morning he was his usual overblown and genial self.

"Shut up, Danel." Celesta pointed toward the woods.

"My queen, the privies are that direction. There's a stream where you can wash. When you get back, porridge is in the pot."

Victoria nodded her thanks, and as she turned to the woods, Danel yelled, "Hey! Give me back my pistols!"

A ripple of laughter went through the camp.

Danel glared around.

Amusement was smothered, but a lot of smiles and winks were sent Victoria's way. Apparently her trick at lifting Danel's pistols while he bullied her had earned their respect.

"The pistols are in the tent." No need to keep them. After all, they wouldn't do her much good without powder and shot. So she headed into the woods.

As she performed her morning ablutions, she practiced what to say to convince Danel to collaborate with Raul. These men needed each other, and for them to remain at odds was a crime. Together, they would guarantee the success of their beloved revolution, for they both were willing to give everything for its triumph.

But when she walked back into the camp, Danel stood gazing toward the edge of the camp . . . and grinning. It wasn't his genial grin, or his angry grin. It was triumph, pure and simple. He waved a hand. "Look, my queen. Your lover has come to avenge you."

She knew what she would see when she looked.

Raul, dressed in the same clothes he'd worn to Tonagra the day before. He had discarded his coat, his cravat, his collar. He had strapped a scabbard at his side, and he gripped his sword—long, well honed, lethal—and pointed it at Danel.

His expression was cool.

His green eyes were murderous.

Danel's people fell back, leaving him an open path to Danel.

In a weighty silence, Raul paced across the camp.

"Give her back." Raul stopped within three feet of Danel, his sword pointed at Danel's throat. "Give her back now."

"I really don't think this is necessary," Victoria said.

The men seemed not to hear her.

"You want her?" Danel grinned, showing all his half-rotted teeth. "After she spent the night in my tent?"

"Nor was *that* necessary." Victoria wanted to slap Danel's smug, nasty face.

But violence simmered between the two men, the situation balanced on the edge of Raul's sword, and she didn't wish to see bloodshed. Certainly not over her.

"Challenge," Raul snapped.

"Accepted," Danel answered.

As if they were performing a refined country dance, Danel's men and women moved in a circle around the clearing.

"Really." Victoria put all her persuasive power in her voice. "If we could discuss this like adults—"

Raul sheathed his sword, then unbuckled his scabbard and placed it in Danel's seat before the fire.

"Very good," Victoria said, relieved. "Now, let's sit down—"

Raul and Danel each pulled a sharp, slender, curved knife from their belts.

Three of Danel's men sprang forward. One accepted the knives and examined them. One drew a circle in the dirt before the campfire. The third tied the end of a long length of white cloth to Danel's wrist, the other end to Raul's wrist, leaving a two-foot length between the men.

Victoria didn't exactly understand the dynamics, but she recognized incipient trouble when she saw it. "Really, gentlemen, this isn't a good idea."

The man with the knives put them behind his back, shuffled them back and forth, and stood waiting.

"You're my guest." Danel gestured with his free hand. "You choose."

Raul nodded, pointed at the man's left arm, and took the knife he was handed.

"Ah, you got mine." Danel accepted the other knife. "It is a good blade."

Raul tossed it into the air. The steel glittered as it spun end over end.

Victoria hissed in fear.

Raul caught it by the handle. "Then you'll be happy to have it cut out your heart."

Danel laughed. If he was afraid, he didn't show it.

"It would be best if we could negotiate a truce," Victoria said.

She might as well have been talking to herself.

Danel's three men each tested the knots that tied Danel and Raul together.

Celesta and one of the women took Victoria by the arms and moved her back to the sidelines, then close to the stump where Danel usually sat. They moved away, leaving her to stand alone like a prize to be won.

The camp buzzed with excitement. Men lifted their children onto their shoulders. The crowd jostled one another, seeking the best views.

She *hated* this. She said, "This is really not the best way to solve an argument—"

Danel's blade slashed toward Raul, a movement so fast Victoria flinched only when it was done.

Yet the point never touched Raul; he moved out of the way too swiftly.

The two fighters went into half squats, holding their blades as if they were extensions of their hands. As they moved within the circle, the cloth between them was first taut, then loose, then taut again. Raul made his move in a flurry of slashes so fast Victoria couldn't see them. Danel leaped and parried, and when the exchange was over, both men were bloodied, Raul on his neck, Danel on his arm.

Victoria gasped in terror.

No one else made a sound. The only thing Victoria could hear was the two men breathing, and the incongruous song of the mockingbird.

The length of cloth drooped between them.

Danel grabbed it and, blade out, yanked Raul close.

Raul's blade clanked against his.

They broke apart.

Now both men had stab wounds to the chest. Not deep, apparently, for neither gave an inch.

But Danel taunted, "So all was not lost when you went to live the soft life in England. You remember a little of your early training."

Raul's white teeth flashed in his tanned face. "I remember I was always faster than you."

It was then, hearing the mockery and bickering, that Victoria realized—the fighters were enjoying themselves.

Yes, they were serious.

This was, no doubt, a fight to the death.

But they were having *fun*.

She had noted many times in her life that men were stupid.

These two were especially stupid.

How these men had managed to work themselves into their positions of power, she did not know, nor did she believe it reflected well on the women that they had allowed such a thing to happen.

She cast her gaze around.

Every eye was fixed on the battle.

The blades clanged together in a steady rhythm. The men leaped and shuffled. Blood seeped from cuts on their faces, their arms, their chests.

Moving guardedly, Victoria picked up Raul's sword. She drew it from the scabbard, and before anyone could stop her, she walked into the circle and approached the two men.

They were so intent on each other, squatting in fight position, that neither saw her coming until she was standing between them.

Then they both froze. They stared at her.

She put the point of the sword to Danel's throat. "Tell him the truth about last night."

Cunning and calculation shifted in Danel's eyes.

"I would gladly kill you," she said. "You know I will. I proved that last night. Now—tell him the truth."

Danel used his knife to push the point away from his throat, straightened, and said, "She spent the night alone in my tent."

"Tell him why," she said.

In dire tones, Raul said, "Woman, you should go *sit*."

She ignored him, gazing right into Danel's eyes. "Tell ... him ... why."

"She stole my pistol!" Danel admitted.

"She stole your pistol?" Raul stopped behaving like a barbarian, stood up straight, and looked between them.

"And she shot at me. If I hadn't jumped out of the way, she would have shot me right through the heart!" Danel appeared truly hurt at the idea.

"But there's only one shot in a pistol." Raul shook his head. "If she shot it, then why . . . ?"

Danel glowered. "Because she stole both my pistols."

Raul passed his hand over his mouth, wiping his smile away.

"She knew how to use those pistols!" Danel almost frothed with indignation. "An Englishwoman! It's unheard-of."

"I do know how to use a pistol," Victoria assured him. "Much better than I know how to use this sword. So I suggest you two stand as far apart as possible and stretch that cloth tight, because . . ." She lifted the sword over her head.

In fear and horror, the two men sprang away from each other.

She brought the sword down with all her might, and slashed the cloth in half. "Now," she said calmly, "stop dancing and kill each other."

Chapter Thirty-six

The entire camp stood openmouthed with shock.

Immobile, Raul and Danel stared at the limp rags hanging from their wrists.

Sword point in the dirt, hand on her hip, Victoria waited.

Raul thundered, "Woman! Don't you know better than to interfere in the business of men?"

"Yes, woman! It's not your place to—" Danel stopped and took a breath. "It's not your place to . . ." He cackled, then put on a stern face. "To instruct us in the art of the fight—"

Raul snorted.

Danel chortled.

They both snickered.

The crowd nudged one another and grinned.

Raul and Danel broke into a guffaw. Then they fell on each other, slapping each other on the back and laughing so hard tears streamed down their faces.

Victoria watched them in disgust, shook her head, and hoped they didn't accidentally stab each other with the knives they still clutched.

In a falsetto voice with a fake British accent, Danel mimicked, "'Stop dancing and kill each other.'" And he brayed with laughter.

Raul staggered away, hooting.

Danel bent from the waist and gasped for air. He finally got control long enough to ask, "How do you stand her?"

Raul straightened up and looked at Victoria, his eyes wicked. "It's like breaking a high-spirited horse. After the initial bucking and resistance, I stay in the saddle and prove I'm the master." His smile faded. "Then the ride smoothes out and I'm mounted on the wind."

Caught in his gaze, she stared at him, and wondered how he could say something so incredibly insulting and make it a seduction.

"Hey!" Danel shoved Raul's shoulder, breaking their eye contact. "You're crazy. Give me a good sturdy mountain pony every time." He sheathed his knife, asked a question in Moricadian.

Victoria thought it was, *Do you want to do . . . something?* She couldn't quite comprehend that last word.

The crowd leaned forward to hear the answer.

With a wry smile, Raul answered in the affirmative.

Once again, every eye turned to Victoria.

Some nodded. Some grinned. Some shook their heads. Some eyed her warily.

Never had she cursed her inability to completely grasp a language.

"It's your funeral." Danel slapped Raul on the shoulder. "Come, cousin, let's break bread together."

As quickly as that, they called a truce.

With a sigh, Victoria relaxed.

Her gamble had paid off. Raul and Danel hadn't killed each other. They hadn't really wanted to. But if she hadn't stepped in, manly pride would have caused a disaster for them both, and for Moricadia.

The crowd drifted away and returned to eating, to washing, to tending the children.

Raul approached Victoria and held out his hands for his sword. "May I?"

Victoria handed it to him, hilt first. "What kind of cousins try to kill each other?"

"Cousins who are fighting over the right to sit on the same throne." Danel stomped to his tree-trunk throne, dragged the rug onto the ground and kicked the cushions atop it, then bellowed, "Hey! We're hungry!"

"You're bleeding, both of you." Victoria untied the remnant of cloth from Raul's wrist and used it to stanch the flow of blood on his face, chest, and arms.

"We need wine!" Danel shouted.

"Water their wine," Victoria instructed Celesta, "or with this blood loss, they'll be drooling in their bedrolls within the hour."

Danel stuck his face into Victoria's face. "Wine!" His eyes were fierce.

Celesta poured wine into two horned mugs, filled them to the brim with water, and handed them to the men. "Wine!" she answered.

"Damn women." Danel took his and drank it down.

Raul lifted his goblet toward Danel. "You can say that again. I wouldn't be here if *someone* hadn't decided to run away."

"I didn't run away; I went for a walk, and I wouldn't have gone for a walk if you hadn't—" Victoria stopped.

Danel leaned forward. "Hadn't what?" he asked avidly.

Now she thrust her face into his. "That is no one's business but ours."

"Humph." Danel held out his goblet and said nothing as Celesta again mixed wine and water.

None of Raul's wounds were severe, and they were clotting. The deepest cut over his heart would require stitches, but for now—she handed him the cloth. "Press that there."

He did as he was told. "Danel, there is no debate about who sits on the throne. I'm the acknowledged heir."

Victoria turned her attention to Danel, who said hotly, "And I'm the one who stayed here, kept the fight going while you were safe in England at your daddy's house."

Like Raul, Danel didn't seem badly hurt, only surface cuts in multiple places—until she saw his elbow. There Raul had peeled the skin away, leaving the joint protruding.

To Celesta, she made a sewing motion.

Celesta nodded and ducked inside her tent, returning with needle and thread.

Danel paid the women no attention, shouting, "You can't just gavotte in here, all pretty-boy and fancy-face, and take the kingship because your mother was older than mine."

Victoria couldn't help her grin.

"Yeah, see?" Danel pointed his fat, grimy finger in her face. "Even your sweetheart agrees with me."

"I didn't say I agreed with you. I simply approve of your turn of phrase." She jabbed the needle through his skin.

He turned a ruddy color, and with his round face and full cheeks, he almost looked like a pomegranate.

But pomegranates didn't swear.

She waited while he reeled off a whole list of Moricadian insults—she understood the gist if not the actual language—then stabbed him again. "I don't know why you two are even having this discussion."

"Because the stupid fool wants to push me aside!" Danel snarled, then gasped as she took another stitch.

"You're making yourself bleed more with all your shouting," she said. "Stop it right now; I can't see what I'm doing and I might sew your wrist to your knee."

In an exaggerated whisper, he said, "Tell us how you would solve this problem, O Solomon."

"You can't be king," she said.

"You're his lover!" Danel spit on the ground to express his contempt for her opinion.

Victoria pointed at his spittle. "Right there; there's the reason you can't be king." She could scarcely contain her disgust. "Look at you! You're dirty. You stink. You're uneducated. You've got half your teeth and that half is rotten. You barely speak four languages, only one of them well."

He scratched his head.

Her voice gained volume. "Your hair is crawling with lice, and there's no way to exterminate them because it's so matted and filthy, no one could get a comb through it. You might as well shave it off!"

"You sound like my mother," Danel said.

It wasn't a compliment.

"You know nothing of finance," she continued, "and your idea of diplomacy is to pull out a knife and have a fight. And if you'd kept fighting, you would have lost!"

"Would not." He sounded like a sulky boy.

Victoria was not to be drawn into that fruitless argument. "At the same time, I've heard Mr. Lawrence admit that you're among the best military strategists in the world."

"You weren't supposed to tell him that!" Raul snapped.

She smiled with satisfaction. "You could have said that my Moricadian is so bad I misunderstood you. But you didn't, and now Danel knows it's the truth."

Raul glared.

Danel roared with laughter. "She's too smart for you, cousin!"

"I'm too smart for both of you, which is not a large enough accomplishment of which to boast." She turned back to Danel. "Without education in any of the ways of government, you would be a disaster as king. Yet if you and Mr. Lawrence banded together, you could unite your whole family and all the people of Moricadia under one banner rather than fail in this most important cause because of foolish pride. I would suggest to you both that only together can you win the upcoming revolution." No one said anything for so long that she glanced up to see Danel's reaction.

He sat frowning like a toad on a log.

She glanced at Raul.

He watched her, his eyes half-closed, as if trying to see the truth about her.

Danel snapped to attention. "Saber, your woman reminds me exactly of my mother. That's why I never go and visit the old harridan."

"Your mother is a frightening woman," Raul admitted.

"She misses your mother." Danel slammed his fist into Raul's shoulder. "I never offered my condolences on your mother's death. You were gone when she faded away, and when you came back, I forgot my manners. She was a great woman, and we miss her."

"I do, too." Raul's sorrow was palpable. "I would have done anything to be here for her."

"You'd rather have been here than in England, living the soft life?" Danel laughed, but he seemed to be asking a real question.

Raul didn't answer right away.

He didn't answer for so long Victoria realized he didn't intend to answer, that his pride wouldn't allow him to plead his own case. But she knew the truth, so she said, "I was a friend of Mr. Lawrence's half sister Belle, and she told me her father beat Mr. Lawrence so badly on the occasion of his grandfather's death that they feared for his life."

"Victoria," Raul said warningly.

"He had a broken arm. Bruises so black they took months to heal. Broken ribs, and that was the thing that scared them, because he couldn't breathe. They thought he was going to die. They believed he wanted to. But after a month in bed, he recovered, and Belle said he was never the same."

Danel scratched the scraggly growth of beard on his cheek. "His father is a right old misery, then."

"He favored his son over his other children." She finished closing the wound on his elbow. "There you go. Be careful how you work the arm. If you rip the stitches, you'll be no good as king or commander."

Danel scratched his head, then hastily lowered his hand. "If I take the post as commander of the army, I get to ride at the front of the victory parade."

"And I will bring up the end," Raul said.

Victoria turned away to hide her smile.

Seven hours later, she wasn't smiling. She was swaying with weariness.

Raul and Danel had been talking—negotiating—the terms under which they would work together. Once that was settled, they discussed how the revolution would progress.

Danel had fought in these mountains and in this terrain his whole life, and he held strong opinions on the best way to finish the de Guignards and take the capital.

Raul knew the classic battle tactics and how they could be adapted to aid in every possible instance during the fight.

Using sticks, the two men drew battlefields in the dirt, discussed Prince Sandre's likely strategies, agreed Jean-Pierre was an opponent to be respected, and decided how to move supplies, what to do if their army was divided, whether it would be wiser to divide their army.

They fought about the date for their initial attack.

Raul said at the next new moon.

Danel insisted they move within the week. "We've already pushed our luck as far as it can go. One of our people is going to be caught and tortured, and they'll spill it all."

"We have to teach your troops and mine to work together," Raul said.

"I can do it in a week. You want me to do the job? Trust me."

They argued some more, then ate some more beans, fresh venison, bread, and cheese, and they drank two gallons of wine mixed with water.

Now they were still talking.

Victoria sat beside Raul, staring into the embers of the fire and trying to subdue her sense of accomplishment.

She had done it. She had taken enemies and made them allies. She had made Raul's victory, if not assured, at least more likely.

"Victoria." Raul's warm voice caught her attention, brought her head around. "Victoria, you're nodding off."

"Didn't get much sleep last night," she murmured.

"Rest on me." He caught the back of her neck in his palm, then with gentle pressure brought her head down onto his knee.

She reclined on her side, eyes wide, as he pulled a blanket over her. Only when he stroked her hair off her forehead did she relax.

Danel laughed. "She's turned the wrong direction."

Victoria didn't understand what he meant, but Raul chuckled, too, murmured an answer, and continued that slow stroking that made her want to stretch and purr like a cat.

The sounds of their voices lulled her; her eyes closed, then opened, then closed, and finally she slept, aware somewhere in her mind that here she was warm and safe.

Chapter Thirty-seven

When Victoria woke, she lay on her side still facing the fire pit. The camp was quiet. The sun pushed through the trees, giving the grove a greenish tint. Her back was warm, pressed up against a man's body—pressed up against Raul, who held her in his arms.

As she watched, the camp began to stir. First an elderly woman hobbled out of her tent and headed into the forest, coming back with kindling she set on the embers. The twigs readily caught fire, and she added more wood, larger branches, until the flames cracked merrily and wood smoke rose in a twisting white column into the pale blue sky.

Now the others stirred, one by one leaving their tents to cook, to tend the horses, to stretch, rub their eyes, gather in small groups to discuss ... something. Something that involved Raul and Victoria, if their smiling glances were anything to judge by.

At last Danel staggered out of his tent, scratching and yawning loudly.

A young woman with dark, flashing eyes followed. Like a cat, she rubbed up against him.

He swatted her bottom.

She smiled and sauntered off.

Another woman, not so young, but very pretty, followed her, tying her hair back in a ribbon. She, too, lifted her face for his kiss, got a swat on the bottom, and staggered away, looking a little more exhausted than the first.

Finally, Celesta ducked out of the tent, her arms full of clothing. She kissed him on the mouth, got the now-familiar pat on the bottom, and walked across the camp and into the woods.

Victoria could scarcely believe the parade.

Raul spoke in Victoria's ear. "Danel has a reputation as a great and inexhaustible lover of women."

The discussion was earthy and embarrassing, but Victoria kept her voice steady when she said, "I see that. Is that all of them?"

"Unless more of them sneaked in after I fell asleep."

"Are they his ..." She paused awkwardly, not knowing exactly how to phrase her question. "That is, is he married to any or all of them?"

Raul chuckled, his chest rocking her. "Not at all. In Moricadia, a man is allowed only one wife. But if he can convince women to visit his tent, the number is limitless. Or so I suppose—I've never been interested in more than one woman at a time."

"That's good." Snuggled together as they were, she knew he was interested in her right now.

That was embarrassing, too. Embarrassing and thrilling and disappointing, for they couldn't indulge themselves in more lovemaking, and while Victoria knew very well she shouldn't want to ... she did.

"I'm interested only in you," he said.

"That's very flattering." She didn't believe him for a minute—after all, when the revolution was over, she would leave Moricadia forever. But she appreciated the reassurance that while she was here, he wouldn't be inviting other women into his tent.

"Come on, you lovebirds!" If anything, Danel was louder in the morning. "Rise and shine. We've got a ceremony to perform!"

As if his words were a signal, the pace of the camp changed, became lively, bustling, and cheerful. Everyone seemed to have a task and they performed it vociferously. The men teased the women; the women teased back. And Victoria understood little but the tone.

Sitting up, she looked down at Raul.

Like her, he was still dressed, but while she felt grubby and wrinkled, he looked wide-awake, anticipating the day with bright eyes and a warmly flushed complexion. Even his hair, tousled and tangled, shone with the light of the rising sun.

"What ceremony?" she asked. Her hair had come loose during the night and hung helter-skelter down her back. She must truly be a sight.

He toyed with one of the strands, examining it as if fascinated by the glisten of gold. "We're transferring ownership of you from Danel back to me."

"What? *What?*" She was incredulous.

"We're transferring ownership of you from Danel back to—"

"I heard you! I mean . . . what do you mean, transferring ownership?"

"He captured you. You slept in his tent. You're his."

"He wasn't in there!" Her voice rose.

"I know." Raul lifted his shoulders. "But I didn't make the rules. We have to have a ceremony."

"For pity's sake. This is most inappropriate, and incredibly vexing." Gathering her hair in one hand, she pulled it over her shoulder, ran her fingers through it until she'd established a modicum of order, then rapidly braided and tied it.

He tugged at the end. "Don't you want to be mine?"

"I am his right now?" Victoria pointed to Danel, who was scratching his private parts with such concentration, he might have been finding gold.

"That's right."

"Then yes, I want to be yours."

"A man can never be conceited while you're around." Raul tugged on her braid again. "Do you know why women rub their eyes in the morning?"

"No. Why?"

"Because they don't have balls to scratch."

She looked at him to see if he was serious.

He winked.

She laughed involuntarily and pulled away from him. She considered a reprimand, then decided against it. "What time did you go to sleep?"

"A very wifely question."

She stared at him, more stricken by his "wife" comment than when he'd made his joke.

He shrugged. "There's no clock out here. Late, I suppose, well after midnight."

Everything about this raised her hackles: that he

would dare equate her with a wife, someone permanent in his life, and that he could look so good on so little sleep.

He added, "Thanks to you and your timely intervention"—he stroked her arm—"Danel and I had much to discuss."

She warmed at his gratitude. "Did you get your differences settled, then?"

"We'll be coordinating our efforts to overthrow the de Guignards. The army is his to command. The throne is mine."

"Exactly as it should be."

She slid out from under the blankets and started to stand.

He caught her hand. "Tell me something. Have you ever swung a sword before?"

"No. You're lucky I didn't chop off your arm." She was glad to see him pale. That would teach him to be so bright and energetic in the morning. She pulled away and straightened her clothes—the clothes she'd been wearing for too long and through too many ordeals.

"Come on." Celesta gestured to Victoria. "We'll go wash."

"Thank heavens!" She was grateful for the chance to escape Raul's gaze. Victoria found her bonnet—the straw had been crushed and now sat catawampus on her head—and hurried after Celesta.

It appeared every woman in the camp was part of their group. The younger ones ran ahead. The older ones trailed behind. But all of them were laughing, calling out, still in that boisterous mood that again made Victoria wish she comprehended more of the language. She would have liked to join in the conversation, but more than that—it seemed as if everything they said concerned her.

She didn't understand why. Yes, she was an anomaly among these dark-haired, dark-eyed people, but their interest seemed so much more than that. It wasn't that they were disrespectful, more that they were kindly mocking her.

Probably it was the way she had handled the sword yesterday. Possibly it was her connection to their future king. But whatever it was, she could only go along with them, smiling and nodding and wishing her linguistic skill hadn't chosen this place and time to abandon her.

Shrieks from the front of the line warned her that the younger girls had found something. She walked around a corner and discovered a whole vista opening before her. She halted, speechless with awe and pleasure.

Never in her life had she seen a place so unspoiled and glorious. A small, pristine mountain lake, surrounded by pines and backed by a rocky cliff that rose bare and rugged against the blue sky. Waterfalls foamed as they flung themselves toward the bottom, and halfway around the water, a doe with two fawns watched wide-eyed as the young girls stripped off their clothes and dove in, naked as Eve.

The way they screamed gave Victoria fair warning that the temperature would be icy, and she thanked heaven that the older women would be more measured and more modest in their ablutions.

Or so she thought, until they started tugging at her clothing.

"No, no." She smiled and brushed them off. "I can undress myself."

They laughed and tugged some more, untying her bonnet strings, undoing her buttons.

"No, really." She used her patented firm-governess tone. "I'm not a young girl who needs help—do you *mind*?"

It appeared they didn't, because no matter how she protested, they kept on removing her clothing, unbraiding her hair, pushing her, ganging up on her, snatching away every bit of modesty until she stood as naked as the young girls, only a good deal more embarrassed. They left her no choice but to jump off a rock into the water.

When she came up, she gave an involuntary shriek. It was as cold as she feared, so cold the water felt as if it were scouring the flesh from her bones. Celesta called her name and tossed her something—a bar of lavender-scented, French-milled soap, a luxury anywhere, but up here . . . a miracle.

Victoria used it on her hair and face; then, ignoring her own modesty and the eyes that watched her so closely, she climbed onto the rocks to thoroughly wash every inch of her skin. Tossing the soap to Celesta, she plunged back into the lake—with grim humor, she noted that the water hadn't gotten any warmer—and rinsed herself.

With no small amount of trepidation, she got out. She didn't want to don her dirty undergarments and wrinkled gown, but what choice had she?

Yet the women who had insisted on undressing her now stood waiting to clothe her, too. Not in her own clothes, either, but in a pale yellow embroidered shift. "I . . . really need my clothes back." Because this was clean and simple, but she saw no undergarments, and the straight lines would expose her every curve.

Then Celesta lifted a dark blue wool cloak off a bush beside the clearing, and Victoria relaxed. "Oh! All right, that'll cover me." She allowed them to dress her in the shift and cover her with the cloak, and the whole of the womenfolk headed back toward Danel's tents.

Chapter Thirty-eight

Danel sat on his tree stump, twitching as he waited.
Celesta brought a basin of hot water and put it in his hands.

Leaning his head against her belly, he smiled cajolingly up at her. "Have I told you you're my favorite bedmate?"

"I won't slit your throat, if that's what you're thinking," she said.

"That's my girl." He handed her a razor and strop.

She started sharpening the razor. "I'm more inventive than that."

Danel turned white.

Raul chortled.

Danel turned on him. "Hey, you! Cousin! *Someone* has to go get my mother."

Raul took his last bite of porridge. "Who would that be?"

"Why, you, my king!" Danel laughed, that loud, braying laugh he used as a diversion.

Not that Raul was diverted, but he knew Danel had a point.

If Raul was to be king, he was also the head of the family, and it was his task to deal with the crotchety ladies who scared the hell out of everyone.

He stood. "I'll bring her back."

"She's as mean as a snake, but she's the family's matriarch, so try not to cry when she talks to you."

"I don't cry when your mommy browbeats me. I'm not you." Raul started up the path.

Danel grinned in appreciation. "Hey, do you know where you're going?"

"I know." Raul turned to see the look on Danel's face when he fired his final volley. "I visit your mother on occasion." He enjoyed the satisfaction of seeing Danel's astonishment before striding into the woods and up to his aunt's house.

When Raul came panting up the mountain, Izba Xaviera was on her hands and knees working in her garden. She looked him over from head to toe, snorted, and said, "Soft."

Compared to her, he was. She was thin as a whip, weathered beyond her years by forty-seven Moricadian winters, and honed by the tribulations of living under de Guignard rule and the loss of so many of her family. She was tough, smart, contemptuous of every weakness, and, above all else, a survivor.

He adored her. "I've come to bring you to Danel's camp."

"Settled your differences, did you?" She held out a hand and he helped her up. "It's about time you lads stopped pouting and played nicely together."

He loved the way she put two powerful men firmly in their places. Next she'd be reminding him that she'd changed his diapers. "Victoria agreed with you, and took the matter into her own hands."

"Victoria?" Izba Xaviera's brown eyes, deep-set in her weathered face, scrutinized him critically. "The Englishwoman who's living at the castle?"

"You know about Victoria?"

"I had a vision."

"Of course," he agreed. In the family, there was talk that Izba Xaviera was a witch.

In his opinion, she knew everything because no one dared keep information from her for fear she would rip the hide off their backs with her scolding.

"The English are feeble," she said.

"Not Victoria." He repeated the story of how Victoria used his sword to break up the fight.

"Good for her. You men are fools." Izba Xaviera cackled. "Still, she's English. Blond, fair skinned, afraid to work hard or get their hands dirty."

"She is blond. She is fair skinned. She's beautiful and strong. And she works; she teaches the children. Didn't your vision show you that?"

"Yes, I know."

"I'm taking possession of her tonight."

"Fool!" Izba Xaviera glared, ire in the depths of her dark eyes. "If she had money or a title, it would be different."

He rubbed the dirt off Izba Xaviera's knobby knuckles and smiled. "What can I do? She fits me, and she'll bring honor and benefit to my court."

Izba Xaviera put her other hand to his face and looked into his eyes. "Do you love her?"

He laughed. "I am my father's son. I do not love. But I keep what is mine."

The old woman breathed heavily, thinking what to say. Finally, she responded. "I was a maid at the hotel where your mother met your father. I never liked him."

"No one likes my father. He doesn't know or care." As Raul remembered, the vision of Grimsborough rose in his mind. The cold face, the indifferent eyes, the sharp cruelty. "But living with him made me strong. I'm not afraid of pain. I'm not afraid of loneliness. I know how to plan, how to look beyond the trouble of this day to the victory of next week or next year or ten years from now."

"You say that, but I see your mother in you." Izba Xaviera slapped his cheek hard enough to sting. "Arrogant, stubborn, reckless, unwavering."

"All good qualities for a king."

"Yes. But also like your mother, you have passion hidden even from your knowledge."

That pricked at his pride. "I know my passions."

"Maybe." Still Izba Xaviera searched his face. "Unlike your father, your mother *did* love."

"It was her weakness."

"And her strength. She would have killed for you. And did." Izba Xaviera pointed at a stump in the yard. "Sit there. I will bring you food and drink."

"Yes, Izba Xaviera." Because she never allowed anyone to visit without feeding them, and considering what he was about to do, he'd gotten off easy.

As he ate and waited for her to change, he knew how deeply unhappy Victoria would be if she understood the ramifications of what was about to happen. But when he had returned to his castle and discovered she had run away, he had been furious. She was his captive, yes, but he'd laid claim to her.

How could she not comprehend what that meant?

Or had she been playing him, knowing the restraints on her would loosen when she yielded?

Then, when Hada told him of Victoria's distress, he had grown absolutely livid.

He understood, of course. He'd been raised in proper English society, and Victoria was a gently bred virgin who, through his guile and seduction, had fallen from grace.

That was her belief.

And she was a decorous woman who valued her privacy, who chafed at having to share his bedroom and disliked being the center of attention at the evening meal. To have the whole castle know of her perceived disgrace—that must have wounded her dignity.

But understanding did not heal his pride.

He had spent weeks luring her into his bed. She by God should have stayed lured.

By the time he tracked her to Danel's camp, he had been murderous. He was going to kill his cousin without a second thought.

Then Victoria had used his own sword to slice through his rage.

He had never imagined a mere woman could make him forget who he was and what he intended to become.

For those minutes when he believed Danel had raped her, nothing mattered—not his ambitions, not his family, not his plans, not Moricadia. Every element of his mind and body focused on her—avenging her honor, getting her back, keeping and comforting her.

He did not like having a woman control him so completely.

Something had to be done to tie her to him. So this afternoon they would perform the traditional Moricadian ceremony, and perhaps someday he would regret his impetuosity, but for now, it would bring him peace of mind. For now, he would be able to concentrate on what really mattered—the overthrow of the de Guignards and the independence of the Moricadian people.

Izba Xaviera appeared, clothed in her good black gown, one he recognized from his youth. She took his plate and cup away, came back holding her white lace handkerchief, and put her hand on his arm. "Let's go meet this Englishwoman of yours."

Chapter Thirty-nine

The women didn't return to Danel's camp right away. Instead they went to a meadow, unpacked baskets full of food, picked flowers, chatted and sang, and generally kept Victoria entertained. As the hours passed, she realized some women were slipping away to be replaced by others. Only when Amya appeared did she note that the component of her guard—for they were her guard—had changed. She recognized that these women were from Raul's castle: warriors and servants. They had come to see the ceremony, and they seemed excessively happy. Jumpy. Sort of . . . jubilant.

With a sigh, Victoria realized that these women were *excited* to see another woman bound to a man in a transfer-of-possession ceremony.

She had fallen into a primitive society. She would be

glad to return to England, the home of civilized behavior. Not too much longer . . .

Odd how that thought made her spirits lower.

At a little past noon, the women decided it was time to go back to Danel's camp.

There flowers festooned the trees. The women had created garlands of blue columbines and pure white mountain meadow flowers, and hung them from the pine branches, creating a bower of sorts.

A lean, brown, weathered woman sat in Danel's seat of honor and gazed at Victoria shrewdly, as if she knew Victoria wore no undergarments beneath the native costume.

The men of the castle had arrived and were gathered in knots, laughing and joking. They had washed and dressed in their finest, which was still remarkably shabby. But they looked excited, as though they were about to see something special. Victoria imagined they were probably more thrilled by the prospect of free-flowing wine after the ceremony.

The castle children had arrived with their parents, mixed with the children in Danel's camp, and now ran screaming in circles of excitement. Many of the children she had taught English and mathematics (and who had taught her Moricadian) stopped their play to watch Victoria's arrival, and she gave them a quick wave and a generous smile.

Prospero was helping Hada make her slow, painful way off his horse, and the big, rude jackass of a man handled his wife as if she were spun glass.

A spot in front of the fire had been cleared, similar to the circle they'd cleared for the knife fight. Danel and Raul stood waiting, and for a moment, she wondered if they were going to fight again. But no, they both looked oddly ... clean. Raul's hair was damp and pushed back from his face, and he wore a crisp white shirt, rough brown trousers that tied at his waist and ankles, and short brown boots.

Danel's head was shaved. So was his face. He looked like a shiny round Shrovetide ball with eyes and a surprisingly small pursed mouth.

Everyone was waiting for something ... waiting for her.

She didn't have a choice. She would reside with either Danel or Raul, and she knew who held her heart....

No. She didn't want to dwell on the emotions that could bind her so tightly that if she tried to free herself, she would break.

She strode forward.

Amya caught her cloak and pulled it off her shoulders, leaving her clad in that ridiculous, revealing native costume. She felt the breeze stir her skirts and press the thin material closer to her slender frame.

But Victoria didn't pause. She wanted to get this *over with*. She stood before Raul, challenging him with everything in her.

The man didn't play fair, though. He reached out, slow and gentle, and smoothed her hair back, tucking a strand behind her ear.

He was lethal.

Once they stood in place, Danel started talking, fast and sure.

If Victoria understood Moricadian better, she would be able to follow along, but the language seemed archaic and formulaic—a ceremony, just as they'd said, and probably from ancient times. She could understand only snippets of Danel's words, and they sounded very formal, words that seemed odd coming from Danel's mouth.

At various parts of the ritual, Danel stopped speaking after what seemed like a question. The first time, the weathered woman sitting in Danel's chair answered "yes" to whatever question was asked. The second time, Danel looked expectantly at the crowd and was met with only smiling silence.

Finally, Danel paused in his speech, and Celesta handed Danel a coil of worn, gold-threaded rope.

Raul tugged Victoria around so she stood with her back to his chest, put his right hand on top of hers, and Danel used the rope to tie their wrists together.

"It's too tight," she said.

"That's so if one of us tries to cut ourselves free, we'll both bleed," Raul said.

She couldn't see his face, but his voice was meaningful. Which made her feel sort of . . . funny. Tearful and incredulous.

But when Raul lifted his arm—and hers with it—and the people cheered, Victoria smiled.

It was what was expected of her.

At her back, Raul chuckled deep in his chest.

The celebration wasn't so much a meal as a constant flow of food and drink. Raul's people and Danel's people joined together to cook, to drink, to laugh, to dance. Musicians from both camps produced instruments and played. Victoria sat on the ground on Danel's rug between Raul's outstretched legs.

She had to sit with Raul. Everyone refused to untie their hands.

She ate from Raul's fingers, drank from his cup. She thought the proceedings were odd; no one else seemed to. In fact, all around the fire, the men fed their women as if it were some Moricadian ceremonial ritual. Truthfully, Victoria had grown somewhat used to Raul's unorthodox dining methods, even finding comfort in the knowledge that he paid such close attention to her likes and dislikes and catered to them at every opportunity, as he had done every day since he captured her and brought her to his castle.

Danel tapped a barrel of strong liquor—according to him, his mother had made it—and the first sip took Victoria's breath away. But she was aware of Izba Xaviera's critical gaze and sipped again.

Actually, after the first glass, she decided the beverage tasted like oranges. Very, very intense oranges.

After the second glass, she decided she liked it.

Raul wouldn't let her have a third glass.

When Victoria felt the need to use the convenience, Raul walked her to the edge of the clearing, untied the knot that bound them, and every woman in the camp accompanied her. Which made her hostile until Raul assured her it was merely tradition. He said, with a twinkle, that in ancient times the possession sometimes made a run for freedom.

"Wise possession," Victoria muttered.

"You'll get your chance," he said enigmatically.

All the while Raul and Victoria ate and drank, smiled and nodded, conversations swirled around them.

"The training is going well."

"Thompson volunteered to stay behind to tend the castle."

"Prince Sandre is afraid to come out in public. They say he stays in his room tending his accounts."

"We attack in a week."

"We attack at the next new moon."

"We attack when we're told."

"Jean-Pierre is quite mad—he's holding the palace guard hostage by putting their families in the dungeon."

Yet the conversation seemed halfhearted, as if the family were watching the sky and waiting for some special event.

Finally, when the afternoon was waning, Izba Xaviera raised one bent finger. "It is time!"

Raul lifted Victoria to her feet.

Izba Xaviera carefully untied the knot. She coiled up the rope and handed it to Raul, then started toward the path that wound into the depths of the forest.

Raul and Victoria followed.

Victoria glanced around.

The entire party trailed behind them.

At the edge of the forest, Izba Xaviera stepped aside.

Everyone gazed expectantly at Victoria.

She looked around inquiringly.

"Run," Hada said, sotto voce.

She glanced at Danel.

He jerked his head toward the depths of the woods.

Victoria glanced at Raul.

He watched her with a furrowed brow as if . . . as if he were the predator, she the prey, and he was waiting to hunt her down.

On a gasp, she leaped into the forest and fled down the path.

Chapter Forty

The whole camp gave chase, hooting and calling out, the women encouraging Victoria to run away, the men shouting for Raul to catch her.

She glanced behind her.

Raul was ten feet back, keeping pace with her.

The rest of the party was behind him, but rapidly diminishing as the path grew steep. Couples peeled off into the woods. Singles turned back to the party.

Soon it was only Victoria and Raul running through the forest. She took one small path, then another. She was lost. She was half-scared because he seemed so intent—but not really scared. Because she was uncontrollably giggling.

The path widened and she found herself in a clear, high, rocky circle where the last of the sun's rays lingered and the surrounding trees were deep and old and quiet. She put her hand to the stitch in her side and turned, gasping, to face him.

He stopped, his shoulders hunched, his gaze intent, his hands cupped and loose at his side.

She backed away, laughing.

He was not even smiling. His chest rose and fell in deep breaths. His green eyes focused on her to the exclusion of all else.

Unhurriedly, he started to stalk her.

It felt like a game . . . a game with one ending. And knowing what he intended made her feel fluttery and foolish and . . . aroused. "No." She thought she sounded, well, not stern at all. More like teasing and flirtatious. So she frowned, shook her head, and backed away. "No, Raul, listen to me. I don't think this is a good idea."

Perhaps he listened to what she meant, not what she said, for he kept walking, one slow step after another.

"Raul, this is ridiculous. We're out of doors!" She glanced behind her.

Apparently, when she stopped he'd immediately assessed the terrain, and shrewdly planned his ambush, for he was backing her into a corner between a towering stone cliff and a tall, smooth boulder.

Her heart rate picked up. She laughed again, breathless with a need as sudden as a summer storm. "Anyone could see us." Her back struck the boulder. The stone was rough, crystalline, warm from the lingering rays of the sun. She inched sideways, trying to stay out of his reach. "Raul, listen . . ."

He grabbed her so fast she was trapped before she knew it. His hands, hot on her waist, held her still as he pressed her between his body and the hard surface. Immediately and without finesse, he pulled her shift up, out of the way. "No one followed us. I made sure of that." His voice was guttural, hard, flat.

She swallowed. She didn't feel like laughing now. She was bare, exposed to the open air . . . and to him.

He pushed his knee between her legs and rubbed his thigh up and down.

At once she caught fire. She grabbed his shoulders for balance in a rapidly tilting world, and moved on him, and moaned his name.

How could she be at a pitch point so soon? What kind of woman grew incited to the pitch point by stalking? Was she an animal?

Was he?

Yes. And yes. Because he tore at the buttons on his trousers. He shoved them down. Gripping her bottom, he lifted her against the rock.

She wrapped her legs around his hips.

He balanced her, used his fingers to probe at her opening. Then both his hands were on her bottom again, and it wasn't his fingers anymore. It was him, his organ, burning her with the heat of his lust.

She was damp.

He was hard.

He breached her at once and started thrusting, moving too fast for her to adjust.

Yet she did, her body unlocking for him, taking him in. She cried out at the sweet frenzy, at the unexpected power of this mating. The stone was rough at her back. The setting sun struck at her eyes, blinding her to everything but Raul, his passion, his power. His dark hair swung around his savage, desperate face as need propelled him on, faster and faster.

She couldn't move. He held her too forcefully. But her body clenched rhythmically, responding without her volition. She squeezed his shirt in her fists, arched her back, and tried to get closer to him when already he was touching the deepest part of her.

She didn't want to be like this, in thrall to a desire she couldn't control. She didn't want to be a creature who responded to this male because he looked like sex, smelled like sex, because he made her live and breathe and *be* as his mate.

It was shameful to be so easy, but he was all she wanted.

He grunted, his face contorting, his organ jerking as he orgasmed.

And at the sight, the sound, the *feel*, she came.

She clawed at him.

And came again.

Some more.

Again.

The pleasure went on and on until tears started in her eyes and she cried aloud, and the forest and the stones absorbed the sound of her ecstasy.

Chapter Forty-one

Raul held Victoria securely pinned between the cliff face and his body. He was inside her as far as he could go. Yet even as he held her, still gasping from the force of her orgasm, her face warm and beautiful with pleasure, he felt as if she were slipping away.

He had to extract a vow now, while she was weak and clinging.

She was an honorable woman. No matter how unfair the circumstances, she would keep her word. "Victoria." His voice was deep and commanding, vibrant with demand.

She opened her cornflower blue eyes and stared at him as if she were still lost to everything but the pleasure they'd found . . . together. Then she lavished a smile on him, and in a languorous voice whispered, "What?"

"Promise me you'll never run away again."

She blinked as if he confused her. "You were chasing me. I thought it was a game."

"No, not that. Not today. I meant . . . promise you'll never run away like you did after we . . . mated the first time."

Her eyebrows went up in surprise, then down in irritation.

Hurriedly he added, "I know that for a gently bred young woman, the intimacies of"—what the hell did they call it in polite society?—"of physical relations are a shock. But I will be temperate"—just not this time—"and help you adjust. I promise to listen if you're unhappy, as long as you will promise never to run away again."

"I told you. I did *not* run away." She sounded, looked, annoyed. "Is that so hard to believe?"

"You have been my captive. Captives run."

"You know better." She struggled against his hold. "I don't run away from my problems."

He clasped her tighter. "Am I such a problem?"

"Yes," she said fervently. "Yes, you are."

He thrust himself at her once more.

She flinched, not in pain but in delight. She shuddered, and inside, the sweet, warm nest flexed and caressed like a silk-gloved hand. "And that's why." She almost seemed to be talking to herself. "Because even when we're finished with the wild passions and are at rest once more, all I can think is, How soon can I feel like that again?"

His cock stopped retreating, began to stiffen again. "Yes. I think that, too."

"Really?" She searched his face, and this time her

smile was timidly pleased. "I'm glad. I'm glad I'm not the only one who . . ."

"No. You're not the only one."

She put both her hands on his face, held it, and looked into his eyes. "I swear to you, when I leave, I will say good-bye to you, to your face."

It wasn't the vow he truly wanted, but right now, it was enough.

Carefully, he lifted her, put her on her feet.

She leaned against the bedrock of Moricadia as if too weak to stand alone, and brushed the skirt down to fall around her ankles.

Swiftly, he pulled up his trousers and fastened them. Seizing her hand, he towed her into the woods.

She stumbled after him.

He stopped. Turned to see her.

Her wheaten gold hair was tousled around her shoulders; her intelligent face was aglow with pleasure. She smiled at him as if she knew how much he was tempted to take her again, here and now.

"No," he told her. Picking her up, he headed into the shadowed hush of the forest, intent on his destination.

They reached it before the sun set, a pine grove set high on a rugged mountain.

Clearly, she knew at once what he'd brought her here to see. Going to the broad trunk of the oldest and tallest pine in Moricadia, she placed her hand on the rough bark and looked up.

"This tree grew here when Attila cut his swath through Europe, when my ancestor stole his saber and fled to give birth to his child in this land." He jumped, caught the lowest branch, swung himself up, then leaned down and extended his hand. "Come on."

"What?" She looked up at him as if he had lost his mind.

"Trust me," he said.

Her face took on an expression he had begun to recognize: jaw set, eyes narrowed, nostrils flared. "Only if *you* trust *me*."

He studied her. He had never said that he believed her claim that she hadn't run away. She had noticed. Of course she had. "I do trust you."

She studied him back.

Their eyes locked, and without his volition, he saw things in her he had never thought to see: resolution, strength, courage, perhaps a little affection, and, most important, faith in him.

She must have seen the same traits, for she said, "All right," and reached out her hand to him and gave a jump.

He pulled.

She grabbed the branch with her other hand.

He hauled her all the way up.

"I've never climbed a tree before," she warned him.

"Another first with me," he teased.

She gave him that patented female *You're treading on thin ice* look.

He wasn't concerned. She had faith in him. And affection. The two of them were almost a couple. "I'll help you. Are you afraid of heights?"

"Not particularly."

Of course not. "Are you afraid of anything?"

For a long, quiet moment, she scrutinized him. "I didn't used to be."

He didn't know what she meant by that. But the sun was setting. They needed to climb before they lost the light. So he pointed up. "We're going there." *There* was a platform constructed of sturdy branches built a hundred feet in the air. "We built it when we were kids, Danel and I," he told her. "If our mothers had known..." He helped her stand on the next branch up, showed her where to put her hands and feet, then followed close after her, ready to catch her if she slipped.

She didn't. In her grace of movement and her coordination, Victoria showed a natural athleticism. Her children would be beautiful, bright, and competent. Her children would be—

But before he could finish the thought, she said, "Building this tree house must have been quite a labor for two young boys."

"It was. We set up a pulley system with ropes to bring the wood up. Prospero and Zakerie found out what we were doing and wanted to help, but we wouldn't let them. It was *ours*."

"Selfish children," she chided.

"Selfish, with a big dollop of superiority. We were rotten to the core, heirs to the throne of Moricadia, and we lorded it over the other lads." He laughed bitterly. "When I got to England, my father beat that sense of privilege out of me."

"Not all of it," she said.

"No. Not all of it." For when he'd wanted her, he'd taken her. And as she climbed, he caught flashes of her ankles, her calves, and, if he was positioned just right, her thighs.

It made for odd contortions as he tried to position himself for the next step, the next hint of her body's glories.

All unaware, she said, "But it would have been easier to exert your mastery over the others if you'd made them build it for you. So perhaps you weren't as wicked as you would like to believe?"

"I was a brat," he said with finality.

She stopped and stared down at him, one foot on one branch, one foot on the other.

He strove to keep his gaze on her face.

"You're still a brat. But only when you choose." She started up again. "Why did you build a tree house? Why here?"

"Because we liked to climb trees. Because we pretended the tree house was a ship we sailed around the world. Because we loved to watch the storms roll in and to scream like girls when the lightning struck close."

She laughed.

"Because up here, we were free." He sobered. "No de Guignards, no starvation, no fighting, no death. We never allowed anyone in this place."

She paused. "No one?"

"I got Danel's permission to bring you here."

She started climbing again. "Did you never fall?"

"Never." Wryly aware of the dangers of trying to see her legs and beyond, he added, "At least, not before today."

They were almost there. She stretched to reach a branch. Her costume rose.

His breath caught.

She looked up. "I know why you built it. Up here, you can see heaven."

"Yes. I can," he said fervently.

She glanced down at him as if he puzzled her.

Hurriedly, he said, "This morning I repaired the platform. You'll be safe up there."

"I never doubted it."

Reaching the tree house, she hoisted herself up onto her stomach. As she looked around, her legs dangled in his face. "There's a rail, so we won't fall off. And you made a bed!"

He had, of fresh pine boughs covered with sturdy canvas. "I brought food, too, and drink."

"So we can really spend the night?" She shimmied all the way up.

He scrambled after her, joined her.

She was standing, frozen, gripping a branch and staring at the vista before them. "My God." She breathed a prayer of awe.

Putting his arm around her waist, he looked, too.

The last rays of the sun spread across the valleys and mountains, the waterfalls that plunged from one high place to the next, the trees that rippled like grass in the breeze. One by one, each snowy peak flamed red with the sunset.

Victoria leaned her head against his shoulder.

He hugged her tightly.

Then, as the sun dipped below the horizon, the light was extinguished like the flame of a candle, and the first stars opened like flowers on a field of darkening velvet.

"I give you all this." He had never meant anything so much in his life.

"It's beautiful. Thank you." She stroked his arm. "I'll never forget these days with you, or this place. Nowhere else on earth could be as beautiful."

She believed he offered her this time here with him.

When, in fact, he had offered her his country, Moricadia, hers for the taking ... as long as she took him, too.

But he didn't correct her assumption.

After all, he could give her only Moricadia forever.

Victoria was the kind of woman who would want his heart.

Chapter Forty-two

Victoria rested on her back on the bed in the tree house and stared at the stars, so bright they might have been burning holes in the tapestry of the sky.

Out here, there was no other light.

Raul slept soundly beside her, his arm flung over her waist, his leg nudging hers. She could hear his breathing, and the call of the owl, and the branches as they rustled in the breeze.

Out here, there was no other sound.

The air was so fresh, she could smell the fragrance of pine boughs beneath her back, and from the north, a hint of autumn with its swirl of crisp leaves.

Out here, there was no other scent.

Although . . . that wasn't really true.

She could smell Raul, faintly sweaty and still warm

from their lovemaking. As night fell, he had seduced her. Then he fed her bread and cheese and wine, and seduced her once again. He had done everything to bring her satisfaction, to bring her pleasure, to make her happy. He had said he would give her his country. In his own way, he'd been trying to tell her he wanted her to stay with him, and she knew that if she'd responded with a modicum of accord, he would have asked her to marry him.

She couldn't bring herself to do it.

Oh, she wasn't afraid that marriage to Raul would be the misery she'd seen her mother endure. Nor did she doubt her own ability to support him in his quest for the throne, or to perform the duties required of his queen when he succeeded. And certainly with him, she would have financial security, respectability, and the constant reassurance that he wanted her body.

But she, Victoria Cardiff, the woman who believed in sensibility above all things . . . she could not do this. She couldn't marry a man who did not love her. Who would never love her. Not when she lay here beside him and knew she'd given him everything in her heart.

If only she weren't so angry.

At him, for not giving her the one thing she so desperately needed.

At herself, for abandoning good sense in the pursuit of something so ephemeral—she had never really believed in true love before, and now she was willing to walk away from money, a throne, and a man as glorious as the stars themselves—for love.

Most of all, she feared what hid beneath the anger—a clawing agony of loneliness and sorrow to last for the rest of her life.

So when his revolution was over and she knew he

would thrive, she'd go to England to see her mother, and she would, she swore, be more understanding of the poor woman. If news of her disgrace had spread—and she supposed it had—she would use her savings to move on. America was a new country with wealthy young women who traveled to England specifically to catch a nobleman. There would be employment for an English governess with experience teaching decorum and etiquette.

She leaned her head against Raul's shoulder and smiled with pained humor.

She had, after all, trained the court of King Saber of Moricadia.

Raul watched the women surround Victoria and walk her over the castle drawbridge, across the courtyard, and through the towering door into the keep. They were symbolically welcoming her to her new home and her new society.

Victoria smiled and spoke to them in her stumbling Moricadian, but she didn't have a clue what these customs meant.

It was better that way.

She was beautiful this morning. Amya had packed clothes for Victoria, and Victoria had gratefully shed the traditional Moricadian costume and donned her dark blue gown, her white collar and cuffs, her leather shoes, and her paisley shawl.

But no matter how she covered herself in civilized English clothing, he knew what she looked like beneath the proper garments. He knew what she felt like, naked against him. He had made love to her into the night, and again in the morning. As he tried to impress himself on her, he felt the sense that time was running out. If he couldn't make her understand what he wanted from her now, on the night before he plunged into the final preparations for war, would a better time ever be delivered to them?

As they climbed the stairs to the great hall, Danel jostled him. "Cousin, you've got a good woman there."

"Yes." But Raul wouldn't discuss her with Danel. He wouldn't discuss her with anyone. She was his, and what they had between them was private, personal . . . important.

So he started speaking in an undertone of what was to come. "Hada says we can fit your people into the castle."

"That's a hell of a lot of people crammed into one household." Danel, too, kept his voice low.

"Hada and Thompson can handle the influx of family. They can handle anything. And it makes sense to use this as our base. From here, we can move out easily to drill and—"

The women stepped into the great hall. They abruptly stopped.

The men piled up behind them.

Silence fell, a silence so abrupt and awkward Raul pushed his way forward.

Jean-Pierre de Guignard sat in Raul's chair at the head of the table.

Behind him stood Bittor and eight well-armed members of the palace guard.

As Raul watched, Jean-Pierre lifted his whip and slapped it on the flat wood surface.

Questions tumbled through Raul's mind. What was Jean-Pierre doing here? What had he discovered? Where were his people, the ones who had stayed behind to care for the castle?

But he had a part to play, and he didn't hesitate. He surged forward, hands outstretched in what he hoped looked like genuine delight. "Jean-Pierre! Welcome to my home. If I had known of your visit, I would not have kept you waiting."

"I prefer surprise visits."

"So you have told me!"

Jean-Pierre observed Raul's genial salutation, then slashed the table again, knocking a goblet of ale over. It ran like gold-brown piss across the table and onto the floor.

"My servants will get you more," Raul said.

To his surprise, Amya hurried to the sideboard and brought the pitcher back to the table, and with many little bobbing curtsies, she poured the goblet full again. She was not as timid as he had thought.

"Did you come to hunt?" Raul asked.

Jean-Pierre rose slowly. "You've been hunting?"

"Indeed we have. If you wish to go, we can go out again!"

"You had success?"

"Great success."

Jean-Pierre looked around. "Where's the game?"

"We roasted venison last night on a campfire in the forest." Raul slapped Danel on the shoulder. "You must come out with me. My huntsman never fails."

Danel stood still and stiff with pride and hate.

Raul squeezed his shoulder hard.

Danel winced, then stepped forward and, like a grateful idiot, he grinned and bobbed his head. "I'm the best huntsman in Moricadia. The smart foreign visitors hire me to lead them to the game. I can find whatever you want, my lord—venison, boar, geese. . . ."

Jean-Pierre's gaze examined the crowd. "So, Lawrence, you feast with . . . *Moricadians*?" His scorn and disbelief were palpable.

"He was trying to impress me with his hunting prowess." Victoria pushed her way out of the crowd of women and made her way to Raul's side. She petted his arm and stared adoringly into his eyes. "As if he needed to do anything so manly to impress *me*."

Raul's heart contracted with fear.

She had called herself to the attention of a man so cruel and dangerous that mothers scared their children with his name. And she had done so purposefully, to distract Jean-Pierre with her pretty face and shapely figure.

"Who the hell are you?" Jean-Pierre snapped.

Victoria looked at Jean-Pierre in hurt surprise. Seeming to remember her manners, she curtsied and said, "Pardon me, Your Highness; I forgot myself in my excitement at meeting you. I'm Miss Victoria Cardiff of England."

Jean-Pierre's pale blue eyes narrowed. "I know that name."

"I arrived in Moricadia with my employers, the Johnsons—"

"That's why I know you!" Jean-Pierre glared with withered disdain. "Mr. Johnson roared like a bull when you disappeared. You've been here all this time?"

Raul held his breath. She had to answer very, very carefully. If Jean-Pierre caught her in a lie . . .

"Not all this time." Her lip wobbled. "I was in the ballroom when those horrible men in black came in and attacked us. I ran through the hotel and outside. Then I was lost until Mr. Lawrence found me. He was frightened, too, so he took me under his wing and . . ." She lavished an adoring smile on Raul.

She was doing a marvelous imitation of an artless *fille de joie*.

Jean-Pierre teetered on the edge of disbelief. "Johnson claimed you were a woman of impeccable virtue."

"I had never met a man like Mr. Lawrence before." She leaned forward and stage-whispered, "He has promised to marry me."

Raul recognized a cue when he heard one. "Soon." He met Jean-Pierre's gaze and winked.

If Jean-Pierre was convinced, he didn't show it. "Lawrence, you were at the hotel all that night."

"Not all night." Raul smiled, man-to-man. "You'll pardon me if, at the time, I didn't explain the treasure I had found in the gardens and brought home."

Jean-Pierre breathed hard, his pale skin flushing with frustration.

And Raul realized Jean-Pierre had not discovered anything incriminating here in his home. Not yet. Jean-Pierre might have his suspicions, but if he really believed Raul harbored rebels or, God forbid, *was* a rebel, Jean-Pierre's men would have shot Raul and Danel when they came through the door.

They were still alive. Soon they would take Jean-Pierre down.

"Why come back to the hotel at all?" Jean-Pierre asked.

"To take my place in the hunt for those villains who so disrupted the ball and to watch their execution." Cheerfully ignoring the fact that none of the rebels had been caught, Raul said, "I cannot wait to see them dangle like fruit from the trees of Moricadia." Then he waited to see if he'd successfully presented himself as an amiable gambler and horse breeder often enough to fool Jean-Pierre with his guileless act.

Jean-Pierre walked up to Raul and thrust his whip into his face. "I'm watching you."

Raul leaned back as if he were alarmed. "Does that mean you don't want to hunt with me today?"

Danel leaned in, breaking Jean-Pierre's concentration. "I've been watching a wild boar for a special occasion."

Jean-Pierre cracked his whip.

Danel leaped back with an agility Jean-Pierre didn't expect, for the blow whistled uselessly through the air.

"Please, my lord, don't hit me!" Danel cowered.

Raul rapped Danel on the head with his knuckles. "I'll hit you instead. Fool!" He turned back to Jean-Pierre. "You know these Moricadians. If you show the slightest bit of leniency, they try to take advantage."

Jean-Pierre glanced around.

Most of Raul's family had slipped away, taking the children. Those who remained stood frozen, wide-eyed and frightened.

They weren't acting, Raul knew. They were terrified, and rightly so.

Jean-Pierre seemed to draw comfort from the familiar cringing forms. "I believe I scared your cook away. And ... sorry about your butler. He wouldn't tell me what I wanted to know." He waved a hand toward the alcove.

A heavy dread settled on Raul.

Signaling to his guard, Jean-Pierre led them out.

When they had cleared the door, Raul ran to the writing desk.

Thompson was nowhere in sight.

Then Raul saw it, leaking out of the tall supply cabinet . . . a trickle of blood that splashed, thick and red, on the wood floor. He yanked open the door.

Thompson fell into his arms—and screamed. Blood stuck his hair together, trickled from cuts along his cheek, his neck, his hands. His cravat had been used as a garrote, and purple bruises circled his neck. "Sorry . . . sir." He gasped the words. "I didn't mean to . . . scream. Not manly . . ."

Raul lifted him.

Thompson screamed again, whimpered, bit his lip. "Sorry, sir. Broken . . . ribs. Didn't realize how much . . . they hurt."

Raul knew. Raul remembered the anguish every breath brought. As carefully as he could, he placed Thompson on the table.

Izba Xaviera got on one side of him, Hada on the other.

Victoria ran away.

Raul didn't blame her. The sight of Thompson wrenched his heart. Thompson wasn't a warrior. He was a butler. And Jean-Pierre had tortured him why?

He'd tormented Thompson just in case. Just for fun.

"Sir." Thompson could barely breathe. "Sir, I didn't tell him . . ."

Raul leaned over the table. "I know you didn't."

"I wanted to tell him. About the weapons in the dungeons. About the training and your plans. But I kept thinking about you, about how your father beat you when you were a lad. The way I beat you on his command. And I knew if you, a little boy, could bear it, I could." Thompson tried to smile. His front teeth were jagged and broken.

Jean-Pierre had used the butt of his pistol on his face.

Victoria returned with a pitcher and bandages, and put them beside Izba Xaviera. "What can I do?" she asked.

"Get the laudanum," Hada said. "Both his arms are dislocated. We've got to put them back in the sockets."

Victoria ran again, but this time, Raul knew she was not running away. She didn't fear the horrors she faced. She would confront them with all the courage in her heart.

"Come on." Danel put his hand on Raul's shoulder. "There's nothing you can do here."

Raul walked with Danel to the window and looked down at his people, gathered in groups in the courtyard, talking and furiously gesturing. "How soon can we put this revolution together?"

Chapter Forty-three

Five days into the training.

The castle was quiet. Raul's and Danel's warriors were in the field, learning to work together, eat together, fight together.

The children had been sent away, scattered among families deep in the forest, out of the line of fire.

Amya had begged for permission to go out and cook for the troops.

Except for Thompson, confined to bed, and the barest of staff, Victoria and Hada were alone in the castle.

They kept busy. They scrubbed out cupboards. They emptied bedrooms, hemmed curtains, mended tapestries, anything to avoid thinking about the revolution, the battles, the injuries and the deaths that would occur while they stayed safe in the castle.

Victoria stayed safe because she was an Englishwoman, untrained in the art of war.

Hada stayed safe because her body had been devas-
tated by de Guignard abuse and she could not fight.

They both suffered an overwhelming and suffocating
sense of dread. They knew of only one way to take their
minds off the coming events—they cleaned.

When it was clear outside, they beat the rugs and the
tapestries until the dust flew, and cleaned the windows
with vinegar and water. When it was damp, they cleaned
the upstairs rooms, rooms Victoria suspected hadn't
been cleaned for generations.

On this day, while rain sheeted the windows and all
the world was gray, they found themselves in the attic, searching for exactly the right hanging to muffle
the empty echo in the upstairs gallery. They worked
their ways through rolls of old carpets and folds of old
drapes.

Victoria had emptied a cupboard, wiped it out, and
now she folded the sheets and blankets, returned them
to the shelves, and talked aloud, blindly, unthinkingly. "I
should leave. Raul said . . . Mr. Lawrence said when the
revolution was ready to start, he would send me away."

"Then you should go." One by one, Hada sorted
through the trunks that stood along the wall. She pulled
out old clothes, old hats, and old shoes. Some pieces she
kept out. Others she put on a rag pile.

"But I promised I would say good-bye to him before
I left." Victoria finished folding and shut the door of the
cupboard.

"You could write him a letter of farewell."

"Yes. I could."

"I'd deliver it."

Victoria considered Hada. "You would?" *The turn-coat!*

"Of course. You are my lady. I live to serve you."

"You're sarcastic."

"No. No, actually, I'm quite sincere."

Their shared situation had made them friends.

But Victoria knew Hada all too well. She wanted Victoria to *think* about a future without Raul, to grieve, to rage, and to resign herself to staying for as long as he wanted her.

Instead, Victoria was determined to leave . . . as soon as she knew he had survived his blasted revolution.

The wind gusted and moaned under the eaves. Victoria and Hada brooded about the misery their comrades suffered out there in the storm, and their guilt built with each crack of thunder.

Hada took the leather handle on the next trunk and tried to drag it toward the window. It didn't move. "This one weighs too much!" she said.

But Hada's old injuries limited her strength, especially on damp days, when her limp was more labored, and when she thought Victoria wasn't looking, she grimaced with pain.

The de Guignards had much to answer for.

So Victoria didn't mind when she had to move the heaviest of items. "Let me." Victoria grabbed the handle and yanked.

She almost fell over. She couldn't budge it.

Hada got on the other side and tried to push while Victoria pulled.

The trunk screeched on the floor and barely moved.

"What's in here?" Victoria asked. "Gold bars?"

The two women looked at the big lock that secured the trunk. They looked at each other.

Excitement rose in Victoria.

Gold bars? Treasure? Could it be true?

Hada jingled the big ring of keys at her waist.

"Can you open the lock?" Victoria asked.

"In the hands of a master, one of these keys will work." Hada leaned against the lid. "I am a master."

"Good to know."

Moving with painful precision, Hada lowered herself to the floor. Kneeling before the trunk, she tried one key after another. Twice she stopped and worked the key in the lock, shook her head, and moved on.

With the seventh key, a click sounded.

The lock slid open.

Hada looked up with a triumphant grin.

Together, they lifted the lid and looked inside. At the top were writing supplies—a pen, a knife, ink, and paper stored on a portable desk.

Victoria lifted them out and set them aside.

Beneath that was a neatly folded man's shirt and trousers, a coat, and a polished pair of well-made black boots.

They were all in the current style, of the finest material and workmanship . . . and Victoria felt a chill of premonition.

Hada removed the clothes and beneath . . . even in the dim light, the gold dazzled their eyes.

Coins. Hundreds of coins.

Victoria picked one up. "French. Forty francs." She swallowed. "Perhaps this is an old, lost stash."

"No." Hada shook her head decisively. "The lid is clean. The ink is wet. The clothes are fashionable."

Victoria looked closely at the coin. "And the coin is newly minted. Whose is this?"

From the doorway, they heard the click of a pistol, and a man's voice said, "Mine."

Chapter Forty-four

The rain had fallen for the last twenty-four hours, an endless deluge of wet that made drill a misery. This noon meal found the men of Danel's unit huddled around one small fire, drinking coffee and eating a watery stew, and Danel stomping up and down, splashing mud with each placement of his big black boot. "Damn that Zakerie. If he went and got himself killed by the de Guignards, I'll chase him clear to hell and make him beg the devil to rescue him from me."

"What if he got himself captured by the de Guignards?" Raul asked.

"Then *they'll* make him sorry," Danel said grimly.

That was the rebels' greatest fear: that one of their people would fall into de Guignard hands, suffer torture, and confess everything they knew.

They'd been lucky so far. With this rain, the de Guignard mercenaries and guards were huddled in Tonagra, leaving Raul's men and women alone to practice warfare.

And practice they did.

They divided up into three sections, one under Raul's command, one under Prospero's command, one under Zakerie's command.

Zakerie's group, the women sharpshooters, practiced in the depths of the woods to hide the sound of their gunfire.

The other two groups mixed and moved according to Danel's orders, learning one another's jobs ("If one of you goes down, the next has to take his place!"), learning hand-to-hand combat from Danel, the dirtiest fighter Raul had ever had the privilege to meet, and learning how to use *anything* as a weapon. As Danel told them, "In the right circumstances, this *mud* can be a weapon. Make it *your* weapon."

Danel didn't subscribe to Raul's kinder policy of training the women in firearms only. "They're good with rifles and with knives, but if they're captured, they need to know where to hit a man and kill him." Danel grinned evilly. "When a guy's got his dick in his hand and rape on his mind, I guarantee he's distracted. A smart woman will hit him in the windpipe and crush it, or smash his nose with the flat of her hand and drive the bone into his brain. Most of these mercenaries don't need a brain, but attack does slow them down."

For the decisive battle, Danel intended to create a distraction and draw de Guignard mercenaries out of the palace and through the narrow pass that led into the city, and slaughter them there. But he had worked out other plans, too, auxiliary plans in case something went wrong.

Raul found himself in awe of Danel's mind. Every possibility and every possible response and Raul's occasional advice based on classical fighting was accepted or batted away according to nothing but merit.

Unfortunately, neither one of them had foreseen this occurrence: Three of the women Zakerie had been training had come in to report that Zakerie had disappeared. To lose one of their commanders now, a man who was deep in their council . . . this was disaster.

Danel sat down to question the women in Zakerie's unit. "When did he disappear?"

After an exchange of glances, the women elected Esti as their spokeswoman. "He was gone this morning out of his tent," she said.

"Did he tell anyone where he was going?"

"No. We thought he was out doing his business." Esti pointed her thumb toward the woods. "Then we wondered if he'd run into a bear. We searched, but found no trace of him. Then we realized his horse was gone. . . ."

Raul and Danel exchanged glances.

So did the three women.

Danel's voice grew sharper. "He was no different last night than usual?"

"He worked us hard yesterday, making sure we knew how to keep our powder dry, telling us to fight the de Guignard mercenaries because we'd be better off dead than to fall into their hands. Thanks to Zakerie, I can shoot the eye out of a squirrel at two hundred paces." Esti shook her head. "I know what you're thinking, sir, but if he's a traitor, why would he train us so well?"

"Someone's coming," the camp lookout said. Then, "*Zakerie's* coming."

"In my tent," Danel told the women. "Don't come out. Don't make a sound."

They ducked low to get inside.

Danel, ever the sarcastic ass, bowed to Raul. "You're the negotiator, my king. Take center stage."

But Raul could handle this. He knew he could. So he bowed back and waited to assess the situation.

Zakerie rode in, waving an arm and calling, "It's awful. I have a message for Saber. It's a tragedy!"

"I'm here!" Raul stepped forward and caught the reins of Zakerie's mare, bringing her to an abrupt halt. "What is it?"

"She ran away again," Zakerie said.

"Who did?" Raul closed his eyes and listened to the tones in Zakerie's voice.

"Miss Victoria Cardiff. She ran away again."

Raul's eyes sprang open and he stood, barely breathing, staring up at his cousin. He didn't need to listen to Zakerie's voice. His soul screamed, *Liar!*

Zakerie continued. "I went after her, but Jean-Pierre caught her. Captured her. My God, he'll rape her, torture her, kill her. Saber, you must go rescue her!"

Raul looked at Danel.

Danel must have read murderous rage in Raul's expression, for he rushed forward. In a tone both jovial and concerned, he said, "For God's sake, Zakerie, get out of the saddle; you're cold and wet."

"I can't stay!" The mare pranced as Zakerie tried to turn her head back in the direction he'd come. "I left my troops to bring you the news, but they're not doing well at all and they need me to drill them."

Liar! Raul's soul screamed again, but he bit down on his anger and fear.

"I insist!" Danel said. "We need the details, where and when you saw Miss Cardiff captured, not to mention the fact that you'll catch your death if you ride back in this downpour." He glanced up at the sky. "In an hour it will clear, and you can return then. I command you, get down!"

All too obviously, Zakerie desperately wanted to ride away, to avoid giving them the details. "My mount needs tending more than I do. I've got a shelter for her in my camp. I'll come back on foot." Under his direction, the mare tried to rear, tried to lift Raul off the ground.

Raul held on, keeping the horse under control. Keeping Zakerie under control.

Zakerie tried again. The mare was getting frantic.

Danel abandoned subtlety and drew his pistol. "I said . . . *get* . . . *down.*"

Zakerie stared at the gun, stared at Danel's grim visage, turned to Raul, blank faced and waiting, and said, "Saber, every minute Miss Cardiff is in Jean-Pierre's hands is one less minute she'll have to live."

"Shoot him," Raul said.

Danel cocked his pistol.

Zakerie froze. "All right. I'll get down. Let me get my saddlebag." He reached behind him, grabbed the leather satchel that hung there, and, as he turned, Danel shot.

Raul released the reins.

The mare reared.

Zakerie grabbed his arm, tumbled backward off the horse and into the mud.

The pistol he'd been retrieving flew into the air.

He'd been planning to shoot Danel. Or Raul.

Danel caught the pistol by the butt and tucked it into his belt. He looked, as he always did, like a brigand and a pirate.

Danel and Raul watched as the mare pranced, her big hooves splashing the mud into the air, and Zakerie scrambled to get out of the way.

When the horse had calmed, one of Danel's men ran to grab the reins.

Zakerie got to his feet, still clutching his arm, and in an imitation of bewilderment, he asked, "What's the problem? What are you accusing me of?" Then, as the three women filed out of Danel's tent, he began to understand. "You can't believe them," he said. "They're *women*."

"Someone's coming," the lookout called again. Then: "It's Hada."

Zakerie's face kindled with fear. He turned to run.

Danel rammed his boot into the back of Zakerie's knee, knocking him flat, and, drawing his sword, he planted himself over him. "I think we should discover why he doesn't want to see her," Danel said.

"I think so." Raul's teeth ached from clenching his jaw.

"Hada's hurt!" The lookout jumped out of the tree and rushed toward the horse.

Hada fell into his arms. "King Saber. I have to talk to the king!" Her gaze fell on Raul and she was speaking even before he reached her side. "It's Zakerie! He has French gold. We found it, Miss Cardiff and I, and he found us. He knocked me out and when I came to—" She took Raul's hand and tears rolled from her eyes. "My king, I beg your pardon; I have failed you. Victoria is gone!"

Raul pressed her fingers. "You could not have saved her."

With her damaged body and the lump on her forehead—a gruesome purple and red—Hada looked like a broken doll. But when Danel picked Zakerie out of the water and shook him like a rat, her eyes caught fire and she struggled to get down. "You! Tell me what you did with her!"

Zakerie fought Danel's hold. "Bitch!"

Raul released his rage.

Where was Victoria?

What had Zakerie done to her?

Advancing on him with murderous intent, Raul seized Zakerie by the back of his neck and slammed his face back into the wide, deep mud puddle. He held his cousin down while he struggled, while the muscles in his back strained and bubbles rose to the surface of the water and popped. Pulling Zakerie's head out of the black water, he shouted, "Where is Victoria Cardiff?"

"She's run away." Zakerie gasped.

"Liar!" Hada limped closer. "Liar!"

Raul dunked him again, leaned against him with the strength of a man possessed by the need for vengeance. Then he brought him up and again demanded, "Where is Miss Cardiff?"

Zakerie gagged and choked. "She's run away."

Raul dunked him again. Let him up again. "Where is Miss Cardiff?"

Zakerie couldn't open his eyes. He spurted mud out his nose. "She ran away," he screamed. "She's a runaway."

"No, she didn't." Raul held the back of Zakerie's neck tight in his grip. "Tell me the truth."

One of the women from Zakerie's unit went back in

Danel's tent and came out with a blanket and wrapped it around Hada's shoulders. She tried to urge her to go in out of the rain, but Hada shook her head. "No. I want Zakerie to tell us where Miss Cardiff is. Then I want to kill him."

Danel sat on a rock, watching the proceedings with fascination. "Tell me, Saber, how do you know your woman didn't run away?"

Raul looked up at his cousin, lowered Zakerie into the mud puddle, and held him there while he thrashed around. "Because she promised me that when she left, she would tell me good-bye."

"You believe her?" Danel asked.

"Yes," Raul said simply.

Danel nodded, then pointed at the hand Raul used to hold Zakerie underwater. "Better pull him out, or he'll be of no use to any of us."

Raul dragged Zakerie out of the mud puddle, pushed on his chest until his eyes rolled open. Leaning down, Raul shouted in his ear, "Where's Miss Cardiff?"

Zakerie gagged and threw up muddy water, but at last he said in a gasp, "I sold her to Jean-Pierre."

It was the answer Raul expected.

It was the answer Raul dreaded.

"Take this piece of garbage." Raul threw him toward Danel. "I have to get ready to ride."

While Raul checked to make sure his powder was dry, that he carried weapons enough to kill every one of the palace guards, Danel pulled his second pistol, pointed it at Zakerie, and said, "Tell us everything."

Zakerie sat there, covered with mud and blood, snarling like a dog that had been kicked one too many times. "I'll tell you. What difference does it make? De Guignard's mercenaries are coming for you now. The French are waiting on the border. When the fighting is almost over and the Moricadian armies are depleted, the French are going to march in and declare that the de Guignards have lost control and take over the country. Because it's a principality, *their* principality. They want Moricadia for the casinos and spas and the money it makes."

"You thought this up? I didn't give you enough credit for cunning." Danel waggled the pistol. "You're family. Why would you sell us out?"

"Why not? I was never in line for the throne. I was never the one everyone fawned over. I was stuck here in the country training a bunch of uneducated bumpkins to fight a revolution they never had a chance of winning. Not even the men—I taught the *women*. Does it get any lower than that?"

His sharpshooters muttered angrily.

"Oh, shut up." He stood up, clutched his arm, scowled. "I trained you well. Saber's forces destroy the de Guignards, the de Guignards destroy Saber's forces, and the French win. *I* win. Why not? What did I have to look forward to? Actually fighting the revolution and getting killed? For you? For them? No. No! I refuse!" He grinned, his teeth white in his mud-covered face. "So, Saber, you can abandon your troops and run after your mistress. You'll be pleased to know she puts up quite a fight, but she never quite had the nerve to challenge me to fire my pistol."

Raul nodded. "Thank you for explaining. I'd never looked at this situation from your point of view before."

The camp froze. Everyone stared at him, aghast.

Danel smiled genially.

Zakerie blinked.

And Raul hit him. Knocked him down, picked him up, and slammed his head against a tree. Letting him go, he watched as Zakerie collapsed, then turned to Danel and said, "Put him in the front line. If he tries to run, shoot him."

Danel saluted.

Using the tree as support, Zakerie got to his feet. "I knew the half-English bastard would abandon his army when it was time to fight."

This time Danel hit him, and when Zakerie went down, Danel put his fat, black-booted foot right in the middle of his neck. Leaning down, he gave a wide, cruel smile. "*King Saber* is going to finish off the de Guignards and rescue his lady. *We're* going to defeat the mercenaries and stump the French."

"What are you going to do with me? Shoot me from behind?" Zakerie spit in defiance.

"No. I wouldn't sully my hands. What I'm going to do is hand you over to the women you taught to shoot and then reviled."

Zakerie's eyes grew wide and horrified.

Danel took his boot away.

Esti replaced it with hers. Leaning over, she said, "Say your prayers, Zakerie, for this is your last day on earth. I guarantee it."

Chapter Forty-five

Hands and feet bound, Victoria sat on an ornate, tall, narrow chair in the Moricadian palace throne room and watched Jean-Pierre give orders to the leader of the mercenaries and to the royal guard. The men stood before the long stone table that almost split the huge chamber in half: Jean-Pierre on one side, his commanders on the other. Maps were spread before them; Jean-Pierre used his whip to point as he spoke.

All three men were armed for war, with weapons stashed on their chests, backs, and belts.

But Victoria was afraid only of Jean-Pierre. Jean-Pierre with those eyes, those pale blue, spooky eyes that made her wonder at the demon inside.

"The rebels have no choice but to bring their cavalry

along the road to Tonagra. Stop them there." His voice was low-pitched and genial.

The mercenary general, a hulking Prussian with white-blond hair, blue eyes, and fists as big as hams, said, "I'll have my troops in place within the hour."

"There are two men to watch for, the leaders of the rebellion. One is young and handsome, quite the lover of the ladies." Jean-Pierre glanced at Victoria, smiling with smooth pleasure. "You've met him, the gambler Raul Lawrence. The peasants think he's their dispossessed king. Kill him first."

She stared back at him, cold and unwilling to let him see her turmoil and terror.

But he knew. Of course he knew. "The traitor who brought the girl said there are women trained to shoot rifles from the treetops, to bring down your men from a distance. Put your shooters to work knocking that female fruit from my trees. When their women are screaming and dying, that will take the heart out of the rebels fast enough."

The ropes cut into Victoria's wrists and ankles. Her fingers were cold, numb, but at the thought of so many of her friends falling, bleeding, she clenched her fists in anguish.

The general grimaced. "I don't know if my men will shoot the women. They like to rape them first."

"Your men will do what they're paid to do," Jean-Pierre said.

"Of course. I'll make sure of it." The general bowed low. "I will die before I fail you."

"Those *are* your two choices," Jean-Pierre said.

The general flinched and bowed again, then scurried, if such a large man could be said to scurry, out the door.

Victoria heard him bellowing his orders.

She took a long breath, fighting to stay calm, brave, unmoved.

Nothing had happened to her yet, and some unconquerable belief in herself and in Raul kept her seeking a way out.

On the far end of the throne room, a tall set of carved double doors opened into the huge, echoing room. Fifty feet away on the other end, an ancient-looking wooden throne rested on a raised dais. There beside the throne, Jean-Pierre had placed Victoria's chair while mocking her aspirations as queen. Between the two ends were polished white marble floors, high windows down each wall, medieval tapestries, and dark metal suits of armor. A fireplace so large Victoria could have stood upright within it held reign in the middle of one side wall, and gargoyles leered from the mantel. Huge oak columns supported the curved beams dark with the smoke of thousands of fires, and colorful heraldic banners hung from the ceiling.

One banner hung behind the throne, and Victoria's gaze lingered on it. She recognized that device, remembered it all too well.

The leader of the royal guard was not so tall as the Prussian, but thin as a whippet, with long white teeth and dark, hostile eyes.

Jean-Pierre turned to him. "You're Moricadian, Bittor. You probably want the rebels to succeed."

"I follow you, Jean-Pierre. You give me what I want." Bittor spoke slowly, enunciating each word as if it required concentration. "Women. A place to kill them slowly. And somewhere to hide the bodies where the smell doesn't bother anyone except your prisoners." His gaze fastened on Victoria and he examined her as if she were nothing more than a pig to be butchered.

Horror closed Victoria's throat.

"Occasionally I enjoy a few minutes of recreation with you, isn't that right, Bittor?" Jean-Pierre asked.

Bittor swallowed and shuddered. "You are very inventive, my leader."

So the rumors were true. Jean-Pierre was the worst of a clan of degenerates and killers.

With a speed that made Victoria recoil, Jean-Pierre lifted his whip and slashed Bittor across the face. "Then why have you not ferreted out the truth about the spies Lawrence has put in place?"

Bittor wiped the blood off his face.

"Maids in the hotels! Servants in the palace! Traitors everywhere! Their heads are still on their shoulders! Their guts are still in their bellies! Find them! Bring them! And I will cut off their hands and feast on their tongues!"

Victoria wanted to vomit. She vividly remembered the torment Jean-Pierre had visited on Thompson. She knew Jean-Pierre intended to torture her until she told him everything there was to know about Raul and his operations. She knew she hadn't a chance of escape or rescue.

Her gaze returned to the banner behind the throne. Although . . . perhaps she could rescue herself, after all.

Jean-Pierre waved Bittor out the door, then turned to her. With a mocking bow, he said, "What an honor to have the new king's whore in the old king's throne room."

Funny. She was in terror for her life, and still, hearing

the accusation of "whore" for the first time cut her to the quick. Was that what her stepfather would say on hearing of her death here? What would he tell her mother? *Thank God she's dead, or she would have brought disgrace on us all with her wanton ways.*

"Do you know what that is?" Jean-Pierre pointed at the suit of armor closest to the throne. "It's said that it was King Reynaldo's armor. It's a bit of a shrine for the Moricadians. The maids polish it with special care. The men touch it for luck. I love to watch them in their surreptitious reverence. Do you know why, Miss Cardiff?"

Wide-eyed, she shook her head.

"Because that's not really his armor." He pointed his whip at the suit that stood in the middle of the row. "That's Reynaldo's armor." He chuckled with pure delight. "The armor to which they're so devoted is my ancestor's. You have to admit it's amusing to think of two hundred years of peasant fidelity given to the de Guignard count who betrayed, tortured, and beheaded Reynaldo."

"It's childish," she said.

"That the peasants are worshipping at the wrong shrine?"

"No, that the wealthy, privileged de Guignards care to play such a joke on people who have so little."

Like a dog about to attack, one side of Jean-Pierre's lip lifted, showing his teeth, and his pale eyes turned almost white.

But no! She had a plan, and she couldn't allow this rabid wolf-man to assault her. Not yet. Not until she had tried to liberate herself. "That banner behind the throne—is that symbolic of your family?"

She had the satisfaction of knowing she had startled Jean-Pierre. "Conversation, Miss Cardiff?"

"Not at all. An honest inquiry. I've seen that emblem before."

"Of course you have." Color returned to his eyes, and he looked almost human again. "It hangs in all the public buildings."

"Not the hotel, though, and I was so briefly in Tonagra I had no time to see anything else. No, I saw that in an account book. My employer had orders to transfer the funds in that book out of this country and into a bank in Switzerland."

She hadn't expected Jean-Pierre to look so startled. "What?" he snapped.

She repeated, "My employer had orders to transfer the funds in the book out of this country and into a bank in Switzerland. So now I wonder—is it you he was working for?"

Jean-Pierre sprang forward so quickly, she slammed her head hard against the high-backed, sturdy chair. But he had her by the throat before she knew what had happened. "You lie," he said.

She shook her head and tried to speak.

He squeezed hard, cutting off her air.

She struggled, convulsing, trying to free herself from him.

"You lie," he said again.

Red spots swam before her eyes.

He let her go. "Tell me the truth now."

She gasped, gasped again.

He reached for her.

Somehow she found her voice and rasped, "No lie. Saw the books. Learned the trade. Am good with accounting. Was going to offer to do the work for you. For freedom."

He stared at her.

He had no reason to be breathing so hard, for his face to be so ruddy and his mouth to hang open as if he were adding two and two and getting five.

He spoke to himself, muttering under his breath. "So. He would do that. *To me.* Yes. Of course he would."

Victoria didn't understand what was happening. She knew only that she had somehow miscalculated, that he was mad—and she was under his control.

"Stay here." He looked down at her tied to the chair, laughed harshly, walked out the doors, and slammed them behind him.

Victoria sat in the eerily silent and empty palace . . . alone and helpless.

Chapter Forty-six

As soon as Jean-Pierre left the chamber, Victoria tried to hop up and down, to propel the chair close to one of the suits of armor, for there a sharp sword gleamed. If she could cut her bonds . . .

But with the horsehair-padded seat and massive embroidery decoration, the tall wooden chair easily weighed one hundred pounds. She couldn't budge it. She tried until she was sweating and trembling, but it never moved.

Why had Jean-Pierre put her in the throne room? She should be in the dungeon or in a bedroom, where she could be raped at Jean-Pierre's leisure, not tied to a chair close to the throne in the most royal chamber of Moricadia.

Then she looked around at the grandeur, the imposing sense of royalty, and was humbled. She was nothing more than bait to catch King Saber. Jean-Pierre intended to lure Raul here and kill him, and forever end the Moricadians' hope for a fair future.

And she couldn't do anything to help Raul, destroy Jean-Pierre, or save herself.

She slumped and closed her eyes in despair.

But when she heard herself whimper, the sound echoing across the marble floor and up toward the ceiling, she straightened and opened her eyes. She would not give up. She had to assume—hope—that Jean-Pierre would release her at some point. Perhaps she could goad him, excite him with the thrill of the chase. In that case, she would need to quickly seize a weapon.

And there were weapons aplenty. Firearms hung on the walls, shiny and bright, rifles and pistols. But she dismissed them as possibilities; although she had shooting experience, she didn't dare depend on their being loaded.

Crossed swords and knives hung there, too. Unfortunately, she hadn't lied when she said she had no experience with swords. She had swung one once in her life, to separate Raul's and Danel's wrists. With a sword, she was likely to hurt only herself.

She'd have better luck handling a knife, but her arms were shorter than Jean-Pierre's and she'd be killed before she could swing.

Of course, she'd seen the pistols on his belt. She'd never have a chance, anyway.

But she didn't know how to die, didn't want to die while Raul was alive. So she had to try to live.

When she heard a quiet footstep in the corridor, she tensed in fear, her gaze glued to the open door.

Then . . . Raul stepped in. Raul, wet and muddy, grim and determined, with a pistol in one hand and an arsenal of weapons strapped on his chest and belt.

She withered in the chair, and tears of relief sprang to her eyes.

She had never seen anything look so good.

She was alive.

He was alive.

Together they could beat any odds.

If he was happy to see her, she couldn't tell.

But she was happy enough for them both.

With a glance, he assessed the situation, signaled for silence, and hurried to her side. Putting his pistol on the floor beside him, he pulled a knife from his belt and went to work on the ropes that bound her.

"I love you," she whispered.

He nodded, concentrating on his knife and the ropes.

"How did you get in? Did you have to fight?" She kept her voice low.

"Two hundred years ago, my family lived here. We have always known all the secret passageways." He glanced up at her, his voice as quiet as hers. "And there are no guards or servants to be found anywhere. They know the storm is upon us, and they are hiding."

"Yes." When her hands were free, she touched his face. "I truly love you."

He glanced toward the door, cocked his head, and listened. Helping her to her feet and giving her one of his pistols, he said, "Get out."

"No." She shook her head. "Come with me."

"I'm on a hunting expedition."

"No." She tried to hand him back his pistol. "Together we have a better chance of escaping."

"I will finish off the de Guignards here and now. It is time for this to be over. It's time to avenge my mother's death ... every Moricadian death." His green eyes were cold and flat. "I can't do that if I have to worry about you."

But you're going to die. You're going to die! Her own voice screamed the words in her head, but she couldn't say them. She knew what he had to do. She even understood it.

He placed the pistol back in her hand. "Shoot anyone who tries to stop you."

But before she could make her decision—stay or leave—a voice spoke from the door. "If only it was going to be that easy."

Jean-Pierre. His rifle was pressed against his shoulder, pointed at Raul. He was going to kill Raul.

Victoria didn't even think. In one smooth motion, she cocked the pistol, lifted it, and shot.

The bullet hurtled fifty feet, from one end of the throne room to the other, and struck at the rifle's wooden butt, blowing splinters into Jean-Pierre's face. The rifle roared, but the shot went wild. Jean-Pierre threw the weapon aside.

Raul sprang across the table and charged.

Jean-Pierre scratched at his injured eyes and reached for his pistol.

Raul plowed into him.

The two men slammed to the floor and slid across the slick white marble, the pistol rolling end over end into the corridor. Raul landed on top, hit Jean-Pierre under the chin, smashed his head to the floor.

Jean-Pierre went limp.

Raul shouted to Victoria, "Get out. Shut the doors. Get away!"

She ran to do what he wanted . . . or at least, some of what he wanted.

He turned back to Jean-Pierre. "This is between him and me."

But he'd lost the advantage.

Jean-Pierre came off the floor and rammed Raul into a suit of armor.

Metal screeched, clattered, and thundered in a storm of ironclad hail.

Raul seized a breastplate and slapped Jean-Pierre across the side of the head.

The metal rang like a bell.

Jean-Pierre's head quivered and he dropped flat on his back.

Victoria slammed the doors shut and slid the defensive wooden bar into the ancient iron brackets.

She wiped the rust off her hands onto her skirt. She was no fool. With the bar in place, Raul could fight Jean-Pierre without the interference of the palace guard. She would see this fight to its end. She could not simply leave Raul to his fate.

Raul flipped the breastplate and swung it, sharp edge out, ready to slice Jean-Pierre in half.

Jean-Pierre rolled away and pulled his sword. He slashed, low and fast.

Raul leaped up and back, and when he landed, he had his knife in his hand. He threw.

Jean-Pierre parried, smacking the knife out of the air.

It skittered across the floor—but blood poured from Jean-Pierre's hand.

The knife had taken its toll.

Victoria couldn't see exactly what had happened, but Raul said, "You won't need that finger."

"You don't need your head." Jean-Pierre swung with both hands.

Victoria slapped her palms across her mouth to cover her scream.

Raul pitched himself backward into another suit of armor.

The suits went down like dominoes, one after another, clattering against the marble columns, floor, walls, in a cacophony of screeching metal that went on and on.

Raul disappeared behind a pile of armor and came up with an antique saber from the rubble, short and curved with a wide, wicked blade.

Jean-Pierre leaped the armor and the men's blades met, the clang somehow clear above the ruckus of falling armor.

And they fought.

This wasn't like the fight between Raul and Danel, the fight between two worthy adversaries. This was ugly and desperate and the outcome would decide the fate of this nation—and of Victoria Cardiff. For if Raul died, she would die, too. She would not once again tamely fall into Jean-Pierre's hands.

When he came for her, she would be ready. This time, she would kill him, and when she had finished, she would escape. Somehow, she would escape, either into the arid life of a withered spinster . . . or into the grave.

Jean-Pierre moved with the grace of a well-practiced warrior; he handled his long sword with its stabbing point with a skill that tore tiny pieces from Raul's flesh.

Raul retreated, blood flowing from a dozen wounds.

Victoria wanted to scream a warning. Instead she ran to the wall and tore down the closest set of pistols. They were not loaded.

She ran to the rifle. Not loaded.

She stood breathing hard. The de Guignards must have lived in fear of assassination. *None* of these weapons were loaded.

And Jean-Pierre was working Raul into a corner.

Raul stumbled on a piece of armor.

Jean-Pierre laughed and went for the kill.

Raul kicked the armor under Jean-Pierre's feet, then swung his wide, curved, single-edged blade; it sang through the air and broke Jean-Pierre's sword in two.

Now the men fought on even terms, teeth bared, sweat flying, in silence, their hatred tangible, tasting sour, smelling rotten.

When Jean-Pierre dropped his sword and went down on one knee, Victoria clapped her hands.

When he came up with a pistol, she screamed a warning.

Raul's blade sang through the air, and the pistol was on the floor, Jean-Pierre's hand with it.

Jean-Pierre lifted the stump of his arm and stared at the blood spurting from it; then with the snarl of a wounded badger, he leaped at Raul.

Raul brought the point of the short, curved saber up into Jean-Pierre's belly, up to his breastbone, and then through his heart. As they were face-to-face, two adversaries at last at an end, Raul asked, "Do you recognize me now?"

Jean-Pierre hung there, staring at Raul's features, recollection lending a last light to his eyes. "The boy . . ." He gasped, and blood trickled from his lips. "The one who ... so many years ago destroyed ... the de Guignard picnic?"

"You do recognize me." Raul nodded and smiled.

With his remaining hand, Jean-Pierre clawed for Raul's throat. But before he could reach his goal, his arm dropped as if it was too heavy. He collapsed onto the floor, the last breath of life rattled in his throat ... and he died.

Chest heaving, splattered in blood, Raul pulled the sword free of Jean-Pierre de Guignard's body. Raul wiped the blade on his shirt, then stood, looking down at his last, best adversary. "It's over," he said. "At last. Two hundred years later. It's over." Lifting his head, he looked at Victoria.

Tears filled her eyes—tears of gratification at his accomplishment—but she wiped her hands across her wet cheeks and nodded. "Yes. It's over. You've done what you came to do."

Raul strode through the scattered pieces of armor, kicking chain mail and jointed knee pieces and breastplates aside to reach her. Taking her head in his hands, he looked at her, just looked at her, as if trying to see with his eyes, his mind, his heart that she was still alive.

Then he kissed her, wildly, passionately, claiming her lips and her mouth, erasing the memory of her anxiety, humiliation, and enslavement at the hands of Zakerie and Jean-Pierre.

He was what she needed, for she forgot everything but him—his heat, his scent, his breath in her mouth, and his hands on her body. He was alive.

They were alive.

Apparently that kiss was what he needed, too, for when he lifted his head, he was smiling faintly. "We've won. We've won the palace, but now I have to go back to the battlefield and win again."

"No." She stroked his hair back from his face. "No, stay with me. Be safe." Immediately she realized that was the wrong tack to take. "Stay with me and keep me safe."

He grinned. He was not so easily fooled. "You, my darling, can take care of yourself. How many times have you proved that?"

"Never," she said in a small, feminine voice.

"It's too late for that. You can't fool me now. After you shot that rifle out of Jean-Pierre's hand, I should have shot him, too. But I had only a pistol, so I had to jump him—my accuracy isn't nearly as good as yours." He laughed as if even now he was astonished by her precision. "You have an amazing eye!"

"I hate to disillusion you, but I wasn't trying to shoot the rifle out of his hand. I was trying to shoot him through the heart."

He laughed again. "You are a remarkable woman."

Yes, but even when you were freeing me from my bonds and I told you I loved you, you didn't offer your love. Even when it was likely we would both die, you didn't offer your love.

But she didn't say that. There was no point.

He kissed her again, and this time he was tender, sweet, breathing her in as if she were his life force.

"We will survive this, won't we?" She lightly touched his still-bleeding wounds suffered in the fight.

"We have won the most important battle," he said. "Together, we won."

Her heart felt as if it expanded in her chest. She smiled tremulously.

He smiled back; his green eyes kindled, and in them she read pride, warmth, devotion, even . . . love?

They were saying things without words, important things, and for the first time she began to hope that, even if he could not speak of his feelings, he *felt* the emotion that filled her.

"Victoria . . ." He traced the curve of her face with his fingertips. "When I was a child, I left behind the warmth of my mother's arms and the wisdom of my grandfather, and came to cold, damp England to live with my father. The first months there, I thought I would die from loneliness and despair, but I clung to the thought that someday I would return to Moricadia and see them again. When they died, when my father . . . discouraged . . . my mourning, I felt as if I'd had a limb amputated. Or my heart cut out."

"Raul . . ." She touched his hair, and wished for the words that could heal him. "I am so sorry."

"I can't give you what I don't have, and I know you believe that England is the only civilized place in the world, and perhaps it is, but, Victoria . . ." He gathered her hands in his. "Victoria . . ."

Boom! Something slammed into the doors to the throne room.

Victoria jumped, stared in that direction.

Boom! The doors swayed and creaked. *Boom!*

"Battering ram," Raul said.

Now? she wanted to scream at the attackers on the other side. *Now? You're interrupting him now?*

Boom! The glass rattled in the high windows.

But sensible Victoria recognized the danger and gave Raul the information to win this fight. "The bar is oak, but very old. The brackets are iron, and also old. It's not going to hold forever."

Leaning over Jean-Pierre's corpse, Raul pulled a pistol off the body and handed it to her.

She checked to see that it was loaded. It was. She nodded.

Boom! The broken masses of armor shivered.

He slid a knife from his boot, pulled the sword from Jean-Pierre's chest.

Boom!

Raul stood in the midst of a gory field of battle, sweat stained, covered in blood, angry, and focused, holding an ancient sword and ready to fight.

She picked up a shield and handed it to him. "No matter what happens, you are always and forever my hero. And I promise to use my shot wisely."

He showed her one wicked, buccaneer smile. "A queen by every definition."

It was a proposal of sorts.

He faced forward.

Boom! The bar broke. The doors smacked the walls.

The palace guard marched in, weapons at ready, Bittor in the lead.

The guard stared at Raul and Victoria.

They stared at Jean-Pierre's broken corpse.

Bittor growled, a deep-throated sound like a pit bull at a dog fight. His bloodshot eyes fixed on Raul. "I will kill you!" He charged into the room.

Victoria took a terrified breath.

Raul lifted his shield and his sword.

And one of the guard said, "Hail, King Saber of Moricadia!"

Bittor swiveled to face them. "*What* did you say?"

The whole guard wavered, then more loudly: "Hail, King Saber of Moricadia!"

"I'll kill you all!" Bittor lifted his hands and lumbered toward them.

In one unified motion, the guards lifted their rifles, pointed at Bittor, and fired.

A blast, and Bittor fell, riddled with bullets.

With their rifles still at their shoulders, the guards stood, staring down at Bittor's broken body. Then like a welcome rain over a barren landscape, their grins broke out and they cheered, "Hail, King Saber of Moricadia!"

Chapter Forty-seven

When French commander François strode into the throne room in the palace in Tonagra, he walked into a methodical bustle and a buzz of low-voiced conversations. The courtiers, a well-dressed and organized bunch, scrutinized him, bowed, and went back to their business in a most civilized manner. One badly wounded fellow—he looked pale and English—sat close to the roaring fire, speaking to an elderly, black-gowned Moricadian widow who hovered over him.

Except for a few lopsided suits of armor propped against the wall, the chamber was large, clean, and orderly.

One gentleman, handsome and well dressed, with dark hair and striking green eyes, stepped away from the very attractive young woman to whom he was speaking, away from the account books spread out on the table, and strode forward. "General François, welcome to my court, and how good of you to be the first person to welcome me back to the throne of my country!"

So. This was Saber. The purported king sported a few injuries from his fight the day before. The fight in which, it was rumored, he had killed Jean-Pierre de Guignard. But all in all, he seemed healthy and far too young to be the ruler of such a wealthy country with so many resources.

Yet here he was.

François, who had this very morning ridden with his troops into the country and the city without seeing any sign of the disruption he had expected, strode forward to embrace Saber. The two men touched cheeks while François struggled to deal with this unexpected situation. "Welcome indeed. I didn't realize you would establish superiority so quickly." He was perhaps abrupt, but he was a soldier, not an ambassador.

Saber laughed and waved the maid forward. When she brought wine and poured it, he said, "Thank you, Amya." The girl curtsied—she was obviously used to service—and departed. Saber offered a goblet to the general and took one for himself, then answered with equal straightforwardness. "Except for a brief hiatus of a few hundred years involving the de Guignards, Moricadia is my family's country. With the de Guignards dead, the French principality is at an end, and with all the accumulated wealth of the country in my hands, there's no doubt who will sit on the throne."

Saber's first intention, obviously, was to clearly inform François that he had secured all Moricadia's money in an unassailable account.

That was bad news, very bad news indeed.

So François sought a reason to doubt Saber. He was, after all, here to conquer Moricadia, not to confirm diplomatic relations. "What about the rumors that your cousin is challenging you for control of the throne?"

"I assume you mean my cousin Danel. Because sadly my other cousin, Zakerie, was killed in action yesterday." Saber's face was untouched by grief.

"I am sorry for your loss," François mumbled.

Saber continued. "Of course, Zakerie was merely a distant cousin, never more than a footnote in our councils."

Another message to François—*If you trusted Zakerie, you were a fool.*

A handsome man, a soldier by the looks of him, walked through the doors and across the floor. He carried a satin pillow and on it a short, curved saber, and he came at once to Saber and knelt at his feet.

The room grew silent with the reverence François associated with a church.

The fellow began to speak the gobbledygook that was the native tongue.

But Saber shook his head. "In French, please, Prospero. We have a guest."

"My king, your sword has been cleaned and is awaiting your hand." The man's French was execrable, but François understood that the gist of his message.

Saber's face settled into an expression of fierce satisfaction. "The blade was not harmed by its time spent in Jean-Pierre de Guignard's heart?"

"I would say it was much improved," Prospero said.

Saber's hand settled onto the plain iron hilt. His

knuckles tightened as he lifted the saber from the pillow and held it with an almost heathen pleasure.

The man Prospero stood, bowed, and backed away.

The sword itself was plain, undecorated, and functional, but François's hands itched to touch it. "I know a bit about swords. This scimitar is of the type carried by the conquerors of old."

"This was carried by Attila, stolen by his concubine, brought here to the wilderness to found this country of Moricadia. Unbeknownst to my family, it was hidden in Reynaldo's suit of armor and revealed to me only yesterday." Without warning, Saber slashed the air.

François jumped back.

But the blade sang with contentment.

Prospero said, "This sword knows the hand of its master."

Saber summoned him and returned the blade to the pillow. "Thank you." He placed his hand on Prospero's shoulder. "How is Hada this morning?"

"Better, knowing her friends executed their duties well enough to make the mercenaries turn tail and run."

Saber turned back to François. "Our women fought from the treetops with rifles, and suffered only one injury in the battle—a broken arm when one of our Amazons fell from her perch."

Horrified, François asked, "You use women as soldiers?"

"Our women are fierce in the defense of their homes and families," Saber answered.

François looked around at the throne room, seeing the people in it with new eyes. Perhaps this cover of civilization was thin. Perhaps the battle that he had envisioned would not have been as brief and easily won as he'd hoped.

Prospero spoke again, raising his voice for all to hear. "Hada was also much recovered when she heard Zakerie died fighting for our cause."

From the center of a group of soldiers, someone snorted.

Prospero grinned.

Saber grinned, too, but with remembered rage. "It's good he redeemed his honor at the end. Of course, he had no choice." Turning, he called, "Danel! Our friend General François would like to meet you."

The bandy-legged, shifty-eyed fellow who strode forward bore no resemblance to the handsome Saber except in his air of authority, which he wore like a well-accustomed cloak.

"Danel, General François of our visiting French troops. General, my cousin Danel, the winner of yesterday's battle against the de Guignard mercenaries." Clearly at ease, Saber leaned against the table and crossed his arms over his chest. "Danel, the general is worried that we disagree on who should occupy the Moricadian throne."

Danel threw back his head and roared with laughter. "No, General, I understand why you'd think that. I am, after all, of the two of us the more kingly." Wrapping his arm around Saber, he grinned a black-toothed smile. "If I'd wanted the throne, I would have taken it, but as you can tell, I'm a soldier like you, and haven't the political skills to serve as king. No, Saber is the head of our family and Moricadia's ruler. All we have left to do is arrange the coronation."

"I think we must do it soon. While I would like to wait until spring and invite my fellow rulers to attend, the people want the security of a king on the throne once more. I was just discussing the funding of such a huge event with my head of finance." Saber smiled at the beautiful young woman. "Miss Cardiff is a genius in the use and control of money. I'm grateful to have her on my team."

The name was a shock to François. "Miss Cardiff? Miss Cardiff is your . . . employee?" According to the spy Zakerie, Miss Cardiff was Saber's inamorata.

"Of course." Saber appeared to comprehend François's bewilderment. "Ah, you're taken aback because I've included a lady in my government. I do realize it's uncommon for one of the delicate gender to work with the evil that is money, but she learned her trade from her employer, Mr. Johnson, a most accomplished comptroller. While he was here on an assignment for Prince Sandre, I lured her away with promises of wealth."

"Being a very practical woman, I accepted." Miss Cardiff's voice was warm and throaty, but François noted that she wore clothes more appropriate to a governess than a royal mistress.

All through this meeting, the French general had become more and more certain that his informant had been a liar, and he himself a fool for believing him. In this case, François was without recourse. He could not declare Moricadia unstable and deserving of annexation, especially when the presence of so many of Saber's troops made a conquest quite impossible and the money the French government desired impregnable.

And since he could not see any way to ask for the return of the small fortune he'd paid Zakerie, it would appear that money was gone.

Saber placed his arm around François's shoulders and walked him toward the door. "As much as I've enjoyed this discussion with you, I find another appointment awaits me. Why don't I give you over to my majordomo to discuss where you and your troops should stay—at my expense, of course—and which casinos would most welcome your presence."

It was a most agreeable proposition. François recognized the wisdom of that course of action and, with a respectful bow, he went on his way.

This would be a pleasant and unexpected vacation.

Raul gave François a comradely slap on the shoulder and handed him over to the Hôtel de Tonagra's concierge, then listened to the thump of the French general's boot heels as the old blowhard marched down the corridor away from the throne room.

Thompson, Danel, Prospero, the family, the palace guards, the servants . . . they all remained, barely breathing, staring at the doors as if afraid to believe they had pulled this off.

When the noise had faded, Raul walked to the great doors, battered but still intact, and shut them. As the latch clicked, he turned to face his people. In a composed voice, he said, "General François would be startled to know that he is paying for his room with the gold he used to bribe Zakerie." And he grinned.

Victoria smiled.

Danel chuckled.

The whole room erupted in jubilation.

They had won.

They had won everything—the battle against the mercenaries, the control of the government, the end of the de Guignards' oppression. The prisoners in the dungeon were freed, Raul would control the hotels and gambling houses and keep the money in his country, and his people would be free and well fed once again.

There would be challenges; everyone knew it.

But the fact remained—*they had won.*

His people had won!

Raul opened his arms.

Danel, Hada, Prospero surged forward. He embraced them, embraced Amya, embraced everyone in his family, both his blood kin and his extended kin. He went to Thompson, still broken but unbowed, and embraced him. He embraced Izba Xaviera.

He embraced them because these were the people who had made his dreams and the dreams of his people come true.

But he was working his way toward Victoria. Everyone knew it. Everyone was glad.

Since the day he had kidnapped her and carried her to his castle, she had won their hearts with her indomitable spirit, her kindness, her knowledge, and her bravery. No matter how much they doubted her—because she was a foreigner, because she looked soft, because she was gently spoken—she had proved herself over and over, and won *all* their hearts.

Had she won his?

No. No. Surely not. His father had early on beaten the emotion out of him. He'd been trying to tell her that, and he knew she understood him.

But he could give her so much. She was a practical woman. She would want what he had.

Yet before he reached her, one of the great doors opened.

An Englishman, a big, barrel-chested man with a florid face, stepped inside.

Victoria stopped laughing, stopped clapping, stopped cheering, and stared at the man as if he were an apparition.

Raul's blood ran cold. He recognized him. He recognized him all too well, and he knew what his appearance represented to Victoria.

The gentleman's stern expression made the merriment die one celebrant at a time. As the commotion faded, he said, "I've come to free Miss Victoria Cardiff from your villainous clutches. Please don't make the mistake of telling me I can't have her. I would hate to take action against this crown."

Victoria stood beside the table, her spine straight, her blue eyes shining with tears. In hushed tones, she said, "Mr. Johnson . . . Mr. Johnson, you came back for me."

Chapter Forty-eight

Stars blazed in the black mountain sky. The bonfire crackled and roared. The scent of wood smoke mingled with the dirty-sock smell of pipe tobacco, and the guitar and drum mixed with the voices of a dozen men roaring out a song about a lonely woman in a field of flowers.

It was not a refined tune.

This was not a refined gathering.

At the first lull in the flurry of Raul's new reign, Danel, Prospero, and Thompson had gathered the men closest to their new king and carried him away into the forest to mourn Victoria's departure to England in a properly drunken bacchanal. The ale and wine flowed freely. They ate fresh-roasted venison and bread with honey and dried berries. They danced around the fire and laughed uproariously when Danel tripped, then helped him up and danced again.

Now the men had settled down to sing, and one by one they fell asleep until only Danel, Prospero, and Raul were left, poking sticks into the fire and talking glumly about Raul's prospects for the future.

"You have to get married. I mean, you know ... in a church with an archbishop and flowers. Not like ..." Danel waved his hand vaguely around at the forest.

"No," Raul answered.

"You're the king," Danel insisted. "The succession falls on you."

"Danel, you're his cousin," Prospero pointed out. "Your son could inherit."

"It's my curse that all women want to bed me but the one who matters will not marry me." Danel wagged his shaggy head in despair.

"Celesta won't marry you?" Prospero asked.

"Smart woman," Raul said.

Prospero snorted.

"Not unless I promise to cleave to her. And that woman can smell a falsehood a mile off. No." Danel sighed. "It's up to Saber to make the next king. Some beautiful young princess from Upper Bruskonia would be thrilled to marry a handsome young bridegroom."

"No," Raul said.

"Where's Upper Bruskonia?" Prospero asked.

"It's a country I made up," Danel answered.

"No," Raul repeated. "It's Victoria or no one."

The two men stared at Raul morosely.

"You're not a man who's meant to live alone." Danel threw his stick in the fire.

Raul appreciated their concern, but—"I'm fine.

Aren't I fine? Aren't I handling my duties well? Aren't I distributing food and helping farmers and welcoming rich visitors and greeting visiting heads of state?"

"You are." Prospero jumped to his feet, shook his legs, and swatted at his butt. "Damn ants."

Raul laughed. See? He could still laugh. He *was* fine.

"Gotta get rid of these." Prospero headed for the forest, dropping his drawers as he went. They got a flash of bare ass that made Danel flinch.

Raul saw a chance to change the subject, stood up, and headed into the woods in a different direction. "Gotta piss," he said.

"Might as well." Much to the objection of one of the lighter sleepers, Danel staggered only as far as the edge of the clearing.

When they were finished, the three men reassembled at the fire.

Raul stretched. "Guess I'll get in my blankets."

"Oh, no, you don't, Your Majesty." Prospero and Danel took him by the arms and sat him back down.

Raul sighed. "Remember England? Cold, rainy, miserable England? Remember how I had to go to England when I was eleven all by myself? I'm used to being alone. I can handle this. I'm fine."

"Yeah, we can all tell." Danel tossed some new logs on the embers.

Raul watched as the sparks flew up and nestled among the stars . . . and wondered if the stars were out in England, or if the autumn rains had set in.

"I don't understand women." Danel seated himself. "I thought Miss Cardiff loved you."

"Hell, *Hada* thought she loved him." Prospero nodded wisely. "And she knows this stuff."

"My women thought so, too."

"Then for her to leave ... like that ... as soon as that interfering bastard Johnson showed up ..." Prospero picked up the pitcher of ale and took a drink.

"You're not supposed to drink out of the pitcher. Give me that!" Raul took it, then figured, *What the hell?*, swallowed the bitter brew, and passed it to Danel.

Danel drank, wiped his chin, and asked, "What did she say? Saber, when she left, what excuse did she give?"

Raul didn't want to talk about this. The memory of Victoria's departure a month ago, on that very afternoon when Mr. Johnson had appeared in the throne room ... it had left him bruised, bleak, and disbelieving. As he had told her during the ownership ceremony, the rope was tied tightly so that if it were cut, they would both bleed.

He didn't know if she was bleeding, but he was. "She said she loved me." Danel still held the pitcher, so Raul groped for the wineskin and drank for a long time, knowing no amount of alcohol could dissolve his misery.

"What did she say when you said you loved her? Did she not realize the honor you bestowed on her?" Prospero waxed indignant. And belched. He pressed his fist to his belly, grinned, and belched again, loud enough to make the sleeping men rumble with discontent. Turning his head to the west, he shook his fist and shouted, "Take that, you skinny Englishwoman who didn't think our king was good enough for you!"

"Not bad manners, just good ale." Danel poked Prospero in the ribs.

Both men dissolved in laughter. And sobered again. Like two bulldogs with their jaws clenched on their unwilling prey, they got back to their questions.

"Okay." Prospero propped his elbow on his knee, put his fist under his chin, and stared fixedly at Raul. "So when you said, 'I love you,' what did she say?"

"I didn't tell her." Terse. To the point. Raul congratulated himself.

The two men turned as if their butts were attached on metal springs. They bobbed for a minute; then Prospero exploded. "You *didn't tell her*?"

"She loves England. She thinks it's the only civilized place on earth."

"She gave you up for *England*?" Prospero sounded incredulous.

"No. Not for England. For other reasons. It's complicated. She doesn't want to be married because of her stepfather, who was cruel to her mother." The truth. Saber was glad for knowing it.

"You *didn't tell her*?" For a confirmed bachelor, Danel seemed completely and totally indignant.

Remembering how he had grabbed her wrist, dragged her to an antechamber, and confronted her about her intentions made Raul feel sick. Because she'd told him again that she loved him. And then he . . . "I tried to tell her what she meant to me. She's my equal—no, my better!—in intelligence, wit, in the way she handles people . . . and the children! They love her."

"You told her you like the way she handles people?" Danel slapped his forehead.

"I told her there was no other woman for me in bed, too!"

The two men looked at each other.

They looked at Raul.

Raul sighed. "I knew what she wanted to hear, but I couldn't lie to her."

"Couldn't lie to her about *what*?" Prospero scratched at his day-old beard.

"I knew she didn't want the responsibility of being queen, either. She wasn't raised to the position. So much of royalty is formality and waving mindlessly to the crowds and . . . Victoria wants her freedom." In letting her go, Raul had done the noble thing. "I owe her that."

"What a steaming pile of horseshit," Danel said.

Prospero covered his nose with his hand. "I can smell the stench from here."

"We've been feeling sorry for you. We've been hating her. And for what?" Danel got to his feet, weaving as if he stood on the deck of a ship. "You didn't even tell her you loved her!"

Raul should have known they wouldn't understand. "She wanted her life. She deserved the life she had envisioned for herself, not the one I forced on her by kidnapping her!"

"More reeking crap!" Prospero staggered up to stand beside Danel. "If you'd begged, pleaded, told her you loved her, she might have stayed." He thrust his chest out and thumped it. "You think I haven't done that with Hada? Every time I'm an ass? You know why I crawl to her? Because I'm nothing without that woman! Nothing!"

Finally, patiently, because if he didn't, they would never stop nagging him, Raul admitted the truth. "I am my father's son. I don't love."

The two men stared, heads cocked. Then they fell on each other, howling with laughter.

Raul watched, offended and astonished that they found this lack in him so funny.

"Y-you don't love her?" Danel tripped over the log

behind him. "I've never seen a man so much in love as you. What the hell do you call it? When you want nothing more than to make her happy? When you're worried about what she wants rather than what you want? When you're miserable without her? Lord almighty, man, that's love!"

"Your love. For her," Prospero clarified. "You're all stoic and dutiful."

"No fun at all," Danel interjected.

"If you'd told her, at least she would have known all she needed to know to make her choice." Prospero pushed his hair out of his eyes. "No woman should have to be queen of an upstart country like Moricadia without love."

"Oh, and please." Danel flung his arms up toward the stars, projecting his voice and bringing almost all their companions out of a dead sleep and up to grumpy wakefulness. "Let's talk about the fact that our brave king Saber is being a coward by not telling her, like a boy who's afraid to ask a girl to dance for fear of rejection."

Raul got a tingling in his fingertips, a buzzing in his ears. It wasn't the wine or the ale, so . . . were they right? Was this the truth? *Did* he love her?

Danel prosed on. "I gotta say, she won my heart when she shot at me with intent to kill—"

Prospero cackled. "And when she swung that sword and told you two to stop dancing and kill each other."

"But I like her better all the time," Danel continued. "To think she would reject our boy and all his beautiful money because he didn't love her."

Raul staggered to his feet and stared fixedly at the fire. Did he love her? *Did* he?

He must, for he heard himself admit, "Hers is the only rejection that matters."

Prospero collapsed onto his back on the ground. "Yes. Too bad you've got no choice. You've got to go tell her. You've got to tell her the truth about everything. The ceremony, everything. You know what I mean."

Raul swallowed. "Yes. I suppose I do."

Danel said, "Because if she wants to marry someone else instead of you—"

"No!" Raul lifted his fists.

Danel insisted, "That woman likes children, and she'll want a few of—"

"No!" Raul's voice grew hoarse and desperate.

"She's beautiful!" Danel said. "You don't imagine she's going to be celibate her whole life?"

Raul reached out, grabbed his cousin by the throat, and pulled him close. "No." It was not an answer to the question, but an instinctive denial to the very idea of Victoria with another man.

The wily old manipulator Danel snapped, "Then you had better do something about it."

Raul let him go. "Yes."

The silence around the campfire was broken by nothing more than the crackling of the flames.

Danel rubbed his throat. "When she finds out the truth . . . about the ceremony, I mean . . . Well, that woman has a temper."

"Yes." A glorious temper. For the first time, Raul's spirits rose.

Reflectively, Prospero said, "I'm really glad I'm not you."

Chapter Forty-nine

"You're going to make your parents proud." Victoria smoothed the skirt of Effie's white gown. "To see you presented to the queen is your father's dearest wish."

"I know," Effie whispered.

The girl was scared to death.

Victoria put her hand on Effie's cheek in reassurance, then turned to Maude. "As you're presented to the queen, the gentlemen who view you will now realize you're a beauty."

Maude looked narrowly at Victoria. "And will they realize I've moved beyond my common origins?"

"I believe so. This is the opportunity you've been seeking."

"Good." Maude straightened her shoulders, lifted her chin. "Then I'll make the most of it."

Since her return from Moricadia two months ago, Victoria had done everything necessary to prepare the Johnson girls for this moment. They knew how to walk, how to bow, the proper incline of the head, what to do if Queen Victoria spoke to them.... No other young lady in England was more honored to be presented than these two.

No other governess in England was more pleased than Victoria to be still employed and untouched by scandal.

On the trip from Moricadia to England, she discovered that after the disruption at the ball Mr. Johnson had brought his family home, then immediately made the return journey to Moricadia to find her. He had been very kind, first asking if she'd been hurt, and when she assured him she'd been treated with the utmost respect, then burst into tears, he had handed her his handkerchief and left her to her misery. The family, Mrs. Johnson and the Johnson daughters, had waited in seclusion until he returned with Victoria, saying nothing about their adventures in Moricadia or the shocking loss of their governess. So Victoria found her reputation intact and the Johnson women sympathetic and generous in their assumptions about her time away. If they privately speculated that their upright, starchy Miss Cardiff could be a fallen woman, they kept those speculations to themselves, and as Victoria remained as she had always been—serene, unruffled, and disciplined—life once more rotated around Maude and Effie.

So now, Victoria was in Buckingham Palace, assisting

the girls in their moments of honor, and blinking with sentiment because these girls, commoners both, would now be respectable enough to present to society, and Victoria had helped accomplish that.

She was proud. Very proud.

Never once did she imagine how, if she were Raul's wife and the queen of Moricadia, she would help many other girls like the Johnsons rise to the top of their potential.

Yet in leaving Moricadia, she had made the right decision.

She knew she had.

So why was she still yearning for Raul as if he were the missing half of her soul?

Queen Victoria's master of ceremonies clapped his hands. "Young ladies, you have one-half an hour. We would like your companions to leave now and take their places in the receiving hall. For our debutantes, I suggest you use that time wisely. The convenience is this way."

Victoria touched each girl lightly on the shoulder, then moved into the corridor with the other companions and governesses.

"Victoria?" The voice was vaguely familiar, the face rounded yet mature, with such sad, sad eyes.

"Belle!" Victoria flung her arms wide, embraced her old friend. "Belle, what are you doing here? Is one of your sisters being presented?"

"No, we can't afford that." Belle's smile trembled. "I'm here with Father. The queen summoned him, and since Mother's illness and his . . . accident . . . I've had to accompany him when he goes somewhere."

Victoria glanced around in search of an alcove and

pulled Belle inside. "I'm sorry to hear he had an accident. What happened?"

"I think . . . I think he owed money to someone, the
wrong kind of person, for Father was beaten so badly
that he . . . Well, his leg didn't heal well, and his face
is quite scarred." Belle couldn't look Victoria in the
eyes.

Appalled, Victoria said, "I didn't know!"

"You can imagine we don't tell most people how the
accident happened." Belle's lip trembled. "Only you,
dear friend."

"But Raul didn't mention it!"

Belle's face lit up. "You saw Raul in your travels?
You didn't tell me!"

Because I didn't want to explain . . . things. "I'm sorry.
I was remiss in not writing you. Yes. I saw him. I spent
time with him." An understatement of sorts.

"How is he? We know he won the revolution and is
king of Moricadia. We read all about it in the papers, and
you can imagine our excitement. I mean, the excitement
my sisters and I shared." Not their father, Belle meant.

"I left before he was crowned, but I assure you, no
one was going to keep him from taking the throne." Victoria knew her voice rang with pride, but she didn't care.
She was, after all, talking to Raul's sister.

"You were there for the revolution?" Belle sank
down on the window seat.

Victoria knew she shouldn't tell Belle the truth. The
tale was too terrible and wonderful and strange. It didn't
reflect well on Belle's brother or on Victoria, Belle's
friend. But somehow Belle's warmth and understanding
wrapped around her and she found herself sitting beside
her friend, relating the whole story: her visit to Morica-

dia, her kidnapping, the strange ceremonies, Raul's constant determination to win the day and her.

When she was finished, she found Belle blinking at her in disbelief. "Raul wanted to marry you, but you left him? *Raul?* You left Raul because he didn't love you?"

Victoria gaped at her friend. "Belle! I thought you would approve. Isn't that what you always said? In school, late at night, when we talked? That you wouldn't marry except for love?"

"I was a fool!" Belle spoke vehemently, wildly. "I would do anything to help my sisters and me escape my father's creditors. It's too late for me to have a life, but my younger sisters deserve a chance. For that, I would marry anyone!"

"Oh, Belle, I'm so sorry." Victoria began to understand the depths of Belle's misery. "Won't Raul help you escape?"

"Father intercepts my letters to him."

"That's not right! When your brother is a king—"

"I should be the sister of a king. Instead I'm the daughter of a wastrel. None of that is right! Or fair." Belle's eyes blazed with frustration and fury. "Neither is what you've done. You could have married *Raul*. He's handsome, he's kind, he has all his teeth, and he's young. Yes, my father hurt him. And Raul may think he doesn't love, yet he loved me; he loved all of our sisters."

Taken aback by Belle's vehemence, Victoria said, "That's true. But that's not a man's love for his partner."

"Couldn't you have married him and been patient?" Belle snapped.

"But what if he never loved?"

"But what if he *did*? His love, so rarely given, would be worth waiting a lifetime for." Belle put her hand on

Victoria's shoulder and stared into her eyes. "Go back. Go to Moricadia and find him, and tell him again that you love him, and that you'll teach him how to love. If he doesn't want you anymore, he'll tell you."

Victoria's breath caught at the anguish of that idea.

Belle saw, and understood. "It's worth the gamble, is it not?"

For the first time in two months, the weight on Victoria's heart lifted. She could take a deep breath, could think beyond the misery that had enveloped her. She could see a path before her that perhaps would end in suffering, but not in doubt. Never in doubt. "Yes," she found herself saying. "Yes. It's worth the gamble. Thank you, Belle. Of course you're right. I will do just that."

Chapter Fifty

Recalled to their surroundings by the bustle of young women lining up in the corridor, Victoria and Belle leaped to their feet, promised to meet later, and hurried into the queen's regal receiving room.

There, courtiers and proud parents lined the carpet where the girls would walk, waiting breathlessly for the newest season's debutantes. At the head of the carpet was the dais awaiting the arrival of the queen.

With polite requests and curtsies, Victoria worked her way toward the Johnsons. They stood in the front with the other parents, lining the rich red carpet like proud flowers along a garden path. When Victoria reached the spot at Mrs. Johnson's right shoulder, she touched her lightly.

Mrs. Johnson turned and gave an exclamation of relief. Linking arms with Victoria, she drew her forward. "Where have you been? We were worried."

"I met an old friend."

"From the glow on your face, I would guess it was an old, dear friend!" Mrs. Johnson smiled roguishly. "What's his name?"

"It wasn't a man." Victoria almost laughed at Mrs. Johnson's blatant disappointment. "It was Belle Lawrence, daughter of the Viscount Grimsborough."

"Of course. They would be here, wouldn't they?"

"What?" Mrs. Johnson was quite scatterbrained, but Victoria didn't understand that at all.

"Shh!" Mr. Johnson glared them both to silence.

Mrs. Johnson squeezed Victoria's arm.

Victoria squeezed back, feeling for the first time since her return to England relaxed and clearheaded.

After she had landed on Britain's shores and reestablished herself with the Johnsons, Victoria had taken the time to visit her family. She had been astonished to discover that her mother kept a book where she pasted Victoria's letters and the map she'd used to keep up with her travels. Victoria's siblings had been impressed by her worldliness. Her stepfather was sullen about her achievements, but for the first time, Victoria didn't notice or care. Instead, she concentrated on building these important, lasting relationships with her brothers and sisters, and, most significant, with her mother. Those relationships made no difference to her career or her future, yet somehow she felt that with her family at her back, she had a solid foundation with which to live her life, and so much old hurt just . . . slipped away.

But for the most part she had been busy with Maude and Effie, their gowns, their manners, the procedures to be followed during the presentation. And every day, she thanked God for her occupation, because every night, she woke up reaching across the bed for Raul. Dreaming erotic dreams about Raul. Most of all . . . longing for Raul.

Now she glanced across the walkway in time to see a path opening to allow Viscount Grimsborough to pass as he made his way to the front row. He leaned heavily on a cane. His face was disfigured. And he carried an air of darkness with him, a heaviness that kept everyone at a distance.

Belle walked behind him, her eyes downcast, her face expressionless.

Victoria hurt for her friend and her bleak life. But soon, perhaps, Victoria would be at Raul's side. She would call his attention to his sisters' unhappiness, and together they would bring them to Moricadia. And even if he no longer wanted her—her breath caught on a shard of pain—she would tell him about Belle's despair and he would rescue his sisters. Then at least something good would come of Victoria's foolish flight from Moricadia.

The room stilled as Queen Victoria was announced. As the crowd dipped in their obeisance, the queen made her stately way to the center of the dais and stood waiting for the debutantes. In stature, she was a small woman, but in her posture and confidence, no one would ever mistake her for anything but the queen of England. Certainly Victoria Cardiff felt wonder as she stood before her monarch, and when it seemed the queen's gaze rested on her, she flushed with awed pleasure.

"Here come the debutantes," Mrs. Johnson whispered.

Maude and Effie walked about midway through the procession, two lovely girls who showed nothing but shy poise and beauty, and were everything that a young Englishwoman in search of a husband should be.

Victoria found herself tearing up. She told herself she cried because she was proud of the part she'd played in their training, and ignored her recent regrettable tendency to cry over little things, like the loneliness that nagged at her.

When the girls had curtsied before the queen, they took their places to the side and watched while the others were received. Then, with a collective sigh of relief, the young ladies waited to be dismissed.

But Queen Victoria had other intentions. In her firm voice, so startling from such a tiny frame, she announced, "Today it is my honor to welcome one of Europe's newest monarchs from one of Europe's most ancient royal families—"

Stupidly, Victoria didn't understand what was happening.

"...a country but recently recovered from a long subjugation..."

A smiling Mr. and Mrs. Johnson cleared a little space in the crowd around her.

"...we are proud to be the first country to welcome the newly crowned *King Saber of Moricadia*!"

And *he* stepped in the door.

Raul.

Dear heavens. Raul Lawrence ... King Saber.

Victoria's heart started to thunder. Her chin trembled. Her hands shook.

She heard a collective indrawn breath, and one of the debutantes unwisely whispered, "My heavens!"

In truth, Victoria didn't blame the girl for her protocol break.

He was gorgeous, regal, noble, and stern, yet at the same time so very, very wicked. And tempting. And, as always, he moved with that long, rolling walk that looked as if he knew everything about how to pleasure a woman.

Which he did. *Oh, God.* He truly did.

Victoria watched in dizzy appreciation as, with kingly dignity, Raul strode up the carpet.

Her knees threatened to collapse in anticipation.

He was going to see her.

But wait. No. She had to move back. She had to hide. If she didn't, he would see her and think . . . think that she had set up this meeting on purpose, when truly, she had had no idea he was even in England, much less London, much less *here.*

Why hadn't the newspapers reported his visit?

She tried to wiggle into the crowd.

But the people behind her strained forward to take a look. Mrs. Johnson held her arm. Victoria was trapped.

Looking neither right nor left, Danel and Prospero walked three paces behind their king. They wore dark, conservative suits, had sober haircuts, and had clearly bathed. They moved like gentlemen, proper gentlemen, poised and confident.

Pride swelled in her heart; she had trained them . . . and she wouldn't have recognized them on the street.

On the other hand, Raul looked more than ever like a fairy-tale prince in a tailored black suit with a starched white shirt and that fiendish cravat. . . . He had tied her up with his cravat and done unspeakable things to her innocent body.

No fairy tale such as she had ever heard spoke of such shocking pleasures.

His stern face had hollows beneath his cheeks, but his lips were the same gloriously plush curves that promised passion and fulfillment. . . .

Don't think of that!

His hair had been trimmed off his shoulders, and it shone with that blue-black, almost iridescent gleam that made her recall its silken texture when she ran her fingers through the strands. . . .

Don't remember. . . .

She waited, panicked, for him to notice her.

But he didn't. Instead, his head swiveled toward the other side of the carpet. There, he met his father's eyes.

He stopped. He stared, his face forbidding.

Grimsborough stared back, equally forbidding, too proud to make the first advance.

But after talking to Belle, Victoria knew it was vital for Grimsborough's family that Raul acknowledge his father, and she held her breath, praying for Belle's sake that Raul would make a gesture of reconciliation.

He did, a short, curt bow of acceptance.

In return, Grimsborough bent his head in respect.

It was a moment awful and wonderful in its significance. It was an act that would buy Grimsborough time to recoup. It was a deed that brought a trembling, hopeful smile to Belle's lips.

Victoria sighed with relief.

Raul walked on to stand before Queen Victoria. "Thank you for England's kind welcome to me, and to Moricadia as it joins the world as a country and a monarchy."

Victoria flushed with sudden warmth. That deep, generous voice recalled nights and days of such freedom and passion as no woman had ever experienced before. . . .

Sternly she told herself, *This is not the time to think such thoughts*. Somehow, she needed to blot those memories from her mind and find a way to escape.

So again she tried to squirm back into the crowd.

Raul said, "I have come to England not only to pay my regards to one of the greatest monarchs in the world—"

Queen Victoria preened under his regard.

Victoria stopped squirming and glared. *The hussy*.

Raul continued. "—but also to beg a boon."

"I will, of course, grant your boon if it is possible," the queen replied.

How odd. It sounded as if they were reading from a script.

Then Raul said, "I want a wife."

Victoria froze.

Shoving ensued among the debutantes.

Queen Victoria turned her stern gaze on them.

The pushing stopped.

The muffled buzzing in the crowd around her made it difficult for Victoria to think, but she had to wonder— Did he mean *her*? Had he come for *her*?

Or had she, Victoria, by some cruel act of fate, been placed here when he came to ask for the hand of some more appropriately noble woman?

She felt sick.

Raul continued. "During the recent revolution, I found at my side a most wonderful woman, a woman of unsurpassed courage and kindness. She is the woman to whom I wish to pledge my life and my kingdom." He turned his head and looked into Victoria's eyes.

Oh. He had seen her. He did know where she was. He did mean her.

He did mean her.

Relief fought with horror.

She didn't want him to marry another woman. *Never.*

Neither did she want him to do this here, in front of everyone.

But in typical Raul style, he was not giving her a choice—and she knew why. He was the kind of man who, when he decided to do something, used every resource at his disposal—in this case, a proposal in the most public of places before her monarch.

A king?

Yes, he was a king.

But he was a knave first. A knave through and through.

She ought to box his ears.

He projected his voice around the great room. "Your Majesty, this most estimable of women is one of your subjects, and I hope to have your help in my wooing of her."

Victoria Cardiff had been duped. She saw that now. Set up. Completely and absolutely misled.

By Mr. and Mrs. Johnson, who insisted on buying her a new gown "as a thanks for your constant care for our daughters."

By Raul Lawrence, who had plotted this nefarious scene.

And by Queen Victoria herself.

"Who is this paragon, King Saber?" Queen Victoria showed a real flair for the dramatic.

"Miss Victoria Cardiff," he answered, and never had she heard her own name spoken with such resonance.

Pretending she didn't know exactly where Victoria stood, Queen Victoria looked over the heads of the crowd and asked, "Is Miss Victoria Cardiff here?"

Victoria took a breath, the first in several minutes. "I am, ma'am." She knew the correct protocols: how to walk forward, how to curtsy. She ought to; she'd been drilling Maude and Effie for weeks.

Queen Victoria, she saw, wore a quirk of a smile, and her eyes crinkled with laughter. She was enjoying the excitement her matchmaking had created. "Miss Cardiff, I believe you know His Majesty, King Saber."

Victoria turned to him.

He bowed.

She curtsied with the same depth she had showed to Queen Victoria. She owed the respect to his crown, if not his person . . . and in truth, she respected him, too. He was an altogether admirable man in every way. And no doubt an admirable king. And most certainly an accomplished blackguard.

Raul waited until she had risen. He smiled at her.

The thunder of her heart grew deafening.

He took her hand, and heat spread outward to her every extremity.

He knelt before her.

The debutantes' sighs of pleasure gusted through the room.

His fingers caressed her palm.

"Oh, don't," she whispered. If only she had decided to return to Moricadia sooner, she would have been spared this melodrama!

"I don't have any family heirlooms to offer you." He spoke to her. Not to the crowd, but to her, and his voice, warm, deep, seductive, wrapped around her, drawing her eyes to meet his where she could wallow in the pleasure of knowing he was here, truly here, on his knees before her and England. "No rubies for your throat, no dia-

monds for your ears, no sapphires to match your eyes.
And you know better than anyone that the Moricadian
treasury should not be spent on jewels, however well deserved they be."

"I know." Her gaze clung to his.

Reaching into his watch pocket, he drew out a ring, a
simple wide gold band.

The debutantes whimpered in disappointment.

"But your throat and your ears are more beautiful
than any rubies or diamonds, and no sapphire could
ever match the sparkle and the color of your eyes."

Out of the corners of her eyes, she saw the debutantes' disappointment fade. Unfurling their fans, they
used them vigorously.

"So I offer this ring, plain and humble though it is."
Putting it in her palm, he wrapped her fingers around
it. "I bought it with ill-gotten gains. But they are *my* ill-
gotten gains."

"Gambling?" she asked.

"And horse racing." He grinned at her. "You know
me too well."

"So I do."

"If with the knowing, you still love me, and you would
agree to wear this ring and be my wife, I can't promise jewels will ever grace your hand, but I can give you
mountains and valleys, cities and wild places. I can give
you Moricadia."

Disillusionment clogged Victoria's throat. She loved
Moricadia . . . but that wasn't what she wanted. She tried
to tug her hand away.

Yet he was still holding her and speaking in that beloved, vibrant, persuasive voice. "I can promise I will
protect you with all the strength of a scarred warrior;

I will cherish you with all the abilities of a mere man; I will worship you with my body." He leaned forward, his green eyes solemn and passionate and true. "And I will love you, *love you*, Victoria Cardiff, for all the years of my life and beyond."

"You love me?" Tears sprang to Victoria's eyes.

Did she dare believe him?

"I didn't recognize the emotion, but I think I loved you from the first moment I set eyes on you. I know I loved you when I saw you teaching the children English. And I was lost in worship when you refused to escape to safety while I fought Jean-Pierre. You're everything that is brave and strong and resolute, a woman worthy to be the queen of Moricadia, and the possessor of my heart." He was absolutely and completely serious, and he looked as if he were prepared to remain on his knees before her for as long as it took to get the answer he wanted.

That wasn't true, of course. She knew him better than that. If she didn't say yes, be damned to propriety—he would pick her up and carry her away and make love to her until out of sheer exhaustion she agreed to wed him.

And as tempting as that sounded, she thought the king and future queen of Moricadia should not make such a scandal in the English court.

She looked around at the crowd.

They observed with breathless anticipation.

She looked up at the dais.

The queen viewed them with plump satisfaction.

She looked toward the debutantes.

They clasped their hands together, silently pleading with her in his cause.

She looked down at Raul.

He watched her with the kind of hungry longing that was love and lust and the promise of joy all wrapped into one.

So she gave him what he wanted. She cupped his face with her hand, leaned down to him, and vowed, "Yes. I will marry you, Raul Lawrence, King Saber of Moricadia, and we will love each other for the rest of our lives and even beyond."

She had thought he would maintain decorum.

She should have known better.

He came to his feet, wrapped her in his arms, and, with a whoop of joy, he picked her up and whirled her around, laughing into her face.

She held on to his shoulders and laughed back at him, knowing that this instant was the true beginning of their happiness.

The court burst into applause, and after a moment of wide-eyed shock, Queen Victoria smiled stiffly and clapped also.

Danel and Prospero backed away, careful not to hinder their king and queen's passionate embrace.

Out of the corner of his mouth, Danel said, "I wouldn't want to be Saber when he has to explain that the ownership ceremony in the forest is the Moricadian marriage service."

Prospero nodded. "Before he tells her, he'd better keep the rope handy to tie her up. That woman's got a temper."

"She does. The first time I saw her lose it, she shot at me. The second time, she almost chopped my hand off, and Saber's, too."

The two men recalled the incidents uneasily.

"Do you suppose she's going to be angry at us?" Danel asked.

"How long do you think she can hold a grudge?" Prospero murmured.

"Surely no longer than the birth of their first child."

"Or their second."

Danel thought for a long moment. "Perhaps we can convince our king to hide Attila's sword."

Prospero threw his arm over Danel's shoulder. "Good idea, my friend. Good idea."

Turn the page for an advance look at
Christina Dodd's

SECRETS OF BELLA TERRA

Available in August 2011

Bella Valley, California

As Sarah Di Luca drove along the winding road out of town and back to the home ranch, she heard the whisper of new leaves struggling to be born from the grapevines. The breeze that blew through her open window smelled like fresh-turned earth and sunshine on fresh-mowed grass, and the cool air slid around her neck like a luxurious fur. The rows of vivid green grapevines made her smile; another year, another spring, another day. At her age, all of that carried a weight and a joy that nothing else could ever replace.

She pulled up to the house, the 120-year-old homestead that stood on a rise at the far end of Bella Valley, and climbed out of her Ford Mustang convertible. She'd bought the car new in 1967. The official color was "playboy pink"; her grandsons called it "titty pink." She laughed at their reaction, figured boys would be boys, and drove more slowly every year. Reflexes, you know.

Old age is not for sissies.

She and her sisters-in-law said that every time they spoke on the phone. If only it weren't so true.

She put her purse over one arm, fished her grocery bags out of the passenger's seat, and looked up the stairs at the wide, white-painted front porch. The treads were narrow and steep, not up to the current building codes, but when the house was built, there were no codes, only immigrants carving out places in the heat of California's central valleys. This house, with its tall ceilings, narrow windows, ornate trim, and root cellar, had been the epitome of the stylish farmhouse, overlooking the vineyards and orchards that spread from one end of Bella Valley to the other. She placed her feet carefully, dropped her purse and bags, and sank into the big rocking chair. She looked over the vineyards. . . . Yes, the rows of grapes that made up the Bella Terra vineyards. But set like a jewel among the rows was the Bella Terra resort, established in the 1930s, during Prohibition, and now the cornerstone of the Di Luca family's wealth and influence.

As she rocked, the floorboard moaned and complained as if it felt the ache in her back and the tremble in her legs.

It made her heart swell with pride to see how thoroughly the Di Luca family had sunk their roots into this valley, to know how the famous and affluent flocked to Bella Terra to relax and vacation.

At the same time, she missed the early days, when the wine country was rural, quiet, homey.

But that kind of nostalgia was another sign of old age,

wasn't it? Just like this weariness that plagued her after a mere trip to the grocery store.

The trouble was, she couldn't let the store deliver, and she couldn't ask one of the kids who worked at the resort to meet her here and carry her groceries in. She'd done that once and her grandsons, all three of them, had found out within an hour and called to see if she was dying of some dreadful disease.

She *was* dying, but it was just old age and it would take its own sweet time about it. These days, eighty wasn't so old.

She groaned and stretched out her legs.

Of course, it wasn't so young, either.

But she'd always been an active woman, and she was still in pretty good shape. If only ... She glared at her shoes, ugly, sturdy things with all the proper supports. Some days she was in the mood to put on heels and dance.

But the bunions had taken care of that.

Still, there was no use complaining. There were people in worse shape, and if she slacked off on going to the grocery store and driving herself to church, her grandsons would soon have her wrapped so tightly in protective gauze that she'd be good for nothing.

So she'd better get to putting those groceries away before the ice cream and frozen peas melted in the heat....

Pushing herself out of her chair, she gathered her bags, opened the front door, and walked down the dim hall, past the parlor on the left and the bedroom on the right, past the bathroom and the second bedroom, and into the big old-fashioned kitchen. The appliances were new, state-of-the-art, but when the boys wanted to do a complete remodel, tear out the counters and the cabinets, change the flowered wallpaper, she'd said no. Because, of course, they would have wanted her to move to the resort to avoid the mess and fuss. She swam in the hotel pool, she enjoyed the occasional massage at the spa, she liked visiting with the guests, but she knew that a woman of her age couldn't move out of her house for a month without pining for the peace and quiet of her own company.

They said she was isolated.

She told them she was content.

Sarah dropped her purse and her bags on the table, briefly noted the cellar door was open—odd, she didn't remember leaving it ajar—and went to the sink to look out the window at her yard.

The boys were always fussing about it as well. They wanted to bring the driveway around to the back door so she didn't have to tote her groceries so far, but to do that they'd have to pull out the live oak in the backyard.

The wide, long-branched evergreen oak had been planted in 1902 by the first Mrs. Di Luca the year she married Ippolito Di Luca and moved into the house as his bride.

Like the house, like the valley, like Sarah herself, the tree had survived storms, fires, droughts, years of prosperity, and years of famine to grow old and strong. Its dappled shade had protected generations of Di Lucas as they played and worked—she wouldn't have it removed. Not it or the rosebushes, now scraggly with age, sent from England in 1940 by young Joseph Di Luca, her husband's cousin; he hadn't survived that war. Oh, and not the amaryllis the boys grew in pots every Christmas and then had planted outside ...

A cool draft wafted across her cheek.

A cold realization struck her.

Wait. The cellar door is open.

She turned to look. Yes, it was open, a dark, gaping mouth with a gullet that led to the windowless basement.

Why is the cellar door open?

She had *not* left it ajar. She knew she hadn't. She'd raised one son and three active grandsons in this old house, and the entire time, that steep stairway and the cold concrete at the bottom had scared her half to death. One tumble and they would have cracked their little skulls. But she didn't tell them that. They would have viewed it as a challenge. Instead she told the boys that she kept her wine down there and the bottles needed darkness and cool to age. They understood. If there was one thing the Di Luca family took seriously, it was wine.

Her wine ... bottles of wine ...

Her heart leaped. Her blood pressure peaked, a nasty feeling that made her light-headed. With her gaze fixed to that open door, she pushed herself away from the sink.

Someone had been in her house. Might still be in her house.

She looked around. Saw nothing else out of place. Saw no one.

She needed to get out.

Her purse and keys were on the table.

Whoever it was is gone. Surely they are gone.

She walked briskly, quietly, to the table and gathered her stuff.

Amazing how the aches and tiredness vanished under the impetus to *get out*.

She turned toward the back door, intent on removing herself from the scene. She opened her purse as she walked, fumbled for her cell phone, and, glancing down long enough to locate it, heard the cellar door creak. As she half turned to see the door swaying, a man in a ski mask ran toward her, a tire iron in his hand.

He swung at her skull.

She flung her arm up.

The bar connected and bones shattered. Pain, bleak and bitter, exploded through her nerves.

Ramming her from the side, he knocked her into the wall.

Luckily the plaster beneath the flower-patterned paper was old and it crumbled under the impact of her head. Luckily . . .

Sarah woke with the sun shining on her face. For a moment, she couldn't remember what had happened, or why she was on the floor in the kitchen, why she could see only through one eye. The light made her head ache.

Then she did remember.

An intruder. Get out!

She sat up. Her forearm flopped uselessly at her side. Agony struck her in waves. It came shooting down her arm. From her head. She wanted to vomit, but she didn't dare. She was afraid to move. She was afraid to remain still. She listened to the house, to the familiar silence, and realized the hot breeze was blowing in her face. Little by little she turned her head to look.

The back door was open.

He was gone.

Slowly, slowly, each inch a new torture, she withered back onto the floor, an old, hurt woman who didn't want to face what would happen next.

She lay there, eyes closed, fighting the nausea, grappling with the reality of her situation.

If he was still hanging around, she was in trouble. But he could have finished her off while she was unconscious, so she would bet he'd hit her and left.

She wondered whether he had instructions to hurt her as some kind of warning or if that had been panic on his part. She hoped it was panic; she hated to think of the state of a man's soul when he willingly sabotaged and attacked an old woman.

She hated even worse to turn her thoughts to the man who must have ordered the attack.

But then, his soul had been damned years ago.

More reality . . . No matter how much it hurt, she had to get up, get to the phone, call . . . Oh, God, her grandsons were going to turn this valley upside down when they heard what had happened.

But she had no choice. There was blood on the floor and she was pretty sure she had a concussion, so gradually she opened her eyes—no, her *eye*—again.

Huh. By some instinct, she'd managed to hang on to her cell phone. *Good job, Sarah.*

Squinting at the numbers on the touch screen, she dialed 911 and talked to the dispatcher—a dispatcher who knew her, of course. Almost everybody in Bella Valley did. By the time the conversation was over, Sarah knew she didn't have to worry about calling the boys. They'd find out quickly through the grapevine.

Instead she went through the painstaking process of making a conference call to her sisters-in-law, one on Far Island and one on the Washington coast.

She didn't waste time with a greeting. She simply said what needed to be said.

"It's started again."